Lennox Morrison is a translator turned TV presenter turned *Daily Mail* staffer and columnist turned celebrity interviewer for *Scotland on Sunday*. With the help of a life coach she has now transformed herself once more – into a novelist. While writing *Re-inventing Tara*, she moved from Loch Lomondside to Glasgow, began working out with a personal trainer – and changed her name. For more information about the author please visit her website at: www.lennoxmorrison.com

RE-INVENTING TARA

TARA

LENNOX MORRISON

timewarner
paperbacks

A *Time Warner* Paperback

First published in Great Britain as a paperback original
by Time Warner Paperbacks in 2002

A CIP catalogue record for this book
is available from the British Library.

ISBN 0 7515 3270 3

Typeset by Palimpsest Book Production Limited,
Polmont, Stirlingshire
Printed and bound in Great Britain by
Clays Ltd, St Ives plc

Time Warner Paperbacks
An imprint of
Time Warner Books UK
Brettenham House
Lancaster Place
London WC2E 7EN

www.TimeWarnerBooks.co.uk
www.lennoxmorrison.com

To Isobel and Angus Morrison

Acknowledgements

This book is the result of re-inventing myself from journalist to novelist . . . with the help of life coach (and now FF – fabulous friend) Fiona Harrold. Within a fortnight of confiding in her my childhood ambition was to write novels, I'd begun *Re-inventing Tara*. After astute editing by FF Irene Macdougall, the first six chapters were read by Giles Gordon of Curtis Brown whose positive response spurred me on through weekends and holidays spent at my laptop.

FFs Jamie Kerr and Ian McCurrach created the perfect five-star writer's retreat for me in Islington; as did FF Anne Dale in the French Alps. At home in Scotland, FF and personal trainer Pam McDonagh kept me fit through the dreichest months. Meanwhile Jamie generously took on the time-consuming role of book buddy, reading each chapter as I wrote it. Thanks to brilliant constructive criticism from him – and from FF Tracey Lawson – my finished manuscript brought me one of the best breaks in the book biz: the glamorous and dynamic Ali Gunn of Curtis Brown as my agent.

She found me the perfect literary match – Tara Lawrence of Time Warner Books – whose elegant and thoughtful editing did for my story what a diamond cutter does for a newly mined stone. Working with her and Joanne Coen is pure joy. As is the security of knowing that in Peter Morrison I have a brother who truly lives up to his first name. In recent months he has indeed been a 'rock'.

P.S. As this debut novel is set in the media I'd like to raise a glass of champers to all the fast-thinking and deep-drinking people I've worked with at the *Mearns Leader*, the *Sunday Mercury*, *Today*, Lomond Television, Scottish Television, the *Daily Mail* and *Scotland on Sunday* . . . and to say thanks to Mary Morrison, my sister, who got me into newspapers in the first place by entering my unpublished work successfully in the *Evening Standard*'s Pakenham awards for young journalists.

PART ONE

THE PURSUIT

Chapter One

London, July 2000

BEHIND-the-scenes at Early Bird TV, Tara MacDonald perched on a slippery leather sofa in the green room, sipping cranberry juice through a straw – to protect her lipstick – and anxiously gathering her thoughts. As the station's celebrity astrologer she was in the studio every morning for her Start-the-Day Predictions, and the windowless hospitality room – with its flowers, fruit bowl and newspapers – was a place she usually felt comfortable. But today was different. In a few minutes she'd be joining Rupert and Jilly on their live mid-morning chat show, *Sofa Talk*, to be interviewed about herself – her least favourite subject and one she usually avoided.

On the widescreen TV in the corner, Rupert and Jilly were interviewing Dolores from Bootle who'd been seduced by the world's first Internet priest. Father Blarney had wooed her through his confessional chat-room, she explained. Now she was pregnant he'd been sent to South America by the Church and she'd been sent to Coventry by her family. What should she tell her about-to-be-born child when it was old enough to ask about its dad?

I've no idea who *my* father was, thought Tara. What

3

if Rupert and Jilly ask about that? I wish I hadn't said I'd do this . . .

Just as she was rehearsing what to say, the green-room door opened to admit two prematurely haggard twenty-somethings: an assistant producer and a researcher, wan-faced and deadline-twitchy.

'Sorry to keep you waiting, Tara. You'll be on after the break,' said the a.p., then glanced at her clipboard and dashed out.

Josh-the-researcher smiled brightly at Tara: 'Tea? Coffee? More cranberry juice?'

Actually I feel sick, realised Tara. Sick with nerves. I've got to pull myself together. Keep the conversation on the straight and narrow and I'll be fine.

'No thanks,' she said, with such a friendly, non-starry smile that Josh felt emboldened.

'Banana-and-turnip smoothie with double vitamins and ginseng?' he teased.

Tara shook her head.

'OK, well . . .' Josh – honours degree in English Lit; post-grad diploma in media studies – began refolding the newspapers on the coffee table.

Poor thing, thought Tara. He looks worn out. Probably studied hard to get here. Yet as far as I can see – newspapers, telly, the Internet – they're just one big gossip session. Not so different from when I was growing up in Glasgow and my mother's friends used to sit in the front room dishing the dirt. As for Rupert and Jilly, their script's exactly the same as it was on Ma's sofa: sex, food and tragedy.

So I shouldn't be nervous, she thought. Just relax

4

and be grateful I'm the star guest . . . and not a skivvy-with-a-clipboard, like Josh.

'OK . . . cocktail of mango-and-parsnip with extra St John's Wort – ice cubes guaranteed organic?'

'No thanks,' said Tara, smiling. 'Why don't *you* have something?'

He hesitated.

Months working here and he's still scared of doing the wrong thing, thought Tara: 'Go on. Have a seat. I'm sure you could do with a wee break.'

With a grateful grin, Josh helped himself to a can of Coke from the mini-fridge and then sank down in the sofa opposite.

So easy to make people feel appreciated, thought Tara. Yet when I was a dogsbody, who ever bothered to do that for me?

The door opened and a further member of the *Sofa Talk* team entered the room. Bouncing in his designer trainers, his clothes said, 'I'm a skateboarding dude,' but his birth certificate said, 'I remember T Rex.' Fast-talking and over-animated, he would've made Tigger look lethargic.

'Nigel Harrington, executive producer. Delighted to meet you, Tara. So kind of you to come on the show. We trailed you yesterday, so ratings a-go-go today.'

He shook Tara's hand. In his other hand she spotted a handkerchief. He used it to catch a sniffle. How old is he, she wondered. Thirty-four? Thirty-five? He's a Josh who's made it. But at what cost? Looks like his energy comes cling-wrapped: sniff-and-go. Maybe I could give him a free astrology reading? Might help

5

him calm down *and* it would give me another fan in high places.

She let go of Nigel's hand slowly and looked up at him, deepening her dimples. 'Everything's wonderful. I'm so pleased to meet you. Jilly told me you'd look after me.'

Tara spoke warmly, calmly, as though she had all the time in the world and he were the most important person in it. Her voice was TV-friendly Scottish: glottal stops pronounced in full and only a hint-of-lilt. It wasn't the voice she'd grown up with, but it was one that landed lightly on English ears.

'You know, that's a bad cold you've got there, Nigel. You should find time to see me. There are things I could help you with.'

Tara looked into his eyes.

Nigel looked away, flustered. Then looked again.

Oh shit, thought Tara. Shouldn't have hinted about the cocaine. Better change the subject. Flirt a little. She looked into his eyes again; smiled prettily.

'They're not,' she said.

'Sorry, I don't . . .' began Nigel.

'They're not really that colour,' said Tara. 'You were thinking: are her eyes really that colour or is she wearing contact lenses. Weren't you?'

'Yes, yes I was,' he fibbed.

She gave him a mischievous smile: 'Or maybe I'm wrong? Were you thinking something else?'

Tara bent forward to flick an imaginary piece of fluff from her silver-painted toenails. As she'd intended, Nigel took the opportunity to look her up and down.

She was short-ish – only five feet three inches – and yet with such massive sex appeal it made his mouth dry.

Her face was girl-next-door, but perfectly presented. With her flawless white skin, collagen-pretty mouth and her hair coloured seven shades of red, she was a walking advert for London's most sought-after beauty therapists. Her body was a perfect combination of 1950s curves and twenty-first-century muscle definition. Her feet were bare, in leather-thonged geisha sandals, with a silver toe ring on one dainty digit. Her legs were untanned ivory, but glistening. Her skirt wasn't short, just above the knee, but it was shiny blue satin, moulded to her, and between it and the powder-blue cashmere sweater lay a hand's span of taut, naked stomach. It looked so succulent, Nigel wanted to bite into it.

'Your eyes, yes, your eyes,' he agreed, unconvincingly.

'I'd love to say I was born with them, but I can't tell a fib,' said Tara. 'They're contact lenses. Green. You'd have to catch me first thing in the morning to see the real colour.'

She let that thought sink in.

Nigel's gaze wandered back to the gap between skirt and sweater.

'They're blue. Plain blue,' said Tara.

His eyes snapped back to her face.

She smiled at him: 'Not everything is as it seems, Nigel. But then you know that as well as I do, don't you?'

7

Sniffing self-consciously, Nigel glanced at his watch. 'You're on. Right after this interview,' he told Tara.

She nodded and looked at the widescreen TV in the corner where Rupert and Jilly were winding up an interview with Joan from Crawley. She had sold her house to pay for Precious, her aging Pekinese, to be cloned in the US. But now Precious and Precious II were both in quarantine kennels while Joan waited alone in a tiny bedsit. As Joan wept, Jilly empathised energetically. Rupert looked concerned. Then he looked at the Autocue: 'After the break, we'll be back with Tara MacDonald, stargazer to the stars.'

As the assistant producer swooped to remove the lachrymose Joan, Nigel ushered Tara into the studio.

Breathe deeply, she told herself. Breathe deeply and relax. Jilly promised this would be a gentle chat. So calm down. Act confident and you'll *be* confident.

'How are you, Sam?' she asked one of the cameramen. Sam beamed at being noticed. 'Ace, Tara, ace. You're looking gorgeous. As ever.'

She smiled back, as grateful for Sam's attention as he was for hers. Then she turned to dimple at Nigel as he propelled her gently to a comfortable chair next to where Rupert and Jilly were sitting on their sofa.

'Rupert, Jilly darling, how are you?' she asked.

Jilly was rubbing her temples. 'I feel Tuesday morning.'

'I know,' said Tara sympathetically. 'Are you coming to see me tomorrow?'

Jilly nodded. Then raised her eyebrows to indicate she was listening to directions in her earpiece.

In the gallery, the PA was counting them in after the break: 'Three, two, one and cue Rupert.'

Fast as a flight attendant, Rupert – the matinée idol of morning television – switched on his smile: 'I wouldn't get out of bed in the morning without catching your Start-the-Day Predictions,' he enthused, reading from the Autocue. 'How do you get it so right?'

Tara sparkled modestly: 'You know, I don't always get it right. But I do care. We all need a little loving guidance in our life. And we need it from someone who cares.' With the adrenaline rush of live TV, Tara's fears were already fading. Expertly, she sought out the right camera, and looked down the lens, soulfully.

'In the last century, astrologers gave people lists of what was coming up for them. But life isn't a soap opera. And I'm not here to give people a preview of the plot. I'm here to give them a spiritual compass, show them the way of kindness and calm.'

'Your rival astrologers say you don't give more detailed predictions because you can't see what lies ahead,' said Jilly.

'I'm not an astrologer in the traditional sense,' said Tara. 'Yes, I use the signs of the zodiac and the stars, but really I do readings based on emotional intelligence. I'm a prophet of the emotions, if you like. If people have an insight into where their emotions are leading them, they can adjust their course, take themselves to a better future.'

'Well you certainly seem to be attracting the stars,' quipped Rupert. 'I'm told Euan McGrigor won't say yes to a new script until he's spoken to you. And that the Countess of Essex has been a regular visitor.'

'I help a lot of different people. They're all very special. I'm grateful for their trust and I would never betray it. You know my great-granny lived in a small village in the Highlands. Everyone could see who went to her door for advice but nobody minded because they knew she'd never break a confidence.'

'That's your great-grandmother from whom you inherited your gift,' added Jilly helpfully.

'Yes, she had the second sight and I've been lucky enough to inherit it. It's a great responsibility. I do my best to deserve it,' said Tara.

'Sounds a bit hocus-pocus, doesn't it?' Rupert was playing the doubter.

'You can call it heightened awareness if you like? Or super-intuition?' said Tara evenly. 'It doesn't matter. What *does* matter is that if people are open-minded enough to let me help them, I know I can. I can show them where their life is going and if they don't like the look of it I can put them back in control. I think of it as power-steering for the soul.'

Across London, in a Docklands warehouse converted into airy high-rental apartments for diplomats and bankers, journalists and computer contractors, a twenty-something man in Calvin Klein boxers was lying on *his* sofa, oblivious of the picture-postcard Thames sailing barge in full sail gliding past his floor-to-ceiling window. With glossy dark hair, and a sleek five feet ten inches of squash-honed body extended to full length, dark brown eyes focused sharply on the Bang & Olufsen TV, he looked like a panther lounging in a tree, eyeing his prey.

Suddenly he leapt up, cracked open a new video-tape, stuck it into the video player and pressed the record button. Retrieving a Biro from the beechwood floor and a newspaper from the pile beside him, he made a note in the margin: 'Power-steering for the soul.'

Nice one, Tara, very nice, he murmured to himself.

No wonder 'the nation's hottest new astrologer' had become so popular so quickly. She talked just like the coverlines on magazines: 'Lose ten pounds in two weeks', 'Find your dream lover on your doorstep', 'Change your life in your lunch hour'. Offer people a short cut to what they want and they'll buy it. If you sell it in style, they won't look too closely for substance.

He should know. As a tabloid journalist he could spin a line with the best of them. He also knew the difference between a celebrity who would be famous for five minutes and one destined for a permanent place in the galaxy of game-show guests. Tara's fame was new, shiny, untarnished. And she was handling it well: sexy not tarty, friendly not fawning, clever but not too clever. Just the right mix of glamour and humility. And with more sincerity than a presidential apology. A class act.

So gorgeous, he thought. So fuckable.

On screen, Tara broke into a bright, green-eyed smile.

So easy to fall in love with, he thought. For men who do that kind of thing.

*　*　*

11

Back in the TV studio, it was Jilly's turn to read the Autocue: 'Yours is a classic story of overnight success, Tara. Everyone reads your magazine column and watches you on TV. Everyone wants you to tell them what the future holds, and yet we know so little about your past.' Jilly looked at Tara expectantly.

'I understand people's curiosity. It's only natural. I suppose because my job is to concentrate on other people I'm not so interested in talking about myself.'

'You were brought up in Glasgow, weren't you?'

'Yes, I was.'

'But your family's originally from the Highlands?'

'Um . . . yes. A tiny village. So tiny it doesn't have a name. Just a few houses really.' To make up for her vagueness, Tara bestowed a dazzling smile on Jilly.

'But near . . .?' persisted Rupert.

'Near Inverness. Although that's stretching the definition of near.'

'How old were you when you realised you'd got second sight?'

'Everyone thought I was just brilliant at guessing things. When my mother realised it was more than that she told me about my great-granny. But she seemed unsettled by it so I didn't do anything with it until relatively recently.'

'So before you became an astrologer, you must've had an ordinary job?'

No way I'm going to talk about *that*, thought Tara.

'Yes,' she said, then, improvising hastily: 'You know, because I've always watched your show I do feel I know you both.' Rupert and Jilly smiled encouragingly. 'So

I'm going to share a little secret with you.'

Sam the cameraman zoomed in on Tara's face.

'My mother loved *Gone With the Wind*. It was her favourite film.' She paused.

Jilly understood she wanted to be fed the next line. 'So she named you Tara, after the plantation?'

'Well, that's my little secret. You see, my real name is Vivien, after Vivien Leigh. I never felt it suited me but because the film meant so much to my mother I didn't want to change my name. Mum died of cancer when I was only eighteen but I still think about her every day.'

She bent her head momentarily. Jilly patted her shoulder.

'So when I changed my name it was really important to make it something my Mum would have liked. I'm Capricorn, an earth sign, so the most appropriate name from *Gone With the Wind* was Tara.'

Jilly was emoting energetically now; her eyes huge with understanding. 'Your mother would have understood.'

Tara nodded, sadly. Then brightened up with a brave smile: 'I've never told anyone that before. So there you go. A wee exclusive for you.'

'Fucking brilliant,' murmured the young man watching from his sofa. She's given them a titbit the tabloids could have uncovered for themselves with all the drama of unveiling a state secret. This woman plays the media game like Max Clifford in fuck-me mules.

Super-intuition? She certainly knows *something*. She seems so calm, so centred. I can see how she gets all the big names coming to her for private consultations. A screwed-up celeb and their money are soon parted. It's not film stars who deserve Oscars, but all the people who prey on them: the therapists and gurus, quacks and diet doctors. Parasites R Us. Unlike me, an honest hack. He chuckled at his own hypocrisy.

On the TV screen, Jilly's face appeared in close-up. The young man shuddered theatrically. Not sure your face is up to widescreen viewing at breakfast, he thought. Not like Tara. Now there's a woman worth freeze-framing: big eyes, big smile and a Barbie-doll body.

On TV, the camera had panned to Tara. He looked at her with real admiration. She knows what she's doing with her life. And she looks like she's enjoying it. Definitely a woman who could keep me interested. And who could keep Roger well amused. He put down his Biro and began stroking his penis.

'Don't worry, Roger,' he murmured. 'I'll get us introduced. Soon as I can work out how.'

Eyes still fixed on Tara, he continued touching himself, firmly, efficiently. Just before abandoning himself to the task in hand, a thought crossed his mind: Wonder if there's a man in her life?

'No there isn't,' Tara was telling Jilly on screen. 'I only wish there were.'

'I'm sure you must've left a few broken hearts behind you in Scotland?'

14

'Well I . . .' Tara tried to get off the hook with a mysterious smile.

But Jilly was too good at her job to let her off that lightly: 'A first love you're having second thoughts about now?'

Got to put a stop to this, thought Tara.

'Well, I wasn't going to tell you this,' she said, 'but I do look into my own future, you know. Not too often, because it's emotionally draining, but I can't resist sometimes. Especially when there's something on my mind and . . . well, I've seen that there *will* be a man, a wee bit younger than I am, coming into my life. Very soon.'

Me, thought Nigel. Me, thought Sam. Lucky man whoever he is, thought Rupert.

'Must be strange to be able to see into your own future,' mused Jilly.

'It is,' agreed Tara, adopting a suitably sage expression.

Wish I really *could* see a man coming into my life, she thought. But who could I trust? What if they found out the truth about me; who I once was – I'd plunge to earth, like a falling star. One final round of interviews to talk about my regrets, and then it would be twinkle, twinkle, goodnight Tara. End of fame, end of fortune . . . then what? I bet Jilly would be amazed to know I haven't even had a proper boyfriend. At school I was the only girl without a lovebite. 'Three-paper-bag job,' was how the boys rated me. When the guidance teacher called me in for the cosy chat on safe sex, the other girls sniggered. 'Going for your wanking lessons?'

15

She felt her cheeks flushing pink at the memory of it.

Smiling at Tara's rising colour, Jilly pressed on regardless: 'But do tell us more about that mysterious first love. Did you meet at—?'

'I'm dying to know too,' interrupted Rupert, 'but we've run right out of time.' He twiddled his earpiece.

'What a pity,' said Jilly. 'Well, thank you so much for coming to see us today, Tara. You've shared so much with us. That mystery man you've seen in your future – you must promise to bring him onto the show.'

Tara smiled: 'Promise. As soon as I know who he is.'

On his sofa, the dark-haired young man with the hand-some-and-knows-it face had put Roger back in his boxers and was murmuring breathily at the TV screen: 'It's me, Tara. It's me. I'll be arriving in your life any moment now.' He chuckled to himself. We'll give you what you need, he thought. Me and Roger. And you'll give me what *I* need. A big, juicy fuck-off exclusive. Business *and* pleasure. Perfect way to get a story. And *this* story will make my name. As long as I get to it before anyone else does. Got to get within close range of Tara, he thought. Then charm the knickers off her.

Jerking himself out of his prone position, he got up off the couch. Shower first, he thought. Then into action . . .

As soon as Harry the studio driver pulled up outside her Primrose Hill town house, Tara – too uptight to

16

wait for him to open the car door – slid out of the back seat of the Granada and hurried up the path. 'Flora! Where are you?' she called, as she stepped into the hallway.

'You were wonderful. I told you you'd nothing to worry about,' said Flora, emerging from her office.

'Really?'

Tara's PA smiled reassuringly: 'Really.'

'God knows what possessed me to start talking about a man in my life. I hadn't planned to say *any* of that.'

'It sounded fine. Absolutely fine. You let the folk at home think they were getting to know you a wee bit better, without giving away anything you didn't want to.'

'I was *so* nervous and Jilly kept straying into dangerous territory.'

'I know. But you couldn't keep on saying no to chat shows – not at this stage in your career. And now you've done one live interview it won't be so bad the next time.'

'Yes, but next time it won't be with Jilly. It'll be someone I don't know.'

'Well, we'll worry about that when it happens. You didn't let anything slip and you looked gorgeous.'

'Thanks, Flora. Sorry to be such a moan. I just feel completely drained.'

'We knew today would be a bit of an ordeal, but you did splendidly. You always do. Now come and have a cup of tea.'

Without giving Tara a chance to refuse, Flora led the way to her green-and-white office-cum-conservatory at the back of the house. Looking through the foliage of miniature palms inside to the newly planted Japanese meditation garden outside, Tara sighed deeply: 'It's beautiful here. Everything I always dreamt of. And it's been such fun putting it together. I just wish I could relax more.'

'Well you *can*. You've done the difficult bit – getting to where you are now. It's time to start enjoying yourself.'

Flora inspected the curves and planes of Tara's newly famous face. Beneath the TV make-up she detected a paleness.

She's come so far, thought Flora. So fast. Maybe too fast.

'Tara, this *is* what you wanted, isn't it?'

'Yes. Well, I'd never want to go back. I've got everything I wanted. Money, recognition, fame. We really turned my life around, didn't we? But . . .'

Flora raised her eyebrows questioningly. 'But?'

'I don't know. I don't want to sound ungrateful . . . Look, don't worry, really, I'm happier than I've ever been.'

Flora kept quiet and waited.

Eventually, Tara's words came tumbling out: 'What happened to love in all of this? I mean, here I am. I've made it. But I'm terrified of getting close to anyone, terrified I'll let something slip which will give me away. D'you know, the only men I get touched by are my masseur and my hairdresser. Oh yes, and the collagen man.' Tara smiled sadly. 'I don't want to be another kiss-and-tell victim so I know the best thing to do would be concentrate on my career and stay away from men. It's just . . . well, the thought of never having anyone. Is that what I've set myself up for?'

Yes, thought Flora. I'm afraid it might be.

'We'll work it out,' she said, patting Tara's arm. 'We *will* work it out.'

Chapter Two

Glasgow, 1986

'GET your head out of that magazine, Scarlett. Your mother needs a wee hand here.'

Scarlett sighed. The flat was too small to pretend she hadn't heard her mother shouting at her. As usual.

Outside on the long street of red sandstone tenements it was a summer evening in Glasgow, clammy with promise. The setting was far from romantic: gardens strewn with rubbish, closes covered with IRA and UVF graffiti. But hormones were in the air.

Girls from Scarlett's school were parading past in stretch-Lycra skirts and crop tops, shoulders red with sunburn, faces orange with bronzing powder. Smoking, swearing and giggling, they were playing *Top of the Pops* on their ghetto blaster and walking with the self-consciousness of adolescence. Although they were only going to the ice-cream van, they acted as though an audience were watching their every move.

They were right. On this street full of men who'd been laid off from the dying shipyards, and women who didn't care what time their children went to bed, nothing happened without other people seeing. Each front room was in full view of the family opposite; each back garden was full of other people's children spying into the back bedroom. In the tiers of cramped flats, stacked atop of each other like sub-divided shoeboxes, there was no escaping the nosy, noisy neighbours. When the old man upstairs from Scarlett lit his first roll-up of the day, his coughing roused the entire close. From then on it was a non-stop cacophony of blaring TVs, wailing babies, footsteps echoing up and down the stone stairs, then the door onto the street slamming shut. In retaliation, Ma played the radio-cassette in her bedroom at full volume: Rod Stewart when she was up; Patsy Cline when she was down.

Scarlett's mother had always been proud of living at 'the right end of the street', where closes were scrubbed and net curtains kept white. At the other end there were boarded-up windows, broken furniture on the pavement, and the one family who kept their garden nice had to chain their wheelbarrow to the railings. With only one bedroom in their two-room flat, Scarlett slept on a sofabed in the living room. Only on nights like tonight, when Ma had people in, was she allowed to sprawl on the apricot satin-look bedspread in her mother's room, reading *Elle*. At the sound of Ma's voice, though, she obediently put down the magazine and went through to see what was needed.

The cramped front room was inappropriately fitted with deep shag-pile carpet, but also, this evening, with wall-to-wall cellulite. In a room the size of a couple of bus shelters, a dozen overweight women were squashed into the Dralon three-piece suite or perched on kitchen stools, their thighs billowing over the edges. Standing in the middle, and centre of their attention, was the only size-ten woman among them. From behind, in her tight white miniskirt, lilac off-the-shoulder top and high heels, her peroxide blonde hair fluffed up as big as it would go, she looked like a twenty-something Barbie doll. But from the front, with her smoker's prematurely lined face, she looked like Barbie's barfly mother. Her make-up was perfect at thirty paces. But close up looked like Max Factor by numbers. Her voice was Glasgow Embassy Regal.

'Right, Scarlett hen, pass round these quiz cards. We're going to find out who knows their calories. Once you know your calorie counts, ladies, you'll think twice about what you put in your mouth.' Mrs Macdougall winked meaningfully and, round the room, double chins wobbled appreciatively. Mrs Macdougall was better than a tonic.

As she said herself: 'I'm cheaper than Weight Watchers and just as good. More pounds off to the pound at Waistwatchers. And that's a promise. If yer man's not chasing you round the bedroom by the time I'm done then my name's not Lola Macdougall.'

Actually, her name wasn't Lola. She'd been christened Lorna. Nor had she ever been married. The 'Mrs' was her own addition. But Scarlett knew better than to say anything. Nor did she correct her mother when she talked about Scarlett having just started secondary school. In reality she was nearly fourteen, but the younger Scarlett remained, the younger Mrs Macdougall seemed. 'And keeping young and beautiful is what it's all about, Scarlett,' her mother never tired of telling her. 'Although *keeping* is not the right word for you, Scarlett, is it? You're young but not beautiful. Wasting yourself. Absolutely wasting yourself, so ye are.' At this point Lola – who saw herself fitting perfectly into the cast of Dallas; ideally as JR's new love interest – would adopt a wistful expression and shake her head sadly.

This evening, though, Lola had no time to fantasise about TV soap operas; she had a real-life audience in her front room. 'Now, ladies,' she was screeching vivaciously, 'time for the answers. Number one: which has more calories, one four-finger KitKat or two two-finger KitKats?

'Think about it, ladies. A four-finger KitKat has an extra sliver of chocolate holding it together. So that's more calories. It just shows, ladies. You can't be too careful. Now, eyes down, question two . . .'

She broke off for a moment: 'Scarlett, did you make up the low-calorie treats yet? No? Aye, well, come on. I've got twelve hard-working slimmers here desperate for a wee nibble. Is that right, ladies?' More laughter.

Scarlett went through to the kitchen. As she left the room, she felt twelve pairs of eyes watching her, twelve appraising glances sizing up her bottom. She knew what they were thinking: 'Imagine Lola Macdougall having a daughter that size. Size sixteen, or is it eighteen? And Lola's so trim and slim. Poor soul. To have a daughter like that.'

It was the same at school. Always had been. Scarlett's

face could go red just thinking about it. When she couldn't climb the rope in PE, when 'Fatty-bum-bum' was shouted at her as she walked across the playground. She had prayed for the name-calling to stop. Recently, it had.

Something worse was happening. She had become invisible. She felt like she took up more space than anyone else in her year, but nobody saw her. Her schoolmates were too busy looking for sex, for drink, for drugs, or all three at the same time. 'You're the Nescafé kids,' their headmaster thundered at assembly. 'You want it all and you want it instantly. You'll ruin your lives before they've started.' Scarlett was desperate to ruin her life, but nobody wanted to ruin it with her. Her classmates wanted their rites of passage in the right clothes, to the right music, in the right company. A fat girl in stretch jeans wasn't wanted en route. Unwanted, unnoticed, she became studious by default. Working hard, she did all right in most subjects and got top marks in English. Her English teacher, Miss Macleod, knew better than to praise her too much in front of the class – that would only have laid the fat girl of the class open to more teasing. But one Saturday afternoon they'd been scouring the same fiction shelf at Partick Public Library. Miss Macleod had suggested some books to Scarlett, then a cup of tea at a café, and ever since – by unspoken agreement – they'd 'happened' to bump into each other in the library most Saturdays. Recently, the conspiratorial flavour of their encounters had intensified, when – over milky tea and Tunnocks teacakes – Miss Macleod had confessed that as well as

24

appreciating Thackeray and Dickens, Grassic Gibbon and Spark, she also had a weakness for *Elle* and *Vogue*, *Harpers & Queen* and *Tatler*. If Scarlett could keep a secret her teacher would be only too happy to pass on copies to her.

Lola, who read only Jackie Collins novels and hairdressing magazines and scoffed at her daughter's interest in literature, had at first accused Scarlett of stealing money from the cash she gave her to go to the supermarket. When reassured they were secondhand copies, she'd pounced on them for her bathtime reading, so that by the time Scarlett got them they were soggy and dog-eared. At least Ma had been pleased with me for once, thought Scarlett. 'All they expensive magazines for nothing? Good on ye, Scarlett. Glad yer learning something at last.'

Abruptly, Scarlett's thoughts were interrupted by a familiar screech: 'I don't hear any choppin', Scarlett. Can ye no find the knife?'

She picked up the bread knife. 'I hope yer gonnae use the right knife this time,' came her mother's voice from the front room again. Instantly, Scarlett put down the bread knife and swapped it for the vegetable knife.

In a pantomime whisper she heard one of the Waistwatchers speaking to her mother: 'Is it Scarlett's thyroid, Lola?'

'No, no,' came her mother's response, at full volume. 'Scarlett's just a gannet, aren't you, hen?'

Scarlett cut through a carrot, slowly. Her face was red. Her eyes were pricking with tears. She fought the urge to cry. Just in time, she realised she'd come to the end of the carrot and was about to cut herself. She chopped a few more, then swept the carrot slices onto a platter and picked up a green pepper. As she sliced it, she looked down with disgust at her hands. They were pink and podgy. Her fingers looked like sausages. Her forearms looked like hams. They couldn't possibly be hers. Why was she trapped inside this heavy, lumbering body? She hated it.

That was why she never did anything about the rest of her appearance: her straggly mouse-brown hair, the unflattering square-framed specs, the spots she always seemed to be sprouting. The only thing she liked about herself was her blue eyes, but lost on her doughball face, the colour wasn't as striking as it was on her mother. The two of them were the same height, five foot three, and shared the same petite build, but next to Lola, it was Scarlett who looked matronly. 'You're my worst advert,' her mother was always telling her. No matter how often she said it, it never failed to hurt Scarlett. She told herself she should draw comfort from the pleasure of displeasing the mother who tormented her so much. But she never quite managed to convince herself of this. And it was minimal revenge for the pain her mother inflicted on *her*.

Her thoughts were interrupted again: 'Scarlett, are ye no done yet?' shouted her mother.

'Nearly. I'm just finishing up.'

On the kitchen counter stood a jar of extra-fruit, low-sugar jam. Carefully, noiselessly, Scarlett opened it and scooped dollops of it into her mouth. It was tasteless.

Swiftly, she put it down and picked up a jar of low-calorie drinking chocolate. She removed the lid, put it to her lips and poured the powder straight into her mouth.

Then, setting aside the drinking chocolate, she hurriedly threw some tomatoes into a colander and rinsed them under the tap before arranging them on the platter, next to the chopped carrots and pepper. From the fridge she pulled out a couple of tubs of cottage cheese dip and some diet lemonade. She found some paper cups, put everything on a tray and carried it through to the front room.

The Waistwatchers fell on it like a flock of obese sea-gulls. Under cover of their screeching, Scarlett took the chance to speak to her mother. 'Have you time now to look?' she asked.

'I suppose so,' said Lola, ungraciously, picking up a paper cup and pouring herself some diet lemonade. Scarlett pulled a brown envelope from her back jeans pocket and handed it to her mother. 'Excuse me, ladies,' trilled Lola. 'This won't take a mo.'

She took the envelope with her into her bedroom – a fuss of peach-and-apricot swagged curtains and gilt mirrors that Lola fondly imagined as Southfork style, but was actually pure trailer park. Following her mother into the furniture-crammed room, Scarlett was so nervous she could feel sweat moistening her palms. As Lola opened the envelope and took out the white card inside it, Scarlett watched her face.

Lola scanned the card briefly, then, catching sight of herself in the dressing-table mirror, put it down and picked up a red lipstick. Expertly, she retouched her lips. Scarlett watched.

'It's not bad, is it?' she ventured.

'Aye, ye've done much worse,' said her mother, reaching for the card and using it to blot her lipstick. 'Why did ye have to show it to me anyway? Am I meant to sign it or something?'

'No, no, it's OK,' said Scarlett. 'I just thought . . . well, Miss Macleod thought . . .'

'Who's she when she's at home?'

'My English teacher. I told you about her.' Scarlett looked at her mother expectantly, waiting for her to agree, but Lola merely sniffed.

'Well anyway,' continued Scarlett. 'She said I should be thinking about going onto college or something.'

Lola couldn't have looked less interested. Scarlett retrieved the report card from the dressing table.

Lola was still looking at herself in the mirror. Then she caught a glimpse of Scarlett's reflection. She inspected her daughter more closely.

'For God's sake, Scarlett. Look at the state of you. What's all that brown stuff on yer face? Are ye growing a moustache?'

With a final glance at herself in the mirror, Lola bustled back to the front room. Scarlett didn't look up till she heard her mother clapping her hands to call the Waistwatchers to order. Only then did she flee to the bathroom and lock the door. Sitting on the toilet seat, avoiding the sight of her own fat face in the mirror, she wept. Silently. She was good at that. And good at getting it over quickly. For in a few minutes the Waistwatchers

28

would want to visit the loo, and woe betide Scarlett if she was getting in the way again.

Forcing herself to lift her head from her hands, to wipe her face with her palms, she caught sight of her mother's toiletries, covering every surface in the tiny bathroom and leaving no room for Scarlett's anti-spot gels and frequent-wash shampoo.

Suddenly, Scarlett felt a tiredness beyond her years. She was tired of her mother's hair dyes and skin creams, her push-up bras and too-tight skirts, and her endless, endless calorie counting. Most of all, though, she was tired of Ma's spectacular lack of interest in her own daughter.

Had Scarlett possessed the least trace of self-esteem, the tiredness she felt would have quickly turned to rebellion. But instead, she slumped further into despair.

Why do I have to be living this dreadful life, she thought. If only I could be somebody else, somewhere else. If only I even had a friend to confide in. But I don't. Ma doesn't want me and nor does anyone else. The only person who seems to have any faith in me is Miss Macleod. And she's probably just taking pity on Fatty-bum-bum.

Just as Scarlett was reaching for a towel to wipe her face, there was a loud rap on the door.

'Scarlett. Hurry up. There's ladies waiting.'

'I'm just coming.'

Scarlett stood up and flushed the toilet as if she'd used it.

Above the sound of the cistern running, she heard

her mother's voice again: 'Hurry up and get out of there or your life won't be worth living.'

It isn't anyway, thought Scarlett. It really isn't. To be born here, to this mother. I hate my life. But how am I ever going to escape from it?

Chapter Three

London, July 2000

BAGEL in one hand, remote control in the other, Jordan Holmes – clad only in boxer shorts – sat cross-legged on his chrome-and-suede sofa, channel-hopping over breakfast. Outside, summer sunlight was turning the Thames a lighter shade of sludge and barges with mysterious loads were chugging downriver, past the glittering corporate towers and the 1980s apartment blocks.

But an on-the-road journalist like Jordan was far too busy keeping up with the news agenda to look at what was going on in the real world. He was clever enough to see the irony in this, but his cleverness didn't stretch to knowing what to do about it. So in the meantime he kept taking the tabloids, washed down with plenty of telly. And he worked hard. Fucking hard. He was never one to wait to be given a story. Always came up with his own ideas.

The phone rang.

Jordan hit the mute button on the TV remote control and spat out a piece of half-chewed bagel – he didn't want to talk to his news editor at the *Daily Brit* with his mouth full. Sitting up to attention, he grabbed the digital receiver: 'Jordan Holmes.' His voice was M25-matey. His tone ready-for-action.

'Jordy. It's me.'

Jordan sat back; recharged his mouth with bagel: 'Sunni. I was just thinking about you.'

'Were you really?' Sunni's voice was voice-coach-improved Brummie. Her tone thrilled-to-be-here. Even without seeing her, you could tell she was wearing L.K. Bennett slingbacks and an animated expression, and you wouldn't be the least surprised to hear she was a satellite TV weather girl.

'I'm *always* thinking about you,' said Jordan – switching on the TV subtitles.

'Did you see any of my bulletins this morning?'

'I caught the five to eight forecast,' lied Jordan, taking another bite of bagel.

'What d'you think of the new graphics?'

'Looked really good.' Eyes fixed on the TV, Jordan resumed channel-hopping.

'D'you think people will understand them, though?'

'Should do.'

'Not too minimalist?'

'Minimalist?'

'Well, getting rid of the fluffy bits and the swirly bits. How are viewers meant to understand what I'm saying? We've had loads of them phoning in complaining. The switchboard was jammed.'

Jordan had stopped watching TV; was giving Sunni his full attention: 'I think it might make a half-decent little story. If your graphics have gone so arty-farty that viewers can't even tell if they need a brolly or not: "Storm over TV Weather"; "Change in Weather Switches off Viewers".'

'Oh Jordy. Not again. Please. Last time you did a story about the station, I got into so much trouble. They wouldn't believe I knew nothing about it until I saw it in the paper.'

'Well you didn't, did you?'

'Yes, but the story was based on something I'd said.'

'It's not your fault if I can spot a story out of nothing, sweetheart. Anyway, there's no such thing as bad publicity. Let's see, "Sunni's Gloom at Changing Weather" or, "Weather Girl Sunni Caught in Storm". Might even get them to run a picture of you. Your gorgeous face in the *Daily Brit*. You'd like that, wouldn't you?'

'Mmmmm . . . OK, Jordy. Just don't tell anyone where you got the idea.'

'Promise. Now . . .' Jordan looked at his watch. 'Sorry, sweetheart, but I've got to run. You still OK for dinner tonight? I'll book a table at Fish. Ten o'clock?'

'But Jordy, you know I've got to be in bed by ten. I've got to be up by four.'

Jordan smiled to himself, then, in a mock-disappointed voice: 'And I won't be finished till ten. If I'm lucky.' He sighed dramatically. 'Our schedules just don't match, do they, sweetheart? Shall I just come round as usual, when I'm finished work? Takeaway in bed? Then I'll leave you to your beauty sleep?'

'Thanks, Jordy. Sorry about dinner.'

'Bye, sweetheart. Later.'

'Bye-bye, Jordy.'

He went for a piss. In the mirrored white-and-white bathroom, he checked his assets: glossy dark hair, labrador eyes, gym-fit body, and of course, Roger, his secret weapon. The regular features destined to make him only cardboard cut-out handsome had been rearranged by a school rugby injury, leaving him with a lopsided grin which catapulted him into the ranks of the devilishly sexy. Of which he was wholly aware. But he also knew there is nothing less attractive than a man aware of his own good looks. So he feigned ignorance. Except at moments like this.

Looking directly at his own reflection, he switched on his best 'I'm-absolutely-fascinated-by-what-you're-saying' expression. Perfect: easy on the eye and easy to talk to. What more did he need? A whopping big exclusive, that's what. Otherwise he'd never get away from the grind of being just another news reporter and into the job he lusted after so much it kept him awake at nights: Los Angeles correspondent for the *Daily Brit*. The present incumbent was due to go on maternity leave in three months' time and the *Brit*'s editor – a man who made Machiavelli look straightforward – hadn't yet announced her replacement. He preferred to let his reporters compete against each other for the most glamorous job on the paper. Jordan was one of four hacks fighting for it as fiercely as prairie dogs over a bone. Yet so far he'd failed to bring in any stories big enough to impress his master.

'It's your fault, Roger. Fucking secret weapon,' Jordan told his reflection.

Six years ago, when he'd been showbiz correspondent on a local evening paper, just about to get a job on a national, Roger had diverted him all the way to Los Angeles, following a B-list actress ten years his senior. She'd seemed so stunning in England but so ordinary in LA, where a series of *Baywatch*-worthy babes and the conceit that he could write a screenplay detained him for six years. He could've stayed there for ever, as kept man to an older woman, but how could he have faced his father, self-made emperor of his own dry-cleaning empire, Same Day Spotless? Or his mother, unceremoniously traded in by his father for a younger model but still queen of her own boutique chain? Not to mention his younger brother, Nathan, the entrepreneurial brains behind Rush Caffeine, the rapidly growing coffee-shop franchise for the dance generation, serving five mood-altering flavours: mellow, wide-awake, hyper, hyper-hyper and snooze (decaffeinated).

And yet at twenty-eight Jordan's own career still hadn't broken the sound barrier. Correction: he was twenty-nine, but his objective was to be LA correspondent by thirty, so he'd given himself a little more time. But now that was running out too.

'Fuck you, Roger,' he told the bathroom mirror. 'I'm on a mission. It's make or break. No more R and R till we get a result.'

He packed Roger back in his boxers and returned to the living area, but his prime telly-watching spot on the sofa was now occupied by a man his own age, in long baggy shorts and T-shirt, dreamily stuffing his face with Frosties. While Jordan's dark good looks and predatory glint gave him a panther-like air, the cereal-eater – six feet two inches, fair-haired with hazel-gold eyes, untrendy specs and a sleepy expression – looked more like a big, friendly bear quietly enjoying a pot of honey.

'Wouldn't jump into my grave so quickly, would you, mate?' challenged Jordan.

'Sorry. I'll shift over,' said the cereal-eater good-naturedly.

It was Jordan's flatmate, Plod. Or rather Swift, David Swift. But Plod was the name he'd been known by since his schooldays. It was Holmes who'd come up with it. On the first day of term Swift had come ambling down the corridor, inspecting the carved wood ceiling, as the rest of the pupils were lined up, waiting for assembly. Holmes had shouted: 'Come on, Swift. Or should it be Not So Swift?' Within a week, he'd shortened it to Plod.

Now, as David swapped the sofa for a chair, Jordan regarded him with a mixture of puzzlement and contempt.

How pathetic, he thought. Why d'you never stand your ground? Still, we can't all be generals. Every army needs its foot soldiers . . .

The instant David had left the sofa, Jordan commandeered it and planted his feet on the coffee table.

He and David hadn't become best mates at St George's, their minor public school in Kent. Jordan had had more money and more girlfriends than David (whose parents were school handyman and matron) could ever keep up with. But top-marks David was so generous at helping out with prep that he was allowed to jog along on the fringes of Jordan's clique. Which was why when they'd spotted each other across the oak-beamed bar of the Prospect of Whitby in Wapping a few months ago, neither of them had looked the other way. Jordan had been stood up by a contact. David was recovering from a stint at the local community centre. This was where his first-class Oxford degree in history had got him, he said.

David's voice was public school mixed with Oxfordshire hedgerow (before the job at St George's, his father had worked at the Cowley car plant, his mother had been a nurse).

'Officially, I'm an outreach worker leading an oral reminiscence project,' said David. 'In reality, I hand out tea and Hobnobs to old ladies who're fed up with daytime telly.'

He'd smiled the self-deprecating smile Jordan remembered from school. But while charm was a commodity Jordan flicked on and off like a switch, David automatically made people feel at ease.

When Jordan responded with a quick one-liner – 'You mean, you're the token toyboy at the Darby and Joan club?' – David's generous laughter reminded Jordan of what easy company he'd been at school.

'Let me do the honours, mate,' he'd said grandly. 'Same again?'

'Thanks,' said David. Wonder what Jordan's up to now? he'd thought, watching his old school friend pushing his way to the bar, past bespoke-clad City types entertaining foreign clients, and East End lads with football-thug faces, nursing bottled beers and grudges.

Looks like he's stepped out of a men's fashion magazine, thought David. What an effort.

Looks like he's still at uni, thought Jordan, returning with a couple of lagers. What a scruff.

'Cheers, mate,' they toasted each other.

'So what are you up to now?' asked David.

Only too pleased to be asked, Jordan produced a copy of the *Daily Brit* and pointed proudly to his by-line, at the top of the main story on Page Three: 'Blind-fold Frolics of Blind Date Girl'.

A tabloid hack, thought David. That's what he's become.

'A national paper,' he said. 'That's brilliant.'

Suitably gratified, Jordan was inspired to show off further. He was living in one of the priciest flats on the riverfront, he explained, because his father – who'd bought it as a London pied-à-terre – was living in tax exile in Guernsey.

'Must be great to live by the river,' said David. 'I'm in Hammersmith, overlooking the flyover.'

'Yeah. And I've got so much space you wouldn't believe it. Fucking humongous,' said Jordan. 'In fact,' – an easy way of making money had just occurred to him – 'it's so big I'd never even notice if someone else was living there.'

Ah, can see where this is leading, thought David. But I'll let Jordan work around to it.

Three lagers later, it was settled: David would move out of his flatshare in Hammersmith and into Jordan's spare bedroom, with his own bathroom and spa bath, and shared use of the kitchen, living area and water-front balcony.

Now, on the few occasions when Jordan glanced out to check what to wear with the weather, all he saw was river and sky, concrete and glass, whereas David, who was writing a book on the Thames, saw something different whenever he looked out. Once it was Roman soldiers, bare-legged and helmeted, marching towards their signal station. Another time it was Charles I, mounted on a magnificent horse, pursuing a stag. Then there were the pirates, draped in chains, being herded towards Execution Dock; the newly paid sailors rolling drunkenly from hostelry to hostelry; the droves of dockers tramping to work to unload tea and tobacco, wine and molasses.

To be so close to the river, to the haunts of Dickens and Pepys, Whistler and Turner, was for David a continual source of fascination. Meanwhile Jordan got what every journalist wants: someone to listen to him being clever. Like now, as he geared up for a new mission. Yes! There she was. His target appeared on the TV screen.

'Don't touch the remote control. This is what I wanted to see,' commanded Jordan. 'Turn it up, mate.'

David obeyed and was about to reach for another spoonful of Frosties, when his attention was caught by the presenter who'd just appeared on screen.

'Good morning. How are you?' said a beautiful red-haired woman in a pink silk summer dress. 'You've chosen to start the day with me. That's your first good choice of the day. I'm here to help you make more. Put down your toast, your teacup, whatever you were going to do next. Sit down, just for a moment. Be still. Think of yourself. You deserve it.'

She's lovely, thought David. Wonder what she'll say about Sagittarians?

'In a moment, Taurus, I have something special to tell you. And Leo, you too. For every zodiac personality, I have an important thought. But now, if you want a better day in sixty seconds, it's time to take that sixty seconds. One minute of quiet reflection, one minute's silence, before you start your day. Let's do it . . .'

David had put down his cereal bowl and was gazing thoughtfully at the screen.

'Wake up, Plod. You're not into that nonsense, are you?'

'Horoscopes? No, not really. But you know, the interesting thing is how many heads of state have relied on them: not just the Chinese leaders, but Ronald Reagan, Charles de Gaulle, François Mitterand, people like that. So historically speaking . . .'

'Yeah, yeah. Shut up, mate. The sixty seconds are over. I want to hear what Tara's saying.'

David raised his eyebrows and resumed his breakfast while Jordan listened intently as Tara dealt with each zodiac personality in turn.

'Totally positive,' David noted aloud.

'Total con,' responded Jordan.

David smiled wryly.

He had heard Jordan claim to be a Leo/Scorpio/Pisces, whichever sign would convince the woman of the evening she was astrologically destined to go to bed with him. So he had no illusions that Jordan wanted to hear Tara's predictions for his sign. Jordan's sudden interest in any subject meant only one thing.

'And finally, Capricorns,' Tara announced. 'Now, what I have to say really *could* change the course of your life, but I know you're the sign of the zodiac least inclined to listen to me. So whatever sign you were born under, if there's a Capricorn you care about and you want to do something that could really help them, join me again, after the break . . .'

'Clever girl, Tara. You know how to keep the nation riveted,' said Jordan, with genuine approval. 'A stargazer with your eyes on the ratings. Not to mention a heavenly body.'

David sighed. 'And I confidently predict . . .'

'Wait for it,' said Jordan, piqued that David should anticipate his next line. 'I confidently predict that you and I are going to make headlines together—'

'—in the very near future,' finished David.

'OK. OK. But keep it to yourself, won't you? This is the story that's going to make my name. Tara's got what it takes to make the scoop of the year, and she's all mine. Totally fuckable, totally mine.'

'Totally fuckable,' agreed David. He enjoyed Jordan's constant re-invention of the English language. 'So when are you interviewing her?'

'No point. She's not at the confessional stage yet. Tara's a bright new star. She's only just arrived.'

'Ah, the rise and fall of the TV celebrity. Your specialist subject.'

41

'Indeed. And she's only *just* got to the top. Nobody knows what she's hiding.'

'What *is* she hiding?'

'No idea. But everyone's got something to hide and if I move fast enough I'll be the first to find out. Girl like Tara could've done all sorts: glamour modelling, escort work, porn movies . . . with any luck she'll have a bitter ex-husband, sister she doesn't speak to any more, father she's never met . . .'

David considered this. 'I saw her on *Sofa Talk* yesterday when I was in the café for breakfast. She said she had a Highland great-grandmother but she didn't specify where. Have you anything else to go on?'

'Not yet. But I will,' said Jordan. 'As for that Highland great-granny. Might be true. Might not. She seems so open, so ready to talk about herself, but I've got a hunch she's not telling the truth. Or at least not telling the full story.'

'And now, I've got some exciting news . . .' said Tara.

Jordan looked round anxiously. Wordlessly, David handed him a pen. Jordan held it above the back of his left hand, ready to take notes.

None were necessary. What Tara had to say wasn't complicated. Yet it had an electrifying effect on Jordan. The moment she'd finished speaking he was punching the air with delight. 'Yes, yes! Tara, you're fucking amazing. Fucking stupendous. You've just shown me the way. You've opened the door for me. I know exactly how to get you now . . .'

'Poor girl doesn't stand a chance,' said David. 'What has she done to deserve you?'

'Don't know yet,' said Jordan. 'But astrology is the ultimate confidence trick. And she's been making a fortune out of other people's futures. So it's time the Great British Public knew about her past. And I've a feeling – Plod, my old mate – it's not what she says it is. Ms Super-intuition. I've got a few hunches of my own. I think she's telling fibberoonis to the Great British Public and it's my duty to let them know. If you want to see a falling star, stick around.'

'But what about the astrology column in your own paper?' asked David. 'Won't it seem a bit odd to condemn Tara for making money out of this nonsense when the *Brit* prints reams of it every week?'

'Never underestimate the hypocrisy of the Great British Tabloid,' said Jordan, picking up a copy of *The Planet* from his pile of newspapers. 'Look: the splash is the result of a sex harassment case, yet it's tits as usual on Page Three. No problem.'

'Double-think.'

'Exactly. Totally *1984*,' said Jordan. 'See, I *was* paying attention in English sometimes.' With a self-congratulating smirk he turned on his heel and strode purposefully from the room.

Without any hurry David switched off the TV, slipped on a CD and contentedly consumed the last of his breakfast.

Quite impressive, he mused. How Jordan skims over the surface of everything, creaming off the key ideas. He didn't do well at English at school – because he didn't do any work – yet he always remembers the essential snippets. Not that a knowledge of literature

43

seems necessary for what he does now. From what I've seen of his modus operandi, a tabloid journalist has to be part-detective, part-stalker, part-Oscar-winning actor.

Poor Tara. Doesn't stand a chance. What she does seems pretty harmless, and she looks orgasmic. If she's re-invented her past a bit, does it matter? Her personal history belongs to her. Doesn't it?

Frosties finished, David settled deeper into the sofa and let the relaxed sound of Moby wash over him.

Jordan meanwhile was in his bedroom, dressing for action and half-listening to Radio 5. Zipping up his black linen Armani trousers, he felt a familiar sense of smugness as he placed Roger in position. A long barrel *and* a large bore. Jordan smiled at himself in the mirror. This was a win-win assignment. If Tara turned out not to have any dire secrets, he could write a flattering features profile designed to charm her under his duvet. She was the most exciting woman he'd seen in ages and he couldn't wait to get his hands on her.

But if she *was* concealing something, then he'd restrain himself on the seduction front and concentrate on getting his scoop. If he could get her into bed before the story was printed, that would be a double-whammy.

The question of what he should do if she had secrets but he genuinely fell for her didn't cross his mind. In the world he lived in, reporters never let sentiment get in the way of a good story. A colleague often boasted about how he'd kept his mobile switched on at his mother's funeral. Jordan checked his reflection one more time. Then, slipping into the war-movie Nazi-speak his news editor affected on big stories, he aimed Roger towards the mirror and intoned: 'For you, Tara, the future is over . . .'

Chapter Four

Glasgow, 1987

SCARLETT was rifling through the top drawer of her mother's dressing table, looking for clues about Lola's future. Carefully, she lifted out the curling tongs, the bottles of nail varnish, the eyebrow tweezers, and put them on the shiny fake-satin bedspread. Then she reached to the back of the drawer and pulled out what she'd been looking for: a thick catalogue on glossy white paper. She leafed through it: dozens and dozens of colour snapshots of clean-cut men, and underneath the mug shots were their potted life histories. On the cover, in bold print, she read:

Southern Gentlemen. Est. 1980. The biggest and best American–Scottish introduction agency. Hundreds of American gentlemen seeking 'lassies' who are longing to be treated as ladies.

So *that's* her plan, thought Scarlett.

Recently, Ma had been boasting about how she was going to high-tail it out of Glasgow as soon as Scarlett hit sixteen. 'My future's in America,' she'd said. Scarlett hadn't been able to imagine how her mother would ever make it across the Atlantic. Now she knew.

Scarlett read on:

No computers. No registration fee for ladies.
A completely personal and confidential service.
If you're a sweet, old-fashioned girl ready to love,
honour and obey the man of your dreams, then let
our experienced matchmakers act as Cupid. We have
single, solvent gentlemen from every state in the
South looking for brides with Old Country values.
If you are 20 to 40, with clean medical records, no
convictions and no dependents, you too could be a
Southern belle. All flights and paperwork paid for by
your beau. Register today and let us arrange your
'happy ever after'.

She's really going to leave me, thought Scarlett, putting down the catalogue and sinking back onto the bed, head between her hands. For years all she'd known from her mother had been the back of her hand, the force of her tongue. She'd been treated more like an unpaid skivvy than an only child. But Ma was all she had.

Where will I go? she wondered. What will I do?

Queasy with panic, she brought her knees up to her chest and hugged them. Can't start crying, she thought. Ma will be home any moment. Makes her mad when I cry. Forcing herself to sit back up she reached for the family-size packet of crisps she'd left lying on the dressing table. As usual she'd been eating steadily but heedlessly all evening. Like a child seeking the comfort of its mother's hand, Scarlett dipped into the bag.

Thank God, she thought. Only half-empty.

Gratefully, she grabbed a handful and transferred it to her mouth. Then another and another. As she ate, she felt her panic easing. She felt numb, but calm. Calm enough to remember to get up, go outside and dispose of the empty packet where her mother wouldn't find it, in one of the communal rubbish bins on the back green.

Feeling better, she returned to Ma's bedroom and resumed reading the Southern Gentlemen brochure:

Franklin Clayton, 52, 5' 11", 210 lbs, divorced, non-smoking, Baptist, $195,000 a year. A successful real-estate agent, the finishing touch to Franklin's beautiful detached home would be a warm-hearted woman to share the good things in life with. Must be slim, 5 ft 3 to 6 with . . .

She stopped reading. What was that noise at the front door? Hastily, she returned the brochure to the drawer, replacing the tongs and everything else. Then she switched off the bedroom light, dashed through to the front room, slipped between the sheets of the Dralon sofabed and picked up the copy of *Vogue* she'd left lying on the floor. Just in time.

The door to the flat opened and her mother stepped unsteadily over the threshold. Scarlett glanced at the clock on the mantelpiece: half past midnight. No wonder Lola Macdougall was having trouble staying upright. Four-inch stilettos and six hours drinking never mixed well.

'Hello, Scarlett. Tucked up in bed? You'll never be a scarlet woman,' said her mother, swaying precariously over the sofabed. She hiccuped, then, recovering herself slightly, sashayed over to an armchair and fell into it.

'Haven't got the equipment for it, have ye? Get yerself stirred and make me a cuppa.'

Scarlett got out of bed and went to make the tea she knew her mother wouldn't drink.

Sure enough. Even before the kettle had boiled, she heard Lola clattering about in the front room, opening the buffet and pouring herself a White Horse. 'Jist a wee nightcap,' she said, as wordlessly, Scarlett deposited a cup of tea (skimmed milk, two Hermesetas) within her reach. Her mother grinned at her. Oh no, thought Scarlett, who knew what was coming now.

Night after night, in short skirts and tight tops, her mother's high heels clicked purposefully as she headed for the lounge bars and the clubs, in search of men. Bad enough when she succeeded and Scarlett had to lie awake on the sofabed in the living room, listening to the bump and grind from the bedroom. But far worse when her mother came home alone. Like tonight.

'Listen to me,' her mother was insisting. 'And look at me when I'm speaking to you, you lazy lump.'

Scarlett obeyed.

'D'ye think I want to be here? Looking a lump like you? I *do* not. Believe me. But I don't have a choice. Haven't had any choices for a long time. Not since you were born.

'You don't know what it's like. Wasting my dancing years on a big lump. A lump I never wanted. I can tell you.

'*Gone With the Wind* we went to. My favourite film. The third time I'd seen it. But the first time I'd been with a man. The very first time. I was in love. Stupid in love. He was tall, handsome, blue eyes, a proper man. Opened my heart, opened my legs, and there you were. You lump. And he was gone. Gone with the wind.

'My proper man. My proper bastard. Never again. Sex is fine. Burns up calories. But love. Never again. Look where it got me. Lumbered with a lump. Scrimping and saving and getting by.'

She poured herself another drink.

'And despite that. Look at me. Look at me, lump!'

Scarlett did what she was told.

'I'm gorgeous. Could get any man I wanted. If I didn't have a lump. A lump that won't even smile when I bring a man home. No wonder none of them wants to take on another man's leavings.'

'Well they won't need to. Because I'll be gone soon. Gone with the wind.' She giggled at the joke Scarlett had heard so many times before.

'Gone with the tide. To America. To my future. Soon as you're sixteen.' Her tone softened slightly. She looked almost kindly at her daughter.

'Soon as you're sixteen, we'll both be free women, Scarlett. That'll be great. I'll have my independence and so will you. I won't hold you back, hen, I'm not boring like other mothers.'

I wish you *were* like other mothers, thought Scarlett; mothers who fuss over their daughters, who write notes to get them off PE when they've got their period, and who take them shopping on Sauchiehall Street, and – having never known any of these things, Scarlett quickly ran out of specifics . . . But – she looked at Ma, talked out now and reaching for the cup of tea – that's never going to happen, is it? And now you're going to leave me. Don't cry, Scarlett told herself. Just don't cry.

Lola took a sip of tea, made a face and put the cup back down. 'Cannae drink this. It's cold.' She kicked off her high heels, heaved herself out of the chair and headed for the bedroom, slamming the door behind her.

Scarlett got back into the sofabed. For a few minutes she lay there, completely still, crying silently. Then – having waited long enough for Ma to have fallen asleep – Scarlett reached under her pillow and pulled out the giant Galaxy bar she'd bought earlier from the ice-cream van. With the desperation of a junkie seeking a fix, she peeled off the wrapper and began sucking the chocolate. As she did so her tears dried up. She stuffed the wrapper down the side of the sofa. So tired now, she thought. But not sleepy. What else can I eat?

She felt under the pillow and down the side of the sofabed, but found only discarded wrappers, among them the one from the Galaxy bar. She pulled it back out and licked off the remaining crumbs.

Then, snuggling down under the duvet, she picked up the copy of *Vogue* and began flicking through the pages: Chanel, Lancôme, Estée Lauder. No mention here of the cosmetic range her mother sold: Mary Ellen Skincare and Beauty. As soon as any of her Waistwatcher women had slimmed down to a 'brand-new body', Lola talked them into buying 'a brand-new face to go with it'. Scarlett knew her mother's sales spiel by heart: 'I'm the exclusive west of Scotland agent for Mary Ellen Skincare and Beauty, as used in Hollywood,'

51

was what she told her clients. 'In horror movies,' Scarlett had started adding silently.

She might be a fourteen-and-a-half-year-old in size sixteen jeans from What Every Woman Wants but she knew her Max Factor from her Miners, her Dior from her Dorothy Perkins. She knew what true chic looked like and it looked nothing like her mother. The more Lola Macdougall did, the worse she looked. She wore appliqué by day, sequins by night, and so much costume jewellery she jangled like a jackpot from a slot machine. She was over-dieted, over-peroxided and over the top.

Looking down at her magazine, Scarlett ran her hand across the glossy colour page; her fingers across the models' faces.

Then – holding the image in her head – she jumped out of bed, ran across to flick off the light, then back under the covers. Lying in the semi-darkness, she tried to keep the picture in her mind, but other thoughts kept intruding.

Will Ma really go? she wondered. What will I do without her?

What if she goes before I've done my Highers? Miss Macleod said it would be a waste if I didn't go to college. But then Ma didn't want me to go anyway. Wanted me to get a job. If Ma went it would be easier for me to do what I want. If I can afford it. If the grant's enough. Need to speak to Miss Macleod. On Saturday.

Cheered at this, Scarlett yawned. Tiredness was finally turning to sleepiness. She closed her eyes, felt her body relax.

A new life, she thought. A life like they have in the magazines. I know exactly what I'll wear and what my house will be like and what I'll have for dinner – not tea – and who I'll invite round and what we'll talk about and everything . . . The only thing I don't know is how to get a life like that. Doesn't say it anywhere. Not in any of the magazines.

Used to look at the horoscopes. To see when things would get better. But they haven't so far.

To block out the streetlight shining through the cheap readymade curtains, Scarlett pulled the duvet over her head.

Then, mentally flicking through her favourite magazine images, she found the one she looked at most – an advert for champagne showing beautiful people laughing together in a cocktail bar – and, under cover of the Littlewoods continental quilt, in her mind's eye, she surveyed the scene.

Got to get a new life, she thought. Got to make it happen. Soon as I can work out how . . .

Chapter Five

London, August 2000

'YOU'D be taking a huge risk,' warned Flora.

'I know,' said Tara. 'But I can't bear any more interviews. They're too unpredictable. This way I get to tell my story, *my* way. The publisher's thrilled – an autobiography will sell far better than a straightforward astrology book.'

'But why hire this man to write it for you?' Flora glanced at the letter Tara had handed her. 'He's a *Daily Brit* reporter.'

'If a tabloid hack writes my book and *he* doesn't uncover the truth then I'll *know* I'm safe. Everyone will assume he's covered all the angles and there's nothing more to find out about me.'

'Well . . .' Flora sounded doubtful: 'You've never told me why you wanted all this secrecy but I know it's important to you, so why put extra pressure on yourself?' She picked up a computer print-out on Early Bird TV stationery: 'Your ratings are higher every week. Do you really need more publicity?'

'The minute you sit back and rest on your ratings, someone else jumps into your slot. Remember that fitness presenter who went on holiday and when she came back Mr Move-It had taken over her job?'

'No. Can't say I remember her.'

'*Exactly*. Which is why I need to keep a high profile. I haven't come this far to give it all up now. I've always dreamed of a life like this. I want to stay famous long enough to start enjoying it.'

'Well, I'm all for *that*,' said Flora. 'And it could be useful to have a contact at the *Daily Brit*. The column in *Gorgeous* is good for kudos, but a national daily would be much more lucrative than a magazine.'

'Six days a week, instead of once a month.'

'Good for the phone lines,' noted Flora. 'Does the publisher know this chap?'

'No. He's just a pushy hack who heard me saying on TV I'd been asked to write a book on intuitive astrology. The next day he approached the publisher and offered to be my ghostwriter. Two days later he submitted an outline.'

'A fast worker.'

'Just what I need . . . the sooner I tell Tara's story the way I want it, the less I'll have to worry about people finding out who I used to be.'

'No doubt he's heard about the huge advance from the publisher,' observed Flora. 'And what if he doesn't accept what you tell him? What if he starts doing his own digging?'

'I'll offer him a good fee and a tight deadline. It'll be in his own best interest to get on and finish the book. Anyway, we've covered my tracks pretty thoroughly. I know it's risky, Flora, but this constant fear of being found out is driving me crazy. I have to do something.'

* * *

From behind her Gucci sunglasses, Tara could see the rooftops of Soho, TV aerials and red-brick chimneys, with pigeons scrabbling between them, and in the distance a church spire with a golden vane. Right next to her, in their summer colours, twenty- and thirty-somethings sat on metal chairs at wooden tables, wearing this month's fashions and talking tomorrow's PR/magazine/telly deals.

She was on the roof terrace of Soho House, the capital's hippest members-only media club.

Tara closed her eyes and inhaled deeply: Silk Cut and the herbal freshness of aromatherapy oils. The unmistakable scent of media London, AD 2000. If they could see me now, she thought. The girls from school who used to sit in that awful café in Scotstoun . . . with the Formica-topped tables, the fug of cigarette smoke, the Pyrex plates. I never dared go in for sweeties when they were there. Knew what they'd be saying: 'Fatty-bum-bum stuffing her face again.' I was so desperate to be sitting with them; one of the gang. Bet they're still there. With their kids. On benefit. Probably fat themselves now.

She opened her eyes to see a figure emerging from inside the club and pausing on the edge of the tiled terrace. He was carrying two glasses of champagne but he wasn't a waiter.

Gorgeous, she thought. And he's coming right towards me. This must be . . .

'Hello. Thought I'd bring up the drinks with me. Saves time. And even if we don't write a book together at least I can say I drank champagne with Tara MacDonald.'

He deposited the glasses on the table.

'Thank you,' smiled Tara.

'I'm Jordan Holmes. May I sit down?'

'Of course.'

Wouldn't normally drink in the afternoon, she thought, but . . . mmmmm. As the first sip hit her tongue she felt a tingle of surprise. It wasn't the house champers; it was Cristal. Not available by the glass. So he'd had to buy a bottle. He clearly meant business.

'Lovely.' She raised her glass to him.

Jordan smiled. The barman had told him it was Tara's favourite. He turned his full brown-eyed gaze on her.

'Glad I made the right choice.'

'I haven't got long, I'm afraid,' said Tara coolly, removing her sunglasses and meeting his gaze: wide-eyed green at full power. He looked back at her: liquid brown at full power.

He blinked first.

Round one to me, thought Tara: 'So tell me, why are you interested in writing a book about intuitive astrology?' Apart from the huge advance from my publisher, she added to herself.

Jordan smiled winningly: 'I'll be honest with you. I haven't ghostwritten a book before.'

Hardly something you could lie about anyway, thought Tara. She waited for him to continue.

'I know you could hire anyone you wanted. There's no real reason to go with me. Except that I've been following your work very closely and I'm a huge fan.'

'Thank you. That's always good to hear,' said Tara. Not that I believe it, she thought.

Jordan kept his tone conversational: 'I'm Leo, you know. And what you said on Early Bird a few weeks ago, about Leos always wanting to charm? I've been thinking about it. I use charm in my job. I have to. So much so it's on automatic pilot now. What you said about charming so many people so often you lose track of who you really care about, well, that struck a chord, you know?'

He scanned her face to see how his script was playing. Tara was listening intently.

Jordan continued: 'And then last week, what you said about status symbols. Well, you're right. I surround myself with them. If you looked at my wardrobe you'd find a designer label on everything. I plead guilty as charged.' He took a swallow of champagne.

Tara opened her mouth as if to say something, but Jordan got in first. He had shifted up a gear, started speaking faster, gesturing with his hands. 'In the autumn, what you said about how Leos interact with other people. That was the best. I can't say it's changed my life but it's made me more aware of myself. It really has.' He couldn't have looked more sincere.

That's his sincere look, thought Tara. 'I'm impressed. You really seem to have followed what I've been doing. And it would be great to have a ghostwriter who's genuinely interested in astrology.'

It was a good moment for Jordan. But he took a risk: 'I'm not,' he said. 'I'm a journalist. I've prepared well. I looked up every column you've written and I got a TV producer I know to give me videos of your shows. I sat up all night watching them. With a couple of bottles of Becks and a Thai takeaway. I'd always been a bit sceptical about astrology, but your readings were spot-on. So I'm a very recent convert. That's the truth. If we're going to work together I might as well be honest with you. Anyway, it would be pure madness to lie to Ms Super-intuition, wouldn't it?'

Very smooth, thought Tara. But she couldn't help smiling.

Jordan continued: 'You see, you were *so* right about Leos. Here I am now, trying to charm you.'

Tara smiled in acknowledgement but reached for her sunglasses to protect herself. 'I must tell you . . . there's been a change of plan with the book.'

Jordan – having made his pitch – waited for Tara to explain.

'My publisher has persuaded me to add a couple of chapters about myself. Not a full autobiography – just a sketch of who I am and what I'm about.'

'Great,' said Jordan.

Or is it? he wondered. If she's happy to tell her own story maybe there's nothing to tell. Still, there's only one way to find out . . .

'I'd be fascinated to work with you on that.'

'Good . . . but there's a very tight deadline. Will you be able to devote yourself to the book full-time?'

'I've already asked my editor for a sabbatical,' lied Jordan. 'If I'm fortunate enough to get the chance to work with you,' he added hastily.

'I'll have to speak to my publisher.'

'Of course.'

'He'll get in touch with you next week – either way.'

Thinking that she was making up her mind, and aware that this was the moment when the best salesmen stay silent, Jordan smiled vaguely at Tara, took a sip of champagne, then pushed back his chair – right into the path of a waiter, who tripped and sent a dish of ice cubes tumbling onto Tara's bare legs.

As she jumped up, Jordan retrieved a pile of paper napkins from another table and – restraining himself from dabbing her legs – pressed them into her hands. The skin where he'd touched her tingled.

Tara lowered her head and wiped her legs dry before sitting down again.

'Sorry. Are you all right?' asked Jordan.

'Yes . . . thanks. No harm done,' said Tara. Except that you're making me nervous, she thought. Just when I need to keep a clear head.

'Good. Is there anything else you'd like to ask me?' he said.

'No,' she said firmly, regaining her composure. 'I think we've covered everything.' Tara shifted her chair to one side, making space to cross her legs. Right over left. Jordan's gaze followed the movement, then flicked up her thighs, skimming over the retro denim skirt and the pale blue cotton vest to the soft, buffed skin of her cleavage, arms and shoulders.

'Would you like another glass of champagne?' he offered.

'No, no, thank you. I've got to go soon,' said Tara, but instead of making a move to leave she reached for her glass, and – although there was only a mouthful of champagne left – deliberately took only the tiniest of sips.

She took off her sunglasses and fiddled with them.

'You know, you don't look old enough to have a book written about you yet,' he ventured.

'I'm thirty-six,' said Tara.

'You look much younger,' he schmoozed. Actually, it wasn't a schmooze. Looking at her close up in the sunshine, with minimal make-up, she genuinely appeared younger than it said in her cuttings.

I can't think of a sexier woman to turn over in print – or in bed, he thought. Must ask my Harley Street contacts if she's had a face-lift.

Tara saw him eyeing her intently and realised he was searching her face for crow's feet. He's sharp as a knife, she thought. And gorgeous. Dangerously gorgeous. Still, nothing I can't handle.

Tara started to move out of her seat but Jordan leaned forward. As she sat back, he grinned: 'Look, I have to tell you this. I've got an ulterior motive for wanting to write this book with you. After you've heard it you might not want to work with me. Why don't you let me take you out for dinner? I can confess all. Then even if the answer's no at least I'll have had the pleasure of dinner with you. How does that sound?'

Sounds fun, thought Tara.

'Sounds fine,' she said.

Jordan smiled: 'Great. Well?'

'I'm not sure when I'm free,' said Tara, finally getting up to go. 'Give me your card and my assistant Flora will call you with the time and the place.'

'I look forward to it.'

Intriguing, thought Tara as she walked away. I

definitely look forward to seeing *him* again. And to hear what he's got to say for himself. I thought I'd heard every line in a journalist's repertoire. But maybe Jordan Holmes has a new one. Can't wait to hear what it is . . .

Chapter Six

Glasgow, November 1997

'LISTEN to this, Scarlett, this is the best line ever. Never fails,' said Rab McGinty.

Scarlett looked up. Sixteen stones of sweaty reporter was standing over her desk: beer-bloated frame bursting out of a smart suit, Bobby Charlton hair draped across his bald pate. At fifty-one McGinty was one of the oldest reporters still on the road, but right now his beefy face was lit up like a little boy with a new Nintendo. Scarlett knew that look: it was the post-coital glow of a hack who'd just turned someone over. Tomorrow's front page belonged to him and there wasn't a shit-hotter reporter in the whole of Glasgow. Until someone else got the next day's splash. So McGinty was making the most of it while the sun still shone out of his arse. Everyone else in the newsroom was bent over their keyboards, intent on their stories. So it was up to Scarlett to be his audience. She understood that. It was part of her unwritten job description. That was how she'd got the job in the first place. Understanding what people really wanted, not what they said they wanted. She'd started here six years ago, as a temp. They hadn't wanted her. She'd been only eighteen, straight from commercial college, and green as a one-pound note. But the editor's secretary had had a nervous breakdown, the Scottish edition of the *Daily Brit* couldn't function for five minutes without her, and Scarlett was the only temp available at such short notice. The first few weeks had been hell.

'Coffee, Scarlett. When you're ready,' shouted the sports editor, interrupting McGinty's story.

'Right away,' she replied. 'You too?' she asked McGinty.

'If you're offering.'

Scarlett switched on the kettle next to her desk, spooned Nescafé into a couple of mugs.

'Anyway,' continued McGinty. 'It's a line I'd used before so I knew . . .'

'Is that coffee on the go?' enquired a reporter sitting nearby, frantically keying in a story.

'Milk and two sugars, aren't you, Jimmy?' asked Scarlett, reaching for a third mug.

'Magic.' Jimmy's eyes hadn't left the screen in front of him.

'So anyway,' said McGinty, testily.

Scarlett turned round, threw him a tell-me-more look.

Keeping them sweet was second nature now, but at the start it had been so daunting: thirty egos packed in an airless newsroom, demanding her attention *now*. But she hadn't panicked. She'd done everything she'd been asked to. Instantly. Eating her way to size eighteen under the watchful eye of a calorie-pinching mother had taken years of ingenuity and determination. Now

Scarlett applied the same skills to her job. McGinty wanted blank restaurant receipts for his expenses? She'd bought a whole pad from a stationery shop. The features editor wanted a 'real person' to test a new bra with pump-up cleavage? She'd phoned a Waistwatcher keen to show off her new shape and slipped her twenty quid from petty cash. The editor wanted his wife to think he was in London on business when he was in Paris with his girlfriend? She'd typed up a fake itinerary and had it on his desk in twenty minutes. 'Scarlett-from-Do-It-All' the hacks had nicknamed her. But six months later, when the editor's secretary refused to return to her post – on medical advice – Scarlett had got the job. The personnel department in London had thought she was too young, but her size made her look older and at only nineteen they didn't have to pay her much. Still, it was a lot more than most girls her age. She'd moved out of her mother's flat in Scotstoun and into the city centre, near the newspaper offices. Soon after, the Southern Gentlemen introduction agency had provided Ma with the man of her dreams: Tyler Dubois from Louisiana. Lola had been so excited she'd even confided in her daughter: 'Look, Scarlett, a self-made oilman with his own apartment in New Orleans *and* a mansion on a bayou.' Tyler's photo showed him standing in front of a brand-new motorboat, brandishing a fish. He looked like he had fifty-inch hips and chewing-tobacco breath but Lola had refused to be daunted: 'Lovely big bear of a man,' she'd enthused. 'Wonder why he's asked me for my shoe size?'

It turned out Tyler had a foot fetish. As soon as he saw Lola's dainty stiletto-shod feet clicking through arrivals at New Orleans airport, he didn't care that the woman walking towards him had a less than peachy complexion and a seen-it-all expression.

Ironic really, thought Scarlett. Ma devoted so much time to improving on what nature had given her, and all Tyler had been interested in were the size three-and-a-half feet she'd been born with. That's what had clinched the deal for her anyway; made her Mrs Dubois.

Well, Scarlett wouldn't be clinching any deals with men. No way. Certainly not with McGinty, who was still standing there, droning on about how he'd got across some poor woman's doorstep and charmed her story out of her. Scarlett flashed him an adoring glance. It was just like listening to children: let them witter on and throw in a few smiles to make them think you're listening.

'So I told her not to worry, I'm not that kind of reporter,' McGinty was saying. 'No way I'm going to pester you.'

Scarlett nodded, gave him another tell-me-more glance.

I can't do this job for ever, she thought. But what else could I do? Miss Macleod's still going on about going back to college. But that secretarial course was bad enough. OK during the day. In class. But afterwards. In the evenings. When the other girls were all chatting, making plans. I was always rushing off. As if I'd something to do, somewhere to go. Couldn't bear hanging around, waiting for invitations that wouldn't come. Not for Fatty-bum-bum. Better alone. In my bedsit. Stuffing my face. Or round at Miss Macleod's. Not too often though. Couldn't let her know how unhappy I am. After all she's done for me. Got a job. Money in the bank. Got away from Scotstoun. But I'm still fat. Still Ma's daughter. Still ashamed of what I did. Terrified someone might talk.

'Can get almost anyone to talk. If you've been in the game as long as I have.' McGinty was still preening himself.

'Just a mo,' said Scarlett, handing him a coffee, then hurrying over to the sports editor's desk with his.

'Ta, doll,' said McGinty. 'Anyway . . .' He waited till she'd sat down again: 'Told her I'd leave her in peace, but I had an awful sore throat and could I just come in for a glass of water. Soon as we were in the kitchen I started coughing and she says: "A hot drink's what you need," and puts the kettle on. Well,' he paused for dramatic effect. 'Before it was boiled she was spilling everything. The whole story. No problem.'

'Brilliant,' said Scarlett. 'You're wasted here. Should be in London.'

'I've had plenty of offers. Plenty. When Fleet Street really *was* Fleet Street. But now? It's all Perrier and press releases. No place for a real reporter. And London? Poofs and pollution. Who'd want to go there?'

I do, thought Scarlett. I do.

Late at night, in her one-bedroom rented flat in the trendy Merchant City, leafing through the glossy magazines, she felt full of confidence, ready for anything. Tomorrow, she told herself, she'd start dieting, go window-shopping in her lunch hour, think about getting away, getting to London. The next day she'd skip breakfast but by lunchtime she'd be having chips and cheese at her desk. And the work was so overwhelming, she'd stay in the building all day, forgetting about her own plans, till ten at night, when she was home again, eating Galaxy bars and reading magazines, resolving to start her new life tomorrow, hating herself for not having started today.

But the next day would be the same as the one before: the shabby open-plan newsroom, crammed with rows of computer workstations, manned by intense, gossipy, wise-cracking journalists, all wanting her to fetch coffee, cuttings, faxes, *now*. The cramped space made Scarlett feel even fatter. She shifted her bulk as quickly as she could across the coffee-stained carpet. Her thighs were permanently bruised from bumping into the office furniture. But that was preferable to being pigeon-holed as a slow-moving fat girl. As each long day wore on she got hotter, sweatier, more harassed. And like chicks squawking in a nest, the journalists continued to pester her for attention. Each of them felt overworked, under-appreciated, and each of them, every day, told her at length why this was the case. As they did so, they cast continual nervous glances at the glass-partitioned office behind her desk, whence, any moment, they expected to hear the barking tones of their master's voice. Like now, for instance. Scarlett flinched as she heard a familiar shout, accompanied by loud banging on the glass. The editor wanted something. 'Excuse me, Rab,' she said. 'Captain Blood Vessel calls.'

She grabbed notepad and pen and rushed to the editor's office. Lonnie McCoy, known to his minions as Captain Blood Vessel, was once more demonstrating how he'd earned his nickname. A scrawny fifty-something, five foot five in his built-up shoes and Boss suit, he was thumping his desk and shouting loud enough for the whole newsroom to hear: 'Where the fuck is that astrologer's copy? Would you chase that fucking useless cunt before I chase her myself?' Beneath his thinning grey hair, the narrow rat-like face was puce with anger and the veins on his neck were bulging alarmingly. The wiry 1970s moustache failed to conceal the nervous twitch in his thin upper lip. With anyone else it would have been the cue to call in a cardiac arrest team. With McCoy, it was business as usual.

Or should that be bollocking as usual? Scarlett knew better than to say anything. She scuttled straight back to her desk, flicked round to 'S' for 'Stars' on her Rolodex, and phoned the lounge bar where Mona McGonagall could usually be found of an afternoon.

'Sorry, hen, she's no here and she won't be here again for a while,' said the barman. 'She's been banned. She went a wee bit over the top last night. I blame Celtic myself.'

'What d'you mean?' asked Scarlett. Surely Mona McGonagall, the ultra soignée mix-and-match queen of Scotland's stargazers, wasn't a football fan?

'It was the fans. After Celtic's win last night they all wanted to buy her Tricolours. And ye ken whit Mona's like. Never refuses a drink.'

'Tricolours?'

'Aye. Brandy, Baileys, and Crème de Menthe. OK in small doses but not by the dozen. She told them Rangers was gonnae win the league and they just went mental. The glazier's been here all day. The boss has banned Mona for the duration. 'Scuse me, hen. I've got customers waiting.' He hung up.

'When's she filing?' Lonnie McCoy was standing over Scarlett's desk.

'She must be at home. I'll call her there,' she said.

'It's fucking seven o'clock. What the fuck is she playing at?'

McCoy turned on his heel and strode off to the back bench.

For once his apoplexy was justified. Mona's copy was meant to be in a week in advance. But the features editor had been on holiday, Scarlett had forgotten to check, and now it was only two and a half hours until the first edition had to be off stone. Scarlett dialled Mona's home number. No answer. She got out the A–Z, checked which bars were in Mona's street, and phoned them. No sign of her. She looked up the electoral roll on her computer, jotted down the names of Mona's neighbours, got their numbers from the phone book and called them. No word of Mona.

'Scar-lett,' shouted McCoy, without turning round from his computer screen.

'I've just spoken to her,' lied Scarlett. 'She's faxing it over.'

She redialled Mona's number, and let it ring. Someone picked up the phone, then put it down again. Scarlett redialled.

'Hello,' croaked a husky voice.

'Mona. It's Scarlett. From the *Daily Brit*. Where's your predictions? The editor's raging.'

'She's not well. She's indisposed. Too ill to come to the phone,' said the voice.

'Mona. I know it's you. What's the score? Have you done them?'

'Nearly. I'm halfway through them. My computer's not working and I've had a power cut and I'm very ill. Extremely ill. Should be in the hospital.'

Scarlett glanced at the clock. Ninety minutes before first edition.

'OK, well, phone me when they're ready.'

'Right you are, darling. I won't let you down. Bye-bye.'

'Bye,' said Scarlett. She'd seen her mother's hang-overs often enough to know that Mona *would* let her down. What now?

'Scar-lett. I'm losing my fucking patience here,' shouted McCoy.

'Her fax isn't working. She's just dictated them to me over the phone. I'll input them right away,' said Scarlett.

Oh God, she thought. Why did I say that? But I can't think of any other solution. It's my own fault. I know Mona needs social working to keep her sober.

71

It's my responsibility and I forgot to take care of it. If Mona's column fails to appear in tomorrow's paper, the phone lines will be jammed with calls from irate readers. And I'll become Captain Blood Vessel's whipping boy of choice for the next few weeks. A scary prospect. Even scarier than the only course now open to me . . .

Scarlett picked up her notepad and walked to the far end of the room, to the features editor's corner. She logged into the computer and opened a new file. 'ARIES (Mar 21–Apr 20),' she typed. Then she looked down at her notepad, as though reading something from it. Her mind went blank.

Come on, *come on*, she told herself. Think of something. You've read horoscopes often enough. It can't be that difficult.

Nothing came to mind.

She began typing in the names of the eleven other signs, leaving space to fill in the blanks. Staring at the screen, desperately awaiting inspiration, she reached Scorpio, her mother's sign. All at once, she visualised her mother in the front room of their flat in Scotstoun, ensconced on the sofa like a houri in a harem, flicking through mail-order catalogues while Scarlett kneeled before her, painting her toenails.

'SCORPIO (Oct 24–Nov 22),' she wrote. 'Watch out for your slave-driving tendencies today. You're overbearing and manipulative and if you don't stop ordering other people around you will end up alone and unloved. In the not-too-distant future.'

No, that was too harsh. People wanted to feel good

about themselves. They wanted to be understood. However little they tried to understand other people. Even Ma. She thought of her again. How did Lola Macdougall, now Dubois, see herself? She'd indulged in so many drunken monologues over the years, it wasn't too hard to imagine. Scarlett thought hard and rewrote the prediction: 'You've had a tough life in many ways. And no one works as hard as you do. Before you throw yourself into today's routine, schedule in some time to pamper yourself. You'll feel better for it and if you're kinder to yourself, you'll be more forgiving of others. Then you'll experience more of the love you deserve.'

That was it. Now, Captain Blood Vessel. She knew his sign: Cancer. Come to think of it, she knew his mother's sign too. He always got Scarlett to buy lavish presents for her on Mother's Day. And on her birthday. Sometimes he sent her flowers for no reason at all. He only did that for his wife when he'd been unfaithful.

'CANCER (Jun 23–Jul 23): People get the wrong impression of you. They think you're permanently angry but really you're a caring person who's too busy to show it. No one knows that better than your mother. Take a little time today to try to show that side of yourself to others. You won't lose respect, but you will win affection.'

'Scar-lett. Where the fuck are you hiding?' McCoy's voice bellowed across the newsroom. Despite the decibel level, the reporters and sub-editors kept their eyes on their stories. They were used to working to the sound of their master shouting.

73

So much for wrong impressions, thought Scarlett. The man is pure 110 per cent bastard. Still, all the more reason for him to lap up a bit of totally undeserved kindness. Always worked a treat with Ma.

Her fingers flew over the keys, tapping out TLC for each sign of the zodiac. 'It's over,' she shouted to McCoy, as she pressed the 'send' key.

He didn't answer. 'Thank you' wasn't in McCoy's vocabulary. The best you could hope for was that he stopped shouting at you. Silence was his way of showing approval.

'Scar-lett!'

She'd relaxed too soon.

'I don't want a fucking replay of this ever again. Make sure all Mona's columns for the next month are on my desk before morning conference tomorrow. Go round and get her to dictate them to you.'

Scarlett looked at the clock. It was 9.30 pm.

'Get a cab on account,' shouted McCoy, with the air of a potentate bestowing a great favour.

'Right, Lonnie, I'm on my way,' said Scarlett. But he didn't acknowledge her.

Veins on his neck pumping like pistons, he was now yelling at the chief sub: 'Call this a headline? My dog could write a better headline than this.'

Scarlett stuffed a notebook in her shoulder bag and waddled rapidly out of the office.

'Night, Scarlett,' said the security guard.

Outside the cobbles were slippery after rain. Vans ready to distribute the first edition were lined up, engines running. Through the porthole in the pub door, she could see The Printer's Devil was already packed with reporters downing a pint between editions and bitching about Captain Blood Vessel. A black cab rumbled to a halt and decanted a hack straight into the pub. He didn't bother to ask if Scarlett wanted the cab.

Wearily, she re-opened the door herself, climbed in, and gave the driver Mona's address. But what was the point? From past experience she knew Mona would be out for the count by now; incapable of stringing a few words together, let alone a month's worth of predictions.

'I've changed my mind,' she told the driver. 'Take me to Waterstone's on Sauchiehall Street.'

'Right, hen.'

She checked her watch: 9.35 pm. Waterstone's closed at ten.

'Would you wait please?' she said as she clambered out of the taxi and, heavy-footed, hurried into the shop. Fifteen minutes later she emerged with a bundle of books.

'That'll keep you out of mischief,' said the driver.

Tired as she was, Scarlett gave him a friendly smile. 'You're right there.'

'Where to, pal?'

'Back to the Merchant City, please. Ingram Street.'

She began leafing through one of the books. At the top of Ingram Street she got out, popped into the all-night corner shop, then walked the few yards to the converted warehouse where she rented a one-bedroom flat. Three flights up without a lift. Arms laden with shopping, she trudged up the stairs. With each step, her thighs chafed against each other. More blisters.

As she closed the door behind her, she sighed. Her stomach was churning with nerves. Could she really pull this off? It was nearly eleven o'clock. She felt hot, tired, weighed down by blubber and the long day behind her. Come on, she told herself. There's no other option. Get stuck in: coat off, kettle on.

She unpacked her purchases and laid them out on the coffee table: three astrology books, a Twix, a KitKat and half-a-dozen Galaxy bars. Where was her notebook? Music? No, she didn't want anything to disturb her thoughts. She needed to think back, to remember.

She pictured her mother's front room in Scotstoun. Ever since she could remember there had been Waistwatchers meetings or Mary Ellen make-up parties almost every evening: a room-full of women talking, talking, talking. They'd shared their fears and dreams, their insecurities and triumphs. They'd talked about their man, their children, their sex life, or lack of it. There were no holds barred.

As Lola rubbed moisturiser into pinched, cigarette-smoking faces, and stroked blusher onto wan, chips-and-white-bread complexions, the women would spill their most intimate secrets. Sometimes there were tears and the eye make-up had to be redone. But her mother hadn't minded. The more they cried, the more products they bought. The more they spent, the more they glowed with gratitude as they left the house. Even as a little girl Scarlett had noticed that.

She smiled wryly to herself. She'd hated her child-hood, hated her mother. Never thought she'd been paying much attention to anything going on around her. But now, remembering, details came flooding back. Fragments of chat came into her head, faces she thought she'd never want to remember. She knew almost every-thing there was to know about these women.

Men? Well, they'd talked about their men too. Their partners were buttoned-up west-of-Scotland males too macho to show their feelings, except on the football terraces. So on the rare occasions when they spoke of their emotions, the women pounced on these utterances like a dog on a bone. They saved them, then dug them up to gnaw over with their friends. The tenacity with which they extracted every nuance of meaning from a few unguarded words would have put a psycho-analyst to shame. So there was nothing Scarlett didn't know about what made people tick. She unwrapped the Twix bar, stuck a chocolate finger in her mouth, then picked up her Biro and started writing.

'Good, very good,' said Lonnie McCoy, leafing through the pile of print-outs Scarlett had left on his desk. She'd been in the office since six in the morning keying them into the computer. Even so, she hadn't expected McCoy to show appreciation. It was completely out of char-acter.

'I've read through them all. She's really got into the nitty-gritty with these. She must have been on form last night.'

'Yes,' said Scarlett. 'I gave her heaps of black coffee. That seemed to do the trick.'

McCoy smiled at her. Then his face went grim. 'Don't fucking lie to me. I know she didn't do them. Don't you realise you can't just copy stuff out of a book? We'd be sued for breach of copyright. What the fuck are you playing at?'

Scarlett was too taken aback to reply.

'Do you think I'm fucking stupid?' thundered McCoy.

'No,' said Scarlett. 'No, the thing is . . . I only wanted to . . . how did you . . .?'

McCoy thrust the final edition of the *Daily Brit* at her. 'Look at the Stop Press,' he commanded.

She looked: 'Popular stargazer Mona McGonagall struck by mystery illness. Mona, real name Morag McGonagall, 46, was rushed to the Western Infirmary in the early hours of this morning after collapsing in a hotel lounge in Glasgow city centre.'

'Oh,' said Scarlett. 'How is she?'

'As well as can be expected for a whisky-soaked cow. There's no fucking mystery about her illness. Get onto the hospital, get her discharged and get her into that drying-out clinic on the South Side. Tell them the *Daily Brit* will pay. And do it discreetly. If this gets into any other paper I'll hold you personally responsible. Now. Where did you lift those astrology columns from?'

'I didn't,' said Scarlett. 'I wrote them myself.'

McCoy looked at her sharply. 'Don't lie to me, Scarlett.'

'But I did. I stayed up all night and I wrote them.'

He picked up a page and re-read it.

Oh God, thought Scarlett. Is he going to sack me?

McCoy finished reading and fixed her with his beady eyes: 'Is that the truth? You didn't take them from a book, or another newspaper?'

'I looked at a couple of astrology books to get an idea of how to write them. But I didn't copy any of the predictions. I made them up myself.'

'Nobody helped you?'

'No.'

'Does anybody know about this?'

'No.'

McCoy beamed at her. Allowed a rare hint of warmth into his voice: 'They're not bad. Not bad at all. We'll run them.' He looked at her appraisingly. 'Mona will be out of the game for at least six months. D'you reckon you can churn it out till then? The same standard? I'll pay you extra.'

'Yes, yes, I'm sure I can,' said Scarlett. Why not? she thought. Once I got going last night I was hardly able to write fast enough to keep up with my ideas. The time just flew past. Although I've hardly slept I feel great. A real sense of accomplishment. And now I'm to fill in for Mona. How exciting. Don't imagine McCoy will let me off my other work but who cares? It'll be fun. Something different. Can't wait to see my name in the paper. That'll show everyone.

'Thank you, Lonnie,' she said. 'This is so great. I won't let you down. I'll get my picture by-line done as soon as one of the snappers gets in.'

'You'll what?' said McCoy. 'You don't think we'd . . .'

What was left of his sense of decency kicked in and he didn't finish the sentence. But he didn't need to. Scarlett knew what he had been going to say.

Eyes downcast, she fought back tears: 'You don't want my face at the top of Mona's column. I don't look the part, do I?'

'No, no, it's not that,' said McCoy. 'It's continuity. The readers like continuity. Mona has her following. We don't want to lose it. Look, I'll make it well worth your while. And you can go home at six every night to make sure you've time to do them. Just don't tell anybody. OK? I'll phone the managing editor myself.'

He glanced at Scarlett's face. A moment ago she'd been radiant. Now she looked stricken.

'Look,' said McCoy. 'I realise how hard you've worked on these. They're good. But will you be able to keep it up? It won't be easy.'

Scarlett's expression hadn't changed.

'If Mona doesn't come back, then you can take over. Promise. OK?'

'OK,' said Scarlett, dully.

'Good girl.'

Scarlett walked back to her own desk, carrying the paper McCoy had given her. She turned to the horoscope page. They'd printed it exactly as she'd written it. It read well. Very well. Her phone rang.

'*Daily Brit*,' she answered automatically.

'Oh hello, hen. Josie O'Donnell here. I read about Mona this morning. Terrible. Would you tell her I'm asking for her. I've just read my stars and she's spot-

80

on, absolutely spot-on. She's magic. Pure magic. She really made me think this morning. I'm praying for her. Would you tell her that, hen? From Josie O'Donnell, Paisley?'

'Yes, Mrs O'Donnell. I'll pass that on. Thanks for phoning.'

Scarlett hung up.

'Scar-lett,' bellowed McCoy. 'Where's my coffee?'

'On its way,' Scarlett shouted back, reaching for the kettle.

The phone rang again.

'*Daily Brit.*'

'Mrs Sanderson here. I'm calling from Haddington. Have you got a telephone number for Mona, your astrologer? I've been reading her column this morning. So full of insights. It's really helped me. I'd like a private reading.'

'I'm sorry, Mrs Sanderson. Mona's unwell. But if you'd like to write to her care of the newspaper I'll make sure she gets the letter. Thank you so much for phoning.'

As she put the receiver down, Scarlett felt a tingly sensation in her stomach. Mid-morning munchies? On reflex she reached into her drawer, retrieved a Jaffa cake and stuffed it in her mouth.

'Scarlett. Any chance of that coffee before lunch-time?'

In response to McCoy's shout, Scarlett picked up the half-boiled kettle and – to speed things up – poured some of the water into the wastepaper bin.

'Just coming,' she shouted back.

No, it's not hunger, she thought. Something else.

The phone rang.

'*Daily Brit.*'

'Helen Lawson here from Aberdeen. Just ringing to wish Mona all the best. That was an awful thing to happen to her. And a rare column from her this morning. Don't know how I'll cope without her.'

'Um . . . well she works a wee bit ahead so we'll be running her column as usual.'

'Well I'm fair relieved to hear that. And I hope she gets well soon.'

'I'll pass that on. Thank you so much for phoning.'

McCoy was banging on the glass now, holding up both hands in exasperation.

OK, thought Scarlett. I'll get your coffee.

But I know what's different, she said to herself. Last night I battered out some advice, and this morning all these women have taken it to heart. I feel . . . it's so unfamiliar I couldn't work it out at first . . . but I know what it is now . . . a small sense of achievement . . . and of power . . . yes, that's what it is.

If people are phoning to say how good I am, I must be good. And yet, she grimaced to herself, here I am, making McCoy's coffee. So nothing's changed really. McCoy will never let me take over from Mona. In a few months she'll have dried out and be back as 'Scotland's most sophisticated stargazer'. And I'll still be the Do-It-All girl at everyone's beck and call. I was Ma's dogsbody. Now I'm McCoy's.

Scarlett sighed so deeply one of the hacks actually turned round and threw her a sympathetic glance. She picked up a pile of paperwork and pretended to read. But her head was buzzing. When am I going to escape? she wondered. And how? When is Scarlett the dogsbody ever going to become a somebody?

Chapter Seven

London, August 2000

DAVID lowered the stylus of the old record player onto the scratched vinyl, then sat back to see what effect the music would have on his audience. The reaction was even better than he had hoped. As the strains of the 1940s hit 'Don't Sit Under the Apple Tree (With Anyone Else But Me') resonated through the brightly painted community centre café, a dozen elderly faces lit up with recognition. Feet that had once stood ten hours a day in munitions factories tapped in time to the music. Edna Hooper, retired pub landlady and life and soul of every pensioners' organisation in the borough, announced loudly: 'The Andrews Sisters. Now they really *could* sing.' Clicking ring-heavy fingers and swaying slightly in her stackable plastic chair, she winked coquettishly at Wilf James, the solitary old soldier in their midst.

But David's attention was fixed on Mary O'Reilly, eighty-three next birthday. A fragile figure in floral summer frock and trainers, she'd allowed herself to be bussed in to the oral reminiscence group for the past three weeks but had sat in mournful silence throughout. Usually she sat head bowed, in complete stillness, ignoring his best attempts at stimulating group discussion. But now, David noticed, she'd raised her head slightly.

'Could show those Spice Girls a thing or two,' declared Mrs Hooper, as the song came to an end.

'Yes indeed,' said David. 'They certainly sold more records . . . and this man,' he delved into the box of crackly 78s he'd lugged back from Brick Lane market in his own time, 'this man recorded the first million-selling record.'

Within three or four bars of the introduction, silver-blue permed heads were nodding and lined faces were smiling. By the sound of the train whistle, people resigned to the forgetfulness of old age were suddenly cheered at their powers of recall. Before the lyrics began, everyone in the room knew it was the Glenn Miller Orchestra with 'Chattanooga Choo-Choo'.

It gets better and better, thought David, surveying the animated faces around him. By the time the song ended, almost all of them were smiling.

'Have you got "In the Mood", son? That'll get us going,' bellowed Mrs Hooper.

She nudged Mr James – ex-Dunkirk, ex-British Rail, now a well-loved but little-visited grandpa. 'You know, there's a song,' he screwed up his eyes, trying to remember, 'there's a song Doris and I loved,' he said. The mention of his late wife gave him pause. Politely, everyone waited for him to continue. 'It was about apple trees as well. I think . . .'

'We've just had that, lovey,' interrupted Mrs Hooper. She attempted to exchange a poor-dear's-losing-his-marbles look with David. Ignoring it, David smiled encouragingly at Mrs O'Reilly. Her liver-spotted hands were anxiously twisting the white cotton sunhat on her lap.

Come on, Mary, he thought. What have you got to say?

'"Don't Sit Under The Apple Tree",' Edna was explaining to Wilf in a would-be sotto voce tone that even the deafer members of the group could hear. 'D'you want David to play that again, lovey?'

Unsure of catching anyone's attention, Mary looked up timidly. David was waiting for her, his friendly glance inviting her to speak.

'Apple blossom,' she said shyly. '"I'll Be With You In Apple Blossom Time".'

'That's the one,' said Wilf, tapping his walking stick in delight. Stiffly, he turned towards Mary and nodded gallantly. 'Such a lovely melody. Wasn't it? Sort of an "our song" for Doris and me.'

'For us too,' said Mary. She smiled mistily.

Yes, thought David. Yes!

'I'll see if I've got that one,' he said. 'Any other requests?'

He looked round the room questioningly. 'George Formby? Vera Lynn? Bing Crosby?'

For once, Edna's time-gentlemen-please voice was not the first to be heard. 'Play them all. Just play them all,' said Mary.

David looked at her wonderingly: her defeated half-asleep expression had been replaced by the hope-filled smile of a teenager. What a transformation, he thought.

'Ah, here it is,' he smiled. 'The Andrews Sisters

86

again.' Carefully, he placed 'I'll Be With You In Apple Blossom Time' on the turntable. Within a few bars, it was clear from the faces of his audience that it was one of their favourites, but just as they were settling back to enjoy it, their memories were interrupted.

'Time's up, Mr DJ.'

'Sorry?'

David turned to see the community centre caretaker – a born-and-bred East Ender his own age – walking towards him, stubby fingers pointing meaningfully at his back-of-a-lorry diver's watch. 'Caff closes at six,' he said officiously. 'Time to wrap up.'

'But the minibus won't be here for another half hour,' said David.

'Should've stayed in your regular room, mate. You're booked in there till half past.'

'I know, but . . .' David indicated the happy group in front of him, temporarily rejuvenated by the music.

'Look, I'm not breaking up the party, mate. You can carry on downstairs in your usual room.'

David surveyed the dozen seventy- and eighty-year-olds in his group: 'By the time we get everyone down there it'll be time to go home.'

'Don't know why you came up here anyway.'

'Well it's just more . . .' David was about to say 'convivial', but stopped himself: 'It's more relaxed up here.'

The caretaker responded with a rules-is-rules shrug: 'Sorry, mate. But the counter staff are only paid till half past, and there's no way the cleaners will do the washing up. Not in their contract.'

David looked at his oral reminiscence group. For the past three weeks the conversation had been dominated by one or two people – but now, as they waited to hear the next record, everyone was engaged in lively chat.

'I'll do it,' he said.

'What? The washing-up?'

'Why not? It's just a few teacups.'

The caretaker was astonished: 'You're not paid for that, mate.'

David smiled and shrugged his shoulders. 'No problem.'

'OK,' said the caretaker. The look he gave David added: you're-a-right-mug-you-are.

David saw it but didn't care. 'Thanks,' he said.

Selecting another 78 and slipping it onto the turntable, he looked up and smiled at his group. 'Right, folks. Who remembers dancing to this one?'

As the Glenn Miller Orchestra swung into 'Little Brown Jug', David joined three of the group at a wipe-clean table and helped himself to a left-over chocolate biscuit, then sat back and surveyed the entranced faces around him. Such an important part of recent popular history, he thought. And yet before the radio and the gramophone, how often did people get the chance to hear music . . . As the record came to an abrupt end he leapt up and rushed to put on another. The first that came to hand was another Andrews Sisters number: 'Beat Me Daddy, Eight to the Bar'.

Interesting, thought David. The title's raunchy enough for a hip-hop crew. And yet each generation thinks the previous one is so innocent. Sitting down again, he noticed Mrs Hooper was pointing at his feet and laughing. 'Got *your* toes tapping too, lovey!'

David smiled and gave her a thumbs-up.

Yes, it's great music, he thought. Never really listened to it before. I'm so lucky to have a job where I make new discoveries *and* get new lines of enquiry for my research.

Making her exit bang on six o'clock, the café assistant waved a cheery goodbye to the room in general, and paused to speak to David. 'I've left the hot water on for you. I'd stay myself but with the kids . . .'

David smiled. 'No problem and thanks.'

He leaned back in his chair. This is the best session we've had, he thought. It'll only take me ten minutes to tidy up . . . and then I'll be finished for the day . . . out into this beautiful evening . . . for a stroll along the river – long before any of the Maserati types in our apartment block get home from the office . . .

I wouldn't mind their salary, he mused. But the hours they do are ludicrous. I once pointed out to Jordan he would've put in fewer hours as a mill worker in the Industrial Revolution, but he didn't see my point. Strange job he does. People-chasing. And now it's that gorgeous astrologer he's after . . . Tara. Don't like what he does, but it's fascinating how he does it. Might see him later at the pub . . . I'll certainly be there . . . a nice cold lager . . . overlooking the river . . . breeze rustling through the weeping willow . . . water lapping against the river walls . . . perfect.

Evening planned, his attention turned back to his

group. He was about to get up to change the record, but then stopped himself.

Advancing slowly but straight-backed to the gramophone, Wilf James was clearly about to take over DJ duties. David occupied himself by taking another biscuit.

In position at last, Wilf rummaged through the box, then held up a 78 in triumph. 'Here it is, Mary. You were spot-on with the title, girl.'

Her little old lady's face blushing like a schoolgirl, Mary O'Reilly nodded her gratitude.

Slowly, with arthritis-clumsy fingers, Wilf set about changing records.

'Sorry, folks,' he said. 'Won't be a mo.'

He glanced apologetically at their group leader, but David just smiled and settled back in his chair.

Don't worry, Wilf, he thought. Plenty of time . . .

Chapter Eight

London, August 2000

AMID the sticky mass of humanity emerging from the Tube, Jordan slalomed his way through a slow-moving huddle of slack-bottomed American tourists. Along the litter-strewn corridor he strode and into the lift, where a crush of strangers succeeded in avoiding eye contact all the way to the surface. First through the doors, he marched out of Chalk Farm station into the pizza-scented heat of the summer evening, then over the railway bridge to Primrose Hill; one of London's 'most wanted' addresses for those with money to make estate agents drool.

Ahead of him lay a high street as pretty and whimsical as an opera set: yellow brick and white stucco Georgian terraces dripping with flower baskets and sun canopies; Mercedes convertibles and Grand Cherokee jeeps sailing past the wine merchant and the perfumery, the interior designer and the antique dealer. Out-pacing a male couple in Bermudas and Birkenstocks – licking his-and-his ice-cream cones – then a schoolboy conducting a mobile phone call from his skateboard, Jordan reached The Queens.

Inside he found a pub in the grip of an identity crisis: an Olde England decor with Moroccan-style snug; pork scratchings and bitter next to ciabatta toasties and Hoegaarden.

'A Diet Coke, mate,' he told the barman.

'Ice and a slice?'

'Please. Take a look at your *Standard*?'

'Help yourself, mate.'

Flicking through the evening paper, Jordan spotted something so upsetting he closed the pages in disgust.

'More lies?' asked the barman.

'Yeah,' said Jordan. His tone was casual, but his face was that of a man whose past had just caught up with him. Leave me alone, he thought. But he couldn't resist re-opening the paper and studying the photo on page nine.

'Jack E and the Boyz lend their name to anti-drugs campaign,' read the caption. '"The E is for energy. It's not our fault if people jump to false conclusions," said club diva Jack E last night; as she and her chart-topping band helped the Prime Minister launch his latest initiative – BAD (Britain Against Drugs).'

Oh Jackie, he thought. Why do you always have to remind me? He re-examined the photo. Yes, you *do* look a bit like Tara, he mused. Not so's anyone else would notice. But then no one else has studied your face the way I have. He took a sip of Coke. Coca-Cola and watery Maxwell House, he thought. That's what your mum used to bring us when we were rehearsing . . .

Like a lonelyheart putting on a CD guaranteed to make him cry, Jordan couldn't resist pressing the replay button in his memory: he saw himself at seventeen, in Jackie's dad's garage with the rest of the band, him on lead guitar, her on vocals. Him telling her to loosen up, to come out for a drink. Jackie staying in the garage, singing her guts out; himself in the snug of The Slipper and Ploughshare, chatting up Chantal, a nineteen-year-old au pair. 'I'm at college. In London,' he'd lied.

He saw himself cock-a-hoop in the role of schoolboy superstud, shuttling between Chantal and Jackie, shrugging his shoulders when Jackie found out and dumped him, not caring about her – or his A levels – until the day Chantal said she was going back to Paris, to the fiancé she'd omitted to mention.

Then, as if awakening from a dream, he'd wondered first what he'd do with such rotten exam results, and second what had happened to Jackie. Except that by then she wasn't Jackie any more.

She was Jack E, the latest discovery of a record company man who'd heard the band at a pub gig and seen pound signs written all over her prematurely knowing voice and curvy wet-dream body. Jackie had gone to London, to be hothoused for stardom. Jordan had gone it alone – without help from his father – and got his first break in journalism by betraying the only girl he'd ever cared about. In his first job as a copy boy on the local newspaper he'd given the news editor exclusive photos of the new singing star Jack E, topless, when she was only sixteen. Just a bit of fun: publicity for Jackie and a reporter's job for him. Not a betrayal, he'd told her afterwards. But she hadn't wanted to know.

A south London voice interrupted Jordan's thoughts: 'Finished with that, mate?'

'Yeah. Yeah. Here you are.' He handed the paper to one of the plaster-spattered workmen drinking next to him.

'Cheers.'

Leave it alone, Jordan ordered himself. Don't waste time with what-might-have-beens. You're on a mission. And – well-versed in the tabloid psychobabble of rent-a-quote therapists – he self-analysed fluently: It's because of Tara I'm thinking about Jackie. There's something about Tara. Something Sunni doesn't have. Something no one else has had. Apart from Jackie. Which makes Tara dangerous. I've got to be on my guard.

'Want another?' the barman asked.

'No thanks, mate. Cheers.'

Jordan left The Queens, continued along Regent's Park Road, past Primrose Hill park, the green slopes strewn with single women and their books, bare-chested men and their beer cans. At Chalcot Crescent he turned left into the elegant curve of town houses. Despite being in the heart of London the crescent was quiet, rose-scented, free of traffic; an oasis of peace, ring-fenced by money. The only people to be seen were two builders on overtime re-doing sash windows and an au pair pushing a pram containing a won't-sleep baby. Each house was prettier than the next: painted pink, lemon, pistachio, with white stucco lintels, wrought-iron balconies and railings: a toy town for millionaires.

Finally he found Tara's door. He stepped into the guardsman's box porch and rapped the brass knocker.

Chapter Nine

London, August 2000

THE door opened to reveal a tiny personage. With her silver-haired chignon, neat tweed suit and upright carriage, she looked like Miss Jean Brodie beyond her prime. But her voice didn't match. It should have been Edinburgh Doily. Instead it was Hebridean Welcome: warm and comforting as a whisky toddy.

'Mr Holmes?'

He nodded.

'Come away in.'

She smelt of talc and eau de Cologne and her powdered face bore the gentle lines of a life lived in moderation. Her glasses hung from a spectacle chain. The only hints of bygone frivolity were the pencilled brown arches marking where her eyebrows had once been.

This must be Flora, Tara's assistant, thought Jordan. An OAP PA. There's a novelty.

He smiled winningly. 'Thank you,' he said, following her into a high-ceilinged hallway. He just had time to take in honey-coloured walls, closed doors and a banistered staircase, before being ushered sharp left.

'You'll be having a cup of tea,' said Flora, leading him into an airy white and cream room scented by stargazer lilies in waist-high ceramic urns. No paintings, no rugs, no clutter. Just two invitingly soft suede-covered armchairs arranged at a small inlaid teak table. 'Sit yourself down,' she said, then bustled away, her high-heeled leather-laced shoes tapping across the maplewood floor.

The table was already set for tea for one, with shortbread fingers and buttered gingerbread. At half past seven in the evening. And now here she was, bustling back in with a pot of Earl Grey and lemon slices.

Hot wet beverages, the final purpose in life of the elderly female, thought Jordan. Better humour the old bat. She's bound to know all about Tara.

'Thank you so much,' he said, submitting to tea and shortbread. 'Mmmm, tastes home-made.'

A charming young man, thought Flora.

'It is indeed,' she smiled – and continued to hover.

Might as well make the most of it, thought Jordan. 'I saw that chap, what's his name, the one who's just left his wife on *Coronation Street*, on my way here,' he said. This was untrue. But he knew the actor was one of Tara's clients and wanted to test her PA's discretion. He beamed up at her brightly.

Hmmm, thought Flora. Perhaps a little *too* charming.

'Did you?' she said. 'I'm not much of a one for the television. I'm a great reader myself.'

'Me too,' he grinned, then – reaching for a second piece of shortbread – enquired politely: 'May I?' He bit into it, nodding his appreciation.

Silly old thing, he thought. She'll be eating out of my hand soon enough.

Under cover of smiling at her, he inspected Flora more closely. Why has the astrologer for the twenty-first century got a wrinkly looking after her? Tara's Highland great-granny is supposedly pushing up thistles and anyway, if they *were* related she wouldn't call her Miss MacDonald. So why such an ancient retainer? Must be at least seventy, if not eighty, and fuck, what's this, her bosom's vibrating. She's having palpitations.

'Excuse me,' said Flora, extracting a pager from under her neat little jacket. Putting on her glasses, she read the message on it. As she looked up again, she caught Jordan checking his watch. 'Don't worry, Mr Holmes. Miss MacDonald *is* at home. She's just buzzed me from upstairs. She'll be down shortly.'

Jordan wiped his mouth with the linen napkin. 'No crumbs?' he asked with a grin. Better keep my charm on, he thought. This old dear could be useful.

If he were chocolate he'd eat himself, thought Flora. She shook her head, then turned towards Tara as she made her entrance in a black and white Armani suit, spike heels and a Louis Vuitton attaché case. The outfit said: 'Don't get any ideas – this is strictly business.'

'Hello there,' she said – tepid as a too-busy woman ticking off the next meeting in her personal organiser.

'Hello, Tara,' said Jordan – with enough warmth to crystallise a crème brûlée at fifty paces.

Definitely far too charming, thought Flora.

'I've booked you into Odette's,' she said.

'Good. That'll save time,' said Tara. 'I've always got

97

to be up so early to get to the studios,' she explained to Jordan. 'Odette's is just up the road.'

'Perfect.'

Jordan followed Tara outside and fell into step with her. Tara flicked a swift sideways glance at him, but not swift enough for Jordan to miss. He looked at her questioningly.

'It's a gorgeous evening,' she said.

And you're a gorgeous woman, he thought. But I'm not going to say anything that obvious.

'Yes it *is*,' he said, putting the unspoken compliment into his eyes.

Half his mind was on his script. The other half had already climbed up her bare legs and was powering into her with a vengeance.

Fuck off, Roger, he thought. I'm working.

'Busy day?' he asked.

'It always is,' said Tara, with a slave-to-my-Psion sigh.

Not too busy to turn a business meeting into dinner though, thought Jordan, who could spot a date-in-disguise – even if Tara couldn't.

'Here we are,' she said as they reached Odette's Wine Bar and Restaurant.

Jordan dived to open the door for her. 'Post-modern gallantry.'

Tara laughed.

'Good evening, Miss MacDonald,' said the maître d'. He led them past diners drinking Bollinger and talking Buddhism in the plush baroque dining room into a less formal area at the back. The prices were the same but the atmosphere was one of contrived simplicity: white-washed brick walls and a tiled floor, with huge hanging baskets of greenery suspended from the ceiling. On one wall a vast painting showed young men reclining in a green meadow under a blue sky daubed with fluffy white clouds.

As the maître d' pulled out a cane chair for Tara and lit the Shaker-style single white candle, Jordan whispered conspiratorially: 'This is al fresco eating for people who don't want grass stains on their Gucci.'

Tara smiled appreciation.

Good, thought Jordan. Got her smiling.

He opened the menu. 'Just as I thought. Simple food made complicated. Look, "Peppered fillet of beef with Pont-Neuf potatoes" and "Potted lemon and vanilla rice pudding with cherries in red wine sauce". Take away the fancy potatoes and the booze in the dessert and you've got beef and rice pudding. Just what we used to get at school.'

Tara smiled politely.

Above their heads, the sliding roof was open, framing a rectangle of darkening summer sky. Jordan and Tara looked upwards at the same time.

Nation's favourite astrologer dines under the stars, thought Jordan.

'Bet I know what you're thinking,' said Tara.

'Go on then.'

'You're thinking: astrologer dines under the stars.'

'Am I that transparent?'

'Not at all. It's just that I used to—' Used to work on a newspaper, Tara nearly said, but stopped herself in time.

Jordan was looking at her quizzically; one eyebrow slightly raised. 'You used to . . .' he prompted.

'I used to do mind-reading when I was a wee girl. As my party piece.'

Is she fibbing? wondered Jordan.

'Really,' he said. 'So do you still do it?'

'Only for myself. I don't tell anyone any more.'

Definitely fibbing, thought Jordan.

'You don't believe me, do you?'

'What makes you say that?'

'I heard you thinking it. Loud and clear. "She's fibbing." Am I right?'

Jordan laughed; held up his hands. 'OK. I confess I'm sceptical. But you're converting me rapidly. Now, what would you like to eat?'

There followed a flurry of menus and ordering, salad of asparagus, Irish rock oysters, baked salmon and Gressingham duck, with Pinot Gris.

Tara ate little, drank less. Jordan mentioned a film he'd seen.

'I've seen it too. Really funny,' she said.

'I know. You went to the premiere. That's why I went to see it. So we'd have something to talk about.'

She looked horrified.

'Only kidding,' he said.

'Oh.'

Interesting, thought Jordan. She's not used to being teased. Almost like she's not used to dating.

'Well, it's semi-true,' he backtracked. 'If I'm going to be writing about your life it's useful for me to share some of your experiences.'

100

'Such thoroughness. I'm glad you're on my side. You *are* on my side, aren't you?'

'Of course,' said Jordan, giving her his best on-the-doorstep trust-me expression.

Tara rummaged in her attaché case and produced three cassette tapes. 'These are my thoughts so far. For the book. I started them last week, after we met.'

He reached for them. Their hands met.

Oh dear, thought Tara.

Oh *yes*, thought Jordan.

Tara slapped Jordan's hand away playfully. Why on earth did I do *that*, she wondered.

'Not yet. You haven't told me,' she said.

'Haven't told you what?'

'Your big confession. The reason we're here.'

He took an exaggerated deep breath. Looked her straight in the eyes. 'The real reason I wanted to write this book is that you're a big star who's going to get bigger. I wanted to ride on the coat-tails of your fame a little. Your name next to mine on a book jacket would do me a lot of good. Help make my name a little bigger.'

She smiled. Looked at him. Waited to hear more. It always worked with her clients.

That old trick, thought Jordan. But fuck it. The more I open up to her the more likely she is to reciprocate.

'It's important to me to succeed. Very important. My father . . .' He broke off, looked into the candle flame, then back at her. 'And OK, timing's wrong, but what the hell. Since meeting you last week I've got a new reason: you're the most intriguing woman I've ever met and I want to get to know you.'

101

Fuck, thought Jordan. Halfway through the well-worn line the words had acquired the unfamiliar taste of sincerity.

'Ambition isn't a crime,' she said. 'And since we're here now, I might as well tell you. I've spoken to my publisher and he's happy for you to do the book. In fact . . .' Tara re-opened her attaché case, 'I've got the contract here.'

Jordan read it through quickly and signed with a flourish. 'I'm now your official ghostwriter. Ready for haunting.' He adopted a thoughtful tone: 'You know, it's interesting how many heads of state have relied on astrologers: the Chinese leaders, of course, but also Ronald Reagan, François Mitterand . . .' Who else had Plod mentioned? he wondered.

'Yes, I'd like the political dimension in my book. I've mentioned all of them on my tapes.'

'So what else is on them? Your darkest secrets?'

'Of course,' she smiled. 'For your ears only.'

'Seriously though, what kind of book do you want?'

'My work as a prophet of the emotions, where I get my inspiration from, how to have a happier future, just like you said in your outline. Didn't like your title though.'

'*Tara's Life in the Stars*? I thought it said it all. But maybe you have a title already?'

'*Re-inventing Fate.*'

'Is that possible? What about destiny?'

'Destiny isn't fixed.'

'I'm surprised to hear an astrologer say that.'

'I'm not your average astrologer.'

102

'I appreciate that. But I thought putting your name in the title was a must. That's what will sell it.'

'Maybe. But so will the idea of re-invention. Everyone wants to re-invent themselves these days.'

'True. But how many people d'you know who've actually succeeded?'

Me, thought Tara. If you only knew. She smiled.

What a lovely smile, thought Jordan.

'Anyway,' he continued, 'whatever you do you can't change your past. It will always catch up with you in the end.'

Oh God, thought Tara. Please, please be wrong about that. She looked away, anxiously.

'Are you all right?' asked Jordan.

'Just thinking about fate.'

'Well if it *can* be changed then we're definitely onto a bestseller.' Jordan raised his wine glass in a toast.

Tara smiled and gently clinked her glass against his. 'To the book,' she said.

To me, thought Jordan.

'To the book,' he echoed. 'And I'm so glad you've decided to add a few chapters on yourself, Tara. Your fans will want to know your life story.'

'It's very dull.'

'I'm sure it isn't. What about your childhood? What were you like as a little girl? I can just picture you.'

Thank God you can't, thought Tara. The idea of *you* seeing me as Fatty-bum-bum. Unbearable. She felt herself redden. Oh my God, she said to herself. What's wrong with me? Blushing like an idiot.

'Excuse me.' She got up and made her way between

103

the chattering tables of diners to the ladies' toilet. It was small, wood-panelled and lined with mirrors. She sat down, catching sight of herself in the mirror. *Can I manage this,* she wondered. She pulled a compact from her attaché case and daubed at her flushed face. OK, she told herself. Be sensible. Now you've gone this far with Jordan, you'll just have to handle him. You're not poor naive Scarlett any more. You're Tara. You're gorgeous, successful and on the other side of the door is everything you used to dream about: waiters dancing attention; a great-looking man. All served up under a rectangle of stars. So what are you waiting for?

She's taking ages, thought Jordan. No different from most women in that respect. But in others . . . well, there's definitely something mysterious about her. As if she's got secrets. She'd better have. I'm going to look fucking stupid if I don't get a story out of this.

Yesterday, when Jordan had told the news editor, John Bullock, he wanted to be taken off the reporters' rota, he was working on a story of his own about Tara MacDonald, Bullock's closed, thin-lipped face had remained professionally deadpan. But the *Brit* was well-staffed enough to allow a good reporter like Jordan to follow his nose, and who knew what he might come up with? If Jordan failed it was his own fuck-up. If he succeeded, Bullock would claim the credit for having set him on the story.

I've got to crack this, thought Jordan. Got to get her talking.

He took another sip of wine.

Right now I'm the journalistic equivalent of a

hackney cab, sitting on the news desk, waiting to be sent out on any old story. But if I can bring in a scoop as big as this on my own initiative, LA here I come. Can't wait: the whopping expense account, the ocean-view villa, the chance to get my own back on all those bastards who wouldn't buy my film script. I'll fuck a few backroom girls at the studios, get them to dish the dirt, and I'll have more showbiz scoops than days in the week. My picture by-line will never be off the front page. That'll show my dad.

His father never tired of telling him: 'You and I are in the same business son – dirty linen. I clean it for them. You hang it out in public. The big difference is it's made me a fucking millionaire. And you're still an *em-ploy-ee*. Camped out on other people's doorsteps at your editor's pleasure. I worked so hard I didn't take a shit for ten years. But I was always my own boss. Always.'

This'll finally impress him, thought Jordan. And my smug bastard brother. Last Christmas, over dinner at their mother's, Nathan had declared: 'I'm expanding Rush Caffeine into Europe. Sounds like coals to Newcastle: coffee to France. But my marketing people tell me it'll be a doddle. We're selling style, not taste.' Nathan had turned to Jordan. 'I need someone I can trust to run things on le Con-ti-nong. I'll take you on tomorrow. Just say the word.'

Patronising bastard, thought Jordan. This'll shut him up. As long as I keep my mind on my mission.

'You look thoughtful,' said Tara, slipping back into her seat with an uncertain smile.

What a lovely subtle smile, thought Jordan. Surely I

can have my story *and* have her too? Why should I resist?

'Just thinking how irresistible our book will be, da'ling,' he said. His tone was Ab-Fab parody, but when he said 'irresistible' he looked straight into her eyes.

Picking up her barely touched wine glass, she lifted it to her lips and took a proper mouthful. Then another.

Hurrah, cheered Roger. That'll open the legs.

Shut it, ordered Jordan. The objective is to get her talking.

Better let *him* do the talking, thought Tara.

So, in the gently probing style she used with her astrology clients, she began quizzing Jordan about *his* childhood. He talked. Reluctantly at first. Then with growing interest in his own story. She listened. Drank some more. He followed her, glass for glass. She wasn't used to drinking. He wouldn't usually have drunk so much when he was working. He talked more about himself. His father. His brother. Even Jackie. With some heavy editing. But enough for Tara to realise he'd been looking for another Jackie ever since.

How could I live up to a first love? she wondered.

'How did you get into journalism?' she asked.

He smiled: 'You've turned the tables. Here I am, Mr Monologue. Telling you my life story. After a couple of questions.'

'I'm a good listener.'

'That's usually *my* line.'

'Two of a kind? Oops, cliché alert,' said Tara. Then relented. 'You might be right.'

Definitely up for it, opined Roger.

106

I'm not so sure, thought Jordan, signalling for the bill. He looked straight at Tara: 'Would you like to go somewhere else for a coffee?'

'I've got to get an early night,' said Tara, feeling for the jacket she'd left on the back of her chair.

Jordan leapt up to retrieve it from where the waiter had hung it up. He helped Tara slip it back on, slowly. 'What a pity,' he said.

Isn't it? thought Tara, as she leaned back slightly and he eased her arms into the sleeves.

'I've *got* to get my beauty sleep,' she declared, moving away from him.

'If you don't mind me saying so,' Jordan fixed her with an old-fashioned Julio Iglesias smoulder, 'that's an outrageous fib.'

And that's an outrageous line, thought Tara. But after almost being in Jordan's arms, she couldn't stop herself. 'I *do* have to get home. But I always have a glass of whisky last thing. Would you like to join me?'

'Love to,' said Jordan. Does she mean what I think she means?

They left the restaurant, strolled towards Chalcot Crescent.

What next? wondered Jordan.

What next? wondered Tara.

Half-listening to Tara talking about how she loved the park, Jordan took in the scene. Out of the corner of his vision he clocked a white convertible Mercedes 280 SL, sporting the personalised numberplates of one of that new species, the FTA: footballer-turned-actor. Does he live here, or is he visiting someone? wondered

Jordan. Have to check that out tomorrow.

Tara was unlocking her front door.

No sign of Flora, noted Roger gleefully.

Stand down, mate, ordered Jordan. This is a sensitive mission. Don't assume anything. Follow her lead.

He followed Tara up the wooden staircase and along a corridor with woven seagrass underfoot and stretched vanilla silk on the walls.

'It's like walking through the pages of *Homes and Gardens*. You've got great taste,' he said, meaningfully.

Do I? wondered Tara.

'Thank you,' she said, leading him into a small, dimly lit room.

'Have you got a light?' she asked. He didn't smoke but she'd guessed a professional charmer would carry a cigarette lighter.

Rightly.

Oh shit, she thought. This *is* a mistake. But it didn't stop her flitting round the room, lighting chunky candles. As she did so, Jordan took in the low Moroccan-style couch wrapped around amber walls, red and orange flowers in beaten copper vases, cushions of many colours scattered on the floor. On a little carved cedar table stood a single glass, a bottle of Glenfiddich and a small jug of water.

Had she expected to come home alone? he wondered. Or did she just want me to think that? Don't know. Just follow her lead.

Tara kicked off her shoes. Sat down on the couch. Surveyed the single glass.

Jordan sat down next to her. Not too close.

'We'll have to share it,' she said.

He smiled. This is going so well, he thought. But for what? For getting her to bed or for getting my story?

'Thanks,' he said, taking the glass of eighteen-year-old malt Tara was offering him. He sipped from it. Handed it back: 'Lovely and smooth.'

Not as smooth as you are, thought Tara. And yet . . .

'The perfect way to end the day,' she said.

I can think of better ways, piped up Roger.

You're right, mate, thought Jordan. Usually, in such a situation, I'd have kissed her already. The angle between my head and hers is just right. But this is dangerous territory. Sex could fuck things up. I *want* her, but I *need* this story.

He did nothing.

'It seems like you've travelled a lot,' he said, indicating the straight-from-the-kasbah furnishings.

'I haven't. But my interior designer has,' said Tara. The angle between his head and mine is just right, she thought. But he's sticking to small talk. What's wrong?

She handed him back the glass.

Jordan was still considering the angle. 'You look wonderful.'

'By candlelight.'

'By any light,' he said. His tone was flippant. His eyes serious.

They looked at each other and laughed.

What are we waiting for? thought Tara.

What are we waiting for? thought Jordan.

Get on with it, prompted Roger.

Just one kiss, thought Jordan. To find out where I stand.

Just one kiss, thought Tara. To feel his lips on mine.

She looked up; he looked down. The distance between their heads narrowed, until their mouths met in a kiss. Light, explorative.

Yes, thought Tara.

Yes, thought Jordan.

Roger had stopped thinking.

More, thought Tara.

More, thought Jordan.

Jordan began reaching towards Tara, to pull her closer to him, deeper into the kiss. This is it, he thought. Roger: we're going in.

Is this it? wondered Tara. Time to stop thinking? Time to let go? Maybe I could trust this man? She drew away from him so she could look into his eyes.

She's pulling back, thought Jordan. Tara's pulling back. Follow her lead, follow her lead. He edged away slightly.

What's wrong? thought Tara. Jordan's pulling back. She could see his face now. He looked worried.

She looks worried, thought Jordan: 'What's wrong?'

'Nothing.' Why's he asking me what's wrong? Why isn't he kissing me again? What's he waiting for?

What are we waiting for? demanded Roger. Why aren't we going in?

Fuck off, Roger. This isn't just another shag. This is Tara MacDonald. My gateway to stardom. But not necessarily through her legs. So don't fuck it up. Stand down, Roger. Stand down!

Get a grip, Jordan ordered himself. Say the right thing. 'Tara, you're so beautiful. I had to kiss you. You understand, don't you?'

'I understand.' No, I don't, she thought. I brought you home, we kissed, and yet you *still* want me to make the next move. Ma always said: 'Offer it on a plate and they cannae refuse.' So something's wrong here. Isn't it?

'I'd like to kiss you again,' said Jordan.

So why don't you? thought Tara.

'I'm really very tired,' she said.

Kiss me, kiss me, she thought.

Jordan reached for her right hand, bent his head and kissed it. 'Whatever you say. I'm only a ghost.' He stood up.

Tara smiled as brightly as she could manage. You bastard, she thought. You're leaving now With your options open. That can only mean one thing. Or does it? Tara was too tipsy, too randy to work everything out, and suddenly, genuinely, too tired. She remained on the couch. 'I'm so cosy here. And so tired. Do you mind seeing yourself out?'

'Not at all.' He looked into her eyes, his gaze liquid brown, almost full power. 'I'm sorry if . . .'

'Nothing to be sorry about.'

'Good. Well . . . good night then.' He smiled warily. Looked at his watch. 'Good morning,' he corrected, then looked at her again: his ultra-endearing not-sure-what-I've-done-wrong-but-forgive-me-anyway look. Quietly he said, 'Good *everything*. I mean that.'

I do, Tara, I do, he thought. You're wonderful. Totally.

What the fuck happened tonight? I can't believe I didn't fuck you. Don't send me into the night.

Why am I sending him into the night? wondered Tara. What happened? Don't look worried, she told herself. Look relaxed.

'Good night, Jordan. Talk to you tomorrow.'

'Good night, Tara.'

Chapter Ten

Glasgow, December 1997

FOR the fourth time in five minutes, Flora Macleod's gaze strayed from her Paul Gallico novel to the carriage clock on the carved wooden mantelpiece. Annoyingly, she had to squint to see the flimsy gilded hands. Bad enough my teaching colleagues should give me such a boring retirement gift, she thought, without inflicting something guaranteed to produce more wrinkles. Everything else in the bay-windowed living room of her hard-worked-for West End terraced villa had been chosen with such care: the discreetly patterned wallpaper, the elegant sofas, the Penguin paperbacks, the paintings by local artists.

You'd have thought at least *someone* in my department would have possessed the imagination to think of something I'd really like, she thought. After a lifetime's service at the same school. But no. A carriage clock was as far as their minds could stretch. D minus for creativity. Didn't even look that expensive. But then one of the recurring themes in the staff room had been how hard it was to cope on a teacher's salary. 'Of course it's different for you,' they'd say. Meaning: you're not married, you don't have children, you're not pressed for money, or time, so you can give generously.

Well, she had. Especially the latter: extra tuition after hours, home visits to talk to parents. Even though, over the decades, with the arrival of drugs, the departure of discipline, teaching English in a comprehensive had felt more and more like the punishment of Sisyphus.

Sisyphus, thought Flora. That takes me back. She pictured herself in the Fifties, a dark-haired young teacher in the first flush of enthusiasm, taking the sons and daughters of shipyard workers way beyond their syllabus, into Greek mythology, usually reserved for the offspring of the professional classes at Glasgow Academy. A scrubbed young face came to mind; an eager voice: 'Please, Miss, Sisyphus was sent to Hades so he was, and he was condemned to roll a great big stone up a hill and when it got to the top it rolled down again for all eternity.'

These days I doubt whether any of the staff at Scotstoun Secondary would have heard of Sisyphus, thought Flora. Let alone the pupils. Putting down her book, she smiled wryly. Now I'm condemned, for the remainder of my days, to watch time ticking by, on that wretched carriage clock. All I have to show for thirty-eight years at the chalk face. Pupils today don't even keep in touch like they used to. Apart from Scarlett. She's here so often my neighbour thought she was my granddaughter. I wish she were. Then I'd feel free to tell her to stop working all the hours God sends and to make some friends her own age. But she's always been a loner. Ever since school. Ashamed of her weight. Put down by her mother. Now she's bullied by that editor of hers. She said she'd be here by nine.

Now it's past half past. Well, I'm all ready.

Under the mantel, the fake coals in the gas fire were glowing. The lamps were lit, and the occasional table nearest her was set for tea: cups, saucers, side plates, strainer, milk jug, sugar and tongs. In the neat fitted kitchen the kettle had been boiled, the teapot was warming, the hot-water pot stood ready, and so did the home baking.

Not that she eats much in front of me, thought Flora. Must do it on her own. Always been such a heavy, clumsy girl. Yet such an agile mind. Should have gone to university, not commercial college. Such a waste. But she doesn't have an ounce of self-confidence. No wonder. The way her mother treated her. She said on the phone she wanted my advice tonight. So nice to be asked. None of my great-nephews and nieces would dream of asking my opinion on anything. So patronising when they deign to visit. Chit-chat from my relatives, small talk in the shops, blandness from the pulpit. Easy listening on every wavelength. Thank goodness for Radio Four, and for my books.

Flora let her gaze drift along the bookshelves lining the room: hardbacks and paperbacks, from Plato to Proulx. My faithful companions, till death do us part. She smiled to herself. What was it Robert Louis Stevenson had said? 'Books are a mighty bloodless substitute for life.' He clearly had no conception how anaemic life could be for a sixty-nine-year-old spinster. What would life have been like if I'd married? she wondered.

Flora looked towards the framed black and white photograph on the mantel. Too far away for her to make out the open expression and the curly hair of the kilted soldier. But she knew Sandy's face by heart. Even though she hadn't seen him since he went into France in '44. He'd been a farmer's son, from the same village on Lewis as herself, off to do his duty for King and country before returning to the island to marry her. She'd been so distraught when he hadn't come back, that her father, against his better judgement, had let her go to the mainland to do her teacher training.

'Once you've seen Sauchiehall Street you won't be wanting to come home,' he'd predicted. And he'd been right.

Here I am, she thought. Still in Glasgow. Watching the clock. For the first time in my life. At school the evenings, weekends and holidays had filled up so easily with marking, paperwork, preparation, summer schools. Now, nine years into retirement, she'd turned into a clock-watcher, constantly inventing new rituals to fill her time: the morning crossword, the afternoon play, the walk to the park, the news at six. She'd allowed herself to develop a mild obsession with home baking: a comforting occupation which evoked happy memories of her own childhood. Not wanting her trim figure to run to scone-fat, though, she donated most of her baking to bring-and-buy sales at church.

She checked the clock again: nearly ten. Better start bracing myself for the disappointment of Scarlett phoning to say she's still at work and won't be coming tonight, she thought. Should have started doing that earlier. But she'd seemed particularly keen to . . . Ah, the doorbell. How could I have missed hearing her come up the path?

116

Flora stood up slowly, smoothed down her tweed skirt, patted her chignon, and made her way to the door. She'd undone the security chain earlier so she didn't have to fiddle with it now. Opening the door she smiled at the hefty-looking young woman standing on the step: 'Scarlett, how nice to see you.'

'Miss Macleod. I'm so sorry I'm late. Mr McCoy, he . . .'

'No bother at all. Come away in.'

Poor lassie looks exhausted, thought Flora. If she were my own I'd hug her. In the hallway she held out her arms: 'Give me your coat, dear. That's grand. Now just you go through and make yourself at home. I'll be right with you.'

As Flora bustled off to make tea, Scarlett sat down in her usual armchair and, as always, scanned the bookshelves for new arrivals. I love it here, she thought. Like sitting in a library.

'Here we are, dear. Help yourself to milk.'

'Thanks.'

'And do have some shortbread.'

Scarlett looked at it longingly. 'I've just eaten, thanks.'

'All right, dear. Now tell me how you are.'

'Fine.'

Smiling kindly, Flora gave her former pupil an I-don't-believe-you look and waited to hear more.

'What's this like?' asked Scarlett, picking up the Paul Gallico novel.

'Very soothing. A wee piece of escapism. Why don't you take it for later?'

'But you're in the middle of it.'

'Och, I've read it a couple of times already. I was just filling in time till you came. That editor of yours works you so hard. You shouldn't let him get away with it.'

'I know,' sighed Scarlett. Then, attempting to sound brighter: 'So have you got any new books?'

Such a defeated sigh, thought Flora. And she looks so weary. I'm not letting this go: 'What's wrong, dear?'

Scarlett sighed again and looked away.

Flora waited.

Scarlett took a sip of tea then, without even looking down, reached for a piece of shortbread, conveyed it to her mouth and guzzled it down.

Oh dear, thought Flora. That's a bad sign. Eating so rapidly. We're not going to sit and talk about books. I'm going to find out what's wrong.

'You said you wanted my advice on something?'

'I did but it's just a work thing. Very boring.'

'Of course your ancient school teacher couldn't possibly help with something happening in your exciting newspaper world,' said Flora.

'Oh I'm sorry, that's not—'

'I'm teasing.' Flora smiled kindly.

'Sorry,' said Scarlett. 'It's just . . . It's quite a long story.'

'Tell me all about it, dear. I love hearing what's going on at the *Daily Brit* and you tell it so well. You were always very good at composition.' Flora settled back in her chair with an I'm-listening expression on her face which demanded a response.

Relaxing into the rare comfort of someone listening

118

to *her*, Scarlett told Flora all about Mona McGonagall falling ill, the excitement of writing the horoscopes, the enthusiastic reaction from readers, the disappointment of being denied the credit because McCoy had sworn her to secrecy and the shame of knowing – here, Scarlett's voice became very quiet – it was all because she was a fat, ugly lump whose face couldn't possibly be inflicted on newspaper readers. At the end of her tale Scarlett sighed deeply once more and reached for a second piece of shortbread.

Flora noticed, and Scarlett noticed her noticing it. Miserably, Scarlett ate the shortbread, her eyes already on the gingerbread.

That's enough, thought Flora. Can't let this go on. First that dreadful mother, now that editor. They're crushing the life out of her. I'm not going to sit by and watch. I've got enough regrets in my life. This is *not* going to be another.

Purposefully, Flora handed Scarlett a napkin. The gesture said: you've-eaten-enough-now. Then, gently, she asked, 'Have you any of these horoscopes with you, dear? I'm not quite familiar with the format. I don't set any store by them myself.'

'Here.' Scarlett handed over a copy of the *Daily Brit*, open at the horoscopes page.

Flora put on her glasses, read the column twice, then looked up: 'These are good. Very good. Top marks for imagination. And I must say, the maturity of insight. I'm impressed.'

How do you know these things? she wondered. At your age.

119

'You should show them to another editor on a different newspaper. Get him to give you a job.'

Scarlett said nothing.

'I've always said you should be thinking of becoming a reporter yourself, instead of running around after them. You were always so good at English and this column shows how well you understand people. Aren't those the things you need to be a reporter?'

'I wouldn't want to be a reporter. Getting people's stories out of them whether they want to talk or not.'

'All right. But what about people who *do* want to talk? What about being a features writer? Or a travel writer?'

'I'd like to do what I'm doing now. Writing the horoscopes. I know it's pure nonsense but it makes a real difference to people. Makes them feel better. Readers are always phoning in about them. I just wish I could tell them I wrote them.'

'Well, that's what you should aim to do: astrology.'

'No point. No one would ever want me.' Scarlett looked down at the floor as though there were a mirror there and she could see her reflection in it. 'I don't look the part.'

She doesn't, thought Flora. What can I say? She hasn't come here for platitudes. I hear them myself, all the time. So wearisome.

'I'm sorry. I shouldn't bother you with all this,' said Scarlett.

'I'm glad you are.'

'You've always been so wonderful. If it weren't for you Ma would never have allowed me to go to college.'

'Have you heard from your mother recently?'

'Not since Christmas. She's always pretty busy.' Scarlett's voice was devoid of emotion: 'And she's not much of a one for writing anyway, you know, so . . .'

Yes, I do know, thought Flora. I remember that time at school when I came round to see your mother. Usually parents were delighted I was taking an interest or angry that I was interfering, but this one asked me why I'd bothered. About her own daughter. I'll never forget Scarlett's face when she heard her mother say that. A slap would have done her less harm. Poor wounded soul. It's my duty to do something.

'You must think I'm pretty useless,' said Scarlett. 'Stuffing my face with shortbread and complaining about how I look.'

'I think you're very clever. And very brave.'

Scarlet didn't acknowledge the compliments. 'Thanks for listening,' she said. 'I suppose I'd better go now. Write up the horoscopes for tomorrow.'

Flora looked at the carriage clock. In the fading light she couldn't read the blasted thing at all. She said nothing. But kept staring at the clock. As though she hadn't seen it before. The silence extended.

'Miss Macleod, I . . .'

Flora turned towards Scarlett and beamed at her. 'Don't go yet. You said you wanted advice.'

'Yes, but the problem's me, how I am. Nobody can change who they are.'

'Yes they can. They do it all the time. Hillary Clinton, Madonna, the late Princess of Wales. They all re-invented themselves. That's what modern women do.

Isn't it?' Flora swung into teaching mode. 'Of course not just modern women: Elizabeth the First transformed herself completely when she became Queen. It's just that modern women have so many more tools at their disposal: collagen and liposuction, silicone and laser treatments.'

'I suppose so,' said Scarlett. How does she know about those kinds of things? she wondered. Her gaze flicked to the magazine rack: the copies of *Vogue*, *Elle*, *Harpers & Queen*.

Flora followed her gaze. 'Yes, my magazines. You remembered. You were always very good at remembering details. That's why your horoscopes are so clever. Very clever indeed. I can't imagine how you've learned so much about life already but no doubt I'll find out when we're working together.'

'Working together?'

'Do you enjoy your job, Scarlett?'

'It's all right.'

'Can you imagine doing it for the rest of your life?'

'That would be a nightmare.'

'Do you like the rest of your life now; when you're not at work?'

'It's all right.'

'Are you sure?'

'No.'

'If you could have the life of your dreams, what would it be like?'

'Don't know.'

'Yes you do. If I'd asked you that when you were at school, what would you have said?'

'I always wanted to help other people; to make them feel better about themselves . . .'

'What else?'

Scarlett blushed. Then looked towards the magazine rack. 'My dream was to be beautiful, to live in a beautiful home, be among beautiful people. *And* to help others.' She smiled wryly. 'I sound like a Miss World contestant, don't I? But that's what I used to dream about. Whenever things were really bad. Whenever . . .' Her voice trailed off sadly.

Whenever *what*? wondered Flora. And why didn't she mention falling in love on her wish list? She looked at Sandy's photograph.

Scarlett followed her gaze. She'd always wanted to ask who he was, but in all the years they'd known each other they'd stuck to safe subjects like Scarlett's studies at commercial college, the books they were reading, what was happening at the *Daily Brit*. This evening, however, Scarlett allowed herself a questioning glance at her former teacher.

'A long time ago,' responded Flora. 'But I grew up with him. So I feel I know him.' She paused. 'Have you ever been in love, dear?'

Scarlett's expression immediately changed. She looked half-fearful, half-horrified. On the verge of tears.

'Sorry, I shouldn't have asked,' said Flora.

My goodness, there's a dreadful unhappiness there, she thought. Better change the subject. 'Have you heard of Becky Sharp, dear?'

Scarlett looked blank.

'She's a character in a book, by Thackeray: *Vanity*

Fair. I'll give you it to take away with you.' She paused, took a deep breath. 'Scarlett, I've got quite a lot of time now at my disposal. You're a great girl and I think you can achieve great things. I'd be very happy to help you get the life you deserve.'

'Deserve? Oh Miss Macleod, you've been so good to me. But I'm not worth the bother. Honestly.'

What a terrible thing to say, thought Flora. Not worth the bother. How do I persuade her?

'You know, Scarlett, I enjoyed my job. Which was very fortunate because it was the only one my father would hear of me doing. I miss it now.' She sighed and looked towards the carriage clock. 'I live a quiet life. Too quiet. It would be a real pleasure for me to help you.'

Poor Miss Macleod, thought Scarlett. Sounds so lonely. And she really thinks she can make something out of someone like me: 'OK, I'll try.'

Poor Scarlett, thought Flora. She's no faith in herself. I don't like playing the lonely-old-lady card but it never fails: 'That's grand, dear. Come and see me on Saturday morning. At eleven o'clock. That'll give me time to come up with some ideas for you.'

'Ideas?'

'I'll tell you on Saturday. Is eleven o'clock all right?'

'Yes, yes. Thanks very much, Miss Macleod . . .'

'Flora.'

Scarlett looked startled.

Flora smiled. 'Teachers have Christian names too. I've been meaning to say that to you for a long time. Call me Flora.'

Scarlett smiled. 'OK.'

'Here's *Vanity Fair*. See if you can find time to read it.'

'Thanks. Thanks very much. I didn't expect . . . Well, this is so good of you. Thank you.' Scarlett heaved herself out of the armchair.

'See you on Saturday, dear.'

Flora closed the door behind Scarlett, put the security chain in place and switched off the outside light. Then she returned to the sitting room and sat down. In a moment, she thought, I'll get up again and draw the curtains. In a moment. She looked at the clock. It was far too dark to read the time, but she stared at it anyway. Why did I build Scarlett's hopes up? she wondered. Can I really help her? If anyone deserves help, it's Scarlett. That dreadful mother, that haunted look on her face when I asked her if she'd ever been in love. Something very wrong there, but I'll wait to be told. Won't pry.

Now, in her tidy mind, Flora began addressing the practicalities: changing how Scarlett looked, making use of that writing talent . . . These are things I can work on, she thought. It'll be a challenge. No need to feel daunted. In fact, it'll be invigorating. I've been living such a quiet life, preparing for death. Such a waste. Frittering away the time God's given me. Now He's offering me the opportunity to be of use. To someone who's very dear to me. If this is my final fling before eternity then I'm grateful. And I'm going to make the most of it . . .

Flora got up out of her chair to close the curtains.

But before she did so she went over to the fire. She picked up the carriage clock from the mantel, looked at it with distaste, then threw it, with some force, into the wastepaper basket.

Chapter Eleven

London, August 2000

TARA'S eyes were closed, her face damp with sweat. As the rhythm of her body grew faster, her breathing became louder, deeper. Her nipples were hard, her legs apart, her hips shifting back and forth. She felt herself on the verge of orgasm, then suddenly splashing into it. Her hips shuddered, her gasps dissolved into a sigh. She sank face down into the couch.

'Tara?' came a voice from the other side of the door.

Hastily, Tara lifted herself up, rearranged her silk knickers and skirt and opened the door.

'All right, dear?' asked Flora. 'I couldn't sleep and I heard Mr Holmes leaving so I wondered if you'd like a cup of tea.'

You mean you wondered how our dinner went, thought Tara, annoyed at the interruption of what had been a very private moment.

But in her pink dressing gown, her long silver hair released from its daytime kirby grips, her face scrubbed clean of rouge and powder, Flora looked touchingly old and girlish at the same time.

'No thanks,' said Tara, 'I'm just finishing my nightcap.' She picked up the glass to finish the whisky; noticing the scent of sex on her fingers. Oh my God, she thought. Flora didn't hear what I was doing, did she?

'So is he the right man, d'you think?'

Is it *that* obvious? wondered Tara.

'To write the book,' finished Flora.

'Oh yes. Well, I think so. We had a very useful chat about the outline, and the autobiographical sections, and he's raring to go. So I signed him up.'

'What about the ulterior motive he was going to tell you about?

'Oh, it was perfectly harmless. He thinks it'll do him good to be associated with a celebrity.'

'I see.' Flora left a meaningful silence.

'What do *you* think of him?' asked Tara.

'Well, I've told you already, dear. He seems very ambitious, very charming . . .'

'You don't trust him?'

'Do *you*?'

'I don't know,' said Tara. 'I feel quite confused. You know we actually had a really good chat. And he made me laugh.'

Oh dear, thought Flora. She isn't falling for *this* one?

'Be careful, Tara.'

'I know, I know. I haven't forgotten he's a hack.'

'He is indeed and you've told me yourself – it's the charming ones you've got to watch.'

Tara looked downward, but then couldn't resist confiding: 'He said I was the most intriguing woman he'd ever met.'

'Well I'm sure you are, dear,' said Flora. 'Any right-headed young man would see that within five minutes of meeting you.'

Tara smiled. 'Honestly, Flora. If you'd been there. There's a lot more to him than the average hack.'

'Well there must be for you to be interested in him, dear.'

'Oh, I didn't mean . . .'

Flora smiled. 'Are you sure you don't fancy a cup of tea?'

'Sure.'

'Oh well, I'd better get back to bed. Good night, dear.'

'Night, Flora.'

The door closed behind her, but instead of getting up and going to her bedroom, Tara remained on the couch, pulling her feet up after her and hugging her knees to her chest. *Should* I have just fallen into his arms? she wondered. Other people seem to go to bed first; fall in love later. I wanted him in my bed. And he wanted to be there. Is that so wrong? Or does it make me as bad as Ma?

Head buzzing, thoughts going round in circles, Tara went downstairs to get an aspirin from the kitchen.

From the kitchen, she thought. Who am I kidding? I know they're in the bathroom. Opening one of the fitted cupboards, she pulled out Flora's home-baking tin: half a loaf of gingerbread. In her mind's eye, a picture flashed: the gingerbread took on the appearance of a big, brown turd. But before it started to steam, hot and smelly, she pushed it from her mind, tore off a piece of gingerbread, stuffed it in her mouth. As the sweet stickiness hit her taste buds, the horrible mental image vanished. Suddenly, her hunger felt genuine.

She took another piece, then another and another,

eating as fast as she could. Then, as though remembering something, she picked up the gingerbread in one hand and moved across to the sink. Gazing out through the kitchen window, into the night-dark garden, she kept on tearing off pieces of gingerbread with her right hand, transferring them to her mouth. When she'd eaten it all, she looked down at her empty left hand with surprise, as though wondering where the gingerbread had gone.

Still in a daze, she turned on the taps to wash away the crumbs. Then she opened another tin: found the baking chocolate. Stuffed it into her mouth. The next time she looked down, the slab was finished. She tore open another packet of chocolate, broke off a corner, stuffed it in her mouth.

Why? Why am I doing this? she wondered.

Her face felt hot. She felt sick. The chocolate melting in her mouth was runny, sticky. An image flashed into her mind of dung, brown and dribbling, steaming from a cow's hind quarters. Shuddering, she spat the half-eaten chocolate into the sink. Then she took a paper towel, scooped up the chocolate from the sink, hurled it into the bin. Moving quickly, she grabbed another towel, wiped the sink, then tidied away the home-baking tin, flicked off the kitchen light.

Almost running now, she went upstairs to her bedroom, through to the en suite bathroom to find the aspirins. She felt too sick to swallow them. Caught sight of her face in the mirror. Strange, she thought. The reflection looks like Tara, but inside I feel like Scarlett. Suddenly, she felt very tired. Tired and heavy. She drank a glass of water. Pulled off her clothes. Sat down on the toilet seat. Peed. But didn't get up right away. Just sat there, looking down at her thighs.

Still toned, she thought. Still slender. Yet I feel as though I were fat again. As though I were still Scarlett. What on earth's happening to me? I've changed my body, my voice, my name, my life. Yet here I am, feeling the same as before: trapped, lonely, unloved. What's the point of the money, the fame, if I'm still not happy? No wonder I understand my celebrity clients so well. Can tune into their fears. They're all lonely, yet so suspicious of other people; isolated by fame. They think I can see into the future. But really, I can see into their hearts.

But what about my own heart? I've been so busy becoming Tara, I haven't had time to think. And now I've succeeded – beyond my wildest dreams – the first thrill has gone. Here I am. Alone again. On the toilet seat.

She looked at the closed bathroom door. Solid wood. Beyond it, her own bedroom. Flora was on another floor. No need for silent tears any more. Tara could cry out loud if she wanted. No one would come knocking on the bathroom door. I might be lonely, she mused. Howlingly lonely. But I've made it. I'm rich and famous. One of the beautiful people. In my beautiful home. Just like the magazines. I'm Tara MacDonald now. Life is good. And even if I feel like crying, so what? I can cry in five-star luxury . . .

Chapter Twelve

London, August 2000

IN Jordan's Docklands flat the digital phone was ringing.

'Hello.'

'Hello, David. Is Jordan there?'

'I think so, Mrs Holmes. Hang on.'

He *was* in, but David was under strict instructions never to divulge such information. Jordan was in his bedroom, transcribing one of Tara's tapes onto his laptop.

'It's your mother.'

Jordan sighed. 'OK. I'll take it . . . Hi, Mum.'

'Hello, darling. You sound very busy.'

'I am. But never too busy to speak to you.'

'How *are* you?'

'Good. How are you?'

'I'm fine, darling. I've just had a call from someone on your newspaper. Said she was doing a feature on glamorous older women and would I take part? Said you'd given her my number.'

'Oh yes. Fabulous at Fifty-plus. Sorry, Mum. Meant to phone and ask you first but I didn't think you'd mind. The features editor said the case histories had to be absolutely stunning so obviously I thought of you.'

'She wanted me to come up to London so they could take the photographs in a studio.'

'It'll be a really professional job. Great publicity for your boutiques.'

'Well, I told her I'd too much on this week but I could come up next Tuesday. Will you be free then, darling?'

'Love to, Mum. But you know what it's like. Never know what I'm doing from one day to the next.'

'I know, darling. Is it all going well?'

'I'm working on something very big just now. So can't really make any arrangements. But if I'm around when you're in London I'll take you to Mirabelle's for dinner. How does that sound?'

'Sounds wonderful. Hope we manage it this time.'

'Yes, I know. I'm sorry about the last couple of times. I hate cancelling so late in the day, but that's just how this job is.'

'I know. It's just that I haven't seen you since Christmas. And we're in August now.'

'Is it that long? I'm so sorry, Mum. I'll make it up to you. I was planning to come and see you for a weekend anyway.'

'That's wonderful. When were you thinking of?'

'Soon as I'm finished this story.'

'So when do you think that will be?'

'Can't say, Mum. Sorry. But it'll be soon. Very soon.'

'All right, darling. Well, I won't hold you up any longer. Bye.'

'Bye then.'

En route to the kitchen to fire up his espresso machine, Jordan dropped the receiver back in its base in the living area with a put-upon sigh.

'Your Mum OK?' asked David.

'Pestering me as usual. Why can't she understand that when I'm on a story I've no time for anything else?'

Runs in the family, thought David, recalling all the times Jordan's parents were too busy building up their respective businesses to visit their son at school. All cyclical, he mused: relationships, history, academic endeavour. So often in my research I know I'm retreading ground covered by previous scholars, but then each era has its own take on the past. What Jordan would call 'angles' and I call 'perspectives'. I'm part of the chain of thought. And the way Jordan treats his parents now is a continuation of the pattern they set for him.

At school, though, I wished I had a father like Jordan's who would zoom up in his Mercedes and take me off on flash trips. I was embarrassed that Mum was the matron and Dad the handyman. Couldn't understand why so many of the boarders spent all their free time hanging around our house. Now, though, I can see why they felt at home with us. Mum and Dad always listened. Took what we said seriously. Encouraged, but didn't push. Compared to most of the other pupils' parents they were a sociological oddity: still married, still talking to each other, still interested in their offspring.

Looking out, David noticed little waves ruffling the murky surface of the river. Mum and Dad would love the view here, he thought. Old Father Thames. The Mississippi is Ole Man River. I wonder if all rivers are male. And why are boats female? David took a note-book from his pocket. On the cover he'd written: *The Time Traveller's Guide to the Thames*. Most of the pages were already covered in his large-looped handwriting. He found a blank page and added a few lines.

'Mind your feet, mate!' It was Jordan, dashing past with a mug of espresso. Minutes later, David heard the clatter of Jordan's computer printer coming from the bedroom.

David smiled ruefully. Heard Jordan come in at half past one this morning, he thought. And he's been in full action since his alarm woke me up again at seven. Must be chasing a deadline. David yawned, stretched, rearranged his six-foot-two-inch frame on the sofa. Hmmm, he thought. Deadline: interesting word, and so appropriate. Deadlines are the serial killers of truth, forcing us to cut short the search for facts because we're running out of time. At least an historian has more time to play with than a hack. I can count the deadline for my book in years; Jordan considers it a luxury if he's got a couple of weeks on a story.

David got up slowly from the sofa, ambled through to the kitchen and assembled the components for a milky coffee.

Fascinating seeing Jordan in action, he thought. Just like he was at school. Only more so. Living life on fast forward. Would I like to be more like him? Sometimes. When I see that look in women's eyes – when I tell them I work at the community centre, live in a mate's flat, that I have a Tube pass, not a car. *That* look. I'd be glad if I never saw it again. But I don't want to whizz through life on turbocharge like Jordan, swallowing everything, savouring nothing. If I could speed up just a little. Before everything passes me by. I'm not stupid. I know the past provides a refuge; a refuge from a present where nothing much is happening.

Taking his coffee into the living area, David went over to the television – past the remote control – and switched it on. Tara appeared on screen: 'And now Cancer. I've been thinking about you a lot recently because I know that . . .'

'Hey, Jordan. It's Tara on TV.'

Jordan's printer was still rattling away in the bedroom, but he emerged from the bathroom, brushing his teeth noisily with a battery toothbrush.

'Don't you want to hear this?'

Jordan shook his head, still brushing. He disappeared, then returned, carrying his sports bag. 'It's all right, mate. Don't need to see her on telly any more. Last night I was with her in the flesh.'

'I see.' David looked more closely at the TV screen. 'Doesn't look like you wore her out.'

'Make-up, mate. Make-up.'

David looked at Jordan disbelievingly.

'OK, OK. It wasn't quite Tara-booms-a-daisy last night. But it will be, Plod, my old mate. Very soon. Seduction imminent. I assure you.'

'Right.'

'That's why I've been up so early this morning. I'm going round to see her this afternoon with some supplementary questions and thoughts on her book. Thought it would look better if I printed them out.'

'I heard the printer earlier on. You never sleep. Do you?'

'No time, mate. No time. You can do my sleeping for me. Why are you up so early anyway? Going round the centre today?'

'No, I'm down to three days a week. Thought I'd go for a walk. Have a look round St Katharine's Dock.'

'Again?'

David smiled and shrugged his shoulders.

'Well, if you insist in taking your exercise in such a strange way,' said Jordan. 'I'm off to the gym. Only two names from the top of the squash ladder now.' He swiped the air energetically, as though wielding a racquet.

Suddenly, an electronic version of 'Simply the Best' resounded through the room. Jordan reached for his mobile phone: 'Kill the sound on the telly, mate. Might be my news editor.'

It was.

'Where are you?' demanded Bullock.

'At home.'

'What the fuck are you doing there? I thought Tara was a Scottish bint. Why aren't you in Jock-land?'

'I'm on the eleven o'clock to Glasgow. Just waiting for the cab to City airport,' lied Jordan.

'About fucking time. Got anything yet?'

'Some very useful stuff. Plenty of colour. I had dinner with her last night, went to her house. That's why I waited till today to go to Scotland.'

'OK. OK. But if I'd wanted colour I'd have bought a paintbox. It's a story I need. Not fucking colour.

137

Unless you fucked her. Did you fuck her?'

'Not yet.'

'Must be losing your touch. Listen, you're on the right track, mate, just get a fucking move on. OK? The editor's screaming for this story.'

Liar, thought Jordan. He won't even have told the editor yet: 'OK, mate. I'm on my way.'

'I've sorted out your advance. Just call Julie in accounts. And I've lined up a leg man to mop up some stuff for you here.'

Can't have one of Bullock's by-line bandits poking around on my story, thought Jordan. He improvised quickly: 'I've got my own leg man. Someone who knows Tara already. Could be very useful. Worth a few shifts.'

'OK, OK. But I want results for my money. I'm not a fucking job creation scheme. Have you checked out the birth certificate yet?'

'I'll do it myself when I get up there. Can't trust an agency to do it. Might blab.'

'OK. But call me as soon as you get to Jock-land.'

'Will do, mate.'

As soon as the call was over, Jordan hit the speed-dial number for a cab, then, with a friendly grin, turned to his flatmate. 'David,' he said.

He's calling me David, thought David. Must want something.

'Look, mate, you said you were free today, didn't you?'

David said nothing. He hadn't told anyone about *The Time Traveller's Guide to the Thames*, so Jordan wasn't to know his riverside walks were really research expeditions.

'And some extra dosh wouldn't go amiss, would it? A hundred pounds a day. You'd really be helping me out.'

'With what?'

'With this story. About Tara. She's expecting me to turn up this afternoon but Bullock wants me in Glasgow pronto.'

Plod glanced at Jordan's mobile.

'Yeah, I know. But he'll ask for my land line up there and call me back. He doesn't trust anyone, that bastard. Anyway, he's right. I *should* be in Jock-land.'

'I thought you were well in with Tara?'

'I am, I am. But . . .' But what, thought Jordan. Where *do* I stand with Tara?

'What leads did you get from her last night?'

'One or two.' Zilch, Jordan said to himself, rushing to the bedroom. Too busy talking about myself, he thought. Fucking unprofessional.

Jordan grabbed his pre-packed overnight bag with one hand, his laptop with the other and slung them over his shoulder. Checking his pockets for mini tape recorder, notebook, wallet, he returned to the living room: 'Anyway, mate. Are you in or are you out?'

David was still considering. Not really my thing, he thought. On the other hand, here's Jordan, living on the waterfront, working in the fourth estate, a twenty-first-century denizen of Wapping, offering me the chance to get an insight into his working life. Could provide a topical postscript for *The Time Traveller's Guide*.

Jordan watched his flatmate making up his mind. Veteran of many doorsteps, he knew better than to interrupt someone's decision-making.

A hundred quid a day wouldn't go amiss, thought David. As long as I don't have to do anything dodgy.

'OK. But I'm not a journalist. What on earth can I do?'

'You're a hero, mate.' Jordan flashed David a thanks-a-million grin, then turned sharply on his heel and made for the front door, where, with the air of a brigadier briefing one of his men, he shouted back: 'I'll work it out on the way to the airport and call you from departures. Stand by the phone . . .'

Chapter Thirteen

London, August 2000

OPENING her eyes sleepily, Tara found herself looking up into a man's face. She gasped.

'Sorry. Didn't mean to give you a fright.' The face was barely a hand's span from her own. As it moved back, daylight streamed into her line of vision, making her blink. 'You looked so peaceful it seemed a shame to wake you.'

Tara recognised the voice. It belonged to Harry, the driver from Early Bird TV who ferried her to and from the studio for her Start-the-Day horoscopes. They were parked outside her front door in Primrose Hill.

Good, she thought. That means I've done my slot.

Vaguely she remembered getting up, being driven to the studio and doing her predictions. She glanced at Harry. He was standing on the pavement, holding open the door of the fleet Granada. As she took a moment to yawn he bent down into the car, once more thrusting his fifty-something face close to hers. Too close, thought Tara, inhaling bacon-roll breath and the Brylcreem holding his remaining hair in place.

'Thought you'd wake up as soon as I opened your door. But you were sleeping like a baby. Had to whisper sweet nothings to get you to open your eyes.' Harry grinned greasily.

That's what I get for always being so friendly, thought Tara. I should start keeping my distance more. Protect myself.

Without a word, she reached for her handbag. Harry took the hint, straightened up again and held the door open wider, but as Tara got out he couldn't resist asking: 'Late night?'

None of your business, she thought.

'Mmmm,' she said vaguely. Then, recalling that snubbed staff have a nasty habit of turning tabloid informer, she summoned up the energy to dispense sweetness-and-light: 'You must have been driving really smoothly for me to fall asleep like that. Thank you.'

'For you, Tara, smooth as silk. Any time.' He beamed lasciviously.

Get lost, thought Tara.

'See you tomorrow,' she said brightly, then looked at her watch with a goodness-is-that-the-time expression, to avoid any more chat.

Fooled by her exit strategy, Harry threw her a jaunty salute – 'See you tomorrow, Tara' – and settled into the driver's seat.

As he pulled away Tara could finally relax and consider how ill she felt. I feel *so* sick, she thought. Hung over? No. I drank more than usual last night, but that's not it. I haven't had this feeling for a long time but I know exactly what it is: that morning-after-a-night-of-binge-eating feeling. Yuck. Never again. Never,

ever again. After Jordan left, the feeding frenzy in the kitchen: the gingerbread, the baking chocolate. Why did I let myself do that?

I feel nauseous, bloated. Worst of all, I feel like Scarlett. Not Tara. And I'm not going to allow that to happen. Being Scarlett was so painful, so humiliating, so . . . No, I'm not going to remind myself of those nights; the nights I'd give anything to forget. I can never tell anyone what I did for Ma. Not even Flora. I'll deal with it on my own. However lonely that feels. Lonely is safe. Anyway, I've no time to be lonely any more.

She glanced at her watch: 9.35 am, Gucci time. It was reassuring to see the sliver of silver on her wrist; elegant proof that she was living the life she'd once dreamt of. Before going in, she paused to take in the facade of her town house. I've made it, really made it, she thought. As Tara. Not Scarlett. Scarlett would never have made it: she was a doormat, letting everyone walk all over her; and a dustbin, stuffing her face with junk food. I'm Tara now. I've got to stay in control. I'm not going to binge again. I'm not going to let Harry talk to me like that. And I'm not going to confide so much in Flora. She helped create Tara, but I *am* Tara. And I work so hard at it.

Taking deep breaths to stop herself throwing up, she lifted her head, stood up straight and forced herself to put a spring in her step. As she pushed open the front door, Flora was there to greet her.

'Hello, dear. Are you feeling more yourself now? You seemed a wee bit tired this morning.'

143

Tara ignored the obvious invitation to talk. 'I'm fine. Nothing wrong with me at all. Who's my first client?'

'Jilly's coming this forenoon, as soon as she's off air.' Flora looked at Tara more closely. 'What will you be having for your breakfast?'

'Nothing. I'm not hungry,' said Tara sharply. 'I'm going to get ready for Jilly's reading.' She turned to walk away.

'Jordan telephoned,' said Flora.

Tara stopped. Turned around.

'He didn't leave a message,' added Flora. 'Said he'd call again later.'

Oh my God, thought Tara. He's phoned already. He couldn't wait until he sees me this afternoon. There *was* something between us last night. Something special.

The phone rang.

Tara was about to pick it up but remembered just in time she didn't answer it herself any more.

She looks like a schoolgirl with her first crush, thought Flora. I always suspected she'd never had a boyfriend; now I'm sure. If she'd a wee bit more experience she'd be more wary of this Jordan character . . . 'Hello,' she said into the phone.

'Hello, Miss Macleod. It's Jordan Holmes again. I wondered whether Tara might be back by now?'

'She is indeed, Mr Holmes. One moment . . .'

Taking the phone from Flora, Tara went up to her bedroom. 'Hello?'

'Tara, good morning. Again. How are you?'

I like the sound of that 'again'; he's flirting with me, thought Tara. 'Fine. How are *you*?'

'Hard at work. Listening to your voice.'

'It's hard work listening to my voice?'

'On your tapes. I'm transcribing them. They're wonderful. I've already got most of what I need for the first chapter.'

'That's good. Great.'

'I know you want the book completed as soon as possible.'

'Yes, yes I do.' Forget the book, thought Tara. What about last night? Have you thought about that?

'Have you thought about adding a chapter on a day in your life: you know, who you see, what you do, when you meditate, your beauty routine, meals, exercise, that sort of thing? You're a role model. Readers will want to know how you keep your equilibrium, how you always look so beautiful.'

He thinks I'm beautiful, she thought. But he's saying it in such a businesslike way. Well, I can do that too: 'Which tape are you on?'

'I'm halfway through the second one. Couldn't wait to hear them. So I listened to the first one before I went to bed. Then started again at six.' He paused to put a smile in his voice: 'If you can do without sleep so can I.'

'Sorry?'

'I'm afraid I missed you on Early Bird today,' he continued.

'Oh yes. Right,' she faltered, thinking of her sleepless night.

'Too engrossed in your tapes,' said Jordan. 'They're fascinating. Really fascinating. I'm very excited about them. The thing is, though, I've got a problem. I don't know how to tell you this . . .'

Here we go, thought Tara. 'Just tell me.'

'You'll think I'm very unprofessional . . . It's my mother. Otherwise I wouldn't dream of doing this to you,' continued Jordan. 'She phoned from the hospital this morning. She's broken her elbow – it's a really awkward break, and they're going to operate straight away. She's going to be all right but, well, I think I told you last night . . . my parents are divorced and she'll be on her own. The thing is she lives on Guernsey and I might be gone for a few days. I feel dreadful vanishing like this when you've only just hired me.'

Tara felt relief wash over her. 'Don't worry about the book. Of course you must get over there. As soon as you can.'

'Thank you, Tara. I was so worried you'd—' Jordan interrupted himself, 'Actually I *knew* you'd understand. It's just that the deadline . . .'

'Don't worry about that. Your mother's far more important.'

'But I *promised* you,' said Jordan. 'And if I let you down . . . well, I just wouldn't do that. I'm not that kind of person. Anyway, I've got a plan. If it's all right with you?'

'Go on.'

'I'm going to keep working on the tapes; get a really detailed outline written up. I'll bring it round next week. Mum will be home by then and my sister-in-law's going to move in with her for a while.'

'Good.'

'But in the meantime, to keep things moving I've asked a friend of mine – he's a freelance journalist; very bright guy – to help me out. I've drawn up some questions, so if you don't mind going through the list with him . . . His name's David, David Swift. Would that be OK?'

'Yes, yes, of course it is,' she said, disappointment plain in her voice. She tucked a stray hair behind her ear.

'Thank you, Tara. And I also wanted to say . . . about last night . . . Last night was . . . Tara, I hope . . . I didn't mean to . . .' He paused. Waited.

She fell into the trap. 'That's all right,' then realised she had no idea what he had been going to say.

'I just want to say. You're wonderful. Truly, Tara. I knew you'd understand.'

'Um, well, I'll see you next week then,' she said.

'And today . . . would it be all right if I sent David round this afternoon?'

'Make it tomorrow afternoon. At two. There's something else coming up this afternoon.' Possibly the contents of my stomach, she thought bleakly.

'OK.'

'Fine, well, I hope your mother's OK.'

'She sounded pretty shaky. But she was glad to hear I was coming over.'

'Of course.'

'And Tara . . .'

'Yes?'

'I'm sorry I'm not seeing you today . . .'

147

So am I, she thought.

'If you've got any questions about the book you can always reach me on my mobile.'

'Yes.'

'Well, thanks again. And I look forward to seeing you next week.'

'All right, Jordan. Well, I've got to go now. Bye.'

'Bye, Tara. See you next week.'

Tara keyed 'end' on the receiver, cradled it thoughtfully in both hands, her stomach churning with worry. She wouldn't see Jordan for days and she was surprised by how upset she felt. And now she had to cope with another hack. Things were starting to get out of control.

The sound of the phone ringing again brought her back. Tara left Flora to answer it, but checked the time: 10 am. Oh shit, she thought. Jilly's coming for a reading this morning and I haven't done any prep: 'Flora!'

No answer.

Tara punched Flora's pager number on the phone, then changed out of the dress she'd worn for her TV slot and into her comfort clothes: silky cargo pants and a cashmere sweater. She yawned, then curled up on the bed. There was a knock on the door and Flora came in. Tara sat up: 'Could you bring my new stuff on Jilly upstairs? I'm going to do my prep here.'

She's getting a little too used to ordering me about, thought Flora. Abrupt almost. Still, she's under so much pressure. Especially with this young Lochinvar to think about.

148

'What time is Jordan coming round?'

'He's not. His mother's in hospital on Guernsey. He's going over to see her. He sounded pretty upset.'

'I see,' said Flora, in the tone she used to use to pupils who made excuses for neglected homework.

'Look, Flora. I know you don't trust him but if Jordan were using the book as a front to get my story he'd never dash off like this, would he? A real hack would stick with the story even if his mother were on her deathbed.'

'I suppose not,' said Flora, sounding unconvinced.

'He's sending a friend round tomorrow to work with me on the book.'

'A friend?'

'Another journalist.'

'*Another* journalist?'

'I *know*. I'm not very keen either. But it's too late to back out. If Jordan gets any hint there's a bigger story to go for, who knows how he'll react? The same goes for David.'

'Is that his friend?'

'Yes. And don't worry. I'll watch every word I say to him.'

'Why didn't you just tell Jordan you'd wait till he got back?'

Tara looked suddenly flustered.

Because you weren't thinking straight, thought Flora. Well, I can remember a few men who had that effect on me.

'Don't worry, dear,' she said kindly. 'I'm sure you won't tell him anything you don't want to. I've known you for years and I still don't have a clue what you're so keen to keep secret.'

Tara looked down and didn't respond.

'Would you like a cup of tea, dear?'

Flora didn't offer anything to eat. She'd been tidying the kitchen, seen the empty cake tin.

'Thanks. Peppermint.' Might settle my stomach, thought Tara, smiling gratefully at the older woman.

Och, she's still the same good-hearted lassie, thought Flora, heading downstairs again. Better for her to be a wee bit arrogant from time to time than to be always apologising for living, the way she used to.

On her return Flora brought a Hollywood breakfast tray bearing a glass of peppermint tea, Tara's notes on Jilly and a small parcel, posted airmail from the US. Carefully she placed the tray on the king-size beech-wood bed.

'Thanks,' said Tara.

As soon as Flora had left the room she picked up the parcel. Surely not, she thought. After all this time. Something from Ma?

Eagerly, she tore open the Jiffy bag.

Of course not, she thought, with another twist of nausea in her stomach. How could I be so stupid?

She picked up the book she'd ordered on the internet and inspected the cover. *Reading People: Secret tips that reveal the truth behind body language.* The authors, said the blurb on the back, had acted as consultants in hundreds of trials – including O.J. Simpson's – helping the defence team choose a jury sympathetic to their client.

Actually, thought Tara, this will be a great help to me. Feeling a flicker of energy returning, she looked at the introduction: 'How to understand people and predict their behaviour – anytime, anyplace.' That's all I have to do, she mused. Stay one step ahead of Jordan Holmes, forget the past and get on with the present. Last night's binge in the kitchen was an aberration. It'll never happen again.

Now – she put down the book – I need to prep for Jilly. Tara picked up an unflattering tabloid photo of Jilly, snapped by a quick-draw paparazzo at the supermarket. This can't have helped Jilly's state of mind, thought Tara. Must rebuild her confidence, remind her she's the best.

She picked up the exercise book on the tray. On the cover, in black felt-tip, it read, 'Jilly: Leo'. Inside were pages and pages of Jilly's personal details: her successes and failures, fears and ambitions, romantic history, husband and children, bosses past and present, confidants and rivals, every weakness and regret she'd ever mentioned. Recorded from the back of the notebook were the times and dates of her readings with Tara, starting with the first session, six months ago. They were accompanied by copious handwritten notes, covering what Jilly's concerns had been, what Tara had said, how Jilly had reacted. Tara read through the latest entries, then closed the notebook, opened the bedroom door and lay down on the bed for a nap.

She was wakened by the front doorbell and the sound of Flora greeting Jilly and ushering her into the reception room.

Tara stretched and checked her watch: 12.30. OK, she thought, I'll give Flora ten minutes with Jilly before the reading. Should I change out of my comfort clothes? No. Jilly will be feeling fragile enough without me glamming up. Got to make her feel good.

Tara stood up and inspected herself in the full-length wardrobe mirror. I'm still slim, she thought. Still in control. Although I've no idea what's in store for me. I certainly won't be consulting the zodiac to find out. I only ever read horoscopes to see what the competition's up to. A lapsed Capricorn; with cynicism in the ascendant. That's me. She smiled wryly at her reflection. Then she checked her watch again: time to see Jilly, to give her the kind of reading which would make her feel good, make her feel it was worth every penny of the outrageous fee, and ensure she would keep up her twice-weekly consultations.

Tara ran her hands through her hair, her fingers over her eyebrows, flashed a bright smile into the mirror. The stargazer to the stars is ready to give a reading, she thought. She'll get back to her own future another time . . .

Chapter Fourteen

London, August 2000

'HAVE you been gingerbreaded?'

'Sorry?' David looked at Tara uncomprehendingly. He'd arrived at her home punctually at two o'clock and had spent twenty minutes waiting for her to make an appearance. Now she was here, but what was she talking about?

'Or shortbreaded. Flora's an obsessive home baker. I don't have a sweet tooth, which is why she insists on force-feeding my visitors,' explained Tara with a smile.

'I see. Well I have indeed been shortbreaded,' said David, gesturing towards the tea tray Flora had brought him. 'But I didn't mind at all. It was delicious. I *do* have a sweet tooth.'

'Lucky you.' Tara sat down next to him. They were in the cream-and-white downstairs salon where she kept all her clients waiting for a few minutes with Flora before coming upstairs to the Moroccan room to hear their future.

Turning towards David: 'So, you're Jordan's leg man?'

'Well yes. Research assistant.'

'How formal.'

'Sorry? I'm a bit new to all this.'

'To research?'

'Well, not to research. Just to this kind of research.'

Wrong answer, he thought. I *told* Jordan it would be easier to stick to the truth. But he said a ghostwriter would never call in an historian so I had to say I was a fellow reporter. I'm rotten at lying though. *So* clumsy.

He's so smooth, thought Tara. Playing the part of the tenderfoot hack. Well if he thinks I'm stupid enough to drop my guard for *that* old trick he's deeply mistaken. Didn't spend all those years working at the *Daily Brit* for nothing.

'What kind of research d'you normally do?'

'History. That sort of thing.' OK, I've blown it now, he thought.

OK, thought Tara. Historical reconstructions. When newspapers run out of living celebs to interview they write about historical figures. Lots of sex, violence and scandal with no danger of the protagonists suing them for libel. And yet they can claim piously to be educating their readers.

'So who've you done recently?'

'Well it's not so much about individual people, it's more about a picture of a whole society, of . . .' Stop talking, David told himself. You're digging your own grave here. She'll realise you're not a reporter at all, but a bumbling academic.

The bumbling academic, thought Tara. He plays it nearly as well as Rab McGinty at the *Daily Brit*. On the doorstep he was Dr Jekyll, high-minded fact-finder in search of the truth, but as soon as he got back to his keyboard he was Mr Hyde, the low-down tabloid hack in search of the front-page splash.

'How interesting,' said Tara. She gave him a wide-eyed gaze. 'I've always meant to read up about the history of Primrose Hill. What can you tell me about it?' Let's see him talk his way out of that, she thought. Bet he says Primrose Hill isn't his specialist subject.

'Well, Primrose Hill isn't my specialist subject,' began David.

Tara smiled sweetly, triumphantly.

What a sweet smile, thought David. 'But it's an extension of Regent's Park, of course, which Henry VIII originally confiscated from the Church to use as hunting grounds. In 1811 the Prince Regent commissioned John Nash to turn the park into what it is today. But the money ran out in 1826 and . . .' He glanced at Tara for encouragement. She looked as though she couldn't believe what she was hearing.

'I'm sorry, I'm boring you,' he said.

'No, not at all. Please go on.' He really *does* know his history, thought Tara. Unless he's making it up.

She removed the look of surprise from her face; smiled encouragingly.

She really *is* interested, thought David. Unless she's being polite.

'Well, there was an interesting scheme in 1829. A Mr Wilson wanted to turn the hill into a necropolis, with a lift shaft running through it for access to the different levels. Of course that never happened but . . .'

Why am I rattling on like this? thought David.

'Why am I rattling on like this?' he said. 'I'm meant to be interviewing you; not giving you a lecture.'

Might have guessed, thought Tara. All the history stuff was just a warm-up, to put me at my ease. Now he's moving onto serious business; trying to wheedle my story out of me. Well he's wasting his time. I nearly went to bed with Jordan but I didn't let slip a single clue. So this guy's got *no* chance.

'Have you heard how Jordan's mother is?' she asked.

'Um . . . very well, I think.'

'Oh good. So the operation went okay?'

'Ye-es.'

'I'm so glad. And it'll be a real comfort to her that Jordan rushed over there.'

'Of course.'

'Well, if you're speaking to him just tell him to stay on Guernsey as long as she needs him.'

So Jordan's moved his mother from Guildford to Guernsey, thought David. And he's invented some mishap for her. He could have bloody well told me.

'It's great he's so close to his mother,' continued Tara.

If you call a once-a-year visit on December 25th close, thought David. But he merely nodded.

Jordan said he and David were friends, thought Tara. Wonder if he's said anything about me?

'Have you spoken to him today?' she asked.

'Yes . . . umm . . . just briefing me about the book.'

Oh well, thought Tara. Maybe Jordan'll call me later.

'He gave me some questions for you. Here they are,' said David, handing over the list Jordan had printed out before he left. 'He said just to ignore the ones you've already covered on your tapes.'

'Fine.'

'I've got a copy for myself so we can go through the list together.' David pulled a Biro from his pocket.

No way, thought Tara. I'll look at these in private. There's no knowing what's on the list or how I might react to it. Maybe that's his plan: to clock my reaction. I'm not going to be caught out like that. 'I'm afraid I don't have time just now. I've got a client coming in a moment. I'll have a look at them later and put the answers on tape.'

'Tapes are fine. Thanks.' Is there anything else I should say? wondered David.

Has he nothing else to say for himself? wondered Tara. He's so subtle. So softly-softly. Leaving pauses for me to fill. I'm not going to fall for that either.

'When would you like me to come back for the tapes?'

'I'll get Flora to phone you. Has she got your mobile number?'

'Um, no. No she hasn't. I haven't got one. Sorry.'

Hasn't got a mobile, thought Tara. As *if*. He's got this bumbling academic number down to a fine art. 'I don't suppose you've got a pager either?' she said teasingly.

'No, I don't, I'm afraid. But I gave Miss Macleod my home number,' said David. 'And there's an answering machine there,' he added helpfully.

'Oh, well, that's wonderful,' said Tara, a tad too sweetly.

Is she being sarcastic? wondered David. I'm sure she realises I'm not a real journalist. Not an operator, like Jordan.

What an operator, thought Tara. He's so convincing. He's even better than Jordan. Look at him, Mr Harmless, staying silent, pretending he doesn't know what to say next.

What should I say next? wondered David. She seems worried about something. Still, I'm the last person she'd want to talk to: the world's worst would-be journalist. S'pose I should go.

'I suppose I should go,' he said.

Tara, still thinking, said nothing. Gave him a reflex smile. Take control, she thought. Take charge. Take him out for a drink and find out what his game is.

'I was just thinking . . . now you're going to be working on the book too I'd like you to know exactly what I've got in mind. I've got a client arriving any moment, but we could meet for a drink later. Say seven o'clock? At that new café-bar on the High Street: Parliamo. Next to the shoe shop.'

'Great.' He grinned at her. 'I'll be there.'

'See you then.' Tara got up out of her chair to media-kiss him, but just before she bent towards him he held out his hand and beamed. She smiled and shook his hand.

Oh God, what a clot, he thought.

Oh God, what a class act, thought Tara. He keeps in character throughout. I'd be convinced myself. If I hadn't spent so long around hacks.

'Another cappuccino, *signore*?'

'Not just now, thanks,' said David. Not at three

158

pounds a cup, he thought. The coffee at Parliamo came in hand-painted Italian china with a Florentine on a matching side plate, but in the East End cafés he was used to he could get a cooked breakfast for less than that.

To fill in the afternoon he'd walked up Primrose Hill, then back down to the High Street where he'd bought a couple of books for himself and also – on complete impulse – Ted Hughes' book *Birthday Letters*, a cycle of poems full of astrological imagery, written for the poet's first wife, Sylvia Plath.

Now, after a walk round Regent's Park and through Camden Market, he'd already had a beer and then a coffee at one of Parliamo's outdoor tables.

Two women in silk dresses and DKNY flip-flops wafted past; each carrying a small bottle of Evian. They were followed by a designer-dressed Asian girl on a chrome micro scooter – and a man in a linen suit, taking the globally warmed summer's evening in his Gucci stride.

Dreamily, David looked into the middle distance. Without the designer sunglasses everyone else seemed to be wearing, he had to screw up his eyes against the light. But he wasn't contemplating the scene. In his mind's eye he was back at school, in the third week of Latin at St George's, and, once more, late for class, with Mr Swanson, the classics master, giving him a telling off. What was it he said again? thought David. Oh yes: how I was Plod by nickname, Plod by nature. Would never amount to anything et cetera, et cetera. Who, in the history of the world, had ever succeeded by being as slow and plodding as I was? When he shouted 'Answer me, boy!' I cited Quintus Fabius Maximus Cuntator, the Roman general known as 'the delayer' because he put off decisive battles against Hannibal's forces until Rome had time to build up strength and beat them. I hadn't heard about him in class, but I'd been reading about Classical history in the school library. The other boys would just skim through the set books, looking for the sex and violence. But I'd read every word. When I spoke up Mr Swanson had said nothing for a moment. Then he'd asked which British socialist group had named itself after Fabius and I hadn't known. 'The Fabian Society. Look it up in the library,' Swanson had bellowed. But after that he never called me Plod again. And he must have said something in the staff room. Before that none of the masters had expected much of me: the handyman's son. But suddenly they all took an interest. Asked me for answers, even though I never got my hand up first.

Dad and Mum were thrilled when I got into Oxford. And blown away when I got a First. But look where my brilliant degree has got me: playing second fiddle to Jordan, who barely scraped through his A levels. Maybe Fabius didn't do me any favours after all.

'Care for anything else, *signore*?'

Well, the least I can do is make full use of Jordan's offer of reasonable expenses, he thought. 'Yes, I'll have another coffee – no, sorry, make that a beer, please.'

'Yes, sir. Another Peroni?'

'Thanks.'

Jordan warned me she'd be pretty self-contained;

playing a part. Like most celebrities. Seemed genuine enough to me, though. Not as confident as I'd expected. A bit distracted; as though she were worried about something. Still, what would *I* know? She's the first TV star I've ever met. Jordan's interviewed scores of them. Not to mention Sunni giving him personal forecasts in bed. Now he's after Tara as well. Wouldn't mind waking up with *her*. She's even more beautiful than on telly. But she seemed a lot smaller. These beers are pretty diminutive too. What the hell. 'Excuse me, another beer please.'

'Right away, *signore*.'

'Hello again,' said a female voice behind him.

'Tara. Hello!'

She *is* a lot smaller than on TV, he thought.

Tara smiled down at him, taking in the empty Peroni bottle on the table.

But definitely more beautiful, thought David. Would a woman like that ever consider . . .?

'Would you like a beer?' he asked.

No, but I see you've had at least one, thought Tara. So I'm the clear-headed person. Perfect.

'A cappuccino would be perfect,' she said.

'Are you happy to sit out here, or would you rather go inside?'

'Inside, I think.' Tara smiled.

Such a sweet smile, thought David.

Smiling back, he got up, nearly knocking over the little table. He caught it just in time but was too late to open the door for Tara as she led the way inside.

'Where would you like to . . .?'

'That booth in the corner looks cosy,' said Tara. 'On you go.'

As soon as they'd sat down, David looked round for the waiter, but already the padrone was making a beeline for their booth. His face lit up as though greeting a long-lost member of his family, Antonio Petri's gold-chained wrists were extended in welcome as he homed in on Tara: 'Miss MacDonald. Mario told me you'd been in a couple of days ago. And I wasn't here. I was so disappointed. But now you're here again. Looking wonderful. *Cara signorina*. It's always a pleasure to welcome someone from home. Especially the beautiful Miss MacDonald. *Bella, bella, bellissima.*'

'Thank you,' said Tara.

Wait a minute, thought David. *What* did he say?

'I'm Toni, Toni Petri. I watch your TV show every morning. Faithfully.' Toni glanced at David: 'But I'm sorry, I'm intruding. What would you like? I'll take care of it myself.'

'A cappuccino, thanks,' said Tara.

David said nothing.

'David?'

'Sorry. I was just wondering.' He looked at Toni. 'You said it was good to see someone from home.' He turned towards Tara: 'I didn't realise you had family in Italy.'

Toni threw back his head and laughed. 'Not Italy. Clydebank,' he said. 'Don't worry,' he added, slapping David on the back, 'I'm always catching people out that way.' As he spoke he allowed his voice to become less Italian, more Scottish. 'I'm sure you spotted the accent, Miss MacDonald?'

162

'I do *now*,' she said.

'So where are you from yourself?' asked Toni.

'Glasgow.'

'Yes, I know. I read that somewhere. But where-abouts? Don't tell me you're a Clydebank girl?'

'I'm not from Clydebank,' said Tara. Oh God, that sounds a bit standoffish. 'Not far away though: Scotstoun.' Oh no, why did I say that? With a hack in tow. Giving away a clue. Still, without my real name it's not much use. She turned to smile at David: 'What would you like to drink?'

'I've got another beer coming, I think.'

'I'll check on it,' said Toni. 'And for you, Miss MacDonald . . .'

'Please – Tara.'

'For you, Tara, something very special with your cappuccino. *Un ricordo della Scozia.* Coming right up.'

As Toni crossed the floor to the bar with dramatic urgency, shouting instructions at Mario in Italian, Tara and David watched him with amusement. Then turned and grinned at each other: 'I dread to think what he's going to bring you,' said David. 'A deep-fried Mars bar?'

'Scotland's not really like that,' said Tara. She smiled again. 'Actually it's worse. Deep-fried pizza, deep-fried haggis and the ultimate Scottish breakfast: deep-fried scone and bacon.'

'You're kidding, right?'

'No, honestly. If it's not come out of a frying pan we don't consider it cooked.'

'Heart attack cuisine?'

'Exactly. It's all part of the *Braveheart* bravado. We

163

don't risk life and limb on the battlefield any more so we do it at the dinner table.'

'It's all to do with Calvinism,' said David.

'How d'you mean?'

'Catholics can sin merrily away with impunity as long as they confess afterwards. But for Protestants the sin begins as soon as you even think about doing something wicked.'

'What's that got to do with the worst diet in western Europe?'

David shifted his spectacles down his nose and peered over the top: 'I was coming to that part of the lecture, Miss MacDonald. Since wine, women and song are banned, the poor old Protestants have to make do with sugar. Scotland has shortbread, Switzerland has truffles, Germany has *Kuchen*.'

'I suppose so,' said Tara. 'But wait a minute – don't all those countries have Catholics too?'

'True. Another great theory bites the dust,' said David, sighing theatrically. He kept his spectacles at half-mast and eyed Tara mournfully. But she was smiling so warmly at him he couldn't keep up the rueful face. Beaming back at her, he pushed up his spectacles.

This is fun, he thought.

This is fun, she thought.

But shouldn't we be talking about the book? they both thought.

Before either of them could change the subject, a fast-approaching cloud of Aramis signalled the return of Toni, smiling like a watermelon and bearing a linen-draped tray. With a flourish he served them a frothy cappuccino, the obligatory Florentine, a Peroni, and a plate of stuffed olives. 'For you, Tara, all the way from sunny Clydebank, handmade by my mamma. Enjoy!' He bestowed a semi-bow on them, rose to his full five feet six inches then, like a matador returning to the fray, he strutted back to the bar.

'You're going to tell me that Florentines were invented in Falkirk,' said David.

'I think *this* is the surprise,' said Tara, turning her saucer round to reveal what Toni had left there.

'Brown sugar lumps? Don't tell me. They're deep-fried.'

Tara smiled. 'These aren't sugar lumps. They're pieces of tablet. It's a Scottish sweetie. Condensed milk, butter and sugar. Pure hard-core calories.'

'Do you eat it or inject it?'

Tara laughed.

'Bite into it and it will remind you of your child-hood,' instructed David. 'It'll be like Proust and the madeleine. Tara MacDonald and the tablet.'

Giggling now, Tara retorted: 'It wouldn't remind me of *my* childhood. My mother ran a slimming club. The whole house was a calorie-free zone. Nothing in the fridge but carrot sticks and cottage cheese.'

'That's nothing. In our house the sweets are kept in safety deposit boxes. Under lock and key.'

'You're kidding.'

'It's true. My mother's a school matron. The boarders have to hand over their tuck boxes at the start of term and Mum opens them after supper.'

'Sounds terribly old-fashioned.'

'Terribly trendy really. The parents fear for their little darlings' dental health. The whole ethos of the school is anti-Billy Bunter: muesli for breakfast, tofu burgers in the refectory. My mum gets letters from parents complaining there aren't enough vegan options.'

'So you're disgustingly healthy?'

'The complete opposite. I'm a Frosties and Guinness man.' David bit into a chunk of tablet. Then took another swig of Peroni: 'But I can see your mother's regime rubbed off on you.' He smiled appreciatively at her. Absolutely gorgeous, he thought.

Absolute disaster, thought Tara. 'Thank you,' she said. And smiled. Lips only. Oh God! What's wrong with me? Flicking off the safety switch like that. I never usually talk about my mother and I've never *ever* mentioned the slimming club. First Scotstoun, then Waistwatchers, why don't I just tell him my entire life story?

'Would you like another cappuccino?' he asked.

'No, thank you. I've got to go soon,' Tara said hurriedly.

Oh, OK, thought David. He glanced at the clock above the bar: quarter to eight. Probably got a dinner date, he told himself. I can't imagine she spends too many evenings alone. 'Um, we haven't spoken about the book yet,' he suggested.

'I know,' said Tara. Then, abruptly: 'Look, I really must ask you a tiny favour.'

'Of course.'

'What I said about my mother's slimming club. Well, I never usually talk about my mother. She died of cancer. And I still find it difficult to talk about her. You

166

do understand?' Tara blinked unhappily as though she was about to burst into tears.

'Of course.'

'So I'd rather you didn't mention anything about that. To Jordan. Or anyone.'

'Yes of course,' said David. You poor thing, he thought.

'Do you really mean it?'

David looked puzzled. 'Of course,' he said quietly.

Tara looked unconvinced.

'I don't say things unless I mean them,' said David. He looked like he meant it.

God, he's so good at that looking-like-he-means-it look, thought Tara.

'I know it must seem a bit over-dramatic but really, anything to do with my mother, it just breaks my heart. I know I can rely on *you*.'

Like hell I can, she thought.

She stood up: 'Don't get up. Please, finish your beer. I'll get Flora to give you a call.' Tara clasped David's right hand with both of hers, bent over and kissed him on both cheeks. 'I wish I could stay.'

Strange, she thought, as she slid out of the booth. I really wouldn't mind staying.

Before David could think of anything to say, Toni was at her side, escorting her fussily through the room, and rushing to open the door for her. The few customers in the café-bar all turned to look at Tara leaving; just as Toni had intended.

David sat staring after her then went to settle the bill, but Toni refused to let him pay.

'For you, *signore*,' he said, ushering David back into the booth and depositing a glass of amber liquid on the table in front of him. 'Lagavulin. On the house. Enjoy!'

'Thank you.'

'No problem. Any friend of Miss MacDonald is used to the best.' Toni gave David a man-to-man grin. 'You're both welcome here. Anytime.' He hovered, hoping for a chat, but David didn't respond. So Toni retreated to the bar, where he poured himself a drink, then raised it towards David: '*Salute!*'

What the hell, thought David. Not as if I had anything else planned. '*Salute!*' he echoed thinly. Then picked up the whisky and administered it to his wounded feelings.

The way she looked at me – like she couldn't bear to leave. And yet really she was dismissing me, he thought. Maybe Jordan was right. Maybe she's just one big performance. And yet – what a performance. I have the feeling she's just played me like a fiddle. Maybe Jordan's right about that too. Maybe these celebrities deserve to be exposed. Taking another mouthful of Lagavulin, he rolled the peaty taste on his tongue. But do I really want to sink to Jordan's level: Judas with a laptop? For a hundred quid a day? And I don't believe that was all show. She was almost in tears when she talked about her mother. I get the feeling she *does* have something to hide. Must be hellish for her. Being so famous. With a secret to keep. And Jordan on her trail. Yet one thing doesn't make sense. The *Daily Brit* is full of celebs confessing their problem with drugs, drink, sex. There's no longer a vice that dare not speak its name. Quite the opposite. Anyone who's anyone has a traumatic tale to tell: child abuse, domestic violence, rape. With enough detail to make a voyeur squirm. As long as there's a whacking great plug for their latest book/album/movie. So what's Tara worried about?

How could such a gorgeous woman have a secret too sordid for the tabloids? And what could she possibly have done – or had done to her – that the world hasn't heard already?

Chapter Fifteen

Glasgow, December 1997

'SCARLETT, Scarlett! Open the door or I'll call the police.'

She doesn't mean it, thought Scarlett. Surely not. She replaced the entryphone in its cradle. Moments later, the buzzer sounded again. The noise reverberated through the low-ceilinged living room of the converted warehouse flat. Although Scarlett was three floors up, too high for anyone to see through the windows from the cobbled street below, she felt like she'd nowhere to hide. As though girding herself for battle, she untied her dressing-gown cord and retied it tighter. Then she picked up the entryphone again.

'You might not think I mean it. But I do,' said a determined voice.

God, she might just do it, thought Scarlett. The police. Here? No way. She swallowed hard: 'Hello. I'm here,' she said into the intercom.

'Thank goodness you're safe.' The voice switched from authoritative to kindly: 'I'm sorry to be so dramatic, dear. I thought something terrible had happened to you. May I come up?'

Scarlett pressed the button to open the metal door at street level, then listened to hear Flora stepping through it and the door clanging shut behind her. There came the slip-slap of sensible-soled winter boots as Flora crossed the courtyard to the stairs.

Scarlett replaced the receiver, then looked around her. The flat was in a mess: magazines, sweet wrappers, Diet Irn-Bru cans and crisp packets were strewn across the ugly black MFI furniture and industrial-use carpet of the open-plan living room and kitchen. Bracing herself for a jolt of self-disgust, Scarlett stood in front of the full-length mirror in the hall. The young woman looking back at her could have been a 'before' picture in a slimming magazine: more than thirteen stones of lumpen misery wrapped up in a frumpy dressing gown spattered with food stains. Her hair was uncombed, her face unwashed and her spectacles smeared with fingerprints.

Normally Scarlett would have looked away in horror. But today she felt nothing. Absolutely nothing. Numb as a sleepwalker, she shambled to the door to answer Flora's leather-gloved knock.

Gracious, what a sight, thought Flora.

'Gracious, how are you, dear?' she said.

'Sorry I didn't answer right away. I was sleeping,' fibbed Scarlett.

'Are you well, dear?'

'I'm fine,' said Scarlett, dully.

'I see,' said Flora, surveying the scene in the living room.

In all the years since she and Scarlett had formed a friendship outside school, they'd met either in coffee shops, or at Flora's comfortable West End home. Given

171

that Scarlett lived above one of the hippest twenty-flavours-of-vodka bars in the heart of Glasgow's see-and-be-seen Merchant City, Flora had pictured her in an equally trendy flat. But although the self-assembly coffee table was laden with interiors magazines, the flat had the transitory air of a hotel room: plain white walls, no ornaments, nondescript prints in cheap frames. And that awful chain-store dressing gown, thought Flora. Scarlett reads all the glossies, earns a good salary and yet this is how she lives. Poor lassie obviously feels she doesn't deserve nice things. It's heartbreaking.

Took me a good three minutes to climb the stairs so she had time to do a quick tidy up. But she didn't bother. Poor soul must be feeling so low. Wonder what's wrong?

As she smiled at her former pupil, Flora inspected her face for clues. Looks dreadful, she thought. But not ill. Obviously been in all day. But hasn't been answering the phone. Not for a fortnight anyway. Since she failed to turn up to see me. When I rang the *Daily Brit* they said she'd been signed off sick and they hadn't heard from her since.

I've been worrying myself daft about what could've happened to her. Silly of me to come over all dramatic on the entryphone but I was imagining all sorts. And goodness, she *does* look like a lost soul. What *can* have happened? I must try not to look at the mess. Discreetly, Flora swept a couple of empty crisp packets off the sofa, and sat down.

'Sorry the flat's not very tidy,' said Scarlett. She looked round, as if seeing the mess for the first time.

172

What a tip, she thought. What will Miss Macleod think? Don't care. What does it matter *what* she thinks of me? What *anyone* thinks? I don't count. Never have. That's how Ma got me to do what she did. Dirty. Dirty. Dirty. How *could* I? How could *she*? Dirty big lump in a dirty dressing gown. That's what I am. And now Miss Macleod can see it too. I don't care. Just want to be on my own. Why did I let her in? Now she's sat down. How will I get rid of her?

Scarlett dumped herself in one of the two armchairs matching the utilitarian dark brown sofa.

'Do you have some tea, dear?'

Why does she bother? thought Scarlett. I'm not worth it. Can't she see that? Tea and sympathy. What use is that? She eyed the older woman resentfully.

'Tea would be nice,' said Flora, pretending not to notice Scarlett's inhospitable glare.

Scarlett got to her feet and went over to the miniature kitchen at the back of the room to put on the kettle. Instead of returning to the armchair, she stood there, waiting for it to boil, rudely turned away from Flora, saying nothing.

She's saying nothing, and I can't think of a thing to say, thought Flora. At least, nothing that doesn't sound like a platitude. What am I doing here? She's not a schoolgirl; she's a grown-up. And yet, I knew her as a schoolgirl, I saw how her mother ruined her chances. I know how clever she is, what she could be. No one else does. And no one else cares. Why did I insist on coming in? Is it because I need a project? Or because I really want to help? Both. And it's such a waste: a clever

173

lassie like that, so unhappy. What's she thinking? She's got her back to me. Obviously doesn't want me here. So why am I forcing myself on her? A cup of tea. To be sure she's all right. Then I'll go.

Scarlett opened the fridge door. Then closed it. 'No milk I'm afraid, Miss Macleod.'

'Flora.'

'Sorry,' said Scarlett, without adding the 'Flora'.

'Not to worry. I'll take it without.'

'I'm afraid I've got to go out soon,' lied Scarlett. So you've got to go soon, she thought. I want to be alone with my misery. Can't you understand that?

'I understand,' said Flora. 'Are you . . .?' she began. Then stopped herself. 'Do you have sugar?'

'Sugar? I didn't think you took sugar.'

No, I don't, thought Flora. And you noticed, you remembered. *That's* why I'm here. You *notice* things. Like I do. And there's so much you can do with that. So much. And you noticed something about *me*; an old lady whom nobody looks at any more. I'm not going to give up. Not yet.

Flora smiled brightly at Scarlett's back: 'Just for a change. Sugar would be nice.'

'All right,' said Scarlett. She reached across to open one of the laminated fitted cupboards. The sugar tin was on the top shelf, to stop her putting sugar in her tea. Totally pointless, thought Scarlett. When I've been stuffing my face with chocolate. She reached for the tin. Totally pointless, she thought. Like everything I . . .

'*Oh God!*' she exclaimed. In reaching for the sugar she'd knocked over the kettle and spilled near-boiling water over the counter, and onto her bare feet. Useless lump, she thought. I can't even make a cup of tea. Can't even . . .

She felt a hand on her shoulder. 'Let me look, dear.'

'It's OK, I'm fine. Absolutely fine.'

'All right, dear,' said Flora gently. 'But you're crying.'

'I'm not crying,' sniffled Scarlett.

'No, dear. Not if you tell me you're not,' said Flora drily.

Scarlett caught the irony. Smiled through her tears.

Flora said nothing more; refilled the kettle; switched it on.

Scarlett wiped the counter. Wiped the floor. Made to rub her nose with the back of her hand. Flora handed her a clean white lace-edged handkerchief.

Scarlett smiled again. 'I knew you'd have a hanky like this.'

'Well guessed.'

Flora made the tea. Scarlett put the pot and cups on a stainless-steel tray and carried them across to the coffee table. They both sat down. Scarlett put her hand in her dressing-gown pocket and, wordlessly, handed Flora a letter. It was neatly folded, over and over again, into a tiny square.

'Should I open it?'

Scarlett nodded. Then poured them both tea.

Flora unfolded the letter, smoothed it out and adjusted her spectacles.

The missive had the neatness of a computer printout, but the signature was handwritten. Flora squinted at it.

'It's from Tyler Dubois. The American my Ma got out of a catalogue. They're married now,' said Scarlett.

Goodness, thought Flora. Out of a catalogue? Scarlett told me her mother had married and gone to the States but she never told me *that*.

'It's a company called Southern Gentlemen. The men pay for the matchmaking but it doesn't cost the women anything.'

'I see,' said Flora, and began to read:

Dear Scarlett,
Your mom tells me you are a very independent
young lady and will not be interested in her news
but I feel it is only right for us to share our joy with
you.

We are truly blessed to have found each other and
I am grateful to the Good Lord for leading us to each
other. Many times I wish He had brought us
together sooner but it is not for us to question His
ways.

For five years we have been praying that He
would bless us with a child and now He has
answered our prayers, but in His own way!!! Thru a
contact in Mexico we have found a little boy who
needs us to care for him. He is three years old and
will come to us when we are settled at our new
home. Your mom is busy picking out a name for
him.

She tells me you have no wish to visit with us
and I respect that. You have started a whole new life
and so have we. We trust the Lord to help you

realize what a wonderful mother you have and to
guide you back to her one day. I have promised her
not to write you again unless you call us. But I
wanted you to have this check and to know that we
pray for you every night.

   God bless you!

Flora stared at the letter for a few moments as if struggling to make sense of it all.

'Poor Ma,' said Scarlett. 'No way would she have wanted a child. Bet she's livid he's arranged this adoption deal.' Her voice was devoid of emotion.

Flora's eyes felt suddenly moist. What on earth can I say? she wondered.

'Where's your mother living now?'

'Their old address is at the top.'

'Oh yes. 1126 Bayou Road, Northville, Lafayette, Louisiana,' Flora read aloud. 'But he mentioned they were moving.' She turned the letter over, looking for a postscript.

'He forgot to give their new address. Or she told him not to,' said Scarlett.

Poor soul, thought Flora. Poor wee soul.

'There isn't a cheque either. Ma must have grabbed that herself. It's her handwriting on the envelope.'

Flora decided to match Scarlett's matter-of-factness: 'That's a pity, dear. Money would have opened up so many options for you. Helped you into a new career.'

'Yes, but . . .'

'But what?'

'But it doesn't matter. Does it? What *I* do doesn't matter. To *anyone*.' Scarlett's voice had a challenge in it, but her eyes were fixed on the floor.

'It matters to me.'

'You're just saying that.'

'No I'm not, dear.'

'So that you don't feel guilty.'

'Guilty?'

'When I throw myself off the Kingston Bridge.'

'I . . .'

Scarlett looked up and smiled. 'Don't worry, I wouldn't do that. I just mean you're safe to go now. I won't do myself any harm. I'm fine. In a couple of days I'll be back at work and life will carry on. As normal. So don't worry. Thank you for looking in on me. It was really kind.' She looked pointedly at Flora's teacup. The older woman followed her gaze. The cup was empty. Flora said nothing.

Take the hint, thought Scarlett. Time to go. Can't keep on acting cheerful. Need to be alone. With a video on. *Gone With the Wind*. And a big bar of chocolate. Then I'll be fine.

'I'll be fine,' said Scarlett. 'You can see that. Can't you?' She smiled bravely.

'Yes, dear.' Flora made no move to get up.

Scarlett waited silently. Go, go, leave me alone, she thought, so intensely Flora could almost hear it.

She spoke firmly to her former pupil: 'I'm about to go, dear. I'm glad to see you're fine. I know you can cope. You're very good at that. And I know you'll get back to work and do an excellent job. You've been coping with a lot of things. For a long time. Some very difficult things . . .'

Oh God, she can't know, thought Scarlett. She can't possibly know. Nobody knows. Apart from me and Ma. And . . . But they wouldn't say anything. No way. They'd be jailed. That's one thing Ma was right about. Scarlett looked stricken: 'You don't know . . .'

Flora got up. Came and sat beside her. 'Look, dear. I don't know anything. And I'm not going to pry. I can sense a sadness about you. Anyone with the least sensitivity would recognise it. If they cared about you. And I do. Very much.' Flora smiled fondly at Scarlett: 'I couldn't care more about you if you were my own granddaughter. I want to help. But only if you want me to.'

'There's nothing—'

'Let me finish. I don't mean help with the past. I mean help with the future.'

'What are you talking about?'

'You'll be back at work in a few days?'

'Tomorrow. I've never been off before. The letter was a shock. I just wanted to be on my own for a wee bit. But I'm fine now.'

'Good. You've got real strength of character, Scarlett. Not many people could cope with something like that on their own. But you have. You don't need me. I can see that. Unless . . .'

Scarlett looked questioningly at her.

'The last time you came to see me, dear, you said you wanted help.'

'Yes, but . . . well, I don't know why I did that. I'm sorry. It's not your problem.'

'But you *did* ask. So I thought about what you told me. I've plenty of time to do that, dear.'

Might as well play the lonely-old-lady sympathy card again, thought Flora. She glanced at Scarlett: yes, the appeal to her better nature had hit home. Scarlett was looking slightly guilty.

'Well,' continued the older woman. 'I came up with a plan for you. How to get credit for your writing talent. More than that really. How to become rich and famous and have beautiful things, just like you said. Well?' She looked expectantly at Scarlett.

'If only . . .' Scarlett smiled wryly.

'It's perfectly possible. I've worked it all out. How you can stop working for that awful editor of yours and make a real career for yourself.'

'But I can't afford to stop work.'

'I've thought about that, dear. I think you've got real talent and I want to invest in you. I'll expect a return, of course, but I know you'll do well. You've always been such a hard worker. You'll be writing your own newspaper column in no time at all.'

'Yes, but it's not just the money. It's *me*. I'll never be able to do anything like that.' Scarlett looked down to where her dressing gown was pulled tight over her sponge-cake stomach, her thick thighs; her ankles were so puffy they wouldn't have been out of place on a geriatric ward.

No more wallowing in self-pity, thought Flora. Her tone was brisk: 'If you don't think *you* can then you'll just have to be someone else.'

'Sorry?'

'You'll just have to be someone else. With the money I have to invest you can be anyone you want.'

Scarlett still looked puzzled.

'Mona the astrologer. That's not her real name, is it?'

'No, it's Morag McGonagall.'

'Right then. So you can choose any name you want. And you can look how you want to look. All these celebrities have a change of image. You've got the money now. You can do that too. It'll be fun.'

'But even if I could change, it would still be *me*.'

'Yes, it would still be you, dear. And you'd be getting the rewards for your own hard work. Instead of running around after other people. Like your editor.'

'McCoy. I'd be so glad to see the back of him.'

'Well you would. You'd be free of him. And all the rest. Nobody's skivvy. Your own person.'

Scarlett, who'd been looking hopeful, suddenly looked downcast again. 'Sometimes,' she said very quietly, 'sometimes I don't like that person.'

Flora took her hands in hers and as though talking to a young child said gently: 'You're a good lass. I know that.'

'But I've done things . . .'

Flora waited.

'I can't tell you.'

'Did you hurt anyone else?'

'I hurt me.'

'No one else?'

'Not really.'

'Not really?'

'I mean no. Just me. No one else.'

181

'Then I won't ask any more, dear.' Flora released Scarlett's hands from hers.

'But if I'm famous, people will want to know about me. Find out about my past.'

Flora looked at the letter. 'Your mother's in Louisiana. Have you any other relatives? What about your father?'

'No idea where he is. Don't even know his name.'

'Your grandparents?'

'Grandpa was an alcoholic. Went out for a packet of fags and never came back. When Ma was seven. Set fire to himself in the end.'

Flora looked startled.

'Smoking in bed. In the Great Eastern Hotel. You know, the down-and-outs' hostel?'

Flora nodded.

'I never met him. And I never met my granny. Ma said she drank even more than my grandpa. Just took longer about killing herself with it. Ma was brought up by Rena – that's her big sister – but she hated Ma because she was the pretty one.'

'What happened to Rena?'

'Got married to a soldier when Ma was fifteen. Went off to Germany. Ma got a job in Fraser's, on the cosmetics counter, rented her own wee bedsit. Best time in her life, she always said. Until I came along.'

Once more, Flora felt like weeping. But she didn't. 'Right,' she said briskly. 'In that case you can be whoever you want to be. In fact—' She broke off. Just had an idea, she thought. When I took drama at school, it was fascinating how some of the shyest children blossomed, acting out a part. 'Scarlett, you can pretend to be anyone you want; play a role. It will give you confidence. Believe me.'

'Anyone I want?'

'Yes, a new name, a new look, maybe even – if you're going to be on TV – a new voice.'

'TV?' Scarlett looked at Flora as if she were mad.

'No, I'm not mad, dear. Anything is possible. Would you like to be on TV?'

'I can't imagine it.'

'Did you read *Vanity Fair*?'

'Sorry?'

'The book I lent you?'

'Oh yes. It was very good.'

'Well then. Becky Sharp. A perfect example of a young woman adventuress.'

'Adventuress? Me? But she was beautiful.'

'No she wasn't, dear. If you read it carefully, Becky Sharp was actually quite an ordinary-looking girl. She just made the most of herself.' Flora looked at Scarlett intently, then, with all the warmth of a favourite granny: 'You haven't even started, dear. If you did you'd be beautiful. No one would recognise you.'

'No one would recognise me,' echoed Scarlett thoughtfully. 'Do you really think so?'

'I do.'

I could be someone else, she thought. Someone beautiful. Not Ma's daughter, not McCoy's Do-It-All girl, not a nobody who gets pushed around. If I were famous – one of the beautiful people – like in the magazines, nobody could boss me about, nobody would laugh at me, nobody could hurt me . . .

As though she felt a weight lifting from her, Scarlett sat up in the armchair, straightened her shoulders. 'You think my astrology columns are good?'

'Very good.'

'And I could look the part? Like Mona?'

'Not like Mona. Much, much better. You're young and pretty and . . .' Flora saw Scarlett frown. 'Yes, you are. Very pretty. You'll see.'

'And nobody would recognise me?'

'They wouldn't. Once you've lost a little weight, got some coloured contact lenses, had your hair done, worked on your voice a little . . .'

'You've got it all planned out.'

'Well, I have a few ideas,' Flora smiled. 'When you didn't turn up last week I was so disappointed. Selfish, I suppose. But you've got so much talent, so much potential, it would give me real pleasure to see you succeed. And it'll be far more interesting investing in you than letting my financial advisor have his way with my savings.' Flora paused and regarded Scarlett kindly: 'But it'll mean a lot of work for you, dear. You must really want to do it. Maybe you're not ready yet. Maybe you need a wee bit more time to get over that letter. Why don't you take a few days to think about it?'

'No,' said Scarlett. 'I don't need time to think about it. I'd love to try. I really would. The letter. You talking to me like this . . .' Scarlett's voice trailed off. She looked out the window. Listened to the noise of the traffic trundling over the cobbles in the street below.

I've dreamt about a different life, she thought. For

so long. Without doing anything. Now here's a chance. To alter fate. What have I got to lose?

'I'm ready,' she said.

Goodness, thought Flora. What am I letting myself in for? But I'm ready. Ready to live a little. At my age, what have I got to lose? 'Wonderful, dear,' she smiled.

'So when do we start?'

'Next week. In Aberdeen.'

'Aberdeen?'

'Yes. It's the perfect place. I've worked it all out.'

Scarlett looked bemused.

'You want to transform yourself. To get a new look. Without anyone knowing. So you need to leave Glasgow for a while. Aberdeen's ideal. The oil city. It may not be that big but it's full of people passing through: English, American, folk from all parts. No one pays a scrap of notice to strangers.' Flora warmed to her theme. In a voice once so used to explaining things, she continued: 'Aberdonians are the least curious folk you'll meet. Very reserved. It's not like Glasgow, dear. People won't ask you any questions. They'll keep themselves to themselves and expect you to do the same. It'll be easy to slip into the background and emerge as a beautiful swan.'

'But where will I live? Will you come with me?'

'I'll make all the arrangements, dear. Don't worry.'

Scarlett shook her head in disbelief. All this effort, she thought. When's the last time anyone did *anything* for me?

'What kind of arrangements?'

'Well, there's quite a lot to work on: you'll have to

know as much about astrology as a real astrologer, and you'll have to have the confidence to carry it off. There's a lot you can do to build up your self-esteem. I've been reading up about it since our last chat. In fact I've written down a few ideas already. A wee bit of a master plan.' She looked at Scarlett, trying to gauge her reaction.

In a voice very different to her schoolteacher tone, Flora added lamely: 'I didn't know if you'd be interested but I did it anyway. I have plenty of free time, you know.'

I know the last time someone did something for me, thought Scarlett. It was Miss Macleod: listening to me going on about McCoy. And before that, writing me references for the job, helping me get into college, coming to my graduation. Even if Ma had still been in the country she wouldn't have come. But Miss Macleod did. She's always been there for me. I saw her as my teacher. But she's been my friend. All along. If she's going to invest her savings in me there's no way I'm going to let her down.

'I can't wait to see your master plan. And I'm very, very grateful.' Scarlett paused, took a deep breath, then leapt across the pupil-teacher divide: 'Flora,' she added.

At last, thought Flora. We've both been too formal for too long.

She looked so pleased Scarlett found the courage to get up and kiss her on the cheek. But as she did so her unwashed hair fell across her face. My hair's filthy, thought Scarlett. And so's this dressing gown. And so's this room. How could I have let everything get in such a state?

'Flora, I'm so sorry about the mess.'

'Och, don't worry, dear. I hardly noticed.'

Scarlett smiled at the obvious fib.

'Well maybe a wee bit. But it doesn't matter.'

'I can't thank you enough. For coming round, for your plan. For everything. You've gone to so much trouble. Just for me.'

'No trouble, dear,' said Flora. 'You're a very special girl. Of all the young people I've ever had in my classroom you're the one who's made the most impression on me, Scarlett. You're very talented, very perceptive and you're good-hearted.'

Special, thought Scarlett. Me, special? She looked nervously at her former-teacher-new-friend, as if expecting her to take back what she'd just said.

But Flora returned her gaze calmly.

Talented, perceptive, thought Scarlett. She sounds like she means it. Suddenly Scarlett felt a burst of energy. Not the jingly-jangly sugar rush she got from a Mars Bar, nor the fear-fuelled adrenaline that jolted her into action when McCoy shouted at her. But an unaccustomed surge of happy optimism. She felt light, bright, ready for anything.

'I'd better have a bath, get dressed, tidy this place up. May I come round to see you later? When I'm clean?'

'That would be grand, dear. Seven o'clock? Would that suit you?'

Scarlett looked at her watch. As she did so she caught sight of her fat-dimpled hands, her hefty thighs bulging under the robe. Like a light being switched off, her

187

surge of optimism died. 'If you really think it's worth the bother. I mean, I don't want to waste your time.'

Flora sighed: 'You wouldn't be wasting my time.'

'But I'm not sure I can . . .'

'I'm sure you can do anything you want. It's up to you whether you want to, dear.'

'Well, if you really think . . .'

'I do.'

Scarlett recognised the closing-the-subject tone in her former teacher's voice.

Flora got up off the sofa: 'Now, dear. We've got a lot to do. You'll need to give notice to Mr McCoy, give notice on this flat. I'll need to start setting things up for you in Aberdeen. It's the perfect place for your transformation. I know just the person to help you and no one else will take the least bit of interest in what you're up to. You can easily lose yourself there . . .'

Chapter Sixteen

London, August 2000

'HELLO, Tara!'

'Hello. How are you doing?'

'All the better for getting through to you at last. I phoned a couple of times earlier but you've been with clients.'

'That's the trouble with what I do. When people want an appointment they want it *now*.'

'Well, no point in hearing a future that's past its sell-by date.'

Tara giggled: 'Absolutely.'

'Talking of which, I've just been reading up about *your* sign. Stop me if you know this already . . .'

'OK.'

'But apparently modern astronomers don't see the constellation Capricorn as a goat.'

'Really?'

'No, they see it as a "smile in the sky".'

'That's lovely. And I *hadn't* heard it before.'

'Very appropriate, I thought.'

He makes me feel so special, thought Tara.

'How's your mother?' she asked – but Jordan could hear the happy smile in her voice.

She *does* have a lovely smile, he thought. You can even hear it.

'On the mend. They should be letting her home next week. So I'll be back then.'

'David said the operation went well.'

Thank goodness he caught on, thought Jordan. Good old Plod.

'Yes, thank goodness,' he said.

'Was it a long operation? You said it was a tricky break.'

Don't make me keep lying to you, thought Jordan.

'Yes, yes it was. But she had the best surgeon on the island. They're very pleased with her progress.'

'Good.'

'And how are you getting on with David? Everything all right?'

'Yes, I think so. Although I haven't had time to go through the list of questions yet.'

'Don't worry about that. We'll catch up when I get back. How does that sound?'

Sounds fun, she thought.

'Sounds fine. See you then.'

'See you, "Smile-in-the-sky".'

'Bye, Jordan,' said Tara, formally.

But as she put the phone down, much as she tried, she couldn't stop smiling . . . So much so that when it rang again she forgot to let Flora answer: 'Hello?'

'Hello, Tara. It's David.'

'Oh, hi there!'

'How are you?'

'Great. But very busy. I'm afraid I haven't had time to look at the questions yet.'

'Oh don't worry about that. I was just phoning to say I'm steaming ahead with research. I've done a lot of reading and I thought – since you're a Capricorn – it might be interesting to start the book with a history of your constellation. The Greeks and Romans saw it as a horned goat, but to the Babylonians it was a goat-fish and to the Indians it was a sea-monster. Oh yes, and some modern astronomers say they see the image of a "smile in the sky".'

'Yes. I've heard that.'

'Oh, of course you have. Sorry. This is all so new to me. And quite fascinating. I'm forgetting you'll know it all already.'

'Well, not all of it.'

'I always go overboard when I'm researching. I was talking to Jordan about it this morning. He said most of the material was coming from you anyway and the stuff I've come up with is far too dull for a bestseller. Still, he liked the image of the "smile in the sky".'

'Really?'

Tara paused, surprised how disappointed she felt that Jordan had only been repeating something David had told him.

'Um, Tara . . . well if you haven't looked at the questions yet I'd be happy to get on with some other research . . .'

'I can't think of anything right now.'

'Well if something occurs to you, give me a shout, won't you?'

'Yes, yes, I will.'

'Good. Well, bye, Tara.'

'Bye, David, and um, thanks for keeping me up-to-date.'

Tara put down the receiver and just stood where she was, thinking.

Chapter Seventeen

Aberdeen, August 2000

TWELVE inches from Jordan's face, a pair of teenage breasts was being held towards him; firm and peachy, with a fold of cleavage so deep, so inviting, he wanted to dive in, scent it, nuzzle it.

Could easily lose myself there, he thought. The girl's hands moved across her breasts, fingers fluttering round the dark brown nipples. Cupping one bosom in her left hand, she thrust two fingers of her right hand in her mouth, then, gazing hard into Jordan's eyes, she ran the moistened fingers around her nipples. Fuck me, thought Jordan.

Fuck, fuck, fuck, thought Roger, jolting to attention.

The breasts moved away, the girl turned her back to Jordan and bent over, so that her long white-blonde hair touched her toes. She thrust her buttocks in the air, almost in his face.

Fuck me now, thought Jordan, shifting on his velvet-covered seat and gripping his vodka glass tighter. Fuck me now, he thought, forgetting to lift his glass, staring as though hypnotised at the smooth young bottom with its dividing sliver of black lace. His gaze slid down the minuscule thong, onto the glistening sunbed-brown legs and the six-inch-high platform shoes. As the girl shifted her weight from one leg to the other, in time to the music, the buttocks bobbed up and down, unambiguously.

Fuck me, thought Jordan.

Fuck, fuck, fuck, thought Roger.

Jordan smiled. Not at the girl. But in self-congratulation. Less than twenty-four hours in unknown territory, he thought, and already I've homed in on the best female flesh in the city. Thank fuck for Roger. More accurate than an Exocet.

For the first time in days, Jordan forgot about his mission and settled down to enjoy the moment. In the notebook in his pocket though, was the summary of his pursuit so far:

Day One: arrived in Glasgow. Located HQ of the
Daily Clyde, Scotland's biggest-selling tabloid
where Tara's first newspaper column appeared,
but did *not* speak to any of the reporters there in
case that alerted them to chase the story themselves. Instead, went to Tartan Television, the
commercial station where Tara had her first TV
slot. Producers there too busy churning out
Gaelic game shows and fluffy features to pad
out the news to follow up Tara's story.
Researchers who resented Tara's success talked
about how she'd 'mesmerised' the head of news
into giving her a breakfast-time slot, then used it
as a stepping stone to the network.

Day Two: Found contract cab driver who'd
ferried Tara between terraced villa in West End
and Tartan TV studios during her six months

there. Cabbie remembered the address. Also recalled Tara saying she'd never complain again about the weather in Glasgow, having just spent nine months in Aberdeen.

Pleased at getting such good leads, but worried a rival newspaper might be on the same trail, Jordan had decided not to hire the services of a news agency: idle talk could cost him his exclusive. Instead he'd hired a private detective to check out the Glasgow address. He'd also tried – and failed – to find a birth certificate, for Vivien MacDonald or Tara MacDonald. So, either she hadn't been born in Scotland or, more likely, she'd changed her name. He'd decided to fly north to Aberdeen . . .

All round the room, in the narrow shower-room-size spaces between the tables, young women were perched on their fantasy-high heels, removing their clothes. On each table a printed card of club rules reminded the punters to behave like 'gentlemen'. There was a champagne menu and list of cocktails with names like Slow Screw In The Jacuzzi; somewhat superfluous, seeing as most of tonight's oilfield 'gentlemen' were drinking lager. Fucking boomtown jocks, thought Jordan. No sophistication. He smirked to himself, took another sip of vodka and, with the self-satisfied air of a gourmet inhaling the perfect truffle, licked his lips at the sight of the juicy young flesh before him.

In the notebook in his pocket was a record of how hard he'd worked today before allowing himself this night of R and R:

<u>Day Three</u>: arrived in Aberdeen. Under pretence of working on a different story, infiltrated cuttings library of local newspaper group but not a single mention of Tara in their files before she became famous. So, posing as a magazine journalist writing a travel feature about Tara's favourite haunts in Aberdeen, phoned hair salons, health clubs, night clubs, boutiques, restaurants and café-bars, telling owners they'd been recommended by Tara MacDonald. Proprietors thrilled but bemused: none of them were aware she'd ever been to Aberdeen.

At 10 pm he had finally allowed himself to call a halt; had eaten a club sandwich in his hotel room as he watched the TV news; then asked a cab driver to take him to where the action was. He wasn't very hopeful. From the little he'd seen of the Granite City it seemed to more than live up to its austere image: grey stone facades and grey-faced people, walking at an angle against a wind which pierced the marrow. And this was *August*.

The first bar the taxi driver had taken him to had been rancid: beer-soaked banquettes and smoke as thick as an offshore fire drill: off-duty oilmen drinking pints of heavy and looking mean. As he'd scanned the room, men had stared back, sizing up whether he'd be good for a fight later. Next stop had been an hotel lounge bar: chrome and glass and screeching girls drinking vodka mixes. When he'd hovered at the door, girls had eyed him expectantly, smiled and looked away. His if he'd wanted them, but he didn't want fourteen-year-olds. Finally, the driver had brought him here, to The Macho club. Not quite Stringfellows, Jordan had reckoned. But still worth fiddling his expenses for: late-night drinking and hot and cold running table dancers. Now, with this pretty girl gyrating just for *him*, he knew he'd come to the right place . . .

Taking another sip of vodka, he savoured the view of the buttocks in front of him. Suddenly, though, they vanished from sight as the girl straightened up and turned to face him. In her hand glinted the shiny cling-wrap mini-dress she'd stepped out of earlier. In time to the beat, she shimmied into it, tucking her breasts away and clipping the halterneck back into place. She did it dreamily, without looking down, all the time gazing directly into Jordan's eyes. It was a big swoony I-adore-you-big-boy look, with minimal fluttering of the mascara-black lashes, and no glancing to the side, always focusing completely on him.

She's hot for me, thought Jordan. She really is. That's not a bored-can't-wait-for-it-to-be-over table dancer look. That's for real. Can't have many men like me come into this club. She's absolutely fucking up for it. Just a matter of how. How will I—?

A garter-clad thigh was being presented to him, long polished nails were fidgeting prettily with the lace. Jordan fumbled for his wallet, fished out ten pounds and slipped it between flesh and garter.

'Thank you. Would you like me to dance for you again?'

'I'd like to buy you a drink.'

197

'Thank you.' She drew up a stool next to Jordan's armchair, sat down slowly, crossing her legs right over left, in his direction. Smiling brightly, she gave him a little-girl handshake: 'My name's Mercedes.'

'Like the car?'

Mercedes dimpled sweetly as though this were a dazzlingly original remark. 'No, like the girl the car was named after. She was the daughter of one of the first Daimler dealers. What's *your* name?'

'James,' said Jordan. He looked across to the next table where an older, heavier girl was gyrating through her routine, then looked back at Mercedes: 'I suppose you're tired of hearing how beautiful you are?'

Mercedes giggled modestly.

'And totally fed up of being asked what a gorgeous girl like you is doing in a place like this?'

Mercedes tilted her head slightly and smiled, as though delighted by a question she'd never been asked before. 'I'm saving up to go to college.'

'To study what?'

'Spanish.' She laughed. 'But don't try any on me now. I'm not ready.'

Well ready to be fucked, though, thought Jordan, watching her cross and uncross her legs then – faux demurely – tug the buttock-skimming mini-dress half an inch down her thighs. Just uncross them again, open wide, then fucking in there and . . . Fuck!

Jordan's view of Mercedes' legs was blocked by a waiter bending forward to pick up his half-finished drink.

Fucking chancer, thought Jordan, as the waiter placed the glass on his tray. But I don't want to appear a cheapskate: 'What will that drink be?'

'A Diet Coke,' said Mercedes. Before Jordan could suggest she have something stronger, she ran one hand over her sweat-moist brow, then rubbed it dry against a bare thigh. 'It's so hot in here.'

'Very hot,' agreed Jordan. 'A Diet Coke,' he said to the waiter. 'And a vodka tonic.'

He turned back to Mercedes, who was smiling at him as though she'd never met anyone so interesting in her life.

'So you're not Spanish,' he said.

Mercedes laughed and flicked her hair: 'I'm not. My Mam just thought it was a beautiful name.'

'For a very beautiful girl.'

She smiled.

'Is that a Geordie accent I detect?'

'You detect right,' said Mercedes, with a gosh-you're-so-clever smile. Then, before the conversation lingered too long on herself: 'I've never seen *you* here before.'

'I only arrived in Aberdeen last night.'

'Are you in the oil then, James? Here for the convention?'

What convention? thought Jordan. Oh yes, the petroleum convention; I saw a billboard. 'Yes, yes, I am.' Seeing she was waiting eagerly for more information, he added: 'I'm with Texaco.'

'You don't look like an oilman,' said Mercedes, with a God-you're-handsome grin.

199

'What's an oilman supposed to look like?' teased Jordan. Then, serious but modest, 'I'm a geologist. Special projects.'

'Oh right. One of the new fields. Deep water. So dangerous.'

'Yes, well,' said Jordan, with a hell-it's-dangerous-but-it's-my-job shrug.

'So you're prospecting the White Zone. How exciting. D'you think it'll be worthwhile?'

White Zone, thought Jordan. What the fuck's that? His brain sent an urgent message to his face muscles not to look bemused.

'With the barrel price the way it is?' added Mercedes.

Barrel price, he thought. Fuck me, should have known better than to say I'm an oilman. Bet even the local whores know the barrel price down to the last cent. This girl's not a whore. But she's definitely up for it. Wonder when she finishes?

'You can't tell me, can you? Top secret?' suggested Mercedes helpfully.

'No, no. I *could* tell you,' said Jordan. He leaned closer to her: 'But then I'd have to kill you.'

It was such a tired old line he always delivered it with an ironic smile. But he needn't have bothered: Mercedes was giving him a you-could-write-scripts-for-Billy-Connolly laugh. Then she picked up her glass, drank the remainder of the Diet Coke and – licking her lips absent-mindedly – fixed Jordan with a come-fuck-me look.

I'll fuck you all right, thought Jordan. Don't you worry.

200

He smiled at Mercedes. She beamed back expectantly.

That's not pretend interest, Jordan decided. She's really hot for me. Fucking hot. 'You look hot. Would you like another drink?'

'I'd love to. But the management only let me have one. Then I've got to dance.' She gave him a God-the-thought-of-leaving-your-side-is-Hell look.

'So dance then,' said Jordan.

Already, Mercedes was getting to her feet, moving her hips in time to the music from the DJ's sound desk. Her eyes were locked on his and Jordan couldn't look away. The rules said you couldn't proposition the girls. But it wouldn't have been the first time he'd pulled a table dancer. Strictly amateur, of course. He wasn't one of those sad bastards who had to pay for sex.

'Crystal on stage in sixty seconds, Crystal on stage in sixty seconds,' announced the DJ.

Jordan glanced away from Mercedes to see Crystal negotiating the steps to the stage on six-inch-high heels. He caught a glimpse of long black hair and snakeskin print, before turning his attention back to Mercedes. She flicked her hair, blew out between pouted lips, unhooked her halter top again, then held her breasts towards him with a you-and-me smile. As she turned around to bend forward at the hips, Jordan's gaze flicked across her buttocks then over to the stage to see Crystal, topless now, wrapping her legs round a floor-to-ceiling chrome pole. The expression on her face was meant to suggest moist-and-ready but she looked more like her shoes were pinching. Great breasts, though. Rock hard and upright, whichever way she moved.

Nothing wrong with a good pair of implants, thought Jordan, comparing them connoisseur-like with the breasts Mercedes was now holding towards him again. Fuck, that's a Jack E number she's dancing to, Jordan suddenly realised. And I don't fucking care. Don't feel a thing. About fucking time. Don't know why I've wasted so much effort thinking about her. Not fucking worth it. No woman's worth it. That kind of distraction. When I'm on my way to the top. Plenty of time to get a fuck-off gorgeous trophy wife when I get there. Right now, all I need is target practice for Roger.

This story will make my name, he thought. Won't let anything get in my way. Not even a fucking amazing woman like Tara. If I fuck her: fine. Icing on the cake. But my mission is to get her story. Not her knickers off. That night over dinner I let myself be mesmerised by her. Wasted time talking about myself. When I should have let *her* do the talking. No wonder this mission is so tough. Fucked up on the first engagement. No more of that. No more dereliction of duty. It's not as if there's a shortage of pussy in the world.

He smiled at Mercedes, who was right in front of him, rubbing her hands up and down her thighs, her fingertips almost, but not quite, touching the triangle of G-string he longed to reach forward and rip off, pulling out Roger and . . . oh fuck, thought Jordan, she's getting dressed again. Time for action.

He reached into his inside pocket, felt for his notebook, and without removing it from his jacket, tore out a page. Looking left and right to check the waiter wasn't watching, he slipped the sheet of paper between the covers of the drinks menu. Quickly, he scribbled a few words, then folded the page into a small square and tucked it inside a twenty-pound note. When the song ended and Mercedes held up her gartered leg, he smiled up at her.

'When do you finish?'

'The club closes in an hour.'

'Like to come to my hotel for a nightcap?'

'I'm not allowed to.'

'I know. Don't worry. The address is in here. Take a taxi. I'll pay. I'll leave now so it won't look obvious.'

He slipped the twenty-pound note under the garter, flashing her his best liquid-brown-how-can-you-resist-me look. But Mercedes missed it. Her attention was focused on another man advancing towards their table. Following her gaze, Jordan saw him too: broad-necked and beefy, dressed in black, a ring in one ear and an earpiece in the other. He had a made-in-the-gym body, and his expression said: I survived Barlinnie, who the fuck are you? His fingers were inked with tattoos.

Fuck, thought Jordan. A psycho bouncer.

'S'cuse me, sir. There's something I need to check. The manager would like a word with you . . .' The words were polite but the voice said: fuck-with-me-go-on-I-dare-you.

203

He can't possibly have seen the note, thought Jordan. What the fuck is this about?

'If you'd just come with me, sir.'

The way he said 'sir' sounded like an insult.

Fucking neanderthal, thought Jordan, who'd never been in a fight in his life and wasn't going to start now.

'What's this about, mate?' he asked.

On hearing the English accent, the bouncer's face stiffened with contempt.

Suddenly, Jordan felt queasy. He glanced round the room. In the clubs he knew in London, bouncers were banned from behaving badly because it would frighten away the pinstripes. But here, the punters were hard-faced, hard-drinking men who looked like a little recreational violence would round off their evening nicely. In his City health club, Jordan felt like an iron man among desk jockeys. Here, among men whose brawn kept platforms pumping, and trawlers at sea, he felt like Mr Sand-in-his-Face.

Added to which, he was a coward.

I'm not a coward, thought Jordan. I'm just too clever to get involved in this caveman stuff.

'Just a wee misunderstanding, sir.' The bouncer slipped his fingers under Mercedes' garter, pulled out the twenty-pound note and put it in his jacket pocket. Slowly, he readjusted the garter, pushing it further up the leg until Mercedes grimaced at the tightness.

'Now hold on a minute,' said Jordan. He glanced towards Mercedes, but she was already teetering off to another table. Thank fuck he didn't notice the note

204

I slipped her, thought Jordan. But since it's not that, what the fuck is this about?

'This way, sir,' commanded the bouncer.

Reluctantly, Jordan obeyed. Following the man across the room he could see more tattoos climbing his neck. And, through the stubble on his close-cropped head, a curious V-shaped scar.

Fucking hell, thought Jordan. Heavy duty. No point reasoning with *him*. Maybe his boss will be more civilised. Nothing I can't talk my way out of.

The bouncer opened a door marked 'Private', then stood aside, motioning Jordan to go first.

Fucking hell, thought Jordan. Tactical error. Should have stayed at the table. There's no fucking manager. He's just going to take me in here and beat me to a pulp. I feel sick. Oh thank fuck, there *is* a manager. And this is his office. Stay cool, stay calm. Stop being over-dramatic.

The door closed behind him. In front of him a man his own age with David Ginola hair, a Boss suit, a fake Rolex and a fake tan, sat at a desk piled with staff rotas and bar returns. You didn't need to see his car to know he had personalised numberplates. He was watching TV. Correction, he was watching a bank of TV screens built into the wall opposite his desk.

'Hi. I'm Keith, the manager here. Hope you've been having a pleasant evening with us, Mr . . .?'

No point lying, thought Jordan. They've got my credit card behind the bar: 'Holmes,' he said. 'And I hope you can tell me what this is all about, Keith.' He doesn't seem to appreciate the English accent either, noted Jordan.

'Sorry to interrupt your evening. But there's something I want to show you,' said Keith. His accent was Aberdeen-trans-Atlantic. If you guessed that *Pulp Fiction* was his favourite movie you'd be guessing correctly. He didn't offer Jordan a seat. Instead, he gestured to the TV screens. Jordan turned round to look at them, nearly falling over the bouncer, who was right behind him. The bouncer stood his ground, forcing Jordan to step back quickly. After the loud music in the club, the office seemed deathly quiet. The bouncer cracked his knuckles, meaningfully.

Bastard, thought Jordan. But I must stay calm. Mustn't give this fucking gorilla the excuse he's looking for. This Keith character seems to think he's in a gangster movie. Hopefully he'll keep his gimp under control. Quick chat, find out what his problem is, get it sorted, then out of here.

'We're very high-tech here. CCTV. Throughout the club. Did you notice the glitter balls? There are hidden cameras in them. With zoom focus,' said Keith: 'Look.'

He pressed a button on his desk. On one of the screens the picture changed from a general view of Crystal dancing on stage, to a close-up of her breasts. The image was so sharp you could see the sweat glistening on them. 'State-of-the-art,' said Keith. 'The thing is, we like to keep an eye on everything that's going on. But we like to be discreet about it. Right, Tam?'

The bouncer nodded.

Oh fuck, thought Jordan. Who'd have thought they'd have a security system like this out in the sticks?

'Look, what's this all about?' he blustered.

206

'This is a club for gentlemen. And it's our job to keep it that way,' said Keith. He looked at Tam, who pulled Jordan's twenty-pound note out of his pocket, removed the piece of paper Jordan had slipped inside it and handed it to his boss.

I'm dead in the water, thought Jordan.

With unnecessary slowness Keith unfolded the little square of paper.

Stop feeling sick; start thinking, thought Jordan.

Keith read the note aloud: 'Love at first sight? Copthorne Hotel. Room 51. James.' He smiled at Jordan with exaggerated politeness: 'Yeah, definitely a misunderstanding here. Did our doorman forget to hand you a card as you came in? With our rules on it?'

Fucking wanker, thought Jordan. He's enjoying this. Best cut it short and get out of here in one piece. Before Tam's medication wears off.

'I'm aware of the rules. But, you know, Keith . . .' Jordan gave him a you're-a-man-of-the-world-too look: 'You can't blame me for trying. I'm sure you understand.'

'No, Mr Holmes. What you need to understand is that if *you* break the rules, *we* lose our licence. And if we lose our licence then my boss would *not* be happy. Is that right, Tam?'

'Dead right.'

'Oh look, Tam, it says Jordan here, not James. Funny that.' Keith had picked up Jordan's credit card from among the paperwork on his desk. He smirked at Jordan: 'Sorry, Jordan, but you're blacklisted. Here's your card. And Tam will see you out. Won't you, Tam?'

Tam looked like a little boy who'd been given a puppy to stone.

Oh fuck, thought Jordan. He's going to take me up an alley and tear me limb from limb. Stay cool, use your head: 'That's all right, I'll call a taxi.'

He reached for the mobile phone in his pocket, but before he could retrieve it Tam had drawn a knife and was holding the blade to his neck.

Oh fuck, I'm going to shit myself, thought Jordan.

He let his hands fall to his side. Still holding the knife to his throat, Tam gave him a one-handed body search. From Jordan's pockets he pulled out the phone, a notebook, a Biro, a wallet, the ladykiller cigarette lighter, and a piece of white card. He flung them onto the desk.

Keith took one look at the card, and motioned Tam to put away his knife.

'My apologies, Mr Holmes. There's a lot of heavy people in this city. We can't be too careful. If you want to meet Mercedes socially, then be my guest. Have a drink with me at my table. I'll tell her to go off duty and she can join us. That'll keep us straight with the licensing board.'

Tam looked like he'd missed the Lottery rollover by one digit and would have to go and glass someone to recover from the disappointment.

Jordan's stomach had lurched back into place but his throat was still dry: 'OK.'

Keith handed Jordan back his Metropolitan Police press card. It was years out of date but he was proud of having got it when he was only a rookie reporter on a regional paper doing the odd news shift in London.

And it was still good for impressing hicks in the sticks. Like now.

'We're cool?' asked Keith.

Fuck's sake, thought Jordan. Scripted by Tarantino. Never mind. I'm off the hook. The power of the Press strikes again. 'We're cool,' he said.

'The licensing board here is very strict,' said Keith.

'I understand, mate. No hard feelings.'

'We've got a lot of friends in the police. Always look after them well.'

He thinks I'm with the Old Bill, realised Jordan. *That's* what saved me. What a moron. Never seen a Met press pass in his life. Just saw the 'Metropolitan Police' bit and jumped to the wrong conclusion. He grinned at his good fortune: 'Glad to hear it, mate. I would have told you sooner but I wanted to see what your routine was like. Professional interest, you know.'

'Sure,' said Keith. 'If there's anything I can do . . .'

'There is actually,' said Jordan. 'CID matter.'

'Right,' said Keith. 'So it's Detective-Sergeant Holmes?'

'I'm afraid so,' said Jordan. 'No relation.'

Keith looked blank.

'To Sherlock,' added Jordan.

Keith nodded sagely: 'Oh aye, of course.' He flicked back his long hair. 'So what d'you want to know?'

Jordan glanced at Tam.

'OK, Tam, I've got it covered,' said Keith. As the door closed behind the bouncer, Keith opened the top drawer of his desk and took out a bottle of Crown Royal and two glasses.

209

'Will you have a drink?'

'American whiskey?'

'Unpatriotic. I know. But it's smooth stuff.'

Keith poured, then handed a glass to Jordan with a look that said: in-my-other-life-I'm-Harvey-Keitel.

'What's the situation?' he asked.

What a prat, thought Jordan. And what a night. He took a swallow of the whiskey. 'Excellent.' Yeah, some fucking night. A good hack's yarn to tell in the pub when I get back to Blighty. In the meantime, though, I'd better finish this scene with my new mate Keith . . .

'Have you ever come across Tara MacDonald?'

'The astrologer woman?'

Jordan nodded.

'Is she in trouble?'

'I really shouldn't say at this stage but' – Jordan gave Keith a conspiratorial look – 'it's really someone she's connected with we're after. Someone she had dealings with when she was in Aberdeen.'

'Brendan Nolan?'

Who? thought Jordan.

'Yes,' he said. 'Brendan Nolan. D'you know where I could get hold of him?'

Keith looked amused: 'Wouldn't want to get too close a hold on him, would you?'

Jordan looked puzzled.

'He's a raving faggot.'

'D'you know where he is?'

'What kind of trouble is he in? Drugs?'

'Look, I really can't say. But if you know his where-abouts . . .'

210

'No worries. We're always pleased to help the CID. Brendan used to work here. Behind the bar. But he was too friendly with the girls.'

Jordan looked puzzled.

'Aye, not friendly *that* way. *Friendly*, friendly. He was always in the rec room with them, chatting. We used to call him Brenda – and ask him when he was going to go back to his singing career.' Keith paused, waiting to be asked for an explanation.

Oh get on with it, thought Jordan, who'd worked it out already.

'Brenda Nolan, the long-lost Nolan Sister.' Keith smirked at his own wit.

OK, better keep you on side, thought Jordan. He smirked back, companionably.

'So Tara and Brendan were close?'

'Very close.'

Yes, thought Jordan. As soon as I saw Tara on TV I knew she had something to hide. And I was the man to uncover it. I was so right. So fucking right. Front-page headline in 140-point bold across the top of the page: 'Topless Shame of Table Dancing Tara'; 'Seedy Past of Star who Reads our Futures'.

'How long did Tara work here?'

'She didn't.'

No, thought Jordan.

'And she wasn't called Tara then.'

Yes, thought Jordan.

'Her name was Scarlett. I forget her second name. But it wasn't MacDonald. Brendan would know. He was her personal trainer. Used to do that in the mornings –

train all his rich personal clients – then he'd sleep in the afternoon and work here at night.'

'Go on.'

'Scarlett never came in here. But I saw her out running with Brendan. I was driving home from a party, half-cut—' remembering he was talking to a policeman Keith stopped, smiled ingratiatingly – 'I mean I was in a taxi, half seven in the morning, and there they were, running along the beach boulevard, in the dark, with head torches. Couldn't see who it was at first, but when I realised it was Brendan I had to stop and have a go at him.'

Head torches? thought Jordan. *Running in the dark?* Tell me more.

'Didn't want his posh clients to know he worked here, did he? So I asked him what time he was coming into The Macho. Just to get a rise out of him, like.' Keith laughed.

'And Tara? I mean, Scarlett?'

'Fucking gorgeous. They didn't want to take a lift from me. But I insisted. Took them back to Brendan's place. Thought I'd have a punt at Scarlett but . . .' He shrugged his shoulders. 'Her loss. Must be a dyke. She *was* staying at Brendan's.'

'Did you see her again?'

'No, that was it.'

'Know anyone else who knows her?'

'Just Brendan.'

'Was it him who told you she'd changed her name?'

'Nobody told me.'

'How can you be sure it was Tara, then?'

212

Keith smiled, man-to-man: 'I forget names. Sometimes faces. But in this business, I never forget a body. Soon as I saw Tara on telly I knew it was that Scarlett.' He warmed to his subject. 'Tits. No two pairs alike. If you know what to look for. Hers are real. Could be bigger. But great shape. And her legs: eight, no, nine out of ten. For her height. Aye . . .' He considered for a moment: 'I'd have given her a job. Definitely. If she'd been the right side of twenty.'

'Is Brendan around tonight?'

'I told you. He doesn't work here any more. Spent too much time talking to the girls. Not what a punter wants to see when he comes here, is it? The girls propping up the bar, getting cosy with a faggot?'

'So where is Brendan?'

'No idea.'

No, thought Jordan.

'But Mercedes will know. She was his best pal. Might know more about Scarlett as well. Want to ask her yourself?' Keith grinned sleazily.

Y-E-S, thought Jordan. Double whammy. I'm going to crack this story *and* get a ride. With Mercedes. *A ride with Mercedes*. Oh fuck. Sometimes I'm just so fucking brilliant it hurts. I was *right* about Tara, *right* about coming to Aberdeen. Torpedoes in the water and heading towards target. Never in the history of journalism has so much been achieved by one man in one night . . .

'Tomorrow's Thursday, should be a few of the local bobbies in then if you'd like to come back,' said Keith. He handed Jordan a VIP pass.

Oh fuck, thought Jordan. What if he tells his cop pals about me and they check with the Met? Or he sees my by-line in the paper and puts two and two together? Maybe it wasn't so clever going along with this CID stuff? Still, bet Mr Smooth here won't want to tell the world he's been taken for a ride. Or that he lets his bouncers carry knives – or that he's as good as pimped Mercedes to me . . .

'Thanks. And thanks for Mercedes,' Jordan leered at Keith. 'By the way, about our friend Tam carrying a knife. You can rely on my discretion. I hope I can rely on yours. Even to your friends in the force here. This is a long-running investigation. As far as anyone here's concerned, I'm James the geologist.'

'No worries, James,' said Keith, with an in-the-know wink.

'What about Tam? Will he understand that?'

'He understands what's good for him,' said Keith. 'And you, you'll let me know?'

'What?'

'If Tara's a dyke or not. I've got a bet on. See that story in the papers today about her boyfriend? It's all for show. She's definitely a dyke. Fucking waste. Body like that.'

Fuck, thought Jordan. What boyfriend, where boyfriend, when boyfriend? That story wasn't in the papers I read on the plane this morning.

'Which paper was that in?'

'The *Evening Express*. Check it out.'

Too right I'll check it out, thought Jordan. Where the

fuck has this boyfriend sprung from? Full of surprises, Tara is. But I'm onto her now. Won't be long before the whole world knows every secret she's ever had . . .

Chapter Eighteen

London, August 2000

'OOOOH, he was the cat's whiskers he was,' exclaimed Edna Hooper. 'With his little moustache and the way he raised one eyebrow.'

Round the four pushed-together tables in the community centre café, Joans who'd long outlived their Darbys smiled as swoonily as teenagers. Even with the right pair of spectacles on, not all of them had managed to make out the vintage film poster David was holding up. But Mrs Hooper's voice was one you didn't need a hearing aid for, and as soon as they heard her description they all knew who was being talked about.

'It was a wonderful film. Everybody was talking about it. There wasn't anyone who didn't go to see it,' continued Edna. '*I* saw it three, no, four times.'

'It *was* too long, though,' remarked Wilf James. 'Terrible long time to sit in a picture house.'

'First time I went was with an airman. Canadian, I think he was. From Winnipeg. No, I tell a lie. He was a Yank. From Wisconsin.' Self-consciously patting her implausibly auburn curls, Edna twinkled coquettishly at the rest of the oral reminiscence group, then – with dainty affectation – reached for her teacup.

As she lifted it to her lips, David grabbed the few

moments opportunity to let someone else get a word in. 'Did *you* see *Gone With the Wind*?' he asked Mary Reilly.

Timid as ever, Mary twisted her cotton sunhat in her near-transparent hands and merely nodded.

Must ask an open-ended question, thought David: 'So what did *you* think of it?'

Out of the corner of his vision he could see Edna fidgeting with her 'genuine diamanté' shopping-channel earrings, but he kept his attention fixed on Mary O'Reilly.

'It *was* ever so long,' she offered shyly. 'It started at six o'clock so I had to go straight from work.' She looked round anxiously for someone else to say something.

Edna had her mouth open in readiness, but closed it again when she heard Wilf James clearing his throat. If it had been any of the women she'd have given them the benefit of hearing *her* opinion first, but when the only man in the company decided to say something – well, that was different, wasn't it?

'Doris came straight from work too,' he said. 'She had her sandwiches with her for her tea. Corned beef they were. With pickle. We didn't get pickle in the mess.'

Edna smiled acknowledgement, then pressed on: 'Three hours, I reckon it was. Or maybe three and a half. But I loved every minute of it, I did.'

'I'm sure you did, dear,' said Violet Jones, a sunken-faced spinster who'd been Edna's plainer-looking and plain-spoken friend since primary school. 'But what about the film?'

'Oooh, you're one to speak,' retorted Edna.

217

The rest of the group relaxed and settled back in their plastic chairs: no need to contribute to the conversation now; this was a double act they'd enjoyed for decades.

'What about that time you got put out of the Odeon? With that G.I. of yours?' Seeing David's puzzlement, Edna added helpfully: 'It was the usherettes, lovey. They used to patrol the back row. With torches. Nowhere else to go. In them days.'

'What about *you*, then?' Violet asked David.

'Me?' he responded, wilfully uncomprehending.

'Are you courting yet?'

Twelve pairs of dim-sighted eyes focused as best they could on their young facilitator.

'Well, um . . . no, not really. No.'

'Oooh, I don't believe you. A lovely young man like you,' cooed Edna. 'I bet there's loads of girls after you. Let's face it. There's not that many nice young men around these days.'

'Not that many nice *old* men either,' added Violet, sighing theatrically.

'Ooh, don't I know it?' said Edna. Then, wagging an admonitory finger at her companions, she added: 'But we mustn't make assumptions. Not these days. Maybe it's not young ladies you're interested in?'

'*Edna!*' chided Violet.

But David grinned good-naturedly: 'It *is* women I'm interested in. But then they've got to be interested in me, haven't they? Otherwise it's a non-starter.'

'So what's her name?'

'I didn't mean there was anyone *in particular*,' began

218

David, but Edna – veteran landlady of three public houses – could squeeze a man's story out of him faster than he could down a pint and scratchings. With an expression that was part-Mata Hari, part-interrogating officer, she stared him out.

Must get back to general conversation, thought David. But as he looked round desperately for inspiration he realised he'd never seen his group looking so alert and interested.

'Well, I *was* out for coffee yesterday,' he conceded. 'With a very beautiful woman. But she wouldn't be interested in me.'

'Well she went for coffee with you, didn't she?'

'It was a business meeting.'

'So you've got her telephone number.'

'Yes, but . . . it's more complicated than that.'

'Not a married lady, dearie?'

'No, no. Nothing like that. But . . . well, I'm meant to be working with her. And even if I weren't, she's way out of my league. *And* I met her through a mate of mine so . . .'

'Is she *his* young lady?'

'Well, no. He's got a girlfriend but . . .'

'Oh well then,' declared Edna. 'What are you waiting for, lovey?'

'Hang on a mo . . .' A thought had occurred to Violet. 'What's this young lady's name?'

David threw up his hands in mock resignation: 'Tara.'

'Has Tara taken a shine to your chum?'

'Probably. Most women do. Anyway . . .' David

picked up another film poster and began to unroll it, but Edna wasn't letting him off the hook that easily.

'The thing is, lovey, unless you ask her out, you'll never know.'

'That's right. No point in being backward in coming forward,' said Violet. 'What's she like?'

'You're ganging up on me,' protested David.

'Well then?' insisted Edna.

'Well, I don't know her very well. Don't know her at all really. But she's fun. Easy to talk to. And although she seems very confident, I think . . . I think she's a little bit lost actually.' He paused, but no one said a word. 'And she's got a *very* sweet smile,' he added. 'But I don't know why I'm telling you all this because it *is* a non-starter.'

'Well, what d'you want out of life, son?' asked Wilf. 'Are you just going to stay single, jog along, wait till there's no one left but the wallflowers?'

'Wallflowers?'

'At some point you've got to cross that dance floor and speak to the one who's caught your eye,' explained Wilf. 'Don't want to be left with regrets, do you?'

'In our day you lived for the moment. Had to. You didn't know if you'd be there tomorrow,' said Edna.

Eleven silver-haired heads nodded agreement.

'It's probably more difficult these days.'

Everyone turned to look at Mary. What *did* she mean?

Although nervous to the point of blushing at being the centre of attention, Mary had an inkling of what was bothering David and she wanted to help. 'Well, in our day we were happy to boil up the copper to do the washing. Nowadays girls expect washing machines and videos and I don't know what else.' This was turning into the longest speech she'd made in decades but she was determined to reassure the young man who'd been so kind to her. 'But none of that matters. Not if you've found the right one. Doesn't matter a jot.'

'Hear! Hear!' chorused the group.

'Car-pie dee-em, son!' added Wilf, with a man-to-man twinkle.

'Sorry?' said David.

Wilf looked crestfallen: 'Must be my pronunciation. Seize the day. That's what I meant to say. Seize the day!'

'Carpe diem! Of course. Sorry, Wilf. You were speaking Latin and I was listening in English.'

Pride restored, Wilf nodded wisely.

'And now, what about this one?' said David, holding up the poster for the 1942 film *For Me and My Gal*.

But Edna couldn't resist a final word of advice. Reaching across the table, she patted him on the arm: 'Car-pie dee-em, lovey. Just make sure you do. I know girls are more forward than they used to be, but there's still some you never know what they're thinking. Sometimes *they* don't even know what they're thinking. Not until you cross that dance floor . . .'

Chapter Nineteen

Aberdeen, March 1998

AS the train pulled into Aberdeen station, Scarlett was in the toilet with two fingers down her throat, trying to make herself sick. But the three Mars Bars, two slices of fruit cake, triple-decker bacon'n'egg sandwich and four cans of Diet Coke from the buffet car remained heavily in her stomach. As she squatted, head down over the toilet bowl, fingers of one hand jabbing towards her tonsils, the jolt of the locomotive meeting the buffers sent her flying. Knees crashing painfully against the toilet seat, she had to grab hold of the wash-hand basin to stop herself falling further. Straightening up, she caught sight of herself in the mirror: her big white dough-ball face, overflowing at cheekbones and jaw, like a sponge baked in too small a tin. To mark the start of her new life she'd applied newly purchased beige Lancôme foundation, and instead of hiding behind her shoulder-length brown hair, she'd pulled it off her face into a sleek topknot. Her spectacles had been replaced by contact lenses. But the make-up had melted, the hairstyle was unflattering and her eyes were bloodshot from the unaccustomed lenses. With her shiny fat face, scraped-back hair and sad expression, she looked more like a defeated sumo wrestler than a twenty-five-year-old star-in-the-making. Below the neck, she was draped in black: a slash-necked tunic over an ankle-length skirt, opaque tights and trendy new ankle boots with square toes and stacked heels. The outfit was meant to say big-but-stylish 1998. But at five foot three and thirteen and a half stones the effect was more Queen Victoria 1898.

In Glasgow that morning, when Flora had waved her off at Queen Street Station, Scarlett had felt tingly with hope, embarking on the first part of their plan. But now – three hours and 160 miles later – she couldn't imagine it working.

Look at yourself, she thought. A fat lump who can't get through a few hours alone without stuffing yourself silly. I feel sick. Yet I can't throw up. Tried for years to become bulimic. And longed for anorexia. But I can't even develop a proper eating disorder. I just eat. Always have. As long as I can remember. That's never changed. So why did I think I could change anything else? I'm stuck with this waterbed body, this balloon face. And now, this crazy plan. Which won't work.

I thought I could do it. But I can't. As soon as Brendan sees me he'll know he can't help me. Then we'll phone Flora and tell her she's wasting her money. I should never have left the *Daily Brit*. At my leaving do everyone said how much they appreciated me. I felt I was letting them down. Especially since they're making do with temps now. No one wants a permanent job with such long hours. McCoy said I was 'irreplaceable'. Couldn't believe he was being so nice to me. He said I could come back any time, so why don't I? Back to where I'm needed and what I know. Not pursuing an impossible dream in an unknown city with a total stranger.

Decisively, she picked up her shoulder bag and unlocked the toilet door. The sooner I find Brendan and explain it's all a mistake, the sooner I can get back to Glasgow and get back to reality, she thought.

Mind made up, she was impatient to get going, but the corridor was full of passengers. Rather than pushing past and drawing attention to her bulk, she waited until everyone else had got off before collecting her suitcase. But just as she was heaving it down the aisle, she saw a cleaner advancing with a bin bag. Sizing up Scarlett in a glance, the cleaner sidestepped into a seat, rather than squeeze past. Scarlett switched on the sorry-I'm-such-an-obstacle smile she used umpteen times a day. Her face was hot with effort and red with shame.

Finally on the platform, she dragged her case across the concourse, against a tide of departing passengers: elderly ladies carrying their own tea in a thermos flask, oilmen with wind-battered faces and plastic bags clanking with cans of Tennents, young mothers sucking on a cigarette as their children clamoured for crisps. There was less of a bustle than at Glasgow Queen Street, though; less chatter. Although the railway continued to Inverness, already there was a sense of being at the end of the line.

They're all watching me, thought Scarlett. They're all thinking how fat I am. In her long black blanket coat she felt like a sweaty bundle of misery: her new boots pinched, her bare hand was chafing on the suitcase handle, her eyes were itchy and her stomach queasy. Stepping outside came as a physical relief.

It was like walking into a deep-freeze cabinet: the cold air numbed the aches, made her feel her body was shrinking beneath her clothes. But the greyness of it all made her want to throw herself into the icy waters of the harbour: the buildings were grey granite, the sky was grey, even the day-old snowfall had turned to grey slush. Wish I could just turn round and get the next train back to Glasgow, thought Scarlett. But I owe it to Flora to go and tell Brendan myself that I can't go through with this.

Turning her attention to the people waiting with her at the taxi rank she noticed they were dressed with respect for the elements: adults in hooded Parkas, fleeces, woollen coats; children swaddled like mini Eskimos. In Glasgow, hats and gloves were an indicator of the middle classes. Here everyone seemed to be wearing them. What was it Flora had said, thought Scarlett: 'Aberdeen's further north than Moscow.' The wind certainly felt Siberian. And to her Central Belt ears, the taxi driver's greeting – 'Foo're ye dae'in'?' – was almost as foreign as Russian. Not realising he'd asked how she was, rather than where she was going, Scarlett replied: 'St Olaf's Flats, King Street.'

Unlike Glasgow, conversation was not included in the fare. Without even nodding, the cabbie drove out of the cobbled car park and up a steep brae onto the city's main thoroughfare, Union Street. The cars were new reg and the cashpoints the busiest in the country, but the forbidding combination of grey buildings, windswept expanse and unsmiling shoppers would have made a Muscovite homesick.

The taxi driver continued down Union Street towards the beach, then turned left into King Street and pulled up at new-build apartments, four storeys, faced in rose-coloured granite. Scarlett paid, collected her case and climbed the steps to the entrance lobby. She buzzed flat 4a.

'Hello?' The voice was male, friendly and reassuringly Glasgow.

'Brendan?'

'Up you come, darlin'. Top floor.'

By the time Scarlett reached the third floor, she was bathed in sweat. A dark-haired man, dressed like a gymnast and smelling of Aqua di Gio, sprang forward Nureyev-style to take her suitcase. 'Welcome to the penthouse,' he beamed. 'I'm Brendan, your new best friend.' He bowed and led the way into a living room so freshly decorated you could smell the paint. The shade – chosen under the influence of too many home-decorating shows – was best described as 'screaming daffodil'. The spanking new furniture – small scale to make the low-ceilinged box-shaped room look bigger – shrieked show flat. The CD player was on full blast: Robbie Williams singing 'Let Me Entertain You'.

Scarlett inspected her new best friend. He wasn't much taller than her, only five foot six, but as perfectly formed as a *Men's Health* cover boy. His body – cling-wrapped in tight silver leggings and white singlet – was a walking advert for two hours a day in the gym. Biceps, triceps, pectorals, thighs: everything that could be worked on had been. But he wasn't beefcake: more Sting than Schwarzenegger. Less subtle was his electric Caribbean tan: testimony to a twice-a-week sunbed habit. And his boy-band smooth chest: the result of rigorous chest waxing. His colouring was Celtic: dark hair close-cropped with a diagonal flash shorn into the stubble; blue-grey eyes twice framed with long curly lashes and heavy black eyebrows. He looked like he spent whole mornings in the bathroom: well-buffed skin and neat topiary on his eyebrows and goatee. But with his pointed ears and jutting Jimmy Hill chin the overall impression was more woodland sprite than urban sex god.

As he leapt nimbly across the room to turn off the music, then flashed Scarlett an impish smile, he looked like a Lycra-clad leprechaun ready for mischief.

Scarlett smiled back shyly: 'I'm Scarlett.'

'Not for much longer.' Brendan perched himself on one of the pair of two-seater sofas and gestured her to take the other. 'I'm going to transform you. Miss M asked me to and her wish is my command.'

Why's he so devoted to Flora? wondered Scarlett.

'I wonder what your new name will be,' continued Brendan. 'It'll be such fun choosing. Miss M said you loved *Gone With the Wind* so my first thought was Vivien, after Vivien Leigh?'

Scarlett nodded.

'But that's far too old-fashioned,' continued Brendan. 'I meant to buy one of those books for naming babies but everything's been so frantic. I had to move out of my old flat, move into this one, buy some weights for you and—'

'I'm sorry but—'

'And wait till you see what you've got in your bedroom!' Brendan pulled Scarlett to her feet, led her back across the tiny hall and into one of the rooms leading off it. '*Voilà* . . .' More doll's house furniture and kindergarten colour: the label on the paint pot must've read 'exploding mango'. At the foot of the undersized double bed was what looked like a circular footstool. Seeing Scarlett's puzzled look, Brendan leapt onto it and started bouncing up and down energetically: 'A one-person trampoline. You're obviously too young to remember Sue Ellen in *Dallas*.'

Scarlett was staring at the contraption in horror.

'Great fun! You have a go,' said Brendan.

'No thanks,' said Scarlett. One bounce and I'd break it, she thought. The sooner I tell him I've changed my mind the better. 'Look, Brendan . . .'

'What am I thinking of?' He jumped off the trampoline, took her by the hand and led her back to the living room. 'Now sit down and I'll get you a drink. What'll it be? Just make yourself comfortable and I'll get it.'

Scarlett sat down. But she didn't look at all comfortable.

Brendan regarded her kindly. 'Tea? Coffee? Tequila? Kahlua? What about a Long Slow Screw Against the Wall? Or a Rampant Russian with a Soft Touch?'

Scarlett failed to smile.

Brendan sat down opposite her. 'Trust me. I'm a barman. In The Macho club. Didn't Miss M tell you? By day I'm personal trainer to rich oil wives. By night

I'm a barman. And now every morning, bright and early, I'll devote myself to you. By the time I'm finished you'll have a new body. And you'll need a *whole* new wardrobe.' He ended with a camping-it-up hand flourish and an encouraging smile.

No response from Scarlett.

Brendan stopped hamming it up, leant over and took her hands in his. 'What's the matter, pal?'

'I'm sorry, Brendan. I'm really sorry. But this is all a mistake. It's not going to work.'

'Don't say you doubt my credentials, darlin'?'

'No, not at all. It's me. I can't do it. My ma ran a slimming class, I was brought up on low-calorie everything. And look at me. Look at the size of me.' Scarlett was close to tears.

Brendan sat back, looked at her appraisingly. 'I can assure you, darlin', compared to some of the ladies I train, you're Kate Moss. Really. These oil princesses, sitting at home all day spooning Mississippi Mud Pie – all that frosted icing – and then they get the car out to cross the road?' He affected a Southern drawl: 'Loaded and lardy, yessirree.' He looked at Scarlett and shook his head: 'You're just not in their league. Not large enough, I'm afraid. OK, you've had a couple of fish suppers too many. But slimming you down will be a doddle. Honest.' He smiled encouragingly.

'I'm sorry. It's not just the diet. It's everything. You wouldn't understand. I'm sorry to muck you about. Flora will pay you anyway. And I'll pay her back.'

'You've no faith in me,' said Brendan, serious-voiced.

'No. I mean, yes. Yes I do.'

229

'You said I wouldn't understand.'

'Well how could you?' said Scarlett angrily. I can't bear this, she thought. He means well but he's no idea what it's like to be me. All this talk about diet and exercise makes me think of my Ma, my size, everything I don't want to think about. I just need to get out of here, get on the Glasgow train and get a Mars Bar in my mouth. Then I'll feel better.

Brendan was saying nothing, looking straight ahead, as though trying to work something out. 'You said I wouldn't understand? What wouldn't I understand?'

'What it's like to be me.'

'You mean to hate yourself?'

Scarlett flinched as though he'd slapped her.

'D'you think it's so unusual to hate yourself? To want to be somebody different?'

Scarlett was looking down at her lap. 'Don't know,' she said quietly.

'I went to your school, Scarlett. Five years ahead of you.'

'Flora told me.'

'But did she tell you why I'd do anything for her? Why her wish is my command?'

'No.'

Brendan took a deep breath: 'My father's a part-time brickie. Full-time Celtic supporter. I've got three elder sisters so I'm the only son. Before I could walk, Da was lifting me over the turnstile, taking me to the game.'

Scarlett looked bemused.

'What I'm saying is: all that west of Scotland male stuff. The wee man. And I was good at football. Got selected for Celtic Boys' Club. My Da was over the moon. But that's as far as I got. Because I was bullied. Big-style. Couldn't take it.'

Scarlett had forgotten her own problems. Was listening intently.

'I wasn't interested in girls, was I? Or fighting. Or any of the things I should've been. So I got a hard time. A very hard time. At the club. At school.' Brendan sighed. 'Any chance they got, they gave me a hiding. Said it was for my own good, to stop me being a jessie. One time they jumped on me in the showers, cut off my eyelashes with a flick knife. To stop me looking like a lassie. I was terrified they'd blind me.

'I'd been brought up not to cry. But I did. So they called me Brenda. Brenda the poof. I didn't know if they were right or not. But I prayed to God not to make me a poof.' He smiled wryly. 'God didn't answer my prayers. And there was no one else to talk to. My Ma might have been OK with it but my Da, well my Da could hardly bear to look at me. To him, poof was a term of abuse. Still is.' Brendan sighed. Looked away.

'Flora?'

'Miss M knew I was having a hard time. Took me aside. Told me that there were men who liked women and men who liked men. And that one day I'd know where I fitted in. But I *would* fit in. One day. So I shouldn't worry.

'She didn't tell the other kids to stop teasing me. That would only have encouraged them. But now and again she'd do a lesson on someone like Alexander the Great, or Lawrence of Arabia, and then just slip in that

231

they really were men's men, by the way.' Brendan ended with an exaggerated Glasgow accent and a big wink.

Scarlett smiled.

'So I *do* understand, Scarlett. What it's like to feel bad about yourself. And what *you* have to understand is that Miss M saved my life. Without her I'd have dropped out of school. Wouldn't have made it to college to do sports management. Wouldn't have found my niche at all.

'She found the course, made sure I did the right subjects to get in. Even got Da on side. Convinced him I couldn't do football training because I was studying for college. When I got in, he was dead proud. Came to my graduation. So did Miss M.

'She's written me a reference for every gym I've ever worked in, every client who's asked for one. She's just magic, you know.'

'Yes I *do* know.'

'This is the first time she's ever asked me to do anything for her. And no way am I going to let her down.' Brendan took Scarlett's hands in his. 'She asked me to show you how beautiful you really are. And you're not going back to Glasgow until we've done that. OK, pal?'

Scarlett was gazing downward again.

Gently, Brendan lifted her chin so she had to look at him. 'OK?' he asked.

'But I can't . . .'

'It's not just about you, Scarlett.' He looked straight at her, tried and failed to raise one eyebrow, then with

Frank Sinatra intonation: 'D'you really think Aberdeen's my kinda town?'

Scarlett smiled.

'I hate it. Cramps my style something rotten. Worse than Glasgow. I'm only here to make money, then I'm off.'

'Where to?'

'Ibiza, Miami, wherever the sun shines and the boys are beautiful.'

Brendan sighed theatrically. Then, serious again, he continued: 'The point is, Scarlett, with you paying the rent here – and nine months' guaranteed personal training – I'll be able to save up and high-tail it out of Dodge. You wouldn't condemn me to living in the grim Granite City for ever, would you?' He stood up and strutted round the living room, singing: 'I'm too sexy for this city, too sexy for this city . . .'

'OK, OK,' said Scarlett, laughing. 'You're a great performer.'

Brendan gave her a glad-that's-settled smile. Then: 'D'you really think so? Miss M always said I should be on the stage. Told me I was well good enough for the youth group at the Citizen's Theatre. That was just when I was about to quit Celtic Boys' Club.' He sighed. 'Couldn't do that to my da. Tell him I was giving up football, and by the way I was off to' – his voice became deeper, his accent broader – 'ponce aboot wi' a bunch o' thespians.' Brendan shook his head. 'The shock would have killed him. It's only last year he stopped asking me if I was courting yet.'

For a moment, he looked downcast. But before

Scarlett could say anything sympathetic, he jumped to his feet and asked brightly, 'By the way, darlin', who would you say I looked like?'

'I . . . I don't know.'

Brendan covered his chin with one hand. 'Seriously, without the goatee. Who d'you think?'

Scarlett shook her head.

Brendan spread his other hand across his hairless chest. 'Don't let this distract you. I'm thinking of letting it grow back in.'

Scarlett shrugged.

'Contemporary singing star? High in the charts?'

'Noel Gallagher? Liam?'

'The Eyebrow Brothers? I'm offended.'

'I'm sorry. I've no idea,' said Scarlett. 'I don't really think you look like him. Just the first name I could think of. I don't know about music. I don't really go out or anything.' Her voice trailed off lamely.

'Never apologise, darlin'. Never explain. You've only confirmed what I was thinking already: the goatee has got to go. Then you'll see the resemblance right away.' He sat down. 'Anyway, no more guessing games. Let me tell you what we're going to do. Are you Catholic? Protestant?'

Scarlett was too surprised by the question to answer.

'Catholicism is better for you. All that genuflecting.' He stood up and executed a deep knee bend. 'So good for the thighs. All the Prods have got is that John Knox finger-pointing.' He stretched out one hand and wagged a finger at her: 'So Motown.'

Scarlett was sitting back in the sofa, entranced by his performance.

234

Brendan smiled, basking in the attention: 'I used to be an altar boy. A very good one.' He swung an invisible string of rosary beads. 'But I've got a new religion now. And I'm going to convert you to it.'

He put his glass on the coffee table, stood up and thrust his hands in the air. 'Sport is my religion. Didn't Miss M tell you? The gym I train at is a converted church. It's called The Temple. Which is fab cos my body is *my* temple, and yours will be too.'

He sat down again, leant towards her conspiratorially: 'Miss M told me it's all top secret. When you change your name no one must ever know who you were before. You can rely on me. I won't tell a soul. That's why you're paying me so much money, darling. Hush money, Miss M called it. Said you were going to be a big star and when you were there'd be more in it for me.'

He paused, chose his words carefully: 'I don't want to do myself out of my hush money, darling. But I don't understand the secrecy. I mean, you read in the papers all the time about the humble beginnings of the rich and famous, how they reinvented themselves: Madonna was chubby, Julia Roberts couldn't get a date. You'll have a really good story to tell: "How Scarlett from Scotstoun became a star-gazing star".'

He waited for Scarlett to smile at his clever headline. But she didn't.

'Isn't that how newspapers work, darling?'

'I know how newspapers work. I used to work for the *Daily Brit*.'

'Don't you think it would be a fabulous story, then?

I told Miss M it would be and she agreed. Wouldn't tell me why you wanted it kept secret.'

'That's because she doesn't know why.'

'But you two are business partners, right?'

'We are.' Scarlett heaved herself to the edge of the sofa, sat up straighter, and sighed: 'And you're right about the story too, Brendan. But the thing about newspapers is, no matter how many good stories you give them, they want more. And they want something different from the rest. The more clues you give them, the more they'll keep digging, until they find the dirt.'

'But surely there isn't—'

Scarlett finished the sentence for him: 'Dirt on me?' She sighed again, looked away.

Sensing she was making a decision, Brendan said nothing.

After a few moments, Scarlett's gaze returned to him. For the first time since she'd arrived, it was she who initiated eye contact. And held it. Her voice was business-like. 'Look, Brendan. I don't just want to become a star. I want a whole new life. I want to be someone else. Do you understand that?'

Brendan nodded.

'My childhood wasn't great. There are things I just don't want to be reminded of. Things that hurt. You know?'

'I *do* know.'

'If I thought anyone would find out about them I'd stop this whole thing. Right now. I told Flora that and she understood. She didn't ask me anything else about it. And I hope you won't either.'

236

Brendan was grinning at her. Appreciatively. Shaking his head.

'What's so funny?'

'I'm just pleased to see how determined you can be when you want to. Makes my job a lot easier. When Miss M told me your plan I wasn't sure about it. A few minutes ago you seemed so negative I thought you'd never make it. But now I can see you've what it takes. You're definitely up for it.' He leant over, took her right hand in his and kissed it. 'You *will* be a star, Cinderella. Just don't dare say anything about fairy godmothers.'

Scarlett smiled; sat back in the sofa.

'Relax while you can, darlin', because tomorrow we go into action.' Brendan clapped his hands with enthusiasm: 'I've got it all sussed: we'll get that weight off and sculpt you a whole new body. We can't go to the gym because we don't want people seeing you close up. The beach will be all right, as long as we go out in the dark. Power-walking at first, then jogging. Weights we'll do at home. And the trampoline of course.'

Scarlett looked anxious.

'Kiri te Kanawa has got one, darling. And *she's* no sylph. All you need is the perfect sports bra and you'll be bouncing like the Easter Bunny.'

'What about the diet?'

'What diet? Did I mention a diet? You'll be so busy I'll have to remind you to eat. Haven't you read Miss M's schedule?' He handed her a piece of paper, marked out like a school timetable. 'Look,' said Brendan. 'Six am: rise and shine; seven am: beach run with Brendan; nine am: dumbbells with Brendan; ten am: telephone

237

date with Miss M for voice coaching; twelve noon: bouncing with Brendan.'

'What?'

'That's the trampoline, darlin'.' He continued reading aloud: 'Two to four pm: astrology; four to six pm: psychology; seven pm: sample columns to write up and send to Miss M; nine thirty pm: bedtime; ten pm: lights out.'

Scarlett began reading the rest of the timetable herself.

'You'll be far too busy to think about food,' said Brendan. 'And anyway, the kitchen's off limits. I'm your personal chef: vegetable soup, baked tatties, bean casseroles . . . lovely, filling, low-calorie food. And if you're tempted to sneak off and buy chocolate and sweeties then I've got a can't-fail trick to stop you eating them.'

'What's that?'

'It's pretty nasty. I'm keeping it in reserve.'

'Can't you tell me now?'

'If you need it, I'll tell you. Don't worry, you'll be going back to Glasgow half the size you are now. Honest.' Brendan smiled a Tony Blair trust-me smile, then, catching sight of the music centre: 'Ooh, nearly forgot. Dancing. We'll be doing lots of dancing.'

'I've never been clubbing. I've never danced.' Scarlett looked down at the floor, ashamed.

'Good. So you won't have picked up any uncool moves. We can't go clubbing, I'm afraid. In case anyone sees you. But we'll be dancing right here in our fabulous downtown penthouse.' He leapt up and pulled

Scarlett into an approximation of a tango: 'Dah-dah, dah-dah, dah-dah-dah-dah, in Brendan's hideaway, olé!' he sang. As he deposited Scarlett gently back on the sofa she smiled up at him admiringly, wondering what he'd think of next.

Not one to disappoint his audience, Brendan darted over to the music centre, flicked on the CD player once more. Robbie Williams came on again, still singing 'Let Me Entertain You'.

Planting himself right in front of Scarlett, arms outstretched, Brendan sang along.

Scarlett suddenly realised something important: 'Robbie Williams. *That's* who you look like.' He didn't, but she'd been so relaxed, enjoying his antics, she'd stopped thinking about herself, started thinking about Brendan and what he'd want to hear.

He bent down, kissed her extravagantly on both cheeks: 'I've suddenly realised who *you* are.'

'What d'you mean?'

'Your new name. It's just come to me.' He sprinted to the kitchen, returned with a bottle of Cava, a tea towel and two glasses. *'Gone With the Wind,'* he said thoughtfully, turning the bottle in the tea towel with a bartender's expertise.

'Thought you said Vivien was too old-fashioned?'

'It *is*. Forget about Vivien. I've got a much better idea.'

Brendan opened the bottle with a muted pop, poured two glasses, handed one to Scarlett, held up the other in a toast: 'With the power invested in me by the Worshipful Church of the Steely Buttock, in the name

239

of health, fitness and the body beautiful, you are now born again.' He clinked his glass against hers. 'I hereby christen you: Tara. Let the old Scarlett be gone with the wind . . .'

Chapter Twenty

Aberdeen, August 1998

'COME on, Scarlett, keep going,' urged Brendan. 'Give me ten more sit-ups.'

Lying flat on the floor in sweatpants and baggy T-shirt, body bathed in sweat, Scarlett gritted her teeth and tried to raise her torso. But it was no use. 'Can't do any more,' she gasped. 'My stomach's aching.'

'Good,' said Brendan. 'That proves your muscles are working. Now come on. Just ten more. You've only done twenty today. Yesterday you did fifty.'

Without even attempting a sit-up, Scarlett heaved herself up on her hands and looked down disconsolately at her stomach. 'It's no use, Brendan. Can't do any more. And it's not making any difference anyway.'

'Yes it *is*.'

But Scarlett had got up and flung herself full-length on the sofa. 'Where's the newspaper? I want to see what's on TV.'

'You *know* the rules. No TV till you've finished your programme for the day.'

'I *am* finished. I'm exhausted. You made me run much faster than usual this morning.'

'That's because I want to speed up your metabolism. Now you've lost so much weight already you'll have to work a wee bit harder to lose the rest. So come on, let's go.'

No response from the figure lying prone on the sofa.

Brendan looked down at it for a moment, then, with a sudden inspiration, leapt across to the wall chart where he'd been plotting Scarlett's weight loss on a graph. From when they'd started training six months ago it showed a sudden dip, followed by a steady downward trend, then a levelling out. 'Look how well you've done. Three and a half stones in six months. You're only ten stones now. That's brilliant. The Incredible Shrinking Woman.'

'Yes, but last week I only lost half a pound. And nothing the week before. This must be the weight I'm meant to be. Anyway' – Scarlett patted her tummy – 'I'm not fat any more. Just plump.'

'You're not plump. You're fabulous. And just because you haven't lost any more weight doesn't mean you're not losing inches. Muscle weighs more than fat, you know.'

'So you keep telling me.'

'Come on, I'll get out the tape measure.'

'No, Brendan. Please. You've done a brilliant job and I'm really grateful, but this is slim enough for me. No way I'll ever get to target weight.'

'Yes you will. Three months left. And only a stone or so to go. You can do it.'

'No I can't.'

'Yes you can.'

'No I can't.'

'Yes—' Brendan broke off. 'All right, I give in. This

is getting too pantomime. Why don't you take the rest of the day off? Forget the work-out, forget your astrology books. I'll phone Miss M and say she needn't bother calling you later for your elocution lesson.'

'What?' Scarlett was so surprised she sat up to see if Brendan really meant what he was saying.

'I mean it. You deserve a break from all this hard work. And from your diet. So why don't you go into town, do a bit of shopping. You said yesterday you'd nothing to wear, everything was too loose. So go on, go downtown, and while you're there, why don't you treat yourself to a cream cake?'

'*Brendan!*' Scarlett was looking at him as though he'd just told told her to run stark naked down Union Street.

'Go on. What are you waiting for?'

On seeing the sign for Evans the outsize shop, Scarlett automatically headed over to look in the window. But halfway across the floor of the mall, she stopped in her tracks. Wait a minute, she thought. I may not be slim, but I'm not outsize. Not any more.

She headed out of the shopping centre and onto Union Street. For the past five months she'd spent all her time either running on the beach or at home working out and studying. Evenings had been spent reading or watching videos. This was her first shopping expedition in Aberdeen. And her first time shopping at this weight. Wonder what shops they've got here, she thought. Whistles, Jigsaw, Episode? Don't want to spend too much, though. What if I put the weight back on?

243

By this time she was outside Top Shop.

No way, she thought. All the mannequins look so skinny.

She walked along to Warehouse.

Just as skinny here, she thought. But those black boot-cut trousers are fab.

Before she could lose her courage she pushed open the glass door, scoured the clothes rails and found the trousers she'd seen in the window. Might have known it, she thought. None in my size.

'Want to try them on?' asked a waif-like assistant, nodding towards the trousers Scarlett was holding.

'Um . . . I'm not sure I . . .'

'They look great on.'

'There aren't any in my size.'

'This is a fourteen.'

'Yes, but I need a sixteen,' said Scarlett, shame-faced.

'I dinna think so,' said the assistant, so matter-of-factly that Scarlett meekly followed her to the changing rooms.

They won't possibly fit, she thought, looking at the sculpted shape, the neat waistband. But while I'm here . . .

She took off her stretch jeans and gingerly fitted her legs through the trousers. Pulling up the zip, she sucked her stomach in hard. But there was no need. They fitted perfectly. Excitedly, she turned round to inspect her bottom in the mirror. Wow, she thought. I look perfectly normal. Not fat, not deformed, just normal. Is that really me? Yes it *is*! And I feel fantastic.

Rushing onto the shop floor, she scooped up a fitted

black top, size fourteen. But back in front of the mirror she could see it didn't fit.

Too baggy, she thought gleefully.

'Could you get me a smaller size?' she asked the assistant.

A smaller size, she thought triumphantly. When did I ever say *that* before?

Will it fit?

Yes, it does.

As though fearful what was happening was a dream and she might wake up at any moment, Scarlett hurriedly paid for the trousers and sweater and – the clothes she'd been wearing earlier stuffed into a carrier bag – rushed back out onto Union Street. Now, she thought. Time to celebrate. Brendan's letting me off my diet for the day. Might as well make the most of it. What do I fancy?

In her mind's eye the first thing she saw was a frothy cappuccino and a big slice of gateau, oozing with cream. But almost instantly another image popped into her head: white maggots writhing in a cup next to a plate of vomit.

Oh God, she thought. Brendan's brainwashed me. Can't even face the thought of anything fattening.

Walking past a mirrored shop front, she caught sight of her reflection: an attractive young woman in trendy boot-cut trousers and a slinky top.

God, she thought. It's true. I really look normal. No. Better than normal. I look really good. Like . . . like someone in a magazine. And I feel fab. Absolutely fab. Ready for anything.

She scanned the street.

That's what I need, she thought, spotting a newsagent's. Purposefully, she marched inside, emerging a few minutes later with a pile of magazines: *Vogue, Elle, Harpers & Queen*.

Who needs cake, she said to herself. *This'll* be my treat: deciding what I'll wear when I'm size ten. If I look this good already, when I get to target weight I'll be *gorgeous*.

It's *really* possible. I really *could* be a star. So famous nobody will hurt me or get at me *ever* again. Well, I'm going to make sure it happens. I'm on my way and nobody's going to stop me. Can't wait to get there – and I can't wait to show Brendan my new clothes. If I hurry I'll get back before he goes to The Macho . . .

Chapter Twenty-one

London, August 2000

'MR Swift. How are you doing?' asked Flora. 'We weren't expecting to see you again so soon.'

David held out a brown paper bag: 'I . . . I just want to deliver this.'

'A first draft already?'

'Oh no. This isn't about the book. It's for Tara. Something I meant to give her when I last saw her but . . .' He handed the package over.

'A book?'

'Yes. I thought Tara might be interested in Ted Hughes . . . the Primrose Hill connection and his interest in astrology, so . . .'

'Oh yes, he used to live here, didn't he? I must confess, I haven't read any of his poetry. Shocking, isn't it?'

'Ummm . . . no, not at all. I mean, why should you have?'

'I used to be an English teacher. Many moons ago.'

Oh dear, thought Flora. Tara told me not to tell these lads *anything*.

'Who's *your* favourite poet?'

Is this him trying to charm an old lady now? wondered Flora. She looked up sharply, but smiling down from his six feet two inches to her five feet two inches, hair flopping forward and his too-loose spectacles slipping down his nose, David seemed genuinely interested in her answer.

'These days I find myself returning to the classical poets,' she told him. 'Especially Horace. He understood people so well. It's all just as relevant today. And the neatness of the language. You can say what you want to in half as many words in Latin. Still, you're too young to know about that.'

'Not at all . . . *Cras ingens iterabimus aequor . . .*'

'Tomorrow we set out once more upon the boundless sea – four words for ten. Yes, that's *precisely* what I mean.' Flora smiled up at him: 'Well, what a pleasant surprise. But let's not stand chatting out here, come away in and give this to Tara yourself.'

She ushered him across the threshold and into the cream-and-white salon, where Tara was reading the card on a spectacular hand-tied bouquet from London's most fashionable florist.

'So thoughtful of Jordan to think of me when he's looking after his mother,' she beamed.

'Um . . . this is for you too,' said David, handing over the brown paper bag.

'*Birthday Letters* by Ted Hughes?'

'Thought it might interest you . . .'

What a lovely thing to do, thought Flora.

What a clever touch, thought Tara.

'Thank you,' she said and smiled graciously.

David beamed back.

'Would you like some tea?' asked Flora.

David looked unsure.

Tara sent her a why-did-you-say-that look.

David saw it. 'No, that's all right, I'll . . .'

'You can't go back into that heat without a wee cup of tea,' instructed Flora in her jotters-out-and-pay-attention voice.

'Jilly phoned two minutes ago to say she'll be late,' she told Tara. 'She's got an emergency appointment with her herbalist. So you've time for a cuppa yourself.' She turned to David: 'Earl Grey, Lapsang Souchong or peppermint?'

'Um . . . Earl Grey.'

'Peppermint for yourself?'

'Lovely,' said Tara, smiling at David and shrugging her shoulders, as Flora bustled out, taking the bouquet with her.

'Compulsory tea break. Hope you don't mind?'

'No, not at all.' David smiled shyly.

Why can't I stop smiling and say something? he thought.

Why won't he stop smiling and say something? she thought. Obviously hoping I'll start gabbling again and give away more secrets. Well, not this time. This time I'm in control.

'How are *you*?' she asked.

'Friendly and relaxed.'

He looked mischievous.

Tara looked slightly puzzled.

'Or so you told me this morning,' he added with a smile.

Tara relaxed. 'Oh, so you watch my slot on Early Bird?'

'Well, I have this week. Ever since meeting you. I'm a recent convert.'

'To astrology?'

To you, thought David. 'To a certain extent.'

Still playing the cautious academic, thought Tara. Well, I'm on my guard now. If anyone's doing any finding out here, it's *me*. Under cover of smiling, she looked deeply into the hazel-gold eyes behind the spectacles. They returned her gaze without blinking.

Strange, thought Tara. Even *I'd* be fooled. Those eyes couldn't look more friendly and open-hearted. Never seen a hack who seemed so much like a human being. Got to watch every word I say.

She flashed him a professional TV presenter's smile: 'Relaxed and friendly . . . that makes you a Sagittarius. Have you ever had a personal reading?'

'No, I . . .'

'Don't believe a word of it?' Tara grinned. 'Don't be embarrassed. Lots of my clients thought it was complete mumbo-jumbo. Till they had a reading with me.'

'Oh, I wouldn't say . . . I mean, historically, astrology has had a definite influence on entire countries. So many heads of state have relied on astrologers: not just the Chinese leaders but Ronald Reagan, François Mitterand and . . .'

Tara was laughing.

She's laughing at me, thought David.

He looks so crestfallen, thought Tara. 'I'm sorry,' she said. 'It's just that Jordan told me the same thing, almost word for word.'

Bastard, thought David. He grinned wryly. 'I see.'

'I suppose you two work together very closely, don't you?'

'Yes, um . . . well, it's the first time we've ever worked together.'

I bet, thought Tara. 'Really? What do you normally do then?'

'I'm working on a book. About the history of the Thames.'

'Does it have a title?'

'*The Time Traveller's Guide to the Thames.*'

'Good title.'

'D'you really think so?'

'Yes I do. Honestly. Bit like *The Hitchhiker's Guide to the Galaxy.*'

David's face lit up like Piccadilly Circus.

Coming in with the tea tray, Flora caught his happy expression: 'Here we are then, you two,' she said, then retreated briskly.

Tara poured. David watched her.

Still not saying much, thought Tara. Well, I'll ask the questions then.

'So how do you do your research?'

'Walking, mostly. I walk every stretch three times: once for the general atmosphere, once with a notebook. Then after I've researched it thoroughly I walk it again. Just to see how it feels with all the information in my head. Then I write it up.'

'Must take ages.'

'Yes, it does. But I love it. I love taking in a place on foot. You see so much more. And anyway, you don't really know somewhere until you've seen it in all the

251

different seasons. Even in the city. I mean . . .' I'm talking too much again, he thought. 'Do you like walking?'

'I can't remember the last time I went for a proper walk. Apart from popping up to Odette's.'

'Or Parliamo,' he ventured.

'Yes.' Probably been back there asking Toni all sorts of questions about me, she thought. Must check with him.

'So what do you do when you're not on TV?'

'I do research too, and all the personal readings.'

'I meant what do you do when you're not working?'

'Oh I see. Well . . .'

Stupid question, thought David. She must be invited to every showbiz party in town.

'You must be invited to every showbiz party in town,' he said.

'Yes, I am. And I've been to a few of them, but . . .'

But what? wondered Tara. Why don't I enjoy them? Why do I always feel like they're hard work?

'You'd be surprised,' she said. 'They feel a bit like work.'

That sounds so pretentious, she thought.

But David nodded understandingly: 'So what do you do for fun?'

Fun? What *do* I do for fun, wondered Tara. She looked out the window as though searching for inspiration.

'You know, stamp collecting, toad sexing, that sort of thing,' he suggested.

'Oh well, both of those, when I've got the time.' Tara smiled at him, genuinely amused.

252

That smile, thought David. She's lovely. If only she weren't Tara MacDonald . . . but how can I ask a woman like this if she'd like to go down the pub?

Tara was still thinking about his question: 'You know, most of the time I'm running just to catch up with myself. It's a full-time job being Tara MacDonald.' She paused, as though taking in what she'd just said.

David waited for her to say more, but as if on cue, the doorbell rang.

Oh no, thought David. That'll be Jilly.

'You see,' said Tara. 'That's Jilly.'

He looks disappointed, she thought. Must be because he didn't get anything out of me this time.

'Excuse me,' she said. 'I have to get ready.'

She pushed her chair back and got up. David got up too but failed to push his chair back far enough and sent the tea tray flying. The teapot was empty but milk and sugar lumps spilled across the floor.

Oh no, he thought. She'll think I'm a complete klutz.

Such a klutz, thought Tara.

'I'm so sorry,' said David, bending down to retrieve the milk jug.

As he looked up to place it back on the table, Tara was struck by his flustered, so-sorry face. He looks sweet, she thought. Like a wee boy who's put his football through the window.

'Don't worry,' she said. 'And please leave it. I've got to go.'

She kissed him rapidly on both cheeks, then left the room, moments before Flora came in with Jilly.

Crouching down, retrieving sugar lumps from the

253

maplewood floor, David looked up to find himself at the feet of the queen of morning TV. 'I'm so sorry,' he said.

Jilly looked smaller and paler than she did on television, and the famous features were drawn with tiredness, but on seeing a new face, she rallied like a pro: 'Hello,' she beamed down at him.

David scrambled to his feet.

'Jilly Wyles,' she said, with the false modesty of someone who knows she needs no introduction. 'Have you just had your reading?'

'David's a journalist,' explained Flora. 'Now don't you bother yourself with that,' she added to David. 'I'll clear it up in no time.'

'Has Tara been telling you all her secrets?' Jilly asked with the big-eyed, you-can-tell-*me* smile familiar in living rooms throughout the land . . .

'Och, Tara's got no secrets,' said Flora briskly. 'Please sit yourself down. I'll just see David out, then I'll tell Tara you're here.'

'Nice meeting you, David,' trilled Jilly with reflex sincerity.

'And you,' said David, genuinely.

Wait till I tell the ladies at my oral reminiscence group, he thought. They'll be thrilled.

'How *is* the book going?' asked Flora as they went into the hallway.

'Slowly but surely.'

Slowly but surely I'm playing my part in Tara's downfall, he thought. If she *does* have secrets juicy enough for Jordan. I so hope she doesn't.

'Well, all the best with it.'

'Thanks,' muttered David guiltily, avoiding eye contact. 'I'm so sorry.'

'Don't bother your head about it,' said Flora, waving one hand dismissively at the milk-and-sugar strewn parquet in the salon.

That's not the only thing I'm sorry for, thought David. Why on earth did I get involved in this? At the door, he hesitated. Flora looked at him expectantly.

'I meant to ask Tara when she'd have another tape ready.'

'I'll phone and let you know before we put it in a taxi.'

'No need for that. I'm over on this side of town quite often.'

'Are you now?'

'Um, yes. Quite often.'

'All right then.'

'Thank you. Thank you very much indeed.'

'Bye now.'

'Bye,' said David, allowing himself a final glance upstairs to see if Tara would re-emerge, then – suspecting Flora knew why he was looking there – he smiled shyly at her and made a hasty exit.

Flora paused for a moment in the hallway. Curious, she thought. To be so upset over some spilt milk. Seems such a nice lad. Tara says he's just pretending to be a good-hearted soul. But after all those years, all those children, can my instincts really be so wrong?

She hurried back to the salon to clear up the mess but Jilly had already retrieved the sugar lumps from

255

the floor and was wiping up the milk with a tissue.

'Oh goodness, no need for that,' said Flora.

'Not at all,' said Jilly, with a good-fairy smile. 'Anything to help. How *are* you, Flora?'

'Oh I'm grand. Thank you for asking. Yourself?'

'Marvellous.'

I don't think so, thought Flora. Not when you're trying so desperately to please. Something must be wrong.

'How's Rupert?'

Jilly's face twitched faster than when she was having her electronic facials. With supreme self-control she managed to pull her features into her sympathy face: 'Poor darling is having a hard time. Working with that new weather girl Sunni Winter. She's only ever been on satellite before. The on-screen chemistry just isn't the same.'

Indeed it isn't, thought Flora. If she inches any closer to him on that sofa she'll be sitting on his lap.

'Indeed it isn't,' she agreed. 'Will you excuse me while I tell Miss MacDonald you're here.'

Jilly forced a gracious smile which self-destructed as soon as Flora left the room.

Upstairs in Tara's Moroccan boudoir, Flora briefed her quickly: 'I've never seen her so insecure. She's frantic that Sunni might be after her job.'

'So she's gone into please-the-world overdrive?'

'Exactly.'

'All right, Flora, thanks.' Tara took a deep breath and exhaled forcefully. 'I know exactly what to do.'

'Good girl.'

With an energy denying her years, Flora trotted back downstairs. Moments later, with heavier step, Jilly appeared. Tara leapt up, put an arm around her, and gently led her to a pile of soft cushions on the low wraparound sofa.

Half an hour later, Jilly stood up smiling. 'You're wonderful, Tara. Better than a flotation tank.'

'No one's ever said that before.'

'And you know, darling, I'm going to take your advice about the pampering. If I leave now I can order a swimming Jacuzzi on the way home.'

'A swimming Jacuzzi?'

'You know, a Jacuzzi so big you can swim in it. If I'm going to do this relaxing thing properly that's what I need. Don't you think?'

'Just what you need,' said Tara. Until the next emotional crisis, she thought.

'Goodbye then, darling.'

'I'll see you out,' said Tara.

Jilly didn't protest.

Behind her back, as they went downstairs, Tara smiled to herself. Not bad, Tara, she thought. Not bad at all.

As the front door closed behind Jilly, Flora appeared.

'How did you get on?'

'Doormat to diva in fifteen minutes.'

'Well done, dear.'

'Ten pounds a minute.'

'Peace of mind is priceless,' said Flora.

Wish I could buy myself some, thought Tara. So lovely to get those flowers from Jordan. But it might be like David's poetry book: just another clever touch. I'm totally confused.

Flora noticed her wistful expression. Right, she thought. Time to find out what's troubling Tara. She's not been herself for days.

'Come and have tea in my sitting room,' she said in a sit-up-and-listen classroom voice.

'Jilly's herbalist could help you with that tea addiction,' joked Tara. But obediently she followed Flora through to the little green-and-white sitting room-cum-conservatory at the back of the house. Like an actor emotionally drained after a performance, Tara collapsed into a cane armchair, rubbing her face with tiredness. Flora sat upright, within reach of a tea tray on an elegant glass table.

'Please, no more tea,' said Tara.

'All right, dear,' said Flora. Slowly, gathering her thoughts, she poured herself a cup.

Tara, seeing the thoughts gathering, waited anxiously. What now? she thought. Can't cope with any more problems.

'What we're doing is a good thing,' said Flora. She considered for a moment. 'People come here troubled and you send them away feeling better about themselves. If Jilly didn't come to you she'd be paying someone else to cheer her up. It's not as if she can't afford it.'

'I know.'

'You've worked so hard for the past couple of years

but you've enjoyed it, haven't you, dear? It's been like some huge practical joke we've played. Yet it hasn't harmed anyone.'

'What is this?' said Tara, sitting up. *'This is Your Life?'*

'I'm having the time of my life, dear. I didn't imagine these years would be so eventful and so interesting and it's thanks to you.'

'It was all your idea.'

'Yes, but you've lived it. It's you who had to do all the hard work. I'm so proud of you.'

'But?'

'But I often think I'm having more fun with this than you are. I thought by now you'd be branching out.'

'Branching out?'

Flora smiled at her own coyness, then spoke plainly. 'I imagined you'd be falling in love by now.'

Tara said nothing.

'You did say you'd like to meet someone.'

'Maybe I already have.'

'Do *you* think so?'

'Don't know. You've known me since I was fourteen. Do I seem like I'm in love?' Tara looked uncomfortable.

Oh dear, thought Flora. Why is this such a difficult subject?

'Not for me to say, dear. You'll have to work it out yourself.'

'I'm too busy to think about it.'

'That's not the problem, though, is it?'

'No.'

'Is there something you want to talk about?'

'No.' Tara began to weep, quietly.

Flora got up out of her chair and gave her a hug. 'I'm sorry, dear.'

'It's all right. It doesn't matter.' Tara took the handkerchief Flora offered, wiped her eyes and blew her nose. 'I *am* happy. Really, Flora. I'm just tired.' Actually I'm exhausted, thought Tara: my clients, the TV show, the book. 'I *am* worried about the book,' she admitted. 'I wish I'd gone with the writer the publisher suggested. I knew it was risky hiring a journalist but I didn't realise what a strain it would be. I keep changing my mind about them. Both of them. D'you think I'm being paranoid?'

'I don't know, dear. Jordan's obviously a bit of a charmer,' Flora said carefully.

Tara looked alarmed.

'But then so are you,' she continued. 'He'll be back next week, won't he?'

'So he said when he phoned.'

'And he promised to have the first couple of chapters written up, didn't he? You'll be able to judge from them whether he's really working on the book or whether it's just a cover to get your story.'

'He could be doing both. He's more than clever enough for that.' Which is what makes him so interesting, thought Tara.

'What about David?' asked Flora.

'What *about* David?'

'He's an interesting young man. And you find him easy to talk to, don't you?'

'That's just the problem. I've got to be doubly careful with him.'

260

'He certainly seems a decent soul.'

'I know.' Tara sighed.

'But even if they *are* doing a story about you, would that really matter? You should be proud of what you've achieved. And they're both obviously interested in you, dear. I'm sure they'd write it up nicely.'

'D'you really think so? That they're both interested in me?'

'It's pretty obvious, dear . . . and I don't mean to pry, but I've never understood why everything's got to be so secret.'

The wounded look Tara shot Flora made her instantly regret what she'd said.

'I'm sorry, dear. I promised not to ask. It just upsets me to see you tying yourself up in knots about something which can't possibly be as bad as you think it is.'

Yes it is, thought Tara. And worse. If you knew you wouldn't even want to know me.

She's going to burst into tears again, thought Flora.

'All right, dear. I won't ask anything more.' She took a sip of tea, then with a deliberate change-of-subject brightness: 'I forgot to tell you. Nigel phoned. He wondered if you'd like to go to dinner on Thursday, Friday or Saturday?'

'Nigel who?'

'Nigel Harrington. Jilly's executive producer.'

'Oh yes,' said Tara dully.

'Must be very keen to see you: a choice of three nights.' Flora smiled encouragingly.

'I'm too busy.'

'No you're not. You're free on Friday night. I checked.'

'I've too much on my mind.'

'Might take your mind off things.'

'Not now, Flora. There's too much going on. I *will* branch out. Very soon. I can't cope just now. I really can't. All right?'

'All right, dear.' Flora picked up her teacup, took a sip, then put it down again. 'The tea's cold. So I've been talking long enough. But romance *will* present itself, dear. I'm sure.'

Tara blew her nose again, flashed a wobbly I'm-OK smile and headed back upstairs. Romance will present itself, thought Tara. So delicately expressed. She must know Jordan came back that night. Yet she's never mentioned it. Was that romance? Ma said I was a natural whore. Flora thinks I'm hearts-and-flowers. If only Flora were right . . .

Chapter Twenty-two

Glasgow, November 1998

AS the Frankfurt plane touched down at Glasgow airport, German passengers peered out into the wet black evening and congratulated themselves on having brought umbrellas. The Scots took one look at the rain and exchanged might-have-known-it shrugs. Almost everyone was travelling for business: row upon row of dark-suited executives, running on overdrafts and self-importance, unaware that their laptops and mobiles hobbled them to their labour like irons on a chain gang. This was the end of a long working day: chin stubble was rising and complimentary gin-and-tonics had been downed. As soon as the seatbelt signs went off, mobile phones began to chirrup: messages from secretaries, wives, girlfriends. Workplaces might be full of women, but business flights still resembled men-only clubs.

With so few females aboard the men quickly calculated that being chivalrous wouldn't delay them too much. Already Scarlett's seat neighbour, a junior manager who'd spent the entire flight playing with his Psion, had retrieved her coat from the overhead locker and was holding it towards her. Scarlett hadn't noticed. She was looking down at her seatbelt as if she'd never seen one before.

'May I help you with that?' asked Junior-Manager-man.

'I'm fine, thanks,' said Scarlett, undoing the buckle.

Still can't believe that toned flat stomach belongs to me, she thought. Looks like someone else's.

Junior-Manager-man was also eyeing Scarlett's body: her slim-but-curvy shape outlined in a black sweater and black boot-cut trousers.

What's wrong? she thought. Why's he staring at me like that? He must want me to hurry up.

She reached down for her handbag, but when she sat up again, Junior-Manager-man was still staring. 'Allow me,' he said, brandishing her coat.

Anxious not to block the aisle as he helped her put it on, Scarlett scrambled up quickly, switching on her sorry-to-be-an-obstacle smile for the queue of waiting businessmen. Thank goodness, she thought. They don't look too annoyed. Or too impatient. In fact they look like they don't care how long I take . . .

Still anxious not to delay anyone, she quickly snuggled into her coat. Last winter it had been just big enough; now it almost smothered her. And there was the novel problem of not having enough belt loops to anchor the belt. Was it overly long?

Don't be silly, she told herself. It's me, the new me: slim, slim, slim. And, judging by the looks I'm getting, that Frankfurt hairdresser did a good job after all. I felt so upset when I saw my hair on the salon floor this morning; all those hours in the colour studio went by like I was in a trance. Could hardly bear to look at myself afterwards. But now – she smiled 'thank you' at the man in the row in front gesturing for her to go first – now, I can't wait to be alone with my new hairdo and a good mirror.

'Bye now, cheerio,' chorused the stewardesses. Scarlett walked through the grey tube of corridor to the airport building and straight into the first ladies' toilet she saw. In the mirror above the sinks she inspected herself: an unfamiliar redhead in a too-big coat looked back at her. She'd got used to the lack of double chin, the glow of running-on-the-beach skin, the startling green of the coloured contact lenses. But now, with her mousey brown shoulder-length hair cut short and fringed, the twenty-five-year-old face in the mirror was one she hardly recognised. The eyes looked baby-huge, and there, clearly visible, was something she'd always wanted and never thought she'd have: cheekbones. With the gamine hairstyle, coloured seven-shades-of-red, the glowing white skin and the emerald eyes, she looked so striking she couldn't take her eyes off herself.

Is that really me? she wondered. Looks like someone in a magazine.

She turned her face to the left, then the right, yet from either angle, the face still looked like it belonged to a model or a film star.

But it *is* me, she thought. The new me I've spent so many months working on. She looked away from the mirror, then back again, to check whether she looked as good on second glance. The door opened and another woman came in.

Come on, Scarlett said to herself. Time to see what the others think.

Back in the corridor, she looked up at the closed-circuit TV screen showing who was waiting in arrivals. Yes, there were Flora and Brendan: the retired teacher in a well-tailored heather tweed coat; her former pupil in a white fleece over silver combats.

But why's he carrying a placard, wondered Scarlett.

Rounding a corner, she saw them in the flesh and smiled broadly. Brendan waved but Flora looked right through her. She saw Brendan pointing her out; Flora peering in her direction and looking bemused. Brendan held his sign higher. Something was written on it in black felt pen: 'Glasgow welcomes Tara MacDonald.'

Who? wondered Scarlett. Then, suddenly understanding, she felt a flicker of irritation: they've chosen a surname without asking me first, she thought.

But then Brendan was upon her, bending over the sign to kiss her and shrieking with enthusiasm: 'Your hair, darlin', it's wonderful! Pure Hollywood.'

'Was it Mr Schneider himself who attended to you?' asked Flora. Her voice contained none of Brendan's enthusiasm; she was frowning at Scarlett as though the younger woman were a hard-to-solve crossword clue.

Oh no, thought Scarlett. She doesn't like it.

'Don't you like it?'

'You look just grand. Like a film star.' Flora's frown changed to a smile and then back to a frown as she fought back tears.

Scarlett wrapped the older woman in a hug.

'Sorry, dear,' said Flora, as she re-emerged from Scarlett's arms. 'It's just such a shock. After not seeing you for nine months, I wouldn't have recognised you. Brendan told me you'd completely changed but seeing you now, you're very beautiful, Scarlett.'

Brendan waved his sign at Flora.

'Sorry. *Tara*,' she smiled apologetically. 'It's such a complete transformation, I'm forgetting my own rules.'

'From this' – Brendan puffed out his cheeks to look fat – 'to *this*' – he pointed dramatically to Tara – 'in only nine months. Five stones off, and every inch toned. Am I the best personal trainer on the planet or am I the best personal trainer on the planet?'

'You're wonderful,' said Tara.

'But I'm not best pleased with *you*, darlin',' he said.

'What's wrong?' asked Tara, falling for his mock-stern tone.

'Covering up that drop-dead gorgeous body in that dreadful coat,' said Brendan. 'I *told* her to get rid of it weeks ago,' he said to Flora. 'Best body I've ever created and she's still wearing that big black duvet. Tragic.' He looked Tara up and down. '*And* those trousers I bought you when you got to size twelve. You're a ten now, darlin'. Have been for weeks.'

'Brendan, you know I couldn't go out shopping in Aberdeen,' protested Tara.

'That's right, dear. Couldn't risk people seeing you out and about when your transformation was nearly finished,' said Flora. 'And we shouldn't be talking like this here either.' She shot an anxious glance at the flow of arriving passengers being greeted by friends, families and chauffeurs.

'Let's go then,' said Brendan. 'Time for your

reunion,' he smiled at the two women. 'And my farewell party.'

They headed for the exit.

'When are you off to Miami?' asked Tara.

'Tomorrow. Bye-bye, Sauchiehall Street, hello South Beach. Can't wait,' said Brendan, thrusting his arms in the air and jolting his hips back and forth as though already out clubbing.

'Well you deserve it,' said Flora. 'You've more than earned your fee with Sca— I mean Tara.' Turning to Tara she said: 'I've got all your things, dear. Brendan brought them down from Aberdeen in his hire car yesterday.'

'This way, girls,' said Brendan, leading them out of the terminal, across the rainswept road to the car park and into his hired BMW.

Driving out of the terminal, he headed west, away from the city.

'It's so great to see you again, Flora,' said Tara. 'How are you doing?'

'How are you?' corrected Flora. 'Remember: you don't want to sound too Scottish. Not if you want to be on national television.' Then: 'Grand, dear. Just grand. I'm having such fun with all this. Someone from the church rang to ask me to bring a sponge to the sale of work on Saturday and I didn't even have flour in the larder. I haven't baked for weeks.'

'That's good, because Tara doesn't like sweet things, do you, Tara?' said Brendan.

'Can't stand them. Not after what you did to me.'

'What *did* he do to you, dear?'

'Visualisation techniques,' Brendan answered for her. 'I call it mind over fatty matter. When I applied for the job in Miami I told the gym director how it had worked with Tara and he loved it. Said his members were just gagging for me to arrive.'

'Well they'll definitely be gagging if you do the same with them as you did with me,' said Tara. 'Every time you want to eat cakes or chocolate you've got to imagine it's something else, something disgusting,' she explained to Flora.

'Dead simple,' said Brendan. 'I served her a chocolate bar on the same plate as . . .' – glancing at his former teacher he chose his words carefully – 'as a little doggy souvenir I found on the beach which should have gone in a poop scoop. She took one look at it and went straight off chocolate. We did the same for all our problem foods, didn't we, darlin'?'

'How clever of you, Brendan,' said Flora. 'And for someone with your powerful imagination, Sca— Tara, so effective. Well done to both of you!'

'Now for something much more appetising,' declared Brendan, turning off the road and through an imposing carved stone entrance onto a floodlit driveway. The sign at the entrance read Cameron House Hotel and was stamped with five stars. The rain had stopped, and as they walked from the car park to the hotel they could see stars twinkling in the darkness above Loch Lomond.

'The bonny banks for a bonny lass,' announced Flora with a fond glance at Tara. 'And laddie,' she added.

Brendan deposited a kiss on Flora's forehead. Then,

steps quickening in the cold, they ascended the wide stone staircase into the turreted mansion.

'Michael Jackson stayed here,' said Brendan.

'And Pavarotti,' said Flora.

'But they wouldn't let Oasis in,' said Tara.

'You can take the girl out of the tabloid, but you can't take the tabloid out of the girl,' said Brendan, as a doorman in Black Watch tartan admitted them to a wood-panelled hallway.

'Tara's days at the *Daily Brit* are going to be very useful to her in her new life,' said Flora.

'We've booked a table for eight o'clock in the Georgian Room,' Brendan told the receptionist. 'But we'd like a drink in the bar first.'

'Of course. May I take your coats for you now?'

While the receptionist helped Flora, Brendan removed Tara's coat, then spun her round, took her hands in his, and held her at arm's length.

'What is it?' she asked anxiously.

'You look fabulous. The face, the fringe, the figure. Absolutely fabulous. So take it from me, darlin',' Brendan squeezed her hands in his, 'it's time to stop being so nervous. You're a star now.'

'No I'm not.'

'You soon will be. So you've got to start acting like one.'

Flora nodded agreement.

'Now, I want you to walk into that bar like you own it,' commanded Brendan. 'Just like we practised.'

Can I do that? wondered Tara. She glanced into the ornate gilt-framed mirror behind the reception desk. A woman that beautiful could do it, she thought. Scarlett couldn't, but maybe Tara can. Let's see.

She patted her hair, took a deep breath, and with head held high, stalked into the country-house grandeur of the drawing-room bar.

As if on cue, a troupe of exceptionally fit young men, tall, dark and tracksuited, ranged round the fake log fire as though poised for a sing-song in *White Christmas*, swivelled their gaze to catch Tara's entrance.

'It's Parma AC. They're playing Rangers tomorrow,' whispered Brendan.

They're looking, they're looking, thought Tara. Dare I look back?

She glanced in their direction, as though taking in the log fire. A pair of dark eyes met hers. She looked away. Directly into another pair of dark eyes. Then another, and another.

They all said the same thing: 'We want to toss our mineral waters into the hearth and leap on top of you. Now!'

Seeing this message repeated in so many pairs of eyes, from such devastatingly handsome men, all at once, after years of being ignored, was like Caribbean sun in winter; champagne after Lent; the first drop of Chanel.

It's *me, me, me*, thought Tara. I am Tara. Tara is me. They all love me. And I can do anything I want. I'm going to be rich and famous and nobody's going to make me do anything I don't want to do, ever again.

Gently, Brendan took her by the arm and steered her towards the far end of the room, to a dark wood table

271

set for cocktails. They settled themselves in the comfortable chairs overlooking the floodlit gardens and the darkness of the loch.

'Did you see the impression you made there?' asked Flora.

The question was superfluous. Tara was glowing.

'I knew you'd be beautiful, but not *this* beautiful,' said Brendan.

'Nor did I,' said Flora.

Nor did I, thought Tara.

Suddenly, an image from the past flashed into her mind's eye: it was the favourite magazine picture she'd daydreamed over so often as a teenager in Scotstoun; the beautiful people in an elegant bar, drinking champagne.

'Are we having champagne?' she asked.

A maroon-jacketed and hair-gelled young waiter was already at their table.

'Bollinger?' suggested Brendan.

'Indeed,' said Flora.

The waiter smiled approval and retreated.

'*Now* I can ask you,' said Tara. 'Why MacDonald? I fancied something more glamorous. MacDonald makes me think of hamburgers.'

'And hamburgers makes you think of something else, don't they?' asked Brendan.

'I think I've heard enough about the visualisation techniques,' chided Flora. Then to Tara: 'But if you want a positive association for MacDonald, think of my namesake, Flora MacDonald. She was clever, brave, original.'

'Created the first royal cross-dresser,' observed Brendan.

'MacDonald is one of the commonest names in the Glasgow phone directories,' explained Flora. 'Ideal for covering your tracks. With all the different spellings as well, that'll add to the confusion nicely.'

'You're right,' said Tara. 'Tara MacDonald. I'm getting used to it already.'

'That's a relief, dear. I've already got you business cards. Now you can get yourself a cheque card and a credit card and change the name on your passport. I've got the application forms for you.'

'Is that all she's got to do?' asked Brendan. 'Won't she have to change her name by deed poll?'

'Not in Scotland,' said Flora. 'I checked with my lawyer. Deed poll is an English procedure.'

'Thanks for taking care of everything,' said Tara. 'Sorry I was so funny about it. It's just all so strange. I never thought . . . never imagined . . .' She looked round the drawing room, taking in the wood panelling, the chandeliers, the waiter returning with champagne, ice bucket and flutes, and sighed happily.

'You deserve it,' said Flora. 'In all my days in teaching I've never seen anyone work so hard, and' – she smiled at Brendan – 'I've never seen such a natural teacher as yourself.'

The waiter served the Bollinger and retreated.

'Here's to Tara MacDonald, star-gazing superstar,' declared Brendan.

They clinked and sipped.

'Here's to the best personal trainer on the planet.

273

Robbie would be proud of you,' said Tara.

'Robbie?'

'Williams. They were separated at birth,' Tara explained to Flora.

Brendan struck a pose, trying and failing to raise one eyebrow. Having now shaved off his goatee, he could just about pass for Robbie's changeling brother, placed in the crib by elves.

Flora was used to young people and their fantasies. '"No Regrets" has a lovely melody,' she said. 'Do you think it will do as well as "Millennium"?'

Brendan and Tara were taken aback.

'I've always watched *Top of the Pops*,' said Flora, pleased at their surprise. 'I like to know what my pupils are interested in. And now of course I need to know about the people Tara will be meeting.'

'She'll be meeting Robbie Williams? Cancel Miami,' announced Brendan dramatically. 'I'll stay here and get an introduction.'

'Glasgow first, then London, then maybe we'll join you in America,' said Flora calmly.

'I don't think . . .' began Tara.

'Why not, dear? Look at you. Your own mother wouldn't recognise you,' said Flora.

Wouldn't she? wondered Tara. I wish Ma could be here – just for a moment – to see what I look like now.

'Your Ma would be proud of you,' said Brendan.

'You don't know my Ma.'

'I know she gave you a hard time, but surely—'

Flora shot him a warning glance.

Tara caught it. 'It's all right,' she said to Flora. Then, turning to Brendan: 'More than a hard time. Much more.'

'I'm sorry . . .'

'It doesn't matter now. Really,' said Tara.

Actually it doesn't, she thought. If Ma wouldn't recognise me, then neither would anyone else involved. Nobody will ever know it was me. It never happened.

'That was Scarlett's mother. Not my mother. Tara's mother is dead,' announced Tara.

Feels strange saying that, she thought. But good. Really good.

She smiled at the other two.

Why are they looking at me so strangely? she wondered.

'Why are you looking at me like that?

'Just drinking in your utter gorgeousness,' fibbed Brendan, raising his glass to her.

How could she say a thing like that? he wondered. About her own mother?

'I'll miss you so much,' said Tara. 'D'you really have to go to Miami?'

'My mission on this planet is completed,' said Brendan with a Mr-Spock-of-Star-Trek voice which went all too well with his Vulcan-shaped ears.

Those ears, thought Tara, then regretted it as Brendan leant over and kissed her: 'You look beautiful, darlin', pure Hollywood beautiful.'

'You do indeed,' said Flora. 'You sound perfect too: just Scottish enough to be fashionable, not too Scottish to frighten the English.'

'Thanks to all the elocution lessons you gave me over the phone,' said Tara.

'And what she doesn't know about astrology isn't worth knowing,' added Brendan.

'I can't wait for the next stage,' said Flora. 'It's so exciting.' Her seventy-year-old face lit up with a girlish smile: 'I haven't had so much fun since . . . since I don't know when.'

'One thing I'm still dying to know,' said Brendan, giving Tara his most engaging smile: 'I feel like I've been working for MI6 for the past nine months. Now I'm leaving the country, can't you tell me what it's all about? This hush-hush stuff?'

Tara's whole body tensed.

Flora gave Brendan her sternest school-teacher look. 'You promised not to ask about that.'

'I know, but—'

'But nothing,' said Flora, in a tone that had quelled classroom riots. 'Tara's thinking about her future. She doesn't want to rake over the past. We must respect that.'

'I'm sorry. Couldn't resist. Don't be angry with me,' said Brendan, beating his chest theatrically. He picked up the champagne bottle, topped up their glasses: 'Here's to Tara MacDonald, woman of mystery.'

Smiling forgiveness, Tara took a sip of champagne. But instead of replacing her glass on the table, she held it in her right hand, staring into the honey-coloured bubbles, as though reading tea leaves in a cup.

In a changing-the-subject voice Flora began asking Brendan about Miami. Snippets of their conversation reached Tara as though from a distance: 'South Beach', 'juice bar', 'Gianni Versace'.

Wish I could tell them what happened, thought Tara. What Ma made me do. But I went along with it. So I'm as bad as Ma. If anyone found out I'd die of shame. Even thinking about people knowing makes me feel sick.

'All right, dear?' Flora broke into her thoughts.

Tara nodded; gave her a fragile I'm-OK smile.

Mustn't ruin the celebration, thought Tara. Must think happy thoughts. Let me see . . .

She pictured herself dancing round the living room in Aberdeen with Brendan, laughing at his extravagant moves. Then she imagined herself walking onto a TV chat show, to rapturous applause from the audience. Practising her smile for the cameras, she tested it on her companions: not a smile-with-the-lips, but a big bright smile, so high-wattage the sparkle seemed to reach her eyes.

'I want to propose a toast,' she said. 'To the two of you for making me into a whole new person.'

They smiled and raised their glasses.

'It's such a big change for you. You'll take a wee while to adjust,' said Flora, not entirely convinced by Tara's smile.

Brendan nodded sympathetically.

'Not at all,' said Tara. 'I look like Tara, I sound like Tara, and I'm one hundred and ten per cent ready to *be* Tara.' Experimentally, she willed herself to turn up the wattage on her smile. The response on the others' faces showed she'd succeeded.

If I can convince *them*, thought Tara, I can convince anyone. Anyway, I *love* looking so fabulous. It won't be long before I *feel* fabulous too. Will it?

Chapter Twenty-three

Aberdeen, August 2000

DUMPH, dumph, dumph. The headboard of the hotel bed thudded rhythmically against the wall. Like a paratrooper piggybacking to the ground with a buddy, Jordan clung onto Mercedes as though his life depended on it. She was kneeling; he was behind her. Teeth clenched in concentration, clinging onto her breasts, he plunged into her from behind, hard and fast. Then harder and faster.

'Oh, oh, oh,' groaned Mercedes.

Pain or pleasure? Jordan didn't waste any energy thinking about it.

'Yes, yes, ye-es!' he shouted, as Roger hurtled towards target and exploded into orgasm.

Still holding onto the breasts he thrust two, three more times, discharging every last drop of semen. His face was relaxed now, sticky with sweat. He groaned deeply, appreciatively. Then abruptly, he let go, pulled out of the body beneath him. Like a soldier under fire, he rolled to the far end of the bed, sat up, removed the condom, tied a knot in it and hurled it across the room as though it were a live grenade.

Mercedes got out of the kneeling position, turned around, moved across to where Jordan was sitting with his back to her. She put her arms and legs around him, nuzzled his neck, rubbed herself against him.

Like a fucking limpet, thought Jordan. Leave me alone. You've come, haven't you? Roger's done his duty.

'Oh baby,' said Mercedes. 'Give me a cuddle.'

Smiling, he turned towards her. Pulled her against him, kissed her twice on the lips: once deeply, once lightly. 'You're so special. So very special. Can't bear the thought of saying goodbye.' His gaze was anguished, his voice sad.

'But we don't need to . . .'

No we don't, agreed Roger. This one would definitely be good for a rise-and-shine blow job.

'It's after three. And I've got a seven-thirty flight to catch,' lied Jordan. 'If I woke up and saw you there . . .' He looked deep into her eyes. 'You don't realise how irresistible you are. Do you?'

Mercedes smiled.

'I'll miss you so much when I'm in Peru.'

'Peru? Didn't know there was oil in Peru.'

'Nor does anyone else yet. You'll keep quiet about it, won't you?'

'Yes, but—'

Jordan interrupted her with a kiss: 'I knew I could trust you.'

A thought occurred to Mercedes. 'Are you married, James?'

'Married? No. I've never found the right—' He looked at her meaningfully. 'Will you call me when I get back?' he asked.

'You didn't give me your number.'

'I'll write it down for you, sweetheart. While you get dressed . . .' Jordan retrieved a lacy bra and panties from the floor and handed them to her.

Get a fucking move on, he thought. I'm knackered.

'I'm so tired, baby.' He looked at her soulfully. 'I'll call you a taxi.' He dialled reception. 'I need a cab right away . . . two minutes? . . . OK, thanks.'

Mercedes began dressing. Then: 'So when did you say you'd be back?'

Wondered when that would occur to you, thought Jordan.

'Wish I knew, sweetheart. Could be months.'

He found his jacket, took out his notebook and wrote down a number. No resemblance to his real phone number. Just a number.

'I'll write to you,' said Mercedes.

'Wish you could. But I'll be moving around, different locations, wouldn't ever reach me.'

'I'll write to you in London. To welcome you back. Remind you I'm here.'

'Remind me?' Thank fuck she's dressed at last, thought Jordan. He got up, wrapped a sheet around himself toga-style, went over and kissed her. 'How could I ever forget you?'

Without adding his address to the sheet of paper, he folded it several times, slipped it into her hand. 'I'm between flats at the moment. But I'll call you as soon as I'm back. OK?' He kissed her lightly on the forehead.

'OK.' She picked up her bag, kissed him, paused for

281

a heartbeat, but Jordan didn't make a move. So she turned to go.

'Mercedes?'

'Yes?' She turned towards him expectantly.

'Your pal Brendan; you don't have any other contact for him do you? Other friends, boyfriends?'

Mercedes looked puzzled. 'No, just the place I told you about. In Miami.'

'The Body Shop on South Beach. Sure that's the right name?'

'Positive.'

'And Scarlett's surname was Macdougall, not MacDonald?'

'No. I told you. Definitely Macdougall.' Puzzlement had turned to disappointment. She smiled sadly. 'Bet you won't call me.'

Don't start that, thought Jordan.

'Don't make bets you'll lose,' he smiled.

He jumped up, and as he kissed her, reached for the door and held it open.

'OK, James. I'll see you.'

Jordan smiled.

She waited another heartbeat.

Your time's up, thought Jordan.

'Your taxi's waiting,' he said.

'Night then.'

'Night then, gorgeous.'

He smiled, closed the door, then picked up his watch from the night table. In and out in under three hours, he thought. Not bad. Not a record. But perfectly respectable. He set the alarm on his mobile for eight o'clock, put the light out, lay down and pulled up the covers, but then promptly sat up again.

Stupid tart was wearing far too much perfume, he thought, wrinkling his nose. He shook out the quilt and settled down again.

Five hours sleep, then I'll . . . fucking hell . . . how could I forget . . . the newspaper . . . the photo of Tara with some bloke . . . wonder who he is . . . should take a look . . . oh what the hell . . . in the morning . . . I'll get up bright and early and bang this scoop to rights . . . Tara . . . Scarlett . . . the man in the photo . . . everything . . . it'll all be clear in the morning . . . fuck no . . . can't sleep . . . have to know *now* . . .

Sleepily, he flicked on the bedside light, picked up the phone and dialled reception.

'Hello, it's Room Fifty-one here. Sorry to ask so late but I need to see a copy of the evening paper . . . none left? . . . the thing is I'm going to a funeral tomorrow and I've forgotten the time, there's a notice in the paper . . . would you look in the office or the kitchen or something . . . right thanks, I'll hold while you do that . . . you have? . . . that's wonderful, thank you so much . . . no, no, you don't need to look it up for me, just bring up the paper, thank you very much.'

Five minutes later there was a knock at the door and a weary-faced night porter handed him the *Evening Express*.

'Thanks, mate,' said Jordan. 'Sorry, I don't have any change—' He gestured to the sheet he was wearing, indicating his lack of pockets. 'By the way, I ordered

283

breakfast in my room for seven-thirty. Could you change it to eight-thirty?'

'No bother, sir. Sorry about your loss. Good night.'

'Night.'

Wide awake now, Jordan flicked through the newspaper. On page five he found what he was looking for: the photo of Tara MacDonald and her 'mystery man'. He read the picture caption: 'Tara MacDonald gets starry-eyed with mystery man. The celebrity astrologer revealed to Early Bird TV viewers two weeks ago she was looking for love. Now the still-single thirty-six-year-old has been spotted enjoying a discreet rendezvous at a café-bar in London's fashionable Primrose Hill. Is Venus finally rising for the Scots-born star?'

The photo, snatched in the street by a paparazzo, showed Tara arriving at Parliamo, smiling down at David, seated at a pavement table.

Thank fuck, thought Jordan. It's only Plod. As if a woman like Tara would have any interest in plodding Plod. So clever and yet so clueless. A natural born loser. Still, he has his uses. I'm doing him a favour really. Letting him do his bit. For my glorious career. High point of his life, this. Getting snapped in the street with Tara MacDonald. Poor old Plod. The man with no plan, no proper job and no idea of how to pick up women. Couldn't bear to be like *him*. I'd sooner shoot myself.

With a self-satisfied sigh, Jordan cast aside the newspaper, thumped the pillows into submission and flicked off the bedside light. In the darkness, he smirked to himself: Every great general needs foot soldiers. And victory is so close now, so close . . .

Chapter Twenty-four

Aberdeen, August 2000

DEE-DEE-DEE *deeh!* Faster than a soldier at reveille, Jordan reached for the mobile phone on his bedside table and sat up to attention. In the last nanosecond before hitting the receive button, he cleared his throat, removing the sleepiness from his voice. No time to look at his watch but however early it was he wanted to sound wide-awake for his news editor.

'Hello!' he said in a been-in-action-for-hours voice.

'Morning, Jordy.'

'Sunni? Thought you were Bullock.' His voice slumped back into just-awakeness. 'What time is it?'

'Time to call and say "good morning, darling, wish you were here".'

'Yeah, but what time is it?'

'Ten past seven. I've just done the morning bulletin. Are you missing me?'

'Yeah.'

'That's good, cos I'm missing you. Still in Glasgow?'

'Sort of.'

'Sort of?'

'Well, Aberdeen actually. But it's all the same up here: freezing cold and they've all got speech impediments.'

'Speech impediments?'

'Joke, sweetheart. They're Jocks, aren't they?'

'So how's your mission going?'

'Proceeding as planned. Although the natives are far from friendly. One of them had a knife against my throat last night.'

'A knife?'

'Sunni, sweetheart, d'you have to repeat everything I say?'

'Sorry, Jordy. But a knife. Are you all right?'

'Course I am. Nothing I couldn't handle. But it was hairy. Very hairy. Anyway, I must get back to the fray, so . . .'

'Thought you said I woke you up.'

'You did, sweetheart. But I was just about to get up anyway.'

'D'you know when you'll be back?'

'Not yet. I'll call you.'

'It's just that we've been invited to dinner tomorrow night by Royce. I said I'd let him know if you could make it or not.'

'Royce your agent?'

'Of course Royce my agent. How many other Royces do I know?'

'Just checking, sweetheart. Who else is going to be there? Any of his other clients?'

'Well there's this new reporter at Early Bird, just joined from Essex Radio . . .'

'I mean anyone I might have heard of. Anyone who's anyone.'

'No. Nobody like that. But it should be fun. Royce has got a new boyfriend, Thor. He's going to do a

287

traditional Icelandic dinner: steaks on hot rocks.'

'Whatever gets your rocks off.'

Sunni giggled: 'But can you come?'

'No way, sweetheart. Won't be back in time. But hey, if I make the last flight, I'll call you. You can come over and welcome me back. Show me what I've been missing. OK?'

'OK. Jordy?'

'Yeah?'

'You haven't asked me how my dinner with Max went.'

'Max?'

'The guy who owns the new satellite station. The guy who decides if I get my big break or not.'

'Dish TV? I thought you wanted to get that gorgeous tush of yours onto the Early Bird sofa. You were so much better than Jilly when you stood in for her.'

'Thanks, Jordy. That's what *everyone* says. But I don't know when I'll get another chance to sit in for her.'

'So what's the deal with Dish TV?'

'Don't know yet. But I told Max I wanted my own show. He said he'd think about it.'

'Great.'

'So d'you think he'll really think about it? Or was he just saying that to keep me happy? And if he thinks about it, d'you think—'

'Sunni, sweetheart. I think you're driving me nuts. That's what I think.'

Silence.

'But I adore you anyway. Truly, madly, deeply. OK?'

'OK.'

'Now be a good girl and let me get on with this mission. I'll call you soon as I'm back in Blighty.'

'Promise?'

'Promise. And sweetheart? Tomorrow, wait until after the nine o'clock bulletin before you call me. OK?' Jordan kissed the air and hit the 'end' button.

Without giving Sunni's call a second thought, he put down the mobile, picked up the remote control and flicked on the TV news: two minutes on BBC 1, sixty seconds on Grampian, a minute on Sky, back to BBC 1 – all that was missing from his early-morning channel-hopping was . . .

He picked up the hotel phone, hit the button for room service.

'Room Fifty-one here. What's happened to my breakfast? . . . no, it wasn't eight-thirty, it was seven-thirty . . . no, I didn't change my mind; the night porter must have confused me with someone else . . . look, I don't want excuses, I want my breakfast and my papers and I want them before lunchtime . . . thank you very much.' Practically shouting at the end of the call, Jordan slammed down the receiver with relish.

After the effort of sweet-talking Sunni, the argument with room service had recharged his batteries. He checked the time: 7.35. If his breakfast wasn't here pronto he'd have another go at them. In the meantime . . .

He punched in another phone number. As it rang out, he returned his attention to the TV news, only hitting the mute button on the remote when his call was answered.

'Caledonia Investigations.' The man's voice was as

Glasgow as Sauchiehall Street, as seen-it-all as Taggart.

'All right, mate? It's Jordan Holmes here.'

'The man from the *Brit*.' Just an observation. No effort to sound more alert.

The insolence of the man, thought Jordan. Disgraced policeman turned private 'tec. Should show more respect for a representative of one of the nation's richest newspapers: 'Took you a long time to answer, Mr O'Connor.' The 'Mr' was ironic. 'Have I woken you?'

'Not much sleep in my game, Mr Holmes.' The 'Mr' was equally ironic. 'Been up all night on a matrimonial. Client's wife kissed her lover on the doorstep an hour ago.' O'Connor cleared his throat with a deep, nicotine-strangled cough: 'Would have brought a tear to the eye of a brass monkey.'

Time-wasting Jock amateur, thought Jordan: 'So no progress on Tara MacDonald?'

'Wasn't a lot to go on.'

'Well I've got her real name now: it's not Tara MacDonald and it's not Vivien MacDonald; it's Scarlett Macdougall.'

'With two Ts?'

'That's right.'

'I'll check out the birth certificate.'

'Don't bother. I'll do it myself. I'm flying down to Edinburgh this morning. Have you come up with anything on that West End address yet? Does it belong to a Miss Flora Macleod?'

'It does indeed. Although the neighbours say she hasn't been around for months. They think she's taken a job, down in London.'

'Don't know what I'm paying *you* for to tell me what I know already.'

'I'll consider our business closed then, Mr Holmes. If you need me you know where to find me.' O'Connor didn't sound in the least bit riled.

'That won't be necessary,' said Jordan. 'Goodbye.'

Won't take me long now, he thought. To wrap up this story. As he jumped out of bed, his feet hit the carpet running . . .

The following day, though, sitting in New Register House in Edinburgh, his investigation had come to a standstill. Despite more than an hour trawling through the files, there was no sign of a birth certificate for a Scarlett Macdougall. His temper didn't improve when his mobile phone rang and staff asked him to take the call outside.

'Hello!' he snapped.

'Mr Holmes.'

It was O'Connor.

'What do *you* want?'

'Just wondered how you were getting on.'

Useless bastard, thought Jordan. Holding me up like this.

'You'll get your fee directly from the *Daily Brit*. I've already told the desk.'

'Aye, well, I might be due more than you've put through.'

'Now look here, I don't have time to waste with—'

'Nor do I, Mr Holmes. The thing is that today I

happened to be in the local register office here in Glasgow, checking out something for another client, and I couldn't resist having a wee look on your behalf. Still, sounds like you've got what you need already.'

'Not exactly,' admitted Jordan reluctantly. 'What've you got?'

'Scarlett Macdougall. Mother Lorna Macdougall. Father's name blank. Born Queen Mother's Hospital, Yorkhill, Glasgow. All on the birth certificate.' O'Connor couldn't have sounded more laconic.

'But I've just checked all the birth certificates,' said Jordan angrily.

'Which years?'

'Sixty to sixty-four.' How dare he treat me like a rookie, thought Jordan. 'She's meant to be thirty-six but I've checked backwards too. These TV types always lie about their age.'

'She *is* lying about her age. She's almost twenty-eight. Born December 29th 1972.'

'She's pretending to be *older* than she is? Women don't lie that way round. Why would she do that?' Jordan's irritation at missing a trick had given way to curiosity.

O'Connor caught the change of tone. The gravel voice became slightly less stony: 'To prevent people like you finding out who she really is. Miss Macdougall knows a thing or two about Her Majesty's Press. Used to work for your own newspaper.'

'She *did*?' Jordan was too taken aback to hide his surprise.

'Got all the gen here. Including the last known

address for Lorna Macdougall before she left the country. Also known as Lola Macdougall.' O'Connor waited to be asked for more.

Bolshy bastard, thought Jordan admiringly. He's done the business all right. Neat trick of Tara's, lying the wrong way round about her age. Won't be caught out like that again.

'Just a minute.' He reached for his notebook.

Brilliant tactics on my part, he thought. Hiring a private 'tec with a brain. He's a real pro. Just like me. Soon as this hits the front page I'll be out of the ranks and one of Bullock's heroes. At last. Tara's done for and I'm on my way to glory.

'Right, mate. I'm listening . . .'

Chapter Twenty-five

London, August 2000

'JORDAN? It's Tara.'

'Oh, hello.'

'Is this is a bad time for you?'

'No, no. Sorry. I'm just in the middle of something. Hang on a moment.' Jordan put down the school photograph of fourteen-year-old Scarlett one of her former classmates was showing him. Fuck, he thought. Should've switched my mobile off.

'Excuse me,' he said to childminder Kimberley McBride, who'd hesitated a full two seconds before inviting the most glamorous man ever to appear on her doorstep into a room full of pre-schoolers high on too many fizzy drinks and too little fresh air. 'The signal's not very good in here. I'll just pop outside.'

He dashed into the street.

'Tara?'

'Yes.'

'Sorry about that. Just getting Mum's physiotherapist settled in.'

'I thought I could hear screaming?'

'She's very strict. Shouts at her patients. Still, I'm told she's very good.' Inspiration struck him: 'I decided to go private. Wanted the best for my Mum.'

'Yes. Of course. How thoughtful.'

'Anyway, how are you?'

'Fine. Very busy.'

'Right.'

He sounds so distracted, she thought. 'I've managed to go through the list of questions, though. And I've recorded another tape.'

'That's great. I want to get cracking as soon as I get back. Won't take us long to put an unputdownable book together.'

Won't take me long to put my scoop together, he thought. Just a bit more digging.

'Great,' said Tara.

He sounds so businesslike, she thought.

'Sorry. Was there something you wanted to check with me?'

'No. No. Just phoning to see how you were doing.'

Just hoping you'd want to chat, she thought.

'Also,' she improvised, 'I'm pretty busy next week so I thought it might be useful to fix a time to meet up.'

'Um . . . look, I'm not sure which day I'll be back. Shall I give Miss Macleod a call when I know what I'm doing?'

Should've gone for it that night when we had dinner, he thought. Now I'll never know.

'Yes. Fine,' said Tara. Maybe he's worried about his mum, she thought. 'Jordan?'

'Yes?'

'Everything's OK, isn't it?' With us, she thought. 'With your Mum?' she said.

'Yes. Course it is. Would take more than a broken elbow to slow *her* down. She's a really happening woman. Got her own chain of boutiques. You'll have to meet her sometime.'

Why the fuck did I say *that*? he thought. And why did you have to phone anyway? D'you think this is easy for *me*?

'Then I can ask her about all *your* secrets,' said Tara.

'Oh, I don't have any,' said Jordan. Two images leapt into his mind's eye: Scarlett's miserable face in the school photo and Tara laughing with him over dinner in Odette's. 'Tara?'

'Yes?'

'You be sure and look after yourself. OK?'

'I always do.'

'Glad to hear it. Well, see you soon, "smile-in-the-sky".'

'See you,' said Tara – but he couldn't hear a smile in her voice.

Chapter Twenty-six

Glasgow, 17 December 1998

'NO, I'm sorry. Without an appointment I can't possibly let you see Mr Sharkey. And anyway, he's still in morning conference.' Sheena, secretary to Jim Sharkey, editor of the *Daily Clyde*, glanced towards her boss's office. Through the glass panels, Tara could see white-shirted men and a solitary trouser-suited woman, seated in a semi-circle around their editor's vast rectangular desk, chuckling dutifully at one of his wisecracks. Jacket off, feet on the desk, Sharkey had the same short stature and rodent-like features as Lonnie McCoy of the *Daily Brit*. But while the scrawny McCoy resembled a rat in a Boss suit, Sharkey, with his expense-account paunch and pouched cheeks, looked more like an unusually alert hamster.

'But I thought straight after morning conference was the best time to talk to an editor?' said Tara, more calmly than she felt.

Sheena avoided agreeing. 'I'm sorry. Security made a mistake in letting you up here without an appointment.' She gave Tara a sharp-eyed once-over: striking face, perfect figure, expensive-looking cream coat and slinky black knee-high boots. Must be a PR woman, she thought. Sharkey loathed meeting PR people; almost as much as he hated any contact with his readers.

'But that's why I'm here,' said Tara. 'To introduce myself and make a proper appointment. I've got a new type of astrology column to suggest to him.'

'The *Daily Clyde* already has an astrologer: Guy Fortune. He's extremely popular with our readers. So there wouldn't be any point in you seeing Mr Sharkey, I'm afraid.'

Come on, come *on*, thought Tara. She glanced again towards Sharkey's office. Conference should be over by now. It's nearly lunchtime.

'But I've done a personal reading for him.'

'I'll make sure he gets it,' said Sheena. She smiled tightly.

Tara beamed back, opened her Enny bag, and rummaged through the contents, pretending to look for the reading.

Hurry up, she thought. Please hurry up. She listened hard for any sounds of conference breaking up.

'Sorry,' she said to Sheena. 'It's in here some-where.'

Ignoring the apology, Sheena picked up her phone and ordered Sharkey's lunch: 'That's right, his usual. Quattro stagione, extra everything, as soon as you can. Thanks a million.'

So she *is* expecting him out any minute, thought Tara. And yes, here they come . . .

As Sharkey's executives came out of his office in

twos, clutching their clipboards, both women turned to watch.

Sharkey stood up, put his head round the door: 'Lunch here yet?'

Tara took a pace back, making sure she was in his line of vision: Notice me, notice *me*, she thought.

'On its way,' said Sheena.

But Sharkey had been successfully distracted. The beady brown eyes inspected Tara with interest: 'Hello. Looking for me?'

'I am. But I'm afraid I don't have an appointment.'

'No need for that.' Like bobbing apples, Sharkey's chubby cheeks lifted upwards in a grin. 'As long as you're not trying to sell me anything.'

Tara smiled back.

Sheena shot him an eyebrows-up she's-a-timewaster glance.

'*Are* you trying to sell me something?'

'Quite the opposite. I've brought you something. For your birthday.' Tara forced herself to look directly into the glittering eyes and to smile the coquette's smile she'd practised so often with Brendan: 'It *is* your birthday today, isn't it?'

'So I'm told.'

'But you're still the youngest national newspaper editor in the country,' said Tara admiringly. To her instant regret. The scornful look on Sheena's face revealed just how much more practice Tara needed in the subtle art of flattery. Oh God, she thought, that was far too obvious.

Sharkey, though, was smiling and stroking his chin.

For him, content had triumphed over clumsiness. 'So you've done your homework. Tell me who you are.'

'Tara MacDonald.' She held out her hand.

Sharkey grabbed it, gave it a fast-and-firm shake, and let her have it back. His gaze swept the vast open-plan office: his staff were at their terminals, taking bites of lunch between phone calls.

'Catch the calls, would you?' he told Sheena. 'Now,' he treated Tara to another bobbing-apple smile, 'come into my office and tell me more.'

Yes, thought Tara. McCoy never refused to see a pretty woman. Now *I'm* that pretty woman.

Sharkey ushered her into his office, gestured for her to sit down, shut the door and sat down himself. In contrast to the paper-cluttered no-smoking work-stations of his minions, his desk was importantly bare: just a computer screen and keyboard, a news list, a framed photo of his wife and two children and an over-flowing ashtray.

Before sitting down, Tara remembered to take her coat off. Underneath the covered-up winter coat she was wearing a curve-hugging cherry red cashmere dress. It couldn't have been more elegant and yet it shouted come-and-cuddle-me-big-boy from every fibre. Her seamless bra did nothing to conceal the response of her nipples to the winds-from-Siberia whipping across the Clyde as she'd entered the building. Sharkey sat up straighter; addressed Tara's breasts: 'So, what have you got for me?'

'I'm an astrologer . . .'

Sharkey's eyes glazed over instantly.

300

'But I'm different from any astrologer you've ever met. And I love reading the charts for very successful people. People like you. Masters of the universe. That's why I've done a reading for you. For your birthday.'

'OK, let's have it,' said Sharkey in a get-it-over-with voice.

'Oh, but I don't put my readings in writing,' said Tara. 'Not for someone like yourself. That's far too impersonal. My great-granny always said that you have to be looking into someone's eyes to tell them their future and that's the way I do it too. The eyes are the window to the soul.'

Sharkey couldn't have looked less impressed.

Oh no, thought Tara. The script isn't working. I've got into his office but that's as far as I'll get.

'We've got a stargazer,' said Sharkey. His own gaze had left her breasts and was now directed at Sheena.

Looking for his pizza, thought Tara. How can I get his attention back? Flora told me to flirt with him. As if *she'd* know anything about it? Not like . . .

An unwanted memory flitted into her mind's eye: it was of her mother, looking doe-eyed and dizzy at some man she'd brought back from the pub, absent-mindedly tugging at the tops of her hold-up stockings and trotting out her usual line: 'The wean has to get to her bed. Ah'm afraid ah'll have tae invite you to sit in my own room. Ah'm awful embarrassed. Dae ye mind?'

'I know,' said Tara. 'Guy Fortune. But . . .' But what? she wondered desperately.

301

Sharkey was looking across again to Sheena, who was holding up a takeaway pizza box for him to see.

She'll never let me near him again, thought Tara. And I can see I'm straining his attention span already. Flora thought my predictions would convince him. But she's no idea how much editors hate reading. I've *got* to grab his attention now. I'm *not* going back to a job like Sheena's. I deserve better. And I'm going to get it.

Sharkey looked bored; a heard-it-all editor's look had settled over his smooth and shiny face.

'But what?' he prompted.

Tara gave him a huge, double-dimple smile: 'But I work very differently to Guy. Let me make a prediction for you.'

'OK.'

'I predict . . .' She uncrossed and recrossed her legs, to show off the slender thighs above the knee-high boots.

Sharkey's eyes followed the movement.

Encouraged, Tara smiled again, allowed her lashes to flutter a little: 'I predict we'll spend the afternoon together.' She stared into his eyes, deeply, with meaning.

Was that OK? she wondered. I've never done this bit before. She searched the beady brown eyes for clues.

But Sharkey was looking away . . . at the newsroom, at the clock, at the family photo on his desk.

McCoy had had family photos on *his* desk, thought Tara. Never cramped his style. With the unambiguous smile of a courtesan she leaned towards him: 'My readings are confidential. One hundred per cent.'

Sharkey responded with a don't-bullshit-me glare: 'Are you looking for a column on this newspaper?'

'Of course I am,' she smiled. 'But first I'd like to give you your reading. In full.' How obvious do I have to be, she thought as, once more, she forced herself to lock her eyes on his. 'Is my prediction correct?' she asked, attempting the Princess Di shy-but-willing look she'd been practising in front of the cheval mirror in Flora's spare bedroom.

Suddenly Sharkey relaxed, breathed out. Without looking down at the picture of his wife and children, he moved it a few inches to one side. With his other hand, he picked up the phone.

Sheena answered, turning to face her boss, but he was looking at Tara, apples bobbing upward: 'Table for two at One Devonshire. Right away. Tell Murdo to have the car at the door. And, uh . . . tell Macaulay to take afternoon conference for me.'

Through the glass, Tara could see Sheena ostentatiously dropping the white pizza box in the waste basket, and calling over to Macaulay, Sharkey's deputy.

Sharkey put down the phone and rubbed his dimpled hands together. 'Now. Let's see what you can tell me. I take it you've time for,' he paused meaningfully, 'lunch.'

'Oh yes,' said Tara. She stood up and let him help her with her coat.

Coat on, she turned to smile 'thank you'. Her smile was genuine now; a smile of triumph. Sharkey's apples bobbed upwards in response. Like a lab rat scenting the cheese at the end of the maze, his eyes were glinting greedily.

At last, he thought. A female who wants to fuck her way onto my paper.

At last, thought Tara. A man who wants to fuck *me*, not my ma.

'You know, I *could* have done your reading over lunch,' said Tara as she got up from the table and allowed Sharkey to lead her out of the dining room of One Devonshire Gardens and towards the hotel bedrooms. Using the key the waiter had brought him with the lunch bill, Sharkey opened a door. 'It's much better like this, though,' said Tara, stepping into a stylish grey-and-cream room with a canopied four-poster, antique furniture and oil paintings on the walls. 'Most people prefer privacy when they're hearing things that are so personal.'

Sharkey closed the door and locked it.

Oh my God, she thought. Can I really go through with this?

'Can't believe you got a room here just like that,' she prattled nervously. 'S'pose you're used to the VIP treatment.'

Can't believe *you*, doll, thought Sharkey. Are you a time-waster or are you really going to do the business?

'I don't like to talk business over lunch,' he said.

'Business? Then you mean . . .'

'I mean it might be time for a change of astrologer at the *Daily Clyde*,' he said, baring nicotine-stained teeth in a mouth-only smile. He opened the mini-bar and inspected its contents with a practised eye. 'Would you like a wee glass of wine?'

'But you haven't heard my reading yet.' Let alone done anything else, thought Tara – genuinely puzzled. 'It's a completely different type of forecast I do. Based on the emotions, and on my own intuition.'

'My own intuition's pretty reliable. And I reckon you'll be spot-on,' said Sharkey. He grinned at her patronisingly, glanced at his watch. Time to find out if she's up for it, he thought. 'Is it red or white then? Or would you like some bubbly?'

'Bubbly.'

Wait a minute, thought Tara. What's the deal here? Flora's plan stopped at lunch. Ma's not here to sort things out. I've got to sort this myself. Before we go any further.

Sharkey had opened the half bottle of champagne, poured two glasses, and was handing one to her with a lascivious smile. The beady eyes swept her breasts, her legs, back to her breasts.

'Cheers,' he said, reaching over to clink his glass against hers. He was sitting on the bed. She was in one of the two chairs at the candy-cane-leg table by the window.

'Cheers,' echoed Tara.

'Come and sit next to me,' he said, patting the quilted cream bedspread. 'Those wee chairs don't look at all comfortable.'

Tara smiled, began to get up, then hesitated. Got to sort this, she thought. What was it Ma always said? 'Nothing for nothing.'

'Are we really celebrating?' she asked innocently. 'Are you going to give me a chance? Your secretary told me Guy Fortune had a lot of fans.'

Aye, but he doesn't have tits like yours, thought Sharkey.

'He does. But maybe it's time for a change.'

What the fuck, he thought. Fortune's contract's up for renewal and he's away ski-ing over Christmas. I'll run Tara's stuff while he's on holiday; let the readers decide. If they want Fortune back they'll get him. Otherwise I'll get that greedy bastard off my back and this doll here onto *her* back. As long as that *is* the deal.

'Is that a deal?' asked Tara. 'What if you don't like my column?'

'I can spot talent when I see it.' That's why I've got shit-hot subs who can turn whatever tosh you write into something fit to print. Now let's get my hands on those tits and get started . . .

'Thank you, Jim. Thank you so much. When do I start?'

'Soon as you like.' With one hand he raised his glass to her; with the other he gestured for her to sit next to him.

That's it, thought Tara. Simple as that. But can I do the rest? On my own? Can I? Smile, smile, she told herself, as she went over to Sharkey, clinked glasses and sat down beside him.

He took her glass from her, set it on the floor with his own. '*You*,' he announced, accusingly, 'are totally gorgeous. And you know it, don't you?'

Smile, thought Tara.

Like a machinist putting an object in a vice to steady it while he works, Sharkey put his hands on either side of her face, then leaned forward to plant an efficient, demanding kiss.

Open mouth, open mouth, Tara told herself.

As Sharkey's tongue probed deeper, his arms fastened around her, his weight pushed her back onto the bed. With the confident touch of a Page Three photographer, he manhandled her so she was lying just the way he wanted; on her side, next to him. Holding her in position with one hand clamped on her buttocks, he groaned with relief and triumph as with the other hand he finally got hold of her breasts. His mouth was overly wet now; his kisses harder and messier.

In Tara's mouth, his brandy-perfumed spittle from after lunch mixed with the acid from the champagne. Stop, stop, she thought. I feel sick.

But like a printing press at midnight, Sharkey was powering through his routine: hand down back of dress to undo bra strap . . . but it's front-fastening . . . OK, ignore technical hitch . . . press on . . . up and under skirt to reach between thighs . . . pause for a moment to roll down stockings . . . then onwards and upwards . . . until finally, with a grunt of exertion, heavily on top of her . . .

In Tara's stomach, tiny bites of asparagus and poached egg and lamb and cranberries mixed queasily with Châteauneuf-du-Pape. I feel sick, she thought. Sick and lonely.

Sharkey had her pinioned beneath him, her dress up around her waist, stockings rolled down. Through her knickers, he pressed his erection against her, panting noisily. He began working his fingers in under her knickers . . .

No, not sick, scared, thought Tara. Sick *and* scared. Can't do this on my own. Stop, stop.

'Take them off, doll,' instructed Sharkey hoarsely, tugging impatiently at the knickers.

Stop, stop, thought Tara: 'Stop!'

Did I say that out loud, she thought. Yes, I did. Did he hear me?

Sharkey removed his hand from her knickers, searched for a breast and rubbed it industriously: 'All right, doll?' he asked, in a no-answer-required mumble.

No, no. Can't do this. Stop, thought Tara. 'Stop.'

Sharkey juddered to a halt, rolled off her and eyed her warily.

What are you up to, bitch? he thought.

'What's the matter, doll?'

'I feel, I feel . . .' Sick, she thought. I'm going to be sick. I've got to get to the bathroom. She sat up abruptly, rearranged her dress. 'I'm sorry. I don't feel well.'

Sharkey made no attempt to stop her, but the beady eyes glinted malevolently. 'OK.' He sat up, swung his feet onto the floor.

OK you bitch, he thought. Nobody fucks me around like this. Nobody. You'll wish you'd never tried this little number on me.

'Bathroom's right there,' he said coldly.

Tara caught the tone. The chill in it cut through her; settled her stomach. He looks so angry, she thought. If only it was like the other times. In the dark. When it felt so good. So secret. Not like now. In the light . . . the light . . . what if . . . ?

She slipped off the bed, went to the window and closed the heavy satin curtains. They did more than block out the daylight; they created the near-blackout darkness demanded by the hotel's jet-lagged celebrity guests.

Tara stood there for a moment, feeling the fabric between her fingers. It felt soft, smooth. In the darkness she could hear Sharkey standing up, knocking over the champagne glasses on the floor.

I feel fine now, she thought. She let go of the curtains, darted back to Sharkey, flung her arms round his neck, pressed herself against the expense-account paunch, the undone belt buckle, the place where his erection had been . . . the place where the erection was returning . . .

Now, she thought. *Now.*

You strange fucking female, thought Sharkey. Before she could change her mind again, he pulled her down onto the bed. She was on top of him, but her hands were on either side, reaching above his head . . . what the fuck was she doing . . . bedclothes . . . she was trying to get under the bedclothes . . .

Suddenly, the instinct for others' weaknesses which had got him the editor's job, clicked in. Who'd have thought a woman like this would want to be fucked in

309

the dark, under the covers, he thought. Doesn't make sense, but mine's not to reason why, mine's just to get my end away . . .

In the rush of understanding, kindness crept into his voice: 'OK, doll,' he said. 'You beautiful doll. It's going to be OK now.'

Careful not to let her go, he rolled them both to one side, pulling down the bedspread and awkwardly manoeuvring them together under the duvet. He got her dress up again, her stockings and knickers off; was gratified to feel her unzipping him, reaching for his erection.

Yes, he thought. Spot on.

He unzipped her dress, pulled it efficiently over her head, coped expertly with the front-fastening bra, carefully massaged her breasts, sucked her nipples until they were hard, then reached between her legs with his fingers . . .

Tara whimpered.

Yes, thought Sharkey. You're wet now, doll. Fucking wet.

His mouth salivating with appetite, he parted her carefully with his fingers, exhaling with relief as he finally plunged into her and began fucking heartily . . .

As he did so, the duvet slipped from his shoulders and slid down his body. Too intent on his task to pull it back up, Sharkey fucked on. But to Tara, his heavy flesh was comfort blanket enough, and the darkness felt so safe, so secret. They couldn't see each other; all they could do was touch, feel and hear . . . just like before . . . just like she liked it . . . a man with every reason not to tell . . . in a room so dark it wasn't really happening . . .

In the blackness, she was able to switch off her brain, to allow her body to remember the moves which had brought release, from being fat, from being with Ma, from being Scarlett, from everything. Except this time, for the first time, it was all her own work . . . nobody would switch the light on, nobody would see. Safe, snug and swaddled in sensation, she groaned in abandonment. It wasn't Tara who groaned, or even Scarlett; just a weightless female floating in the warm waters of impending orgasm . . .

'. . . and so I'll be in the *Daily Clyde* from next week,' announced Tara triumphantly.

It was six o'clock and she was back in Flora's comfortable terraced villa in the West End. Dark outside since half past three, the curtains were drawn and the two women were in the bay-windowed living room, drinking tea by lamplight.

Flora shook her head in delighted disbelief. Thank goodness, she thought. Tara was so sick with nerves this morning I thought she was in for a let-down. Yet now she's fairly glowing with confidence.

'Excellent work, dear. The very first newspaper on our list and they've given you a column. You must have really charmed that Mr Sharkey.'

'I suppose so,' said Tara evenly.

If you only knew, she thought.

'I knew you'd manage to get him out to lunch. Men

311

are so easily distracted,' continued Flora blithely.

Men, thought Tara. What does she know about men? Let alone distracting them?

'Did you like him at all?'

'I don't know,' said Tara, surprised. 'I didn't really think about that.' She considered for a moment. 'Never crossed my mind. I knew I'd just one chance to persuade him. I saw it so often with Lonnie McCoy. If you couldn't convince him first time you'd lost his interest for ever. So I was just concentrating on getting our first column.'

'Well I'm so proud of you, dear.' Flora's softly lined seventy-year-old face was lit up like the mother of the dux at a school prize-giving.

You wouldn't be so proud if you knew how I got it, thought Tara.

'It's only for a fortnight, while Guy Fortune's on holiday.'

'Oh, I see,' said Flora, slightly disappointed, but rallying immediately: 'Well, you'll just have to work hard to impress Mr Sharkey.'

'I think I'm all right there.'

Why's she so sure of herself? wondered Flora. It's grand to see, but it's so sudden. She's a different person to the lassie I had to buoy up this morning.

'I want to hear all about it, dear. What did he say to your reading?'

'My reading?' Tara looked away. 'He thought it was spot-on.'

Wish I couldn't tell so easily when folk are fibbing,

312

thought Flora. But after all those years teaching I just can't help it.

'I see,' said Flora. 'Well that's grand.'

Can't ask any more, she thought. Don't want to force her into more lies. And I don't want to dent that hard-won confidence. Must change the subject: 'So that's you well and truly started on your new life, dear. We'll have to celebrate.' Flora smiled.

'Yes,' said Tara, not quite so brightly.

What's wrong? wondered Flora. A moment ago she seemed like she'd blossomed in an afternoon. Now she's got that guilty look about her again. That glow when she came in, could it have been? Would she have? With Sharkey?

A picture flashed into Flora's head: of herself, more than 30 years ago, in her thirties, with Bill, with Iain, their hands reaching up to pull the kirby grips out of her dark hair, her hair tumbling down, and their bodies tumbling into bed, the two married colleagues she'd had consecutive affairs with, quietly, discreetly, without hurting anyone, without anyone in the staff room knowing, whatever their suspicions, when they saw her glowing, like Tara had earlier . . .

'Would you like more tea?' asked Tara.

'Just half a cup, dear.'

I wonder, thought Flora.

Why's she looking at me like that? thought Tara. Has she guessed? How could she? She's no idea. Never been with a man in her life. She'd be so shocked if she knew.

She'd be so shocked if she knew, thought Flora. The secrets I had to keep.

'Is there any more hot water, dear?'

Tara looked at the jug: 'It's empty. I'll get some more.' She took it through to the kitchen.

I didn't want Bill, or Iain, for myself, thought Flora. Just borrowed them from their wives. For a wee while. I didn't love them. But I *did* like them. A lot. Not like Tara with Sharkey. How could she sleep with a man she didn't even like? No, stranger than that: she didn't even stop to think whether she liked him or not. In all the years I've known her, there's never been mention of a boyfriend. Yet unless my instinct is failing me, she's bedded Sharkey to get this column. And she seems to have enjoyed it. Is it wrong for me to let her do this to herself? Who am I doing this for anyway? Is it really for her? Or is it because I wanted a last big project?

'Here you are,' said Tara. She'd returned with a full hot-water jug and had refilled Flora's cup.

'Thanks, dear. I'm a real tea jenny, aren't I? Still, it's not the worst of vices.' Oh dear, thought Flora. Not what I meant to say.

But Tara merely smiled: 'I forgot to tell you. I've got to go into the *Daily Clyde* tomorrow, to get my by-line picture taken. It'll be in their studio: hair and make-up and everything. I'll have to think about what to wear.'

She looks so happy, thought Flora. And she deserves to. Poor girl. The mother she had, the childhood she had. That something in her past she can't bear to talk

314

about. Now she's got another secret. How will she cope?

'How are we going to celebrate?' asked Tara.

'Have you any ideas, dear?'

'Actually,' said Tara, with fake puzzlement, 'I'm suddenly really tired.' Yawning, she put down her teacup. 'I'm sorry, but d'you think we could celebrate tomorrow night?'

'Of course, dear.'

She *does* look tired, thought Flora. No wonder. Never seen a lassie whose emotions went up and down so quickly. Must wear her out. All those secrets to keep. And the effort of transforming herself. Is it all too much for her?

'Good night,' said Tara.

'Night, dear.'

Tara stood up and made to leave the room, but at the door she hesitated, returned to Flora's chair and swooped down to kiss her on the cheek.

'Thank you, Flora. I'm so excited about everything. I would never have done this on my own.' Without waiting for a reply, Tara turned and hurried off upstairs.

The older woman sighed and put down her teacup.

She's right, thought Flora. She *wouldn't* have done it on her own. Scarlett was such a defeated wee soul. Selfish of me. Wanting to see how big a change I could help her make. Well, I succeeded. She's half the size she was. And far more confident. But she's still weighed down by whatever it is in her past. And now this afternoon. How could she be so businesslike about sleeping with a stranger? I *know* she's not a bad person. But I

315

also know the kind of mother she had. Whatever's left that poor lassie so mixed up, I'm sure that woman's to blame . . .

Chapter Twenty-seven

London, August 2000

AS David followed Flora into the cream-and-white salon he smiled politely at the well-groomed thirty-something Sloane already sitting there sipping organic green tea. She jerked her lips upwards in a for-form's-sake smile but then picked up a copy of *Vogue* and began studying it as though her life depended on knowing which face powder Gwyneth Paltrow favoured.

'I'll just get that tape for you, David,' said Flora. 'Won't be a moment,' she added to the other occupant of the room. A mumbled 'yah' emerged from behind the magazine.

Wonder who that is, thought David. Looks familiar. Bit like that TV presenter who was murdered. Got it: the Countess of Essex, Posy Rees-Jones. So she *does* come to Tara for readings. No wonder she's trying to hide her face in a magazine. Just the kind of info Jordan told me to look out for. Not that I'll pass it on. Had enough of doing his dirty work. Makes me feel like a fifth columnist. How can Jordan sleep at night? And how could a woman like Tara fail to see through him?

His thoughts were interrupted by a loud, angry voice from upstairs: 'You idiot. You must be out of your mind.'

Can't possibly be Tara, he thought.

'How could you be so stupid? After all the times I've told you.'

It *was* Tara. In the hallway now and sounding like Boadicea with PMT.

David glanced at the Countess. Still hiding behind the magazine yet she couldn't *but* hear the shouting on the other side of the door.

'I don't know why I put up with you. It's time I got another assistant.'

That was Tara again.

And the sound of someone sobbing.

Oh no, thought David. It's Miss Macleod. How could Tara speak to her like that? Poor old lady. Incredible. I would never have thought it.

The door opened. Pink-eyed, pushing a white lace-edged handkerchief back up her sleeve, Flora entered. She went over to the Countess, who lowered her magazine just enough to make eye contact.

'I'm so sorry. I promise you this young man will make no mention of your visit,' said Flora, shaky-voiced. 'I can't apologise enough.'

'I'm sure he'll be discreet,' said the Countess, finally discarding *Vogue* to direct an imperious glare at David.

'Mr Swift?' Flora looked at him imploringly. 'May I have a word?'

'Of course.' He followed her into the hall.

'I made a terrible mistake there. Tara promises her clients complete confidentiality. I should never have shown you into the same room as herself.' Flora nodded towards the salon.

318

'Don't worry. Shan't say a word.'

'I know it's your job . . .'

'You can rely on me. Honestly.'

'Thank you.'

Hearing footsteps, he glanced up to see Tara coming back downstairs. Beautiful as ever, he thought. Then looked away quickly, as though dazzled.

'Hello, David.' Tara had paused halfway down and was beaming at him as if nothing had happened. Her smile was front-of-the-footlights.

'Hello.' He looked up, and, curiosity giving him courage, gazed directly into her eyes. In the relative dimness of the hall his own eyes were more dark pupil than hazel-gold: why did you do that? they said. The intensity of his gaze made Tara flinch.

Don't look at me like that, her eyes said back.

He looked away.

'I was just seeing David out before bringing herself upstairs,' said Flora gently. 'Was there something you were needing?'

'No,' said Tara. 'I . . .'

Just wanted to ask after Jordan, she thought. How is he? When's he coming to see me?

Tara assembled a businesslike smile: 'How's Jordan getting on?' she asked.

Don't ask about him, thought David. 'He's fine.'

'He told me he was working flat-out.'

Always is, thought David. With some woman or other.

'He's a fast worker,' said Flora.

Does she mean what I think she means? wondered David.

But Flora's face offered no clues.

'He said we'd really get cracking when he gets back,' said Tara. 'So I've recorded another tape. It's got the list of clients he asked for. They're all people who've given their permission. But they don't include the Countess, so . . .'

'I understand. Miss Macleod explained.'

'Good. Well, bye then.' Tara flashed a for-the-cameras smile and swept past David. The professional coldness of it made him flinch.

Goodbye, Tara, he thought. 'Goodbye,' he mumbled to her back as she went into the cream-and-white salon. 'Posy!' he heard her exclaiming brightly, before closing the door behind her.

'I'm sorry me being here created problems,' he said to Flora.

'Don't worry. It wasn't your fault.'

'I know, but . . .' He glanced at the salon door.

'She was quite right to be angry,' said Flora. 'It was a bad mistake for me to make.'

'Even so . . .'

'I'm so glad the book's going well. Can't wait to read it,' said Flora formally.

David said nothing.

'I don't think Tara will have time to record any more for a wee while. But I'll call you if she does. You'll be wanting to pick up the tapes yourself, of course?'

'Yes,' said David. Will I? he thought. Will I want to spend time on a woman who's probably already fallen for Jordan? A woman who's as big a bully as he is?

'Well, goodbye then,' said Flora.

'Goodbye.'

Walking along Chalcot Crescent he tried to make sense of what he'd just witnessed. How could I be so wrong? he thought.

Reaching Regent's Park Road, he glanced towards the green slope of Primrose Hill. Can she really be such a bitch? Maybe she and Jordan deserve each other after all? Two of a kind? And yet there's something about her.

Back in Wapping, outside Jordan's apartment block, David hesitated. He considered continuing the few yards to the Prospect of Whitby, but then remembered he'd beer in the fridge.

As he opened the door the phone was ringing.

'Hello,' he said, jamming the receiver between left ear and shoulder as he took a Budweiser from the fridge.

'All right, mate,' said Jordan. 'How's it going?'

'OK.' David took a swig of beer. 'Just been round to Tara's.'

'Ah, the lovely Miss Monday.'

'Miss Monday?'

'Tara had her chance on Monday. Thursday was the hottest little lap dancer in the north. Tonight . . . who knows who the fuck *du jour* will be?'

Smug bastard, thought David. He said nothing. Took another swig.

'So how *is* Tara?' asked Jordan. 'Pining for me?'

'Not so you'd notice.'

'Must be. Must be pretty desperate. To go for a drink with *you*.'

David took another gulp of beer. So they've been talking on the phone; talking about me; probably laughing over me, he thought bleakly.

'*She* suggested it.'

'Well I know you wouldn't have had the bottle to ask *her*. Poor girl. She looked bored rigid.'

What does he mean, she *looked* bored rigid? 'Quite the opposite . . . but how . . .?'

'You got snatched on the way in. Don't you ever read the papers?'

Tara and he were in the papers? 'Which one?'

'In the evening papers on Thursday. And the *Sun*, the *Mirror* and *Daily Brit* yesterday: "Stargazer starry-eyed over Mystery Man." Fucking hilarious. *You* and Tara. As if.'

As if, thought David, finishing the beer and opening another. Well, he's right there. Bastard. What's he want anyway? Wouldn't be phoning if he didn't want something.

'Anyway, why are you phoning?'

'To find out what she had to say for herself when you had your little drink.'

Not telling, thought David. I promised her I wouldn't, so I won't: 'Not much.'

'OK, mate,' said Jordan. His voice was suddenly friendly. 'Didn't expect you'd get anything out of her anyway. Just thought I'd check. Don't worry. I'll tell Bullock you came up with something good. Make sure you get your money.'

Patronising bastard, thought David. I've spent a lot of time on this; time I could have been working on the

322

book. 'Actually, I did get a couple of things.'

'Yeah?' Jordan couldn't have sounded more sceptical.

Bastard, thought David. I'll show him: 'The Countess of Essex is one of her clients. I saw her there this afternoon.'

'She was snapped coming out of Tara's house weeks ago,' said Jordan. 'But don't worry, mate. Soon as I'm back, Tara will open up to me. No problem. Wouldn't have expected her to talk to *you* anyway.'

But she *did*, thought David. *I'm* the one women talk to; you're the one they fall for. Ever since school. Tara's no different from the rest. So why the hell am I protecting her? He took another mouthful of beer, then, deliberately casual: 'She talked about her mother, where she grew up, that sort of thing.'

'Really?' Jordan didn't sound particularly interested.

What the hell, thought David. She doesn't give a damn about me: 'Said she grew up in a part of Glasgow called Scotstoun. And her mother ran a slimming club.'

'Did she tell you where in Scotstoun? The name of the club?'

'No.'

Oh God, should've known he'd want more, thought David. Wish I hadn't said anything. Why the hell couldn't I keep my mouth shut?

'Did you ask?'

'No, no, I didn't.' No, I didn't keep my promise to you, Tara, he thought. Though you were practically in tears when you asked me.

'It was Earl Street. And the club was called Waistwatchers.'

323

You bastard, thought David. All that agonising about breaking my word, and you'd cracked the story already. 'You've cracked it already?'

''Fraid so, mate. Just wanted to see if you'd cut it as a hack. Don't worry. You were on the right track. Just a bit slow. But you did your best. I appreciate it.'

My best, thought David. More like my worst: betraying Tara, breaking my word. I'm as big a bastard as Jordan, but not as good at it. Not just a bastard. A useless bastard.

'Hey, Plod. All right, mate?'

'Yeah.'

'Don't worry about your dosh. Bullock will put that through no problem. I've had a major breakthrough here: got Tara's real name, date of birth, mother's name. Won't take me long to bang her to rights.'

'Tara's real name?'

'Need-to-know basis, mate. Sorry. Can't risk it getting out. Not at this stage in the game. But it proves that I'm right. That she's got something to hide. She wouldn't try to cover her tracks like that if there weren't some serious muck lying around. One way or another I'm going to bring her down. Told you, didn't I?'

'Yes,' said David. Yes, you did. You told me what you were going to do to her and I went along with it. Wasn't much use to you. But not for the want of trying.

'I'm in Glasgow now. Tying up a few loose ends.'

'And Tara?'

'What about her?'

'I thought you two were . . .'

'Business and pleasure. Sometimes they mix.

Sometimes they don't. This is going to be a very big story, mate. Very big indeed. She had her chance with me, and she missed it. Poor girl.'

'I see.'

'See you, then.'

'See you.'

David dumped the phone on the kitchen counter, picked up his second beer, went to the living room to look out at the river. Despite the blue sky the water was grey. Dirty old Thames, he thought. Got some serious muck running through it. Has Tara really something to hide? Something so bad it'll make a story? Even if she hasn't, Jordan will twist things round, make it seem like she has. What was it he said? One way or another he's going to bang her to rights. He talks like it's a game. But it's not. It's her life. And my conscience. She'll be hurt. Dreadfully hurt. And I can't really bring myself to believe she deserves it . . .

Chapter Twenty-eight

London, August 2000

'PLAYING a role is very hard,' said Tara. 'But sometimes it's easier than being yourself. It all depends on how happy you are being *you*.' Eyes wide with understanding, she took the Countess's hands in hers. Seated next to Tara on the low couch in the Moroccan room, Posy Rees-Jones sighed deeply. 'I know,' continued Tara. 'It's so tiring putting on a one-woman show, twenty-four hours a day, three hundred and sixty-five days a year. But you'll find the strength for it, I know.'

'How do you know?' the Countess challenged, but Tara caught the reassure-me edge to her tone.

In her mind's eye she tried to transport Posy's sturdy body to Scotstoun, to a Waistwatchers meeting in her mother's front room.

No, she thought. Doesn't work. I can't imagine Posy parting with good money to let Ma boss her about. Who was it who used to say that? Got it. Mrs Docherty from two doors down: built like a battleship but resisted all Ma's attempts to sign her up for slimming. Mrs Docherty was too busy tongue-lashing her bus-driver husband until one day she left him for a scrap merchant who installed her in five-bedroom luxury in a posh suburb. She never looked back. Not even for her two sons; her ex got custody. The street was scandalised but Nancy Docherty never looked better; driving around in her lover's Mercedes: 'DUMP1'. 'Size eighteen but she snared him anyway,' Ma had declared wonderingly. 'She's a force of nature, that Nancy.'

Tara looked deep into Posy's eyes: 'Can't you feel the strength in your own character? You're a force of nature.' Letting go of the other woman's hands, she touched her fingertips either side of the broad Saxon face and smiled encouragingly.

'You're right. You're so right,' said Posy, sitting up straighter. 'You know, I feel full of energy again. Ready for anything.'

I feel exhausted, thought Tara. Fit for nothing. 'Good. I'm glad,' she said, sinking back against the cushions.

'Gosh, is that the time?' said Posy, jumping up like a hockey captain late for bully-off. 'Must go. I'll pop in next week if I've time.'

Striding out of the room and heading downstairs – Tara in her wake – Posy flung an afterthought over her shoulder: 'I take it you'll deal with what happened earlier.'

'Earlier?'

'The chap I ran into. Who was he anyway? Looked quite sweet.'

'Sweet? He's a journalist. But don't worry. He won't say anything. He's working on my book.'

'Funny. Wouldn't have guessed he was a journalist. And I'm pretty good at spotting them, I can tell you.

Frightful species. Still, if he's working for you I'm sure you've got him house-trained.' At the front door now, Posy chortled energetically at her own joke.

Flagging inwardly, but outwardly bright, Tara forced herself to join in: 'Remember. If you feel your morale slipping, just give me a call,' she offered.

'My morale is *always* a hundred per cent,' said Posy blithely. 'But I *did* enjoy our little chat.' Restored to full confidence, she bestowed a dismissive 'goodbye' smile, then bounded down the path to her chauffeur-driven Rover without a backward glance.

Patronising cow, thought Tara, closing the door and slowly reclimbing the stairs. She took so much out of me today. I feel drained. One-woman show; twenty-four hours a day; every day of the year. She's got the strength for it. But have I?

She lay tummy-down on her bed, propping up her head with her hands. Look how easily I slipped out of character earlier on, she thought. One glance from David and I lost the plot. As though he could see right through me. Why did that happen? Jordan's the one who confuses me. But what is the deal with David? When he looked at me earlier I got the strangest sensation he wanted to help me. I can't read him at all. He seemed upset I'd been shouting at Flora. Made me feel rotten about it. But why should his opinion matter?

Lost in thought, Tara didn't hear Flora's knock on the door.

'Tara dear.'

'Flora. You gave me a fright.'

'Sorry, dear. Just wanted to check you were all right. There's so much on just now. I'm worried that taking on the book has been a wee bit much for you.'

'If there really *is* a book there isn't a problem.'

'What d'you mean? You said they'd both been on the phone, talking about the research they'd done.'

'I know. But if they got any clue there was a big story to tell they wouldn't rest till they'd cracked it.'

'I know, dear. But you said yourself, you've covered your tracks so well. How on earth would they find out? And what about the contract Jordan signed? It's very generous. They'll be far better off writing your book than taking your story to the papers.' Flora smiled: 'And anyway, David seems such a decent young man. Not like a reporter at all.'

'So people keep telling me. But that's what makes him all the more dangerous.'

'He's doing a good job of appearing very fond of you.'

'He didn't look very fond of me after I'd been shouting at you.'

'Exactly.'

Tara shook her head impatiently. 'You're not even making sense, Flora. The point is, I can't trust either of them a hundred per cent. And since David seems so harmless, he's the one to watch.'

'What about Jordan?'

'If he'd been trying to get a story out of me he wouldn't have rushed off to see his mother like that. No, my problem with Jordan is not so much about the book, it's . . . well, I don't know. When I last spoke to him he sounded so distracted.' Tara sighed: 'But I'm so wound up about everything I'm probably over-reacting.'

Flora sat down on the bed next to her and gave her a quick hug. 'I wish I could help you stop worrying so much. Your story's a very strong one, I know. But it's hardly front-page scandal.'

Tara said nothing.

'I know there's something you're worried about people finding out, dear. I promised I wouldn't ask what it is and I won't. But I've known you for years, and I know you're a good person. Otherwise I wouldn't be here. Doesn't my opinion count?'

'Very much,' said Tara. Which is why you must never know, she thought.

'You know I'd do anything to help you. Don't you?'

'Yes, I know.' Tara sat up and kissed Flora on the cheek. 'Thanks, Flora. Thanks for everything.'

'Is there anything I can get you? A cup of tea?'

Tara smiled: 'Just wait till those two do an exposé on your tea addiction.'

'I need my tea, dear. Lapsang Souchong or I get with-drawal symptoms.' Flora looked at Tara fondly: 'Why don't you get under the covers? Have a wee nap. Your next reading isn't till eight o'clock.'

With a final pat on Tara's arm, Flora got up to go. At the door, she paused: 'I'm always here, dear. Always on your side.'

Without waiting for a response, she left the room.

Always on my side, thought Tara. Because you don't know who I really am. You think because you knew

330

Scarlett that you really know me. But you don't. Only Ma really knows me. And she should be as ashamed as I am . . .

PART TWO

THE SCOOP

Chapter Twenty-nine

Glasgow, August 2000

EAGER as a honeymooner, Jordan slid the plastic card into the electronic lock of the hotel bedroom.

Click! It sprang open.

Bang! He shut the door behind him.

Dumph! He put down his overnight bag.

Then he inspected the room: an executive-size double bed with a card offering a choice of pillows, a TV with pay-per-view movies and a well-stocked mini-bar. The framed prints and easy-to-vacuum-round furniture reminded Jordan of scores of other overnights. Even though he'd just checked in he had to look at the notepad by the phone to double-check where he was: Holiday Inn, Glasgow.

He'd got just the room he wanted: no smoking, no traffic noise and no problem pulling out the phone and plugging in his modem. For two long days he'd been tramping the streets of Glasgow, putting together Tara MacDonald's past. Now all he wanted was peace and quiet and twenty-four-hour room service so he could finally get his scoop out of his notebook and onto the front page.

Itching for action, he took off his jacket and assembled the essentials for the night ahead: laptop, notebook, lager and roasted nuts from the mini-bar. As soon as they were laid out to his satisfaction on the dressing table-cum-desk, he drew up a chair and with the satisfied sigh of a man sinking into the arms of his lover, he pulled the Toshiba towards him and pressed the 'on' button. The first words were always the sweetest: 'EXCLUSIVE by Jordan Holmes' . . .

Afterwards, as the longed-for sense of release crept through every cell in his body, he sat back and re-read what he'd written. He knew he should leave headline-writing to the sub editors, but on a night such as this he hadn't been able to stop himself getting completely carried away:

SECRET PAST OF SEXY STARGAZER:
MILLIONS START THE DAY WITH HER
PREDICTIONS, BUT EVERYTHING TV TARA
HAS TOLD US IS A LIE
—HOW the *Hello!* crowd fell for the fake
astrologer with 'the most believable eyes in the
world'
—SHE doesn't even possess an astrological
chart, let alone a Highland great-grandmother
EXCLUSIVE by Jordan Holmes

FLINCHING with shame as cries of 'Fatty-bum-
bum' pursued her down the street, 14-year-old
Scarlett Macdougall battled to hold back the
tears. At 13 stones, with unflattering spectacles

336

and lank mouse-brown hair, no one would have predicted that the clumsy teenager from the mean streets of Glasgow would succeed in turning herself into one of the most alluring and highest-paid stars of the small screen. Nor was there any hint of the ruthless ambition which would drive her not merely to transform her appearance but to lie about every detail of her life . . .

He read it to the end: three thousand well-crafted words which would be the ruination of Tara MacDonald and the making of Jordan Holmes. Not before time, he thought, hitting the 'save' and 'close' commands. Pushing thirty and only now getting the LA job, he thought. Should have nailed it years ago. Never mind. This is it. This is finally *it*.

He got out of his chair and pulled back the curtains. As summer morning light flooded into the character-less room, he surveyed the morning-after mess: empty lager bottles in the wastepaper basket, a tray with a half-eaten 2 a.m. sandwich. He opened the door, put out the tray and then went to the mini-bar for a cele-bration beer. Nothing left but miniatures and Moët.

Well this *is* a celebration, he thought, opening the champagne and pouring it into a whisky tumbler. He toasted himself in the dressing-table mirror, piled up the pillows against the headboard, then reached for the TV remote control and began channel-hopping.

By the time he'd settled on a chart music show, he'd finished the Moët, the mini Bell's and Martells, and had started on the Gordon's. Which was why, when a familiar face filled the screen, his defences were lower than he usually let them fall. 'So loved up I can't cool down, so loved up when you're around,' sang Jack E through cupid-bow lips glistening with gloss. Perched on stacked heels, leaning vertiginously forward, it looked like she was about to tumble out of the TV and into his arms. She bent over just far enough to bring the leather-bodice-packed breasts centre-screen before arching back, dipping down, and, with a lascivious look at the lens, shaking her twisted-Levi's-clad hips back into the dance routine with the Boyz. 'Can't cool down, When you're around, Can't cool down, When you're around.'

Eleven years since I kissed those lips, thought Jordan. Eleven years since she spoke to me as though she knew me. Eleven years since she made the big time and for me to get to – he picked up the notepad by the phone – the Holiday Inn, Glasgow.

'And that,' breezed the presenter, an androgynous teen-something in Glastonbury flares, 'was Jack E and the Boyz with the song of the season. If you miss them this summer you won't be seeing them live for some time. Jack E's so loved up with Internet music publisher Charlie Heyman she says she's chilling out at home to have his babies.'

With a snort of disgust Jordan changed channels and reached for the Gordon's. In too much of a hurry to fiddle with tonic, he was drinking it neat. Even before the gin connected with his taste buds it sent a shudder of queasiness to his stomach, but he gulped it down and chased it with another.

338

Fuzzy-headed, he lay back against the pillows. Then he checked his watch, hit the 'mute' button, picked up the phone and punched in a number.

'Hello! Sunni Winter here. Or rather not here. Please leave a—'

Where the fuck is she? he thought. At this time in the morning. He punched in her mobile number.

'Hello?'

'Sunni, sweetheart. Good morning.'

'Jordy? Thought it was someone from Early Bird. It's quarter to five.'

'I know, sweetheart. Thought I'd make sure you were bright and early for your bulletin. Aren't I a good boy?'

'You're a very good boy but I don't have time to speak right now. We're doing the bulletin from Brighton beach this morning. There's a car coming in an hour.'

'Doesn't take you five minutes to make yourself beautiful, sweetheart. Plenty of time to celebrate with me.'

'What are you celebrating?'

'Wrapped up my story. The big one, and . . . what's that splashing sound?'

'Water.'

'You're in the bath? You never take a bath in the morning.'

'It's not a bath. It's a swimming pool.'

'Where are you?'

'At Max's. The Dish TV guy?'

'I *see*.'

'You don't see anything. I came round for dinner last night and he suggested I sleep over and have an early-morning swim.'

'I *do* see.'

'No you *don't*. He lives in Sussex so there wasn't any point going back to London. And we slept in completely different wings. This is a mansion, Jordy. Even bigger than Jilly's place. You've no idea.'

'I think I do.'

'I told you. It's not like that. He's *not* after my body. We were celebrating me joining the station. It's so exciting, Jordy. Can you *believe* it? Six months ago I was just desperate to get to London. Now I'm going to have my own TV show. Can't wait to tell Mum. You know all those model agencies who said I was too short? Wait till they see me with my very own series.'

'What kind of show is it?'

'Max says it'll be the first genuinely twenty-first-century TV show and that I'll be the first genuinely twenty-first-century presenter. And guess what? He *loves* my Birmingham accent. Says I shouldn't try to hide it any more. Says it's totally . . . what was it . . . totally post-post-modern . . . whatever that means. The perfect touch.'

'Perfect *touch*.'

'Stop it, Jordy. It's so exciting. Completely new concept. It's the show that's going to get everybody talking about Dish TV and he's giving it to me.'

'Stop talking in innuendoes, sweetheart.'

'What?'

'Never mind. Congratulations.'

'Thanks. Hang on a minute . . . just getting into the Jacuzzi . . . Where are you anyway? Still in Inverness?'

'It was Aberdeen, sweetheart. Anyway, I'm in

Glasgow now. Cracked the story. All written up and ready to roll. A big fat exclusive. Going to bring down one of the biggest stars in the country.'

'Who?'

'Need-to-know basis, sweetheart. You can read all about it in the *Brit* in a couple of days.'

'That's what you always say. Feel a bit sorry for whoever it is. Now I'm going to be a star myself. Know what, Jordy?'

'What?

'Max says Dish TV is going to be so big Jilly will be begging to be on *his* sofa. But she's history, he says. *I'm* the future.'

'Good for you.'

'And you know what else?'

'What else?'

'Max says everyone in the country will be talking about my show. It'll make *Who Wants to Marry a Millionaire?* look tame.'

'Really? How's that then?'

'Wish I could tell you. It's so brilliant. But I'm not meant to tell anyone.'

The words 'not meant to tell anyone' had a powerful effect. Like an actor with tonsillitis regaining his voice on stage, Jordan suddenly felt completely sober. Lightly, almost dismissively, he remarked: 'Topless weather's already been done, you know.'

'It's nothing like that, Jordy. Much classier.'

'OK, but if it's a game show get it written into the contract that you've got something to say, otherwise you'll just be smiling and twirling.'

341

'It's not that kind of a game show, Jordy. "It's more than a game show, it's the rest of your life." Isn't that great? Max came up with that.'

'So what will you be doing?'

'I'll be fronting the whole thing, asking the couples questions, getting them to relax. Max says I'll be just like Carol Dimple, but younger.'

'Just like Carol Dimple. So Dish TV's big new concept is just another version of *Changing Rooms*?'

'Oh Jordy. It's much much better than that. Funny you should say *Changing Rooms*, though, cos that's part of the concept. Sending up all the old-format TV series from last century. Max says there's a whole new audience out there. A post-post-modern audience.'

'Max must be a genius.'

'Oh he is, Jordy. He is.'

'I'm sure he is. That's why he's signed you up, sweetheart. He's got the sense to see you're the face of the future. An icon for the twenty-first century: Sunni Winter.'

'Oh Jordy. D'you really think so?'

'I really think so.'

'This show, Jordy. If I told you what it's about you'd know right away how big it's going to be. Bigger than *Blind Date*.'

Jordan said nothing.

'It'll make my name. Overnight.'

'I'm sure it will, sweetheart. And I'm so thrilled for you. I always knew you wouldn't be a weather girl for long. You're far too talented, far too beautiful. That's been your problem really: you're so much better than all the rest that people like Jilly are jealous. They've been blocking you. Well they won't be able to do that now. You're going to soar way above them all. I just know you will. And you know what?'

'What?'

'You'll soar way above me, sweetheart. You'll forget all about me. But I don't mind. Cos I love you so much. Love you more than I've ever loved anyone. I know I haven't said so before but that's because I love you so much it scares me.'

'Oh Jordy.'

'You don't love me the same way, do you?'

'Oh Jordy.'

Jordan said nothing.

'Look, you won't tell. I know you won't. I just have to tell you. It's called *Changing Grooms*. Isn't that brilliant?'

'*Changing Grooms?*'

'We get two couples who're about to get married. Guarantee to pay for a dream wedding. Whoever they marry.'

'Whoever they marry?'

'The brides have to change grooms. For a fortnight. We take them on the most amazing dates, help them get to know each other, pay for their wardrobe, everything. At the end of that some of them are definitely going to change their mind, realise how easily they could have fallen in love with someone else. Most of them will just call off the wedding, but if we're really lucky, some of them will fall for the other person's partner. Won't that be great?'

'Great.'

343

'Apparently, just before your wedding you're very susceptible to falling in love with someone else. That's what the psychologists say. There'll be a psychologist with me throughout the series, making sure everyone's OK. And afterwards as well. Everyone who wants it will get post-show counselling. For up to six months. TV with a conscience. That's what Max says. He really cares about people. Says we're making programmes *with* them, not *about* them.'

'Sounds like a great guy.'

'You won't say anything, will you?'

'You don't trust me? When I've just told you how I feel about you?'

'Sorry, Jordy. Look, I've got to go now. I'm going to be late. When are you back?'

'I'm flying home this morning. Take you out to celebrate tonight?'

'Not tonight. I'm having dinner with Max and a couple of his money men. He says they like to meet the stars they're investing in. I've got to be there.'

'Tomorrow night then? Early evening. Just like you like it. So you get your beauty sleep?'

'Oh Jordy. I think Max said something about tomorrow night. I'll have to check.'

'OK, sweetheart. Well, I'll call you anyway. OK?'

'OK.'

'Love you, sweetheart.'

'Me too. And Jordy?'

'Yeah?'

'Call me on the mobile. Cos I don't know where I'll be.'

'OK.'

'Bye-bye.'

'Bye.'

Bye, Sunni, thought Jordan. You don't know where you'll be. But I know exactly where you'll be. With Mr Dish TV. Yesterday you were madly in love with me. Today you don't know when you'll have time to see me. What a difference your own TV show makes. Didn't even try to get me to say what my story was about. Usually you're dying to know. Still – he glanced at the notepad he'd been scribbling on since she'd mentioned *Changing Grooms* – not a bad kiss-off. Not bad at all. Sunni Winter superstar. Only too glad to meet me at your very first photo call when you got the weather-girl job. Suddenly too good for me now you're going to be a star.

If she's going to be a star. Wonder if she's signed anything yet? Don't think Max Golding will be too impressed when he sees his top-secret concept splashed all over the *Daily Brit*.

Jordan yawned contentedly. Not a bad night's work, he thought. Mission Tara successfully completed, and enough ammo to stop Sunni in her tracks. Serves her right for treating me like that. Stupid bitch. What's Golding got that I haven't? Apart from a whacking great media empire, half a dozen homes, and his own yacht . . . Makes Dad's business look like a corner shop. And my brother's. Golding could buy and sell Same Day Spotless and Rush Caffeine before breakfast. *And* Max isn't much older than I am. No wonder Dad thinks I'm a failure. Even that LA job's not going to impress him much. I should've been an editor by now. I would be if I hadn't fucked about. Should never have wasted all that time in Los Angeles. Six years and not one of those studio fuckers wanted my film script. Bastards.

Plenty of pussy, though. More than most men get in a lifetime. Even though I was living with what's-her-name. Not a loser as far as pussy's concerned, eh Roger? Not a loser at all. Compared to poor old plodding Plod.

Jordan picked up the phone, punched in his own home number.

'Hello?'

'Wakey wakey!'

'Jordan? What's going on? Why . . .?'

'Mission completed, Plodders. While you were sleeping. I'm all written up and returning to base.'

'Tara?'

'Banged to rights, mate. Back in Blighty by nightfall. With the biggest story of the summer.'

'Right.'

'Permission to sound excited, Private Plodders.'

'It's half past five in the morning.'

'Sorry, mate. Thought you'd want to know. I'll take you out tonight to celebrate. Courtesy of Her Majesty's *Daily Brit*. Expense no object.'

'So what's the story with Tara?'

'I'll email it to you now. Just don't say a word to anyone, OK? Idle talk and all that. Still got to get a snapper round to pick up some pics. They'll probably want to run it Saturday, when there's plenty of space.'

'What did Bullock say?'

'Haven't spoken to him yet, mate. I'm going to print

this out and take it into the office myself. Make sure the editor realises who's brought this one in. Otherwise Bullock will grab all the glory himself.'

'Can't trust anyone in your game, can you?'

'Dead right, mate. You're finally catching on.'

'OK. Well, well done and all that.'

'Thanks, mate. Stand by your computer. I'll email you right now. Then I've got to grab some shut-eye.'

'OK. See you later.'

'Over and out.'

Jordan put down the phone with a flourish. What a loser, he thought. Didn't sound the least excited I'd cracked the story. After all I've done for him. Getting him shifts. Letting him watch a real operator in action. Isn't there anyone better to share my moment of triumph with?

Yawning, he went to his Toshiba, emailed the story to Plod. Then, suddenly tired, he closed the curtains and got undressed. In bed, he set the alarm and turned off the lights. But sleep wouldn't come.

Too fucking tired, he thought. Six in the morning and I've been working all night. Moment of triumph but I'm too shagged out to enjoy it. So what if I get the LA job? Still have to work my balls off.

Jackie's taking the rest of the year off. To have that bastard's babies. While I'm working like a dog. Last time I saw her at a press conference she treated me like a pariah. They all do. Stars versus Press.

Wonder what it's like on the other side. To be rich and famous and sought-after. Instead of doing the chasing. One of the *Hello!* crowd.

I could have been there with Jackie. She was special. Haven't met anyone as special as her. Apart from Tara.

Tara? Otherwise known as Scarlett Macdougall. Re-inventing herself like that. Clichés aside: she's a very special woman. Shame I won't be able to . . . Wait a minute. Why not? Why the fuck not? Such a huge fucking opportunity here I almost missed it. Me and Tara. Tara and me. The perfect media couple. She's famous, I *should* be famous. She's a rich, gorgeous, intelligent, self-made woman, and I bet she shags like a dervish. Fuck's sake: I'm already half in love with her and I didn't realise it. Been working too hard to figure it out.

Fuck's sake. I *am* in love with her. One hundred per cent. No doubt about it. All I've got to do is tell her. Tell her, marry her, write another film script, at my leisure . . . It's all so clear now. Why didn't I see it before? Suddenly energised, he sat up, phoned the *Daily Brit* travel agent, booked an earlier flight. Reset the alarm. Out of the corner of his eye he caught sight of his Toshiba.

Thank fuck I haven't filed the story, he thought. I'll print it out and give it to her. Show her how much she means to me. Course we'll have to tell some of the story sometime . . . to stop some other bastard turning her over. But I'll take care of all that for her. She needn't worry about a thing.

He thumped the pillows into position, got under the bedclothes, smiled to himself. Can see it now, he thought: 'Tara MacDonald, the nation's favourite stargazer, and her screenwriter husband Jordan Holmes, pictured at the Cannes premiere of his latest blockbuster.'

348

Wait a moment, he thought. What the fuck am I thinking of?

'Jordan Holmes, Hollywood's hottest new screen-writer, with his beautiful stargazer wife Tara MacDonald, pictured at the Cannes premiere . . .'

He yawned contentedly. I feel so good, he thought. So fucking good. This is love. Definitely love. And to think I nearly fucking missed it . . .

Chapter Thirty

London, August 2000

CROSSING the little railway bridge into Primrose Hill, David strode past a sweaty-faced estate agent in a tight suit and a tearing hurry. But on Regent's Park Road he slowed down to his normal pace, keeping just ahead of two mothers pushing all-terrain three-wheeler prams. Eventually his progress was so halting he was overtaken by a thick-ankled Greek-Cypriot grandmother laden down with the delicacies her English daughter-in-law failed to make her son.

A convict boarding the ship for Botany Bay wouldn't have walked any slower, mused David. Or a condemned man passing through Traitor's Gate.

Stop it, he told himself. Stop seeking refuge in other eras. For once in your life face up to being right here, right now. Too slow, too late, but at least you're taking action.

Nothing I can do to save her now, he thought. But forewarned is forearmed. Soon as I've put this through her letterbox I'll go home, pack my stuff and start looking for another room to rent. Could've done with the shift money but no way could I accept it now.

At Chalcot Crescent he checked his watch: nearly noon. I must get a move on to get sorted before Jordan gets back, he thought. Should've asked him what flight he'd be on.

Outside Tara's town house David glanced nervously towards the windows. No one in sight. Good, he thought. I don't want to run into Tara or Miss Macleod. But I *do* want them to read this as soon as possible. I'll ring the bell and scarper. By the time Miss Macleod gets to the door I can be round the corner and into Chalcot Square. Taking the sheaf of computer print-outs he'd been carrying, he started to shove it through the brass letterbox.

Come on, come *on*, he thought, as he pressed the rolled-up papers flat to squeeze them through the narrow opening.

As soon as they were through he put his hand up to the bell, but before he could press it, the door opened.

'David?'

'Tara.'

'What are you doing here?'

'Just wanted to deliver something.'

'This?' Tara bent down to pick up the roll of print-outs on the floor.

'Don't look at it now. Please.'

The desperation in his voice made her pause.

'Why not? What's the matter?'

'I didn't think I'd see you. Please read them after I'm gone.'

'Is it my book?' Tara pulled off the elastic band and unfurled the first page.

'No, it's . . .' David reached out to take the page away, but Tara, having already seen the headline, recoiled as though he'd been about to hit her.

Then, in a strangled whisper: 'I can see what it is.'

'Tara I . . . I wanted to . . .'

Her face was blank; her eyes expressionless. 'Just go now. Leave me alone.'

'Tara, please . . .'

But he was interrupted by the sound of someone running up behind him.

Tara saw him first. In an instant her face went from betrayed and desolate to surprised but hopeful.

David turned to follow her gaze.

Advancing towards them, holding a vast bouquet of long-stemmed red roses in front of him like a shield, was Jordan . . .

PART THREE

THE REAL STORY

Chapter Thirty-one

Glasgow, September 1987

HEEDLESS of her elegant gown, Scarlett knelt down in the field and plunged her fingers into the ploughed earth. 'Tara, Tara,' she cried, holding aloft a handful of soil. Then, having drawn new strength from the land, she arose, and with a glow of fresh hope on her beautiful, tear-streaked face, declared bravely: 'After all . . . tomorrow is another day.'

Watching from her sofabed, tears streaming down her face, Scarlett set the video to rewind and plunged her fingers into a family-size bag of Maltesers. Rhett, she thought. I love you, Rhett. *I'd* never let you go. Never.

Stuffing the final handful of Maltesers into her mouth, she slipped the empty packet down the side of the bed, with all the other sweet wrappers, then turned onto her stomach, pulling the duvet over her head.

The quilt blocked out the glare from the streetlight outside, muffled the sound of Friday-night drinkers staggering home, softened the tick of the alarm clock set to rouse her in time to serve her mother morning tea in bed. Two cups: one for Ma and one for the man from the night before. Whoever that might be.

Don't think about that, thought Scarlett. Think about Rhett. About being with Rhett. Right hand reaching between her legs, she closed her eyes and kissed the pillow, tasting the familiar mix of cotton and chocolate as she pressed her hips into the bed, and then, with both hands, rubbed the place between her legs that was so warm and moist and full of sensation, until, hot and breathless, her hips squirmed out of control and she felt the feeling that made her feel lovely all over: lovely and heart-faster and gasping and light . . .

Light as Vivien Leigh with Clark Gable's hands round her tiny waist, light as any of the girls at school with the boys' hands all over them behind the bicycle sheds, light as Scarlett only felt in the quilted darkness, with the duvet over her head, and the lovely feeling washing through her, making her forget how fat she was, how clumsy, and how no matter how much she tried she could never find the right thing to do to make Ma love her . . .

'Move over.'

'Mmmmm?'

'C'mon, Lola, shift yourself.'

Scarlett felt a tug at the duvet, naked flesh against hers; legs seeking the warmth of hers, chest against her back, a hairy softness pressing against her bottom, muscular arms reaching around her and large hands touching her nipples, making them hard, making her not want to wake up, making her disappointed when they moved away, when the arms dropped down, the body edged away and a man's voice, beer-befuddled and accusing: 'Yer not Lola.'

Don't stop, she thought. Please don't stop.

She turned around, put her arms round his neck.

Do it again, she thought. Do it again.

Eyes tight shut, she burrowed into the body next to her, pulled it closer, till she could feel the soft hairiness against her stomach. She pulled herself up against the other body, till the hairiness was between her legs, till she heard a groan – of pleasure and surprise – and the man, warily: 'Ye want it, don't ye?'

Yes, she thought. Yes.

A hand reached between her legs; felt the moistness. She heard the voice; goal-scoring triumphant: 'By fuck ye want it. Yer soakin'.'

Then came the hardness against her, and the fingers probing, more insistent, and the mouth on her nipples, sucking and biting, and the weight of him, bearing down, and the fingers opening her up, and a pushing, a kind of pain she'd never felt before, but over fast, hardly noticeable, in the excitement, which made her want to move, to open up, to take in the hardness, to feel it right inside her and to feel it rubbing against her, till she felt that lovely, light feeling all over again, except this time there was hot breath against her neck and a man's voice in her ear: 'A'right, darlin'. A'right.'

Rhett, she thought. 'Rhett!' she cried.

No duvet around her now, but his arms holding her tight, and her eyes closed, her face buried in his chest, feeling him, smelling him, listening to his heartbeat, feeling safe and light and . . .

Suddenly the door opened, the light was switched on.

'Scarlett!'

357

'Ma!'

'Lola!'

'What the fuck are yous two doing?'

In the doorway, hands on hips, all fake tan and peach nylon negligée, fired up with White Horse and indignation, stood her mother.

'She wanted it. God's truth. She wanted it.'

The man jumped up, taking the duvet with him, wrapping it around himself.

'Ma, I'm sorry. I'm so sorry.'

Marooned on the sofabed, naked and cowering, legs folded to chest and head bowed, Scarlett looked like a concentration camp inmate bracing herself for the wrath of a sadistic guard. The last thing she expected was Lola rushing over, pulling the duvet off the man, wrapping it round her daughter, giving her a whisky-scented cuddle, sitting down next to her and saying gently: 'It's all right, pet. Yer Ma's here now.'

Then turning, lioness-with-her-cub angry, to the man: 'Just what do you think you're about?'

'I got up to piss and I took the wrong door. But she was up for it. I swear. Weren't you?'

Scarlett felt something she'd never felt before: her mother's hands, stroking her hair.

'Don't worry, my wee pet. Yer a'right now.'

The man took a step towards the living-room door.

But Lola was up and past him and at the door before him: 'Hold it right there, John Crawford.'

'Just want my trousers.'

'Bet you do,' spat out Lola, eyeing his penis.

He covered it with his hands.

'Now sit down,' she commanded.

He stepped back towards the sofabed.

'Not there, you bastard. Over there.'

He sat in the armchair; put the cushion on his lap.

'Now Scarlett, pet, tell John how old you are.'

What should I say? thought Scarlett. My real age, or the age you say I am when you're pretending you're younger? She looked at her mother questioningly.

'Go on, Scarlett. Tell him how old you'll be next birthday.'

'Fifteen.'

The man's head sank into his hands: 'Christ.'

'So how old does that make you now, pet?'

'Fourteen.'

'Jesus Christ.' The man shook his head and looked at the floor.

With the dramatic air of a woman who watches too many made-for-TV movies, Lola pulled open the living-room door and reached behind her to pick up something from the hall floor, all the time keeping her eyes on the man.

'Here's your trousers,' she said, flinging them across the room at him. 'And your belt.' It hit him full on the face. 'And your shoes.' He ducked out of the way of the first one, but was too slow to avoid the second hitting him on the shin. 'And your shirt. Now get dressed. And be on your way.'

He hurried to put on his clothes: 'This is not my fault. I didn't know,' he said to Scarlett.

'On yer way,' ordered Lola, standing guard at the doorway.

As he approached, she handed him his jacket. He fumbled in the pockets for his cigarettes. But they were gone. And so was something else.

'Where's my pay packet?'

'Must have lost it.'

'Give it here. I'm not going home without it.'

'Scared of what your wife'll say?'

'Just hand it over.'

'Tell her you lost it on your way home.'

'She won't believe me.'

'Well tell her the truth. Tell her you've just had sex with a fourteen-year-old. What's the right expression? A minor. Aye, that's right. Sex with a minor. Underage sex. Rape. Whatever you want to call it.'

'You bitch.'

'Language! Scarlett's only fourteen. In case you'd forgotten.' Lola smiled at him brightly: 'Which reminds me. It's Scotstoun Secondary your daughter's at isn't it? Same as Scarlett. Is there a Crawford lassie in your class, Scarlett?'

'No.'

'Och well. Maybe she's in another year. But it's definitely Scotstoun Secondary, isn't it, John?'

'You bitch. You set me up. You're a whoor. And so's your daughter.' His face was twisted in anger. He raised his hand to hit her but at the last moment found the self-control to divert his fist to the door, smashing it with such force the wood splintered.

'Good night to you too,' said Lola, stepping aside as he marched across the hall and out the front door to the close.

As the outside door clattered shut behind him, Scarlett eyed her mother with trepidation. Now, she thought. Now I'll be for it.

But to her amazement, she found herself inhaling a cloud of White Horse and Giorgio Beverly Hills as her mother drew her into a hug. 'First time, pet? A wee bit strange, isn't it?'

Not wanting to risk anything which might end the mother-daughter embrace, Scarlett said nothing. Like a torture victim offered a post-beating cigarette, she held her breath to see what would come next.

'It *is* your first time?' Lola released her daughter to look at her questioningly. Scarlett nodded. 'Course it is,' said Lola. 'My big fat lump.' The familiar insult, but in this unknown friendly tone, confused Scarlett completely.

'Never been kissed. And no wonder.' Lola ran her fingers appraisingly across Scarlett's over-fed face, her fleshy double chin.

Then she sat back and smiled: 'You fair enjoyed it, though. I was right outside the door. Listening to the two of yous.' Lola shrieked dramatically: 'Rhett! Rhett!'

Scarlett hung her head. Her face felt red with shame; her eyes prickled with tears.

Lola extended a cerise-taloned hand to her daughter's chin and forced it upwards. 'Oh aye, pet. I heard it all. But don't worry. That bastard won't tell a soul. And nor will I. No one else will ever know. OK?'

But I don't understand, thought Scarlett. Wasn't it bad what I did? Why isn't Ma angry?

'OK?'

Seems to be, thought Scarlett. Seems I've done the right thing for once. 'OK,' she agreed.

'Fine,' said Lola. 'Now why don't you . . . no, why don't *I* make us a nice cup of tea.'

What? thought Scarlett.

'What's the matter? You look like you've seen a ghost,' said Lola. She laughed; her best sitting-on-a-barstool laugh. 'Been some night, I suppose: losing your virginity, seeing a naked man prancing round the lounge.'

No, thought Scarlett. *That's* not it. It's *you*: can't remember the last time you offered to make me tea. Not since I was old enough to boil a kettle.

She looked at her mother and burst into tears.

Lola put her arms round her daughter, hugged her close. 'There, there, pet. I know what you're worried about. But don't you fret. If that bastard's got you pregnant I'll sort it out. We'll have to get you fixed up anyway. For next time . . .'

Next time? wondered Scarlett. Wiping her eyes, she pulled out of the embrace and looked at her mother with surprise.

'Oh aye, pet. Plenty of next times. But I'll tell you all about it in the morning . . .'

Chapter Thirty-two

Glasgow, March 1988

WITH the air of a film director checking the *mise-en-scène*, Lola turned to inspect her reflection in the gilt-framed dressing-table mirror. The light from the pink-toned bulb of the bedside lamp picked out the platinum highlights in her hair (courtesy of L'Oréal at Boots the Chemist), and cast a rosy glow over her bare nut-brown skin (thanks to the Electric Beach on the Dumbarton Road). It softened the shininess of the satin-look sheets (from a market stall at the Barras) and the sun-starved whiteness of the soft-paunched male body she was straddling (courtesy of the lounge bar of the Quarter Gill in Partick). Pursing her lips the way she did when assessing the excess poundage of a new Waistwatcher, Lola surveyed the flaccid male member curled beneath her like a sleeping dormouse. Then, like a cat addressing a saucer of milk, she dipped down to lick the soft ribbed pinkness until it hardened into porn-movie readiness.

Only when completely certain it would remain hard did she remove her mouth and work her way up the body, licking the stomach and chest and reaching up to scratch behind his ears with her long, lilac-painted nails.

'Mmmmmh,' he groaned. 'Fuck me again.'

'What about my friend? Can't she fuck you too?'

'What?'

'D'you want her to? D'you want her to fuck you?'

Lying on top of him, Lola felt his hips writhe in expectation. He sat up and kissed her hard on the mouth: 'You're fucking amazing. Pure amazing.'

'She's in the front room, waiting for you.'

'Bring her in.'

'She's waiting for you. Go on. I'll come and join yous. Here . . .' She reached over to the night table, picked up an unwrapped condom, and expertly rolled it into place.

'Mmmmmmh . . . Lola.' Kissing her hard and wet, he was sitting up, trying to pull her onto his lap, to arrange her on top of his erection. With the unembarrassed touch of the pornographer, Lola pushed his face from hers, patted his penis aside and put her hands on his shoulders. His ordinary, unhandsome face was glowing like a wee boy who'd never dared believe in Santa Claus, but now heard sleigh bells jingling: 'You're an amazing woman, so you are.'

'C'mon,' said Lola, taking him by the hand, out of her bedroom and across the little hallway to the front room. Opening the door, she took hold of his penis and moved her hand firmly up and down. 'Don't switch the light on. She likes it in the dark. OK?'

'Mmmmmmh. OK. What's her name?'

Lola removed her hand from his penis; patted him playfully on the bottom. 'Go on now. I'll be through in a minute. To join yous . . .'

Obediently, he stepped into the semi-darkness of the front room, felt his way onto the sofabed and onto Scarlett, who threw her arms round his neck, and her legs around his, guiding the erection inside her.

'Oh God, oh God,' he gasped. He propped himself up on his arms and thrust forward and back, forward and back, pounding into the soft broadness of the young body beneath him.

'Yes, yes,' said Scarlett. Rhett, Rhett, she thought.

Eyes closed, concentrating hard, she felt herself getting closer and closer to the lovely light feeling, but not quite there, not quite . . .

Suddenly, she felt a deep, sledgehammer thrust, then a warm, heavy weight on top of her, as arms buckling, thighs quivering, the man reached the conclusion of his second orgasm of the night.

Nearly, she thought. Nearly there.

The man had rolled to one side, was gasping for air. Scarlett laid her head on his heaving chest.

Much quicker, she thought. Quicker than the others. Heart's pumping very fast, she noted. And he's sweating a lot. Came very quickly. I'll come myself. Soon as he's gone. Soon as Ma's got him out of here.

In the darkness, Scarlett kept her eyes closed, her head on his chest, her ears open for the sound of the door, the light switch, her mother's voice.

Right on cue, Lola appeared in the doorway to deliver the next page of her script: 'What the fuck d'you think you're playing at?'

Scarlett didn't need to open her eyes to know how

the scene would unfold: she and Ma had played it so often now.

Sometimes there was a technical hitch: the man didn't have enough money in his wallet and had to be sent to the cashpoint on the corner. The first time that had happened Lola had feared he wouldn't come back. So she'd shown him Scarlett's birth certificate.

'You're off your fucking head. This is blackmail and I'm going straight to the police,' he'd shouted.

'Can't you shout a bit louder?' Lola had suggested. 'Don't think the whole street will have heard you yet. Still, they'll all hear about it when it's in court, in the papers, all round your work. Fine by me. I'm off to America. Soon as I've got enough money. Won't be me who has to put up with folk talking.'

Within twelve minutes he'd put his clothes on, been to the cashpoint and was back with ten crisp Bank of Scotland twenties.

'Here, pet,' said Lola, handing Scarlett one of them. 'Take this to school. Buy something nice for your play piece.' The words 'school' and 'play piece' she always lingered over, eyeing the man as she did so.

As soon as he'd left she'd turn to her daughter. 'A'right, pet? Mind giving me that back? I'm a bit short this week. You can keep it next time. OK?'

Scarlett would hand back the note.

'Thanks, pet. You're a big help to your Ma. A great big help. Who'd have thought it, eh?'

This time, though, after the man left, Lola fetched her purse, took the twenty-pound note from Scarlett,

366

and, with a Lady-Bountiful smile, gave her back a fiver: 'Here, pet. This is for you.' Then, inspecting her daughter's face with an intensity usually reserved for giving new cosmetics customers a Mary-Ellen make-over, Lola asked: 'You *are* all right, aren't you, pet? You're enjoying yourself fine. Helping your Ma?'

Scarlett looked away before answering: 'Yes.'

'That's a good girl. That's your Ma's good girl,' said Lola, giving her daughter a swift sinewy-armed hug, then sitting back to look at her.

Scarlett still wouldn't meet her gaze.

Thoughtfully, Lola retreated to the armchair, sat down and lit an Embassy Regal: 'Fancy a fag?'

Scarlett shook her head.

Lola got up to open the buffet and pour herself a White Horse: 'A dram?'

Scarlett shook her head.

'I know, pet. No vices. Except food.' Whisky in hand, Lola went over to where Scarlett was sitting on the sofabed, wrapped in her duvet. With her left hand, like a cannibal testing for tender flesh, she prodded her daughter on the upper arm. Fat-as-a-shank-of-ham, said Lola's disdainful expression.

Scarlett hung her head, drew the duvet closer around her.

'And, of course, men,' said Lola, meaningfully. 'Can't say you're not a scarlet woman now, can you?'

Despite the warmth of the duvet, Scarlett shivered.

'Don't worry, pet. I won't tell. And *you* won't tell either, will you?'

367

'Oh no, never.' Scarlett looked stricken at the very thought.

'Good,' said Lola. She sat down again, retrieved her cigarette, blew out a perfect smoke ring and watched it waft towards her daughter. 'Cos the thing is, pet, you're a very, very bad girl. Very bad indeed.' Lola blew out another smoke ring. '*I* understand why you're doing it. To help your Ma. *I* appreciate that. But nobody else would ever believe you.'

Lola administered another swallow of whisky; smacked her lips in satisfaction. Then, conversationally: 'Imagine your pals at school hearing about this? Or your teachers? Specially that interfering one. The one you spend so much time with. What's her name? Miss Macleod. Imagine her knowing about this. What d'you think she'd think?'

Like a streetwalker whose punter has just pulled a knife to avoid paying, Scarlett – violated and helpless – looked at her mother in total terror. Then, lying down and curling her bulky body into itself like a baby in the womb, she turned her face to her pillow and wept. Silently.

'Exactly,' said Lola, as though *she* were a teacher and Scarlett a pupil who'd just understood a particularly important lesson. Lola stubbed out her cigarette, drained her whisky glass: 'No decent person would want to speak to you again. Ever.'

Yawning with the contentment of someone who'd just completed a good night's work, Lola got out of the armchair. At the door, just before switching off the light, she cast a glance at her daughter, huddled under the duvet, still silent, but her body shaking with sobs.

'Night-night, pet. Better get some sleep. I'm shagged out. Aren't you?'

Chapter Thirty-three

London, August 2000

'I'VE got something to tell you, Tara,' said Jordan, shoving David aside to get to where Tara was standing on her doorstep. Thrusting the roses at her, Jordan caught her gaze with his, looked deep into her eyes: I love you, love you, love you, he wanted them to say. Actually, they said: I want you, want you, want you.

But Tara – so inexperienced in love – failed to spot the difference. Looking back at him hopefully, she wondered: Rhett? Is it really going to be all right? After the hurt, the happy ending?

Left stranded behind them on the path, David looked at Jordan looking at Tara; Tara looking back at him.

Jordan turned to David: 'What are *you* doing here?'

'Tara. I've got to explain something. Before you read it,' said David.

'Read what?' asked Jordan.

Wordlessly, Tara held up the print-outs in her hand.

'I see,' said Jordan, firing a fuck-you look at David, then swivelling his gaze back to Tara: trust me, trust me, I can explain everything.

'If you'll just let me say something first . . .' began David.

'No,' said Jordan in a commanding-officer voice.

'What *I've* got to say is urgent.' His brown eyes fixed on Tara: 'You need to hear this. You need to hear it *now*.'

Yes Rhett, thought Tara. Anything.

'Let's go inside,' said Jordan to Tara.

Fuck off, his eyes flashed David.

'OK,' said Tara.

No, thought David.

Jordan stepped forward, ready to put a guiding arm on Tara, but was diverted by the rumble of a taxi drawing up and someone getting out of it.

'Flora,' said Tara.

'Hello, dear.' Are you all right? her eyes asked.

No, said Tara's. No, I'm not.

'Well now, gentlemen,' Flora addressed Jordan and David. 'Why don't you come inside where we can talk?'

'I have to speak to Tara urgently. Alone,' said Jordan.

'So do I,' said David.

Tara looked from one to the other helplessly.

'Right then,' said Flora. She looked up at the two privately educated young Englishmen towering over her; treated them both, separately, to the gaze that had subdued decades of welders' and boiler-makers' sons; tenement-bred bare-knuckle boys. 'We're going inside. We're having a cup of tea. And then I'll ask you both what you've got to say for yourselves.'

Without waiting for agreement, she turned and led the way inside, into the cream-and-white salon.

'Sit down,' she told them. 'Tara. Give me those papers. Where are my glasses?'

David handed her the glasses lying on the table.

'Thank you.' Flora took the sheaf of print-outs,

371

skim-read the first page. 'On second thoughts, I won't be making tea.' She turned to David. 'Now then, what have you got to tell us?'

Where do I start? thought David.

'It's quite simple,' said Jordan. 'I—'

Flora glared at him. 'David? Perhaps you'd better start by telling us who you really are, what you really do?'

'Well, um, what I really do is I'm an historian. I'm doing some work on an oral reminiscence project. And I'm writing a book about London.'

'So you're really not a journalist,' said Tara. She looked at David in surprise.

'No,' he said. 'I'm sorry. I got involved with something I shouldn't have. Doing Jordan's dirty work.' He looked at Flora and Tara: 'I lied to you both about the book. There is no book. Jordan's just using it as a cover to get close to you both, to get your story, and I'm helping him. I'm as much to blame as he is. And I'm sorry. Truly sorry.' David came to an end; raised his hands towards the two women in the age-old forgive-me gesture.

Seeing his chance, Jordan broke in: 'But you've nothing to worry about, Tara. Nothing. This story will never be printed. That's what I came to tell you. I came as quickly as I could. As soon as I realised how much I love you. How much I want to be with you and make everything wonderful for you.' He stepped closer to Tara, took both her hands in his. 'I'm sorry if reading my story has hurt you. But I can't be sorry I wrote it. Because if I hadn't I wouldn't have got to know you. And to fall in love with you.'

372

That's exactly what *I* wanted to say, thought David. If only I'd found the words.

That's exactly what I wanted to hear, thought Tara.

'From the first moment I met you, I wanted to be with you,' said Jordan to Tara.

Yes, thought David. Exactly.

'I've never met anyone as gorgeous as you. Ever,' continued Jordan.

No, never, thought David. And I never will again.

'But I haven't read your story,' said Tara. 'I don't know what it says.'

Do they know? she wondered. Did they find out?

She looked at Jordan and David, who were both looking at her.

They can't have, she thought. They can't know. Otherwise I'd see it in their eyes, wouldn't I?

'It doesn't matter what it says,' said Jordan. 'No one will ever read it now. And no one will ever write anything bad about you. Ever. I know how this whole game works. I'll look after you, protect you, make sure no one ever hurts you. You and me. Against the world. *I'll* be your agent. We'll make a wonderful team.'

'You're forgetting something,' said Flora; her tone dry as chalk dust. 'Tara's already in a team. I'm the other half. Where do *I* fit into your plans? And how do you expect Tara to believe anything you say, after you've deceived us like this?'

'I know I've deceived you both,' said Jordan. He looked genuinely contrite: 'It's something I've done so often I did it without thinking. I wish with all my heart I hadn't. You must believe me. You must believe how sorry I am, how important you are to me, Tara.'

His eyes looked at her, pleading.

David looked at Tara to see if Jordan's look was working.

Jordan *does* love me, thought Tara. But does he love me because he doesn't know, or does he love me *despite* what he knows?

He *thinks* he loves her, thought David. But is that because she's Tara MacDonald or because she's Scarlett Macdougall?

Maybe it's going to be OK, thought Tara. As long as Flora doesn't read that story.

It's going to be OK, thought Jordan. As long as that old bat doesn't interfere any further.

'We need a wee talk, dear,' said Flora.

'May I have the story?' asked Tara.

Flora handed it to her.

Tara looked at Jordan; then at David; tried to read what was in their eyes. So easy to do with clients, yet now she felt so confused, so worried about how much they knew: 'Promise you won't print this?'

'Promise,' said Jordan.

Tara looked at David, but Jordan jumped in again: 'It's not up to him. I promise you, Tara. Not a word of this will appear.'

But what if you two know, thought Tara. How am I going to bear it? Without wishing to she suddenly heard her mother's voice: '*I* understand why you're doing it. To help your Ma. *I* appreciate that. But nobody else would ever believe you . . . and anyway, you like it fine, don't you?'

374

Never seen anyone look so desolate, thought Jordan. 'Tara?' he said.

Never seen anyone look so desolate, thought David. 'Tara? Scarlett?' he said.

That desolate look again, thought Flora. 'Come on, dear.' She held out her right hand to her protégée. Like a drowning woman sighting a life ring, Tara looked at the hand longingly. But didn't reach for it.

Tara, Scarlett, whatever, she thought. Ma's wee whoor. That's who I am. Ma's wee whoor.

Tara looked at Flora sadly. If *that's* in the story then I'll have lost you for ever, she thought.

And there *is* no Rhett, she told herself. Not for me. She glanced at David and Jordan. Do you know about me? she wondered. *Really* know about me? If you do I'll never be able to look either of you in the eyes again.

'Come on, dear. Let's go upstairs,' said Flora.

'Stay right where you are,' she commanded David and Jordan. 'We'll be back down in a few minutes. Then *I'll* have something to say. Your story won't be complete without it.'

'There isn't going to be a story,' protested Jordan.

Flora gave him one of her fiercest you're-still-on-probation glares. It was the look she used to give the bad boy of the class, and Tara recognised it.

Please no, she thought. Please don't say I shouldn't trust Jordan. Please don't say that story might still be printed . . .

Chapter Thirty-four

London, August 2000

WHITE-FACED and trembling, Tara read the final line of Jordan's story, then set the pages aside and wept. Not her usual silent tears, but loud, violent sobbing which convulsed her whole body. It was so fierce, so intense, Flora hesitated to throw her arms around the younger woman lest she be pushed away.

I'm to blame for this, she thought. Without me she wouldn't be going through this pain. I'm selfish, selfish, selfish. Emboldened by self-reproach, Flora threw both arms around Tara, and held her tightly. Eventually the sobbing subsided.

Face pressed against Flora's bosom, Tara's words emerged muffled and tearful: 'I'm sorry. So sorry. I just can't take any more. Can't cope.'

'They've found out about the thing you won't talk about?'

'No, no, they haven't.' Tara withdrew far enough from Flora's embrace to sit back and smile grimly. 'I was so terrified they would and they haven't. I should be relieved. But I just feel drained; exhausted. I can't cope with this any more. I just can't cope. I'm so sorry. I'm letting you down. After all you've done for me.'

'No, dear. *I'm* sorry. For leading you into all this.'

Flora surveyed her former pupil: beautifully slim and perfectly groomed, in a wisp of an Armani frock and Salvatore Ferragamo sandals, sitting amid the filigree lamps, the silken hangings and the hand-tooled leather of the chicest Moroccan boudoir in London. Hard to equate this woman of the glossies with poor gauche Scarlett from Scotstoun, thought Flora. But that's the problem. I was so carried away with helping her re-invent herself I didn't do enough to help her adjust. Too busy chalking up a final success as a teacher to take proper care of my pupil.

'You realise that in their different ways both the young men downstairs are convinced they love you?'

'I don't think I know what love is. I don't think Ma ever . . .' Tara's voice trailed off; she shook her head sadly.

'Some people aren't capable of showing love,' began Flora, handing a clean white handkerchief to Tara. But then, seeing the don't-lie-to-me look in Tara's eyes, decided to speak plainly: 'Maybe your mother wasn't even capable of feeling love. However much you sought her approval. It broke my heart to see it. And to see you slaving away for that editor, trying to get approval from him. I'm sorry you're so unhappy now, Scarlett.'

Tara blinked at the sound of her old name.

'Scarlett, Tara, it doesn't matter, dear. I care about *you*. You know that, don't you?'

Tara nodded.

'And I'm so proud of you. Proud of what you've achieved.'

'I don't want it any more. I want . . .' Tara looked

377

up, then right and left, as though searching for something. 'I want, I want . . .'

'To be in love? With someone who loves you?'

Tara looked startled.

'Do you think I've never been in love, dear?'

'Sandy?'

'Yes, there was Sandy. But we were barely past being children when he died. We were never even lovers.'

Tara looked double-startled.

'I *know*, dear. We've never talked about these things. Maybe we should have.' Flora smiled. 'Not the kind of thing you expect to discuss with your teacher, is it? Even now.'

Tara waited to hear more.

'I've been in love, dear. More than once. In lust sometimes. Always the wrong men. Always married. But we didn't do any harm, didn't wreck any homes. I felt guilty. But not too guilty.

'I'm only telling you because I want you to know that I understand about love and passion and wanting a man to be with you. You've never wanted to talk about it, so I haven't. But maybe that was a mistake. I think it's time for you to put these things to rest. Time for you to find your happiness.

'You're like a granddaughter to me, Scarlett. And a good friend. A very good friend.'

'As a friend then' – Tara had brightened considerably – 'what d'you think I should do about Jordan and David?'

'As your friend, I wouldn't dream of answering that for you. You'll find the answer yourself.'

'And the story. Will they publish it?'

'No. Not when Jordan hears what I've got to say.'

'But what if there are other reporters trying to get my story?'

'You mean, will they find out what you don't want them to know?'

Tara nodded.

'Don't worry, dear. Jordan is one of the most ambitious young men I've ever met. He's an excellent reporter and he works for one of the richest newspapers in the country. If he couldn't uncover your secret then I'm sure no one else will.'

'I still feel I'm really letting you down.'

Flora looked puzzled.

'By giving all this up.'

'You don't need to give anything up.'

'Yes I do. I've had enough with all the pretence. I'm exhausted. I don't want to be famous any more. Don't want to be on TV. And I never, *ever* want to have to listen to another celebrity droning on about their imaginary problems.'

'Are you sure, dear? I thought this is what you always wanted.'

'It is. When I was a wee girl in Scotstoun all I wanted was to be someone else, to be beautiful, to live like the people in the magazines. Well, I've got all that now. But it's not how I thought it would be. Nothing at all.'

'What do you want to do, then?'

'I don't know. But not this. Not any more.'

'Well, you're rich now. You've got plenty of choices. And you've got me on your side. Whatever you do.'

'I know. I'm so sorry for giving up. After everything you've done. Don't think I'm not grateful.'

'Don't be sorry, dear. And it's I who should be grateful. The past couple of years have been such fun. You've given me a new lease of life. I was turning into a very dull old lady. A very dull old lady indeed.'

'Oh, but—'

'Yes I was. I know I was. But now I feel . . . Well, I feel I could do anything. And there *is* something else I'd like to do, something quite daring.'

She's glowing with excitement, thought Tara. Positively glowing.

'Go on then,' she encouraged.

'Well, this might come as a surprise to you – and I'm sure Jordan and David will be amazed – but it's something I've been wondering about for a while. I'll tell you my idea and if you're happy with it then we'll go downstairs and tell them together . . .'

Chapter Thirty-five

London, August 2000

AS Flora stepped into the downstairs salon David, sitting back in one of the chairs, sat up straighter. Jordan, who'd been pacing the room, returned to his seat.

It's like walking into a classroom, thought Flora, seeing Tara slip into position against one wall, as though she were an assistant teacher, watching how it should be done.

Tara's face was tear-streaked; the two men looked tense. But Flora felt fabulous. my audience, she thought.

'Sorry to keep you waiting, gentlemen.' She smiled warmly; made eye contact with them. 'It's time to announce the truth.'

Jordan's hand was halfway to his notebook before he remembered he was a reformed character and returned the hand to his lap.

'No need to take notes, Jordan. If this story ever appears in print *I'll* tell you how it's to be told.'

Looking at Jordan to gauge his outrage, David caught Tara doing the same thing. They would have laughed out loud but Flora intercepted their exchange of glances. Then, clearing her throat, she began her lecture: 'Your story,' she addressed Jordan, 'is more or less accurate, but bears no relation to the truth. It's true that Tara used to be Scarlett. And it's true that she's not really an astrologer. She doesn't have second sight. Nor does she have a Highland great-granny.' Flora paused; was gratified to see Jordan and David sitting bolt upright, hanging on her every word.

'But *I* do. I was born on the island of Lewis, in the Outer Hebrides, within sight of the Standing Stones of Callanish. I can see into people's hearts, predict where their emotions will take them. The forecasts have always been genuine. But we thought people would pay more attention if they came from a beautiful young woman, rather than her old teacher.'

Flora smiled to herself in remembered amusement: 'Do you remember, Jordan, when you first came round to see Tara? The look on your face when you saw she had an old wrinkly for her assistant?'

'Oh, but—' began Jordan.

'Don't deny it. That's what you think. That old people are past it. That we should be invisible. That all anyone wants to see in newspapers, on TV, are pretty young faces.'

Jordan smiled sheepishly.

'I don't like being invisible. But it has its uses. I'm just a harmless old lady. Someone the celebrities can patronise a little, when they're waiting to see Tara. Except they can't help talking about themselves, because that's their favourite subject, and everything they tell me, I tell Tara. So when they go in to see her, she knows everything that's on their mind. Before they say a word.' She paused to let the revelation sink in.

'Of course as you both now know, Tara has had a hard life. She understands people and she knows instinctively what to say to them to make them feel better about themselves. She takes what I've seen about their futures and interprets it for them in the kindest possible way.'

Jordan was looking at Flora with respect. But David seemed puzzled.

'Yes, David?'

'That day, when Tara shouted at you, when you were in tears, was *that* real?'

'No, no, it wasn't. It's a wee piece of play-acting we do regularly. To make people think Tara's the boss and I'm just a skivvy. Makes them feel they can confide in me without it getting back to Tara.'

'So you deliberately showed me into the same room as the Countess?'

'It's well known she consults Tara but I knew she'd be put out to have someone waiting with her and it would be an excuse for Tara to pretend to be angry with me. It's a little scene we've played lots of times.'

'But that day it was for my benefit?'

'Exactly. To keep you off the right track. The truth is that Tara and I are partners.'

'And best friends,' said Tara.

'And best friends,' agreed Flora.

David was beaming, but Jordan looked uncomfortable: 'Look, I don't want to say the wrong thing' – he glanced anxiously at Tara – 'but how do you expect anyone out there,' he looked out the window, 'to believe

383

what you've just said, about the second sight, the standing stones?'

'I'm sure you'll find a way.'

'Me?'

'Don't you want the exclusive? Of how Tara MacDonald was just the front woman for her shy, wrinkly old teacher; but now, now the old lady's ready to share her gift with the nation herself?'

Jordan was listening hard.

'Timing couldn't be better,' continued Flora. 'Third agers are in the ascendancy. Looking for a role model. Here's a shy old lady who thought she was past it, finally finding the confidence to step out into the limelight, to make the most of her seventh decade. Isn't that a story for the twenty-first century?'

Like a good pupil, David developed the theme: 'A chance to catch the zeitgeist.'

'Wait a minute,' said Jordan. 'Is this the *real* truth? That it's been you all along?' He looked at Flora, but she said nothing.

'OK, well, I'm a bit confused. Do *either* of you take this astrology thing seriously? Or have you just been making everything up?'

'Interesting question,' observed Flora. Then, with feigned innocence: 'I suppose if I don't answer it to your satisfaction you would have a problem presenting the story to your readers?'

'No. That's *not* what I'm saying. Just curious. About the truth.'

'Of course you are,' agreed Flora drily.

'What I'd like to know . . .'

384

'Yes, David?'

'Well, why? Why d'you want to tell people now?'

'Because I don't want to be Tara MacDonald any more,' said Tara. 'I might keep the name – because I like it – but I don't want the lifestyle. It's not what I thought it would be. It's not making me happy.'

'I love you, Tara. *I* can make you happy,' said Jordan, jumping to his feet and going over to where Tara was standing at the edge of the room.

As he did so, she stepped back.

Jordan moved closer. 'Believe me, Tara. I *do* love you.'

This doesn't feel right, thought Tara. This isn't how I imagined it. She looked at Jordan, then at David, then back at Jordan: 'You do?'

Speak up, David, thought Flora.

Back against the wall, pink-eyed and pale-faced, Tara looked more like she was facing a firing squad than two men vying for her heart.

David couldn't bear to see her so upset: 'Yes, he does.'

What? – thought Flora, Jordan and Tara.

'I know he does, Tara. You can't believe everything Jordan says, but that bit is true. I know it is. He really does love you. Or at least he thinks he does – as much as he's capable of loving anyone.' David paused for a moment. 'I can see why, because I, I . . . I care about you too. More than anyone I've ever met. More than anyone I'll ever meet.' David smiled directly at Tara; a big, open smile.

'The thing is, Tara, lots of men will fall in love with you. Not just because you're beautiful. But because of

385

how you are. You're intriguing and vulnerable and strong and fragile and . . .' David looked at Tara adoringly. 'You've no idea how attractive that is. How attractive *you* are. I always wondered why you didn't realise that. It wasn't until today, when I read Jordan's story, about Scotstoun, about Scarlett, that I began to understand.'

Seeing Tara flinch at the mention of the story, David's courage faltered, but he finished what he wanted to say: 'You could have any man you wanted, Tara. I just want you to know that.'

'That's so nice of you. *You're* so nice,' said Tara.

'Not *that* nice. The things you told me, about Scotstoun, about your mother, I passed them on to Jordan. I was angry at you. Disappointed. When you shouted at Miss Macleod I believed it was real.'

David smiled ruefully: 'In the end Jordan didn't need my help. But I was ready to help him. Ready to expose you. I'm ashamed of it now. Wish I hadn't done it. But we've all done things we're ashamed of; things we want to fade away.'

Jordan couldn't hold back any longer. He went across to Tara, took her in his arms: '*Now* do you believe me?'

Tara pushed him away; gently but firmly. She looked at Flora, then addressed David and Jordan. 'I believe you. Both of you. But everything in my life is about to change. Again. I need to be on my own for a bit. To work out what I really want. Get it right this time.'

'Whatever you decide, I won't run a word of your story – unless you want me to,' declared Jordan.

'How can I trust you on that?'

'You don't need to,' said Flora. 'I've done plenty of research on Jordan. Just like I did for all your clients. I've got enough proof of his dirty tricks to get him hauled in front of the Press Council several times over.' She looked at Jordan sternly. 'I know your editor doesn't care how you get your stories as long as you're not caught, but now he's chairman of the Press Council he's got to be seen to care. And you can't afford to be an embarrassment to him. Not at this stage in your career. Not with the chance of going to Los Angeles.'

'But how do *you* know . . .?'

Jordan looked so alarmed Flora almost felt sorry for him.

'Don't worry. I'm sure there won't be any need for that. Not when we're working together.'

'Working together?'

'Don't you want to tell this story, and all the other stories I've got, from Tara's clients, secrets they've never told but would like the public to know, to win sympathy, to keep themselves in the limelight? Stories they'd never tell a reporter, but would trust me to pass on to you, in the way they want them told?'

In his mind's eye, Jordan could suddenly see his picture by-line, in colour, on the front page, again and again and again. He looked at Tara, looked into her eyes, but all he could see was his own name, in bold print, with the coveted strapline 'Exclusive' above it.

He turned away from Tara and for the first time looked into Flora's eyes, properly; saw the strength in them, the mischievousness, and what was it – yes, he'd interviewed enough showbiz people to know that look

– Flora's eyes were bright with ambition, the ambition of a performer who'd always longed for a bigger audience than could fit in a classroom.

As Jordan was working this out, David found the gap in the conversation he'd been waiting for. 'This second sight thing, Flora. Do you really have it? I mean, do *you* believe you have it?'

Flora's face was serious: 'Oh yes indeed.' Then she relented; smiled playfully: 'That is, I have as much second sight as anyone who makes a study of the human heart, who watches where people's emotions take them. You'll know that yourself as an historian. If you want to know the future, study the past.'

'Yes of course,' agreed David.

With the reporter's knack for taking in what's being said while thinking about something else, Jordan was writing headlines in his head. SECOND SIGHT FLORA REVEALS SECRET PACT BEHIND TARA'S SUCCESS, he thought. Yes, that would be the splash. Accompanied by an inside spread: FUTURE IN HER HANDS: LIFE BEGINS AT SEVENTY FOR TV'S NEWEST STAR. Then there would be all the other exclusives Flora had mentioned; about Tara's clients. Who would become Flora's clients of course. And feed her more stories. So many stories. To be had so easily.

Jordan was so busy visualising his glittering future that it took a moment for him to realise Tara was looking at him. A big, green-eyed look; full power.

So lovely, thought Jordan. So lovable. But not the only one. Surely not? So many women out there. Never thought I'd find another Jackie. But then Tara came along. Must be another one. Somewhere. Sometime. When I've got more time. When there aren't so many stories. Just waiting to be written. When I'm not in the middle of such a crucial mission.

I *could* win Tara over. Course I could. But I don't have time. Not now. Not when I'm so close to victory.

With the sad-but-decisive air of a soldier departing for the battlefield, Jordan pulled Tara tight against him, placed his lips on hers, and kissed her hard. But his mouth didn't linger. The instant he'd delivered the kiss, he turned on his heel, walked smartly across to Flora, took her right hand, raised it to his lips and kissed it carefully, almost reverently.

Aha, he thought. Last time I got this close she was wearing eau de Cologne. Now it's Chanel No. 5. And those shoes . . . don't look so sensible as before. Definitely designer. Old girl's got plenty of go left in her. And she's a fuck of a lot sharper than most of the hacks I work with.

Raising his head just enough to look into her eyes, he fixed her with his ultimate, liquid brown, we-can-do-things-together look: 'You're the best operator I've ever met.'

'Thank you.'

He straightened up, still holding Flora's hand. 'I underestimated you so badly. I'm sorry.'

Flora nodded in acknowledgement; removed her hand from his.

Jordan deployed a full-charm smile. 'I'd love to work with you. I hope you'll be able to trust me.'

'I've got more sense than that,' said Flora sternly.

Is that stern-stern, or just acting stern? wondered Jordan.

He affected a crestfallen expression.

Is he play-acting or is he genuinely crestfallen? wondered Flora.

'You're an extremely clever young man. Working with you will keep me on my toes,' she smiled.

Jordan smiled back; extended an arm towards her in invitation.

Flora smiled questioningly at Tara.

Tara didn't hesitate to respond: 'You two will make a great team,' she said. 'Unbeatable. On you go. Both of you.'

Jordan picked up his cue: 'Come on,' he said to Flora. 'Let's grab a cup of tea and talk about this.'

'Tea?' said Flora. 'What makes you think I'd like a cup of tea?'

Jordan didn't miss a beat: 'Sorry. I meant . . . a glass of champagne.'

Flora nodded happily.

'Come on,' repeated Jordan. 'Can't wait to start making headlines together.' As he and Flora left the room arm-in-arm, Tara watched in amusement, but David looked dazed.

He heard the front door closing behind Jordan and Flora and realised he was alone with Tara. He glanced across at her but she looked lost in thought. What should I do now? he wondered.

'What should I do now?' he asked.

Tara looked at him kindly. 'Leave. You should say goodbye and leave.'

'You want to be on your own?'

'Yes.'

'Sure?'

'Yes.'

David nodded; turned to go; then turned back, raised his right hand to his mouth, kissed his fingertips, reached over and gently stroked her face with them. Then, with a final glance at her, he turned and left . . .

Chapter Thirty-six

London, August 2000

AS soon as David had left Tara sat down on one of the chairs, kicked off her shoes and pulled her feet up, hugging knees to chest. Usually, when she found herself alone, she felt like an actress returning to her dressing room after a performance. But now, for the first time in a long while, she felt just the same as when the others had been in the room.

Not Tara; not Scarlett; just myself, she thought. At last. Ready to be myself. But what do I want to do? Stay here and help Flora become a star? No need. Jordan will see to that. And anyway, I don't want to be part of the media circus any more. Not even behind the scenes.

Go to Florida and see Brendan? He's always on at me to visit.

Tara smiled at the thought of Brendan; and of how far he'd come since their early-morning runs along Aberdeen beach. He was still in South Beach. Miami. In his last email he'd said he'd left the gym, set up his own business. Not as a personal trainer, but as a 'body designer': 'prêt-à-porter bodies for the rich'; 'haute couture bodies for the super-rich'. Would be fun for a holiday, she thought. But not for any longer than that. Florida's too close to Louisiana. No way am I going to live on the same Continent as Ma. Not now I'm finally sorting myself out.

So what next? she wondered. I've got plenty of money. But nowhere to go. And no one to go with. Her head sank onto her knees.

Then jerked back up as she heard a knock on the salon door.

David came into the room.

Tara unfolded her legs; sat up properly. 'You're still here?'

'Sorry. Didn't mean to give you a fright.'

'Thought you'd gone.'

'I've been sitting on the front doorstep. With the door open. In case . . .'

'In case what?'

'In case I needed to come back in.'

Tara smiled. '*Needed?*' she asked.

'To see that you were OK.'

Tara looked at David, then gestured him to sit down next to her. She didn't prompt him any further; just continued to look at him.

'To see that you were OK and . . .'

Still Tara said nothing.

'And to spend a few more moments with you,' said David in a rush. Then, as if keeping talking would cover up the importance of what he'd just said, he continued rapidly: 'It's going to be such a big change for you. Giving up the TV show, the fame, everything. I just thought you'd be wondering what you were going to do next, where you'd go.' He glanced at her. 'Or maybe you've got that all worked out?'

393

'No. Not at all. That's *exactly* what I was thinking about.' Tara smiled. 'You could be an astrologer yourself. Reading people's thoughts like that.'

'But it's not that difficult, is it?'

Tara gave him a mock-injured look.

David realised she was teasing but apologised anyway: 'Sorry. I didn't mean to be rude about your former profession. But for people like us, it's not that hard to guess what other people are thinking, is it? And anyway, everyone wants the same things: to love and be loved, to be happy. Don't they?'

'People like us?'

'You're such a brilliant observer, always watching people, taking in the clues. I do that too. Watch from the sidelines. You're not on the sidelines now. You're in the spotlight. But I imagine, well, I might be wrong, but I imagine you must have spent a good part of your life in the background, watching.'

Have I said too much? he wondered.

Keep talking, thought Tara.

'And sometimes, maybe, I don't know. Sometimes the background can be a bit of a lonely place?'

'Yes. Yes it can be.' She smiled straight into his eyes. 'And you're right about the other thing.'

'The other thing?'

'About everyone wanting the same things. To be happy, be loved.' She looked away, smiled to herself, then looked back at him: 'I always wanted a real love story. Like *Gone With the Wind*. Me and Clark Gable.'

David laughed.

Tara shot him an injured look; genuine this time.

'Sorry. I'm so sorry. But *Gone With the Wind*? When did you last see it?'

'Not that long ago. I told you: it's my favourite film.'

'Oh dear.'

'Why? What's the matter?'

David hesitated.

'Go on. Tell me what you're thinking.'

'Well . . .' David looked at her kindly; sighed: 'It's a dreadful film. Racist. Sexist. Puts a false gloss on a society based on slave labour.'

'OK. You're right about the Old South. But what about the romance? Rhett and Scarlett?'

'A battle of egos. Selfish. Greedy. Controlling. Where's the kindness? The tenderness?'

Wow, noted Tara to herself. Kindness? Tenderness? The thought showed in her eyes.

David saw it; had a sudden rush of courage: 'I'm not an expert on romance. But Rhett and Scarlett?' He shook his head. 'That's not what I call a great romance. I could offer you far better than that.'

'You could?' asked Tara quietly.

Under the intensity of her green-eyed questioning look, David's courage faltered. 'Of course there's nothing wrong with liking *Gone With the Wind*. Everyone needs a bit of fantasy, a bit of escape. My escape is history. I intellectualise it. Turn it into projects. But really I'm just retreating into the past. Like some people retreat into *Gone With the Wind* . . .'

Tara was looking at him expectantly.

David smiled: 'And yes, to answer your question, I could.'

He sighed, looked away, then looked straight into her eyes. When he spoke again, his tone was matter-of-fact; resigned.

'Since the first moment I met you I've been interested in everything about you because . . . because I was intrigued by you . . . and then I realised I cared about you. I know we hardly know each other but . . . well, I want to change that. I want to get to know you. I can't bear the thought that once I walk out that door I'll never see you again.' He paused, but then, as though ticking off things he wanted to say on a mental list, continued in the same objective tone: 'Oh yes, and I realise you think you've got something to be ashamed about, some secret you don't want people to know. But I don't care. Did you do something that hurt someone else?'

'No.'

'That damaged them in any way?'

'No.'

'So it's you who were hurt. No one else?'

'Yes.'

'That's what I thought.'

Tara looked relieved, but wary.

'Don't worry. I'm not going to ask you what it is. I would never do that.' He smiled. 'Interrogation over. D'you feel better?'

'Much better.' Tara smiled a relaxed smile; stretched and yawned. 'You know,' she said. 'I don't want this to be the last time we see each other. You're good for me. I can be myself. And you make me feel . . .' She searched for the right word: 'Peaceful.'

'I'm glad.'

'It was so good of you. To come back. Listen to my woes. I don't know what I'm going to do next. But I'd like to see you. Sometimes.'

'That's very tempting. But . . .' David sighed. 'I made the mistake of being Jordan's leg man. Now you're asking me to be your agony uncle. Much as I want to see you, I don't know if I could handle that . . . I want to be so much more to you.'

'I don't know if I'm ready for that.' Tara looked at him sadly.

David looked equally sad. 'I know. So you said.'

A new thought occurred to Tara: 'But I don't like the idea of not seeing you again.'

David looked at her hopefully.

'What about being my friend? Not a shoulder to cry on; not an agony uncle. A real friend.' She smiled at him brightly.

'I still want to be more than that.'

Tara's face fell.

'But I'm willing to start from there.' David got out of his seat, hunkered down next to her, drew one hand down her face to close her eyelids.

Breathing out slowly, Tara felt calmer than she could ever remember.

Gently, David kissed her eyelids.

When Tara opened her eyes, he was beaming at her; his big, open, boyish grin: 'Come on, Miss MacDonald. Forget the past. Forget the future. Let's see what it's like living in the present . . .'

PART FOUR

THE FOLLOW-UP

Chapter Thirty-seven

Eighteen months later . . . on Rupert and Jilly's morning TV show . . .

AS though they were at home on their own sofa, Rupert turned to Jilly conversationally: 'What's happening this morning?'

Jilly smiled brightly in the direction of the Autocue: 'Flora will be here as usual, to tell us what the stars have in store . . . but first we're going to catch up on all the showbiz gossip with our new man in Hollywood, the deeply dishy Jordan Holmes . . . Jordan, tell us the latest.'

The director cut from the studio to a location shot of Jordan, white-toothed and suntanned, in linen shorts and T-shirt, under an azure sky.

'Well, I've got a bit of a surprise for you . . . I'm not in LA . . .' Jordan sounded relaxed and natural, as though talking to someone next to him. On screen, the shot opened out to reveal he was standing on the deck of a boat, moving slowly through a green Biblical landscape.

'I'm on the Nile . . . and the even bigger surprise is who I've got with me.'

The shot opened wider to show a happy young couple sipping mint tea on the sun deck.

Back in London, Rupert and Jilly looked surprised and thrilled.

'Tara! What a surprise!' said Rupert.

'We're thrilled,' said Jilly.

'And such a scoop for you, Jordan.'

'Well yes, Jilly, it is,' agreed Jordan modestly. 'Since Tara MacDonald did her vanishing act this is the first time she's been back on TV.'

'How are you, Tara? And who's that with you?' asked Rupert.

From Egypt, Tara smiled straight down the lens. 'Well, I promised you last time I was on the show that when I met the right man you'd be the first to know . . . so here he is.'

Looking slightly awkward but happy, David smiled for the camera.

'And this Nile cruise isn't just a holiday, is it, Tara?'

'No, Jordan, it's not. We've got two very special reasons for being here. The first is that David's working on a new book—'

Jordan interrupted her: 'David Swift of course is the author of *The Time Traveller's Guide to the Thames*.' He smiled at David: 'Loved the book, David. So unusual for a history book to be a bestseller, but you really brought London alive.'

'Good. Well, I'm as surprised as anyone.'

Jordan smiled encouragingly and waited for more, but David failed to pick up the cue.

'So now he's been asked to write a series. The Time Traveller's Guide to the Mississippi, the Amazon, the Nile . . . we decided to start with the nearest,' said Tara.

'And tomorrow you've got a very special port of call,' prompted Jordan.

'Yes we do.' Tara smiled into David's eyes: 'We're stopping off for a few days to get married in Luxor.'

In the studio, Jilly brought her hands together in excitement; Rupert flicked back his hair and beamed.

'That's wonderful news,' exclaimed Jilly.

'Wonderful,' said Rupert. 'Thank you, Jordan. All the best you two!'

Rupert smiled at the viewers at home, then read the Autocue: 'Jordan, you'll remember, is the only journalist Tara would talk to when she suddenly decided she wanted to give up astrology and disappear for a bit.'

'And it was he who revealed that it was Flora's second sight which helped make Tara's predictions so accurate,' added Jilly helpfully.

'Well,' said Rupert, nodding his head in acknowledgement. 'That was some exclusive. Direct from the Nile. How do we follow that?'

'In a moment we're going over to Miami to meet the new fitness guru who's in vogue with the world's top fashion designers and models.'

As Jilly spoke, a clip appeared on screen of a smiling, Lycra-clad Brendan, doing tummy crunches with an A-list actress.

'And then we're asking: sex in the afternoon – are daytime chat-show hosts going too far?'

The screen cut to a clip from a rival chat-show: to the oohs and aaahs of an over-excited American audience, a hugely overweight man was on his knees, nuzzling the dainty bare feet of a peroxide blonde with an over-made-up face and a hard-as-nails expression. The text along the bottom of the screen read: 'Lola Dubois: Why I married a foot fetishist.'

'Well, that's certainly a bit steamy,' said Rupert.

Jilly looked unimpressed. 'We'll be seeing more of that later. But first we've just got time for a final word with Tara. Tara – are you still there?'

With only seconds remaining on the satellite link, the director in the gallery managed to get the Nile cruiser back on screen.

'Hello again, Jilly.'

'Great to see you so happy, Tara. I'm just dying to know. What are you up to next? After your wedding, what does the future hold? Will you be coming back to team up with Flora again?'

Tara nodded. Then looked at David with a we've-rehearsed-this-bit look.

'Yes, we've spoken about that a lot.' She smiled. 'And we both decided we'd had enough of the future just now. We're going to live in the present a little . . .'

'Well all the best to you, Tara. And to you, David,' beamed Jilly.

'We've got to take a break now, but we'll be right back with Flora's predictions,' added Rupert.

As the adverts rolled, Rupert and Jilly sat back on the sofa and exchanged weary glances.

'You used to get readings from Tara. Do you think she and Flora are for real?' Rupert asked.

Jilly shrugged her shoulders. 'I used to think so. Now I don't know.'

She sighed. It was a sigh never heard on screen; a deep, world-weary, seen-it-all, heard-it-all sound, straight from the heart.

'Does it matter?'